KU-441-930

WILLOW

WILLOW

LINDA LAEL MILLER

THORNDIKE
CHIVERS

This Large Print edition is published by Thorndike Press, Waterville, Maine, USA and by AudioGO Ltd, Bath, England.
Thorndike Press, a part of Gale, Cengage Learning.
Copyright © 1984, 2010 by Linda Lael Miller.
The moral right of the author has been asserted.

ALL RIGHTS RESERVED
This book is a work of fiction. Names, characters, places, and incidents either are the product of the author's imagination or are used fictitiously. Any resemblance to actual events or locales or persons, living or dead, is entirely coincidental.
The text of this Large Print edition is unabridged.
Other aspects of the book may vary from the original edition.
Set in 16 pt. Plantin.

LIBRARY OF CONGRESS CATALOGING-IN-PUBLICATION DATA

Miller, Linda Lael.
  Willow / by Linda Lael Miller. — Large print ed.
    p. cm. — (Thorndike Press large print famous authors)
  ISBN-13: 978-1-4104-3875-1 (hardcover)
  ISBN-10: 1-4104-3875-9 (hardcover)
  1. Large type books. 2. Brothers and sisters—Fiction. 3.
United States marshals—Fiction. 4. Montana—History—Fiction.
I. Title.
PS3563.I41373W56 2011
813'.54—dc22   2011017760

BRITISH LIBRARY CATALOGUING-IN-PUBLICATION DATA AVAILABLE

Published in 2011 in the U.S. by arrangement with Pocket Books, a division of Simon & Schuster Inc.
Published in 2012 in the U.K. by arrangement with Simon & Schuster Inc.

U.K. Hardcover: 978 1 445 86021 3 (Chivers Large Print)
U.K. Softcover: 978 1 445 86022 0 (Camden Large Print)

AudioGO   7·12·11

Printed in the United States of America
1 2 3 4 5 6 7 15 14 13 12 11

*For Steve and Debbie Korrell,
my longtime friends,
with much love and gratitude*

PROLOGUE

Montana Territory
Spring, 1865

The other men wore masks, but Devlin Gallagher's face was bare to the chilly midnight wind. His insides churned, and bile stung the back of his throat. Though he had no love for the condemned, Gallagher dreaded what they were about to do to Jay Forbes. Gallagher was, after all, an officer of the court, duly licensed to practice law, and he'd sworn an oath to *uphold* justice, not make a travesty of it. And for all that, here he was, riding with an unlikely band of vigilantes, fixing to hang a man, and not in broad daylight, either, but secretly, in the dark of night.

Forbes stood quietly in the bed of an old wagon, his murdering hands tied behind his back, his ice-blue gaze fixed on Devlin and glittering with fear, but there was mockery in those eyes, too. When the posse had finally run him to ground, only a few hours before, after he'd robbed a freight wagon and killed the driver, Forbes had laughed, a crazy, cackling sound that sent shivers down Devlin's spine.

"You're doin' this 'cause I took away your woman, Gallagher — 'cause it was me she wanted 'stead of you."

It was true that Devlin had more reason to hate Forbes than the others did, but the once-sharp edge of his fury had been blunted by time; he hadn't seen Chastity, his former wife, in over three years. Since then he'd divorced her, courted and married Evadne Jessup Marshall, a young widow he'd met in San Francisco, and come back to Virginia City, backbone straight, head high.

Devlin's jaw tightened a little; it still gave him a twinge of sorrow to remember Chastity's betrayal, though he'd given up on her long ago. Not a day went by, though, that he didn't yearn to set eyes on his son. Steven had been a small boy when he'd seen him last, only four years old. "This has nothing to do with Chastity," Devlin finally rasped out, "and you damn well know it."

One of the other vigilantes climbed up into the wagon bed to stand next to Forbes and fling a rope over a sturdy tree branch, testing it with a hard pull. Forbes's star-shaped badge flashed in the bright light of the spring moon as he shifted his stance, as if bracing himself against the inevitable.

The springs of the buckboard creaked under the weight of the two men, and the shadows of leaves danced, silver edged, over both of them.

"You people is killin' an officer of the law!" Forbes burst out, finally accepting the gravity of his situation, and his throat worked spasmodically as the noose was slipped around his neck. His long hair was stringy, his lean jaws marred by scars from an early bout with the smallpox.

Devlin didn't wonder what Chastity had seen in Forbes, way back when, because he reckoned he knew. Some women favored meanness in a man, figured they deserved such, maybe, and even seemed to find it exciting.

With a wrench, he brought himself back to the task at hand, grim though it was.

Right or wrong, he'd be glad when Forbes was dead, because a dead man couldn't thieve and rape and kill. Forbes had done plenty of all three, though Devlin hadn't known the true extent of his crimes until recently. He would never have eaten or slept or rested if he'd been privy to the truth.

He'd tracked Chastity and Forbes to Montana, turned the whole territory upside down, looking for his boy, with no luck at all. The worry chewed at his gut, when he let himself think about all the things that could be happening to Steven.

As wild as she was, how could Chastity have put her own pleasure before the safety and well-being of her *child,* and Devlin's? He'd begged her to leave Steven with him when she went off with her outlaw lover, a man she'd met in a backstreet beer parlor. She'd flaunted her penchant for Forbes, thrown him up to Devlin, almost daring him to turn her out onto the streets, said she'd be going away for good as soon as the arrangements were made. At the time, the heartbreak had been almost more than Devlin could take, and fool that he was, he'd still cherished the hope that Chastity might change her mind, come to her senses, and stay.

They had a good life, a nice home, a son.

Chastity had wanted for nothing.

She'd made up her mind about leaving, though it took some time, but she'd promised, sweetly, tenderly, and tearfully that she'd leave the boy behind with Devlin when she left.

It would be better for Steven to grow up

there, in San Francisco, with his father, she'd said.

But then one day Forbes had come for her, and Chastity had sneaked out of their fine house, with its beautiful view of the Bay, and they'd taken young Steven with them. According to the note Chastity left for Devlin, Jay Forbes had always wanted a son and she couldn't deny him anything.

There had been one insane encounter with Chastity, during the intervening years, but Devlin had never again laid eyes on his boy.

"Murder!" Forbes ranted on, struggling against his bonds now. "It's cold-blooded *murder,* what you're doin' here! You've gotta let me go."

"Don't you go yammering on to us about murder!" raged Mance Pickering, the editor of Virginia City's fledgling newspaper. "You've shot four men that we know of, and Lord knows how many we don't. That freight driver you gunned down two days ago was barely twenty years old, you son of a bitch, just married and the wife with a babe on the way!"

Forbes shook his head quickly, like it was all an unfortunate misunderstanding. He was sweating hard now, and his gaze kept shifting off into the distance, as if he was expecting to be saved. "He drew on me," he argued, almost whining the words. "It was kill or be killed."

"You're a liar," Pickering spat out. "Tom wasn't wearing a sidearm or carrying a rifle, and you probably put that bullet through the poor kid's heart before he even had a chance to *think* about going for that old squirrel gun he kept stashed under the wagon seat."

Forbes's voice took on a pleading note, a mite on the shrill side. "You gotta listen to me — this is all a mistake, I'm innocent! Gallagher here, he just wants to see me swing from the end of a rope 'cause his woman's livin' with me — his woman and his boy!"

None of the others so much as glanced in Devlin's direction, but he could feel their embarrassment, sense their awkward sympathy. All of them knew the story, or some version of it.

"Where is my son?" he asked hoarsely. "Where is Steven?"

For all his quaking, a smug look crossed Forbes's face. "You'd like to know that, wouldn't you, Gallagher? Well, you ain't gonna hear it from me, not unless you let me go, like you know you ought to do, 'stead of takin' the law into your own hands this way."

Devlin merely stared up at the man. He didn't say a word.

"You'll go to hell for this!" Forbes croaked out.

"I'll see you there, if I do," Devlin told him.

Forbes began to blink rapidly, and the front of his shirt was soaked, even though it was cold out. "There's a lot you don't know," Forbes went on, almost blathering now. He turned his head, rubbed his beard-stubbled chin awkwardly against one hunched shoulder, as though it itched. "You hear me, Gallagher? There's a lot you don't know."

"I reckon there is," Devlin agreed evenly. He couldn't rightly say he cared overmuch about Chastity's situation, though he had once — she'd made her bed and she could damn well lie in it — but his fear for Steven was like a spear through his middle. It had been seven years, which meant the boy was eleven years old now.

"We've got two boys of our own, Chastity and me," Forbes said. "Coy and Reilly. They need me, Gallagher. They need their daddy."

For once in his miserable life, Devlin figured, Forbes might be telling the truth. "A boy needs his pa," he said quietly. "I

13

never got a chance to say good-bye to my son. I guess you and his mama must have told him I wanted no part of his raising."

The noose was drawn tight around Forbes's neck, and Pickering, who had put it in place, climbed into the seat of the wagon itself and took up the reins. "Let's just get this over with," he said.

"Wait a minute!" Forbes begged. "Wait — I got somethin' more to say!"

"Ya, and you'd talk all night if you thought it would save your hide," said Swede, the blacksmith.

"No," whined the onetime lawman gone bad, "you gotta listen, I tell you! Gallagher, I know where your boy is, and your little girl, too! Don't you want me to tell you where Chastity's got 'em hid?"

The hanging would have proceeded if Devlin hadn't held up one hand to delay it. "What little girl?" he demanded in a gruff undertone.

Forbes laughed like the madman he was. "*Your* little girl, Gallagher — your baby daughter. Chastity calls her Willow."

A tremor went through Devlin Gallagher's sturdy frame. Almost three years before, he'd caught up with Chastity, his runaway wife, at Bannack, where he'd had a mining claim. He'd begged her for news of Steven.

Devlin had shared one night with Chastity — she'd cried in his arms and said she'd made a terrible mistake by leaving him, but in the end she'd slipped away, taking a poke of his gold with her while he still slept. Come the rueful morning, he'd known no more about his son's whereabouts than before.

"He's just stalling, Dev," argued Pickering. "Trying to buy time."

"Where are they?" Devlin asked, with a calm that belied the churning emotions inside him. "Where are my children?"

Forbes shrugged. Even now, when he was about to die, there was something cagey about him. Probably not surprising, Devlin thought.

"Most of the time, Willow lives with a Mexican woman we know," the outlaw allowed slowly. "Chastity thinks the baby oughtn't to grow up in hideouts and on the trail. Maria looks out for her."

"Damnation," the storekeeper broke in. "Devlin, Forbes is lyin' to you! There probably ain't no little girl or no Mexican woman, neither."

A cloud drifted over the wide moon, and every man there shivered. It was then that they heard the eerie screaming.

She rode down through the gulch at a

15

breakneck pace, did Chastity, her thick, fair hair trailing out behind her, her slender frame draped in a dark cape. She might have been a ghost or a beautiful demon just escaped from hell. Her disjointed shrieks of outrage and desperation were etched forever into the minds of everyone there to hear them.

Reaching the scene, Chastity fairly leaped off the back of her lathered black mare, flung one frantic look at Jay Forbes, then stumbled toward Devlin. She wore trousers, like a man, and a ragged white shirt that was open at the throat. "Stop them!" she sobbed, grabbing at him, clutching his lapels. "For God's sake, Devlin, don't let them do this!"

Devlin stared at her, stunned. She was like a specter, a mirage. He couldn't believe she was real.

She was fevered, her eyes wide and imploring. "Please!" she cried, in a keening hiss.

Devlin didn't — *couldn't* — speak for a long moment. Then slowly, sadly, he shook his head.

"Hang him," he said.

Chastity flung herself at Devlin then, a fierce creature, not entirely human, it seemed to him, clawing and kicking and biting, screaming obscenities. As they

16

grappled, she somehow, wild in her terror, managed to catch hold of his Colt .45 and wrenched it out of the holster. "I'll kill you before I let you do this, Devlin!" she screamed. She had the gun, gripped it in both hands. "I'll kill you all!"

At that moment, the driver of the wagon yelled and slapped the reins down onto the backs of the nervous team. Forbes gave a strangled shriek and Devlin lunged for Chastity, desperate to wrest the pistol from her hands.

She was remarkably strong for such a slight woman, and the struggle was ferocious. When the gun went off and Chastity flinched and then fell, Devlin froze, unable to believe she'd been hit.

But she had.

The bullet had torn a crimson gash in her middle.

Eyes wide with disbelief, Chastity slipped out of Devlin's hold and slumped slowly to the ground.

With one ragged sob, Devlin sank to his knees in the dirt and gathered Chastity close. Her blood drenched him, soaking through his clothes, hot against his skin.

"Weren't your fault, Dev!" cried the storekeeper. "We all saw that it weren't your doin'!"

Devlin rocked Chastity's lifeless form in his arms, weeping unashamedly into her hair. It would be a long time before he could think of this night without numbing himself with whiskey beforehand — and even longer until he found his children.

1

Montana Territory
June 9, 1883

The church was a weathered, unpainted structure surrounded by undulating summer grass. Organ music wheezed out into the bright June day.

Gideon Marshall kicked at the ground with the toe of one boot and groaned. The last thing he wanted to do was walk into that modest wooden building and interrupt a wedding, but as things stood, he didn't have much choice.

Much choice? Thanks to his older brother, Zachary, thanks to his own youthful high spirits, he had no choice at all.

He squared his shoulders and approached the open doors of the sanctuary.

Might as well get the unpleasant duty out of the way.

Willow would be furious, of course. Who could blame her?

19

Grimly, Gideon climbed the sloping, rough-hewn steps and entered the church itself.

He paused in the shadows, letting his eyes adjust to the dimmer light — or so he told himself. The bride stood at the altar with her groom, and the sacred words were beginning.

"Dearly beloved, we are gathered here . . ."

The pit of Gideon's stomach quivered, and he cleared his throat, tasted something sour on the back of his tongue. Whether or not this farce was Zachary's fault, *he* was the one who would have to make it right, have to take the ultimate responsibility.

Nothing new in that.

All their lives, Zachary had been the one to instigate trouble. He had a gift for making some wild enterprise sound like a good idea, Zachary did, and when he was younger, Gideon had often gone along with his brother's suggestions.

After all, no one had ever died.

Or been arrested.

Well, okay, arrested. But never actually tried and sentenced.

Irritated regret rose in Gideon. Had it not been for his surroundings, he would have sworn roundly, and at volume. Of course, he couldn't do such a thing, even though he was not a religious man. And he'd done enough swearing since finding out the true scope of the prank his brother and their mutual friends had played on him, two years before, in San Francisco.

There were a lot of people crowded into the narrow pews, and Gideon imagined how they would turn and stare at him, once his mission became clear. By nightfall, the story would be all over the territory — and if Willow didn't kill him personally, her father probably would.

It seemed to Gideon that time had frozen. He stood at the back of the little church, wishing he could vanish, preferably in a puff of smoke like a stage magician.

Of course, that wasn't going to happen.

It would be entirely too easy.

Once again, he centered his attention on the circuit preacher's words and their portent.

"If anyone can show just cause," boomed the clergyman, "why these two should not be joined in marriage, let him speak now or forever hold his peace."

Oh, God, thought Gideon. And then he cleared his throat again and said, "I can show just cause," in a clear voice that carried through the small sanctuary and brought an immediate halt to the proceedings.

Nobody breathed, as far as Gideon could tell. At least, *he* didn't.

The bride turned first, her face — which Gideon remembered as heartstoppingly beautiful — hidden by the dense veil of fine lace. At her cue, the groom and all the guests turned, too.

"I beg your pardon?" demanded the preacher, arching one eyebrow as he glowered at the interloper.

Fully aware that he was as unwelcome in that place as the devil would have been in heaven, Gideon walked slowly up the aisle, wishing that the splintery floorboards would part, Red Sea style, and swallow him whole.

He paused between the first two rows of rough-hewn pews and cleared his throat loudly and, he hoped, with some authority. "Miss Gallagher cannot legally marry," he said, in that same clear voice. "She is, as it happens, married to me."

The bride's bouquet of violets and summer wildflowers tumbled to the floor in a cascade of color, and a wave of excited chatter surged through the congregation, blending with the rustle of sateen skirts, the bumbling buzz of flies, and the speculative whisperings of the men.

The groom, Norville Pickering, a skinny young fellow with an unfortunate complexion, glared at Gideon.

Before he could speak, however, Gideon raised both hands in a diplomatic gesture. "I'm sorry," he said. "I know this is an inexcusable interruption, but as I said before, the lady is married to me and I have the papers to prove it."

Slowly, Willow Gallagher lifted the veil from her face — even more exquisite than he remembered — and her expression was unreadable. She simply watched Gideon with those wide, amber-colored eyes that had nearly undone him, back home in San Francisco, just two years before. Her lush, dark-gold hair was done up and threaded through with sprigs of baby's breath, and there was a beguiling apricot tone to her flawless cheekbones.

"You," she said, without inflection of any kind. And then her eyes rolled back and her knees gave out and she collapsed to the church floor in a faint.

Willow opened her eyes and stared up into her father's face, amazed and shaken. The little room reserved for the pastor's use seemed close and musty, even though a window was open to the summer breeze.

"Was Gideon speaking the truth?" Devlin Gallagher demanded, though his blue eyes were kind. "Are you his wife?"

Willow had never expected to see Gideon Marshall in the flesh again, especially not today, of all days. With great effort, she had put the humiliation and the pain of the joke he and his brother had played on her out of her thoughts, for the most part, anyway. It was rather hard to forget him *completely,* reprehensible as he was.

"No," she said, with resolution, sitting up and drawing a deep, sustaining breath. "I most certainly *am not* Gideon Marshall's wife!"

At that moment, the door of the small room opened and Gideon himself walked in, looking strained and very determined. His clothes were good but not formal, and the fabric looked rumpled, as though he'd been traveling in earnest and in haste. His hair was darker than she remembered, the color of tarnished brass.

And he was still so damnably good-looking that Willow had no trouble recalling why she'd fallen for the cruel joke he and Zachary and a few of their friends had played on her.

She'd wanted *so much* to believe that he loved her, even though they'd barely met.

Spent only one romantic — and wholly innocent — night together, exploring the city in a hired carriage.

Willow had been seventeen at the time, fresh from the wilds of the Montana Territory, and very naive.

Gideon, a full decade older, with a college education and a trust fund, had been, by contrast, sophisticated. Even worldly.

"Hello, Judge Gallagher," he said easily. The nod he spared Willow had to serve as a greeting.

Judge Gallagher squared his massive shoulders and clasped his hands together, probably to keep from closing them around Gideon's throat and strangling him on the spot. "Were you not my wife's son, Mr. Marshall," he said evenly, "I would snap your spine like a chicken bone. What in God's name is the meaning of this?"

Gideon's jaw tightened and his green-gray gaze skirted Willow's. "Believe me, sir," he told her father, "I didn't want to do this. I had to, however, for your daughter's sake as well as my own."

Willow lowered her eyes, unable to look at Gideon. Dear God, what a fool he'd made of her that long-ago night, and how keen the pain was, reawakened after all this time.

Gideon cleared his throat and went on.

"Several years ago, Judge, when your daughter came to San Francisco with our mother, my brother and I decided to play a joke on her. I had just gotten home from Europe and — well, the unflattering truth is, we were drunk.

"In any case, I met Willow at a party soon after I got back, and —" He paused, cleared his throat, and finally went on. "I was very taken with her. We meant to persuade one of our friends to pose as a minister and . . ." Gideon paused as embarrassed color surged into Willow's face, aching there. "For a reason I will probably never understand, Miss Gallagher agreed to marry me."

Willow felt her father's questioning gaze touch her and shivered. God, if only a person could will herself to die. She would certainly have done it then.

The judge's voice was remarkably calm, considering the circumstances. "Did you defile my daughter, Gideon?" he asked forthrightly.

"No," Gideon replied. "I did take her to a hotel and . . ." He stopped and cleared his throat again. "And I realized what I was doing. I couldn't go through with it, of course."

"Of course," agreed the judge, with raspy disdain. "I could hang you, you realize; no father on the face of the earth would blame me for it."

"Yes, sir," answered Gideon, with dignity. "I guess you could."

An uncomfortable and protracted silence ensued, which the judge eventually broke. "If the marriage was a farce, what are you doing here now?"

At last, Willow was able to look up, to search the handsome face that she had loved for years and years — ever since her first sight of the portrait that hung in Evadne Marshall Gallagher's fussy sitting room, right there in Virginia City.

She waited, every bit as interested in his answer as her father was.

Gideon met her eyes squarely, then sighed. A muscle jumped in his strong jaw, settled down again. "I became engaged to a woman in San Francisco recently — her name is Daphne Roberts — and she and I have been pledged to each other practically since we were christened. When the official announcement was made, my brother was prompted to intercede. The joke was on me, it seems, as well as Willow. The minister was a justice of the peace, and the ceremony was legal."

"My God," breathed the judge.

Willow was torn between launching into a screaming rage and clasping her hands together and offering a prayer of gratitude.

She had had no choice but to accept Norville Pickering's proposal of marriage, but now she would have a respite. For a few weeks, maybe even for a few *months,* until an annulment could be secured, anyway, she could keep Norville at arm's length.

Convince him, somehow, that she'd been looking forward to their honeymoon and lengthy marriage — till death did them part, for heaven's sake — and was bitterly disappointed that their plans had been thwarted.

If she chose every word carefully, Norville would believe her.

And Steven, the brother she adored, would not be in danger.

"You could have sent a wire or something!" growled the judge furiously, lowering his bristly eyebrows as he glared at Gideon. "Good God, man, what if you hadn't gotten here in time? What if . . . ?"

He reddened and fell silent.

"I *did* get here in time," Gideon said reasonably. Now, he seemed more amused by the situation than apologetic. Of course, he'd had time to get used to the idea, which was more than anyone could say for the rest of them. "From my mother's letter," he went on smoothly, "I thought the wedding was slated for July. Since I was coming to the Territory on railroad business anyway, I believed I had plenty of time. In any case, something this — delicate — should be dealt with in person, don't you think, instead of over a telegraph wire?"

Willow, sitting up now but still a little dizzy, sighed and looked down at her hands, which were clasped in her lap. A tear she hadn't known she'd shed glistened on the curve of one thumb.

Her father patted her shoulder tenderly. "I'll go out and explain — or try to," he said. And then the door opened and closed, and he was gone.

Gideon came to Willow; he crouched before her as he had once before, in a faraway hotel room, when she had been willing, so embarrassingly willing, to share his bed. He caught her hands in his and squeezed them gently, just as he had done then. "I'm so sorry, Willow," he said, and that, too, was an echo from the past.

There was a great stir in the sanctuary beyond as the news was delivered, and Willow could hear Norville shouting in outrage. She prayed that he would not confront her now, that he would not be angry enough to go back on their bargain.

Willow forced herself to meet Gideon's eyes. Suddenly, inexplicably, she longed to touch Gideon's butternut hair, learn the texture of it, trace the firm lines of his clean-shaven jaw. She kept her hands together in her lap. What did one say in a circumstance such as this? Should she thank him for the unwitting rescue? Could Gideon Marshall see it in her face, the foolish love she still felt for him, after all this time and in spite of so many things?

At that moment, the door crashed open, causing Willow to start violently, and Norville Pickering filled the chasm, his face taut and red with fury.

Gideon rose slowly from his crouching position before Willow. He turned to face Norville.

"Are you truly married to this scoundrel?" the thwarted groom demanded. He spoke with such force that spittle flew from his mouth.

Willow lowered her head again, lest he see the contradictory emotions in her face. "It would seem so," she said softly.

Norville's rage seemed to pulse in the small room. "I will have satisfaction for this, my good man," he said to Gideon.

Gideon's aristocratic mouth twitched slightly and then he spread his hands out wide. He was willing to accept Norville's challenge, obviously, though Willow, watch-

30

ing him from out of the corner of one eye, had to concede that he was trying very hard to be gracious. "There is nothing I can say in my defense," he confessed.

Norville's manner, indeed his entire countenance, was petulance at its most essential. He threw back his thin shoulders and tugged hard at the cuffs of his suit coat. "I will not overlook this," he vowed, and then he raised his fists like a prizefighter prepared for battle. "I *will* have satisfaction, sir, and I suggest you prepare to defend yourself."

Willow stood up now, her head held high. "Don't be an idiot, Norville. Fighting won't solve anything, and this is God's house, after all."

Norville's Adam's apple bobbed up and down, but he lowered his fists to his sides. Turning to Willow and looking as though he might actually burst into tears, he protested, "This is intolerable — good Lord, Willow, how could you deceive me this way?"

Willow swallowed all the things she might have said. After all, Norville Pickering still had the power to destroy her brother. She could not endanger Steven's freedom, perhaps even his life, by speaking her mind. "I-I truly didn't mean to deceive you, Norville," she said gently. "Surely you realize that this cruel trick was more devastating for me than anyone. Imagine how I felt, Norville, why *just imagine!* I was young, I really believed that Mr. Marshall cared for me and had only the most honorable of intentions . . ."

Gideon thrust out an eloquent breath and rolled his eyes heavenward.

Willow flashed him one scathing look and insisted, "I *did!*" before turning her attention back to soothing the badly ruffled Norville. "Please" — disgust gathered into a lump in the back of her throat — "*darling.* You must believe that I was an innocent victim of this-this vicious and unconscionable deception."

Norville lifted his receding chin. "And I will avenge your shame, my dear," he promised, turning fiery eyes on Gideon once again. "I swear it. If it's the last thing I ever do, I will restore your honor —"

Gideon made a sound that could have been either a chortle of amusement or a gasp, probably thinking, as Willow was, that if Norville ever raised a hand to him, it would indeed be the last thing he ever did; he turned away, his coat straining across his broad shoulders as he folded his arms.

Evidently believing he'd made his point, Norville turned as well, without another word to Willow, and stormed out, leaving the door to the sanctuary gaping open.

Willow immediately strode over to Gideon Marshall, raised her foot, and kicked him, hard, in the back of his right leg.

After one howl of stunned anger and, she hoped, severe pain, Gideon whirled to face her.

"Why the hell did you do that?" he rasped.

Willow glared up into his face. "Why the *hell* do you think I did it?" she shot back.

A reluctant grin curved Gideon's fine lips, and those familiar eyes, the ones she'd looked into so often, in her favorite dreams, assessed her frankly, going as far as her full breasts before returning to her throbbing face. "I guess I deserved it at that."

"That and more!" Willow spat out, infuriated. God knew she was the subject of enough talk as it was, without this. By nightfall, everybody in Virginia City and for miles around would have heard about the ruined wedding and know what a fool this man had made of her, not once but *twice.* "You should just be thankful this is a church, because if it weren't, I would have kicked you somewhere else!"

Gideon grinned that maddening grin and waggled one index finger in amused reprimand. "But this *is* God's house, darling," he reminded her.

"If God were minding His business, the roof would have already fallen in on your head, you-you dreadful man!"

He sighed and his hands came to Willow's shoulders with an odd tenderness, his touch engendering a riot of inadvisable feelings within her. He gave a ragged sigh, and the look in his eyes was gentle. "What I did to you was unforgivable, I know. And I'm sorry, Willow, I really am. Since I can't change the past, my apology — and subsequent efforts to make amends — will have to suffice."

Willow's heart leaped into her throat and pounded there so hard that she couldn't speak.

Gideon arched one eyebrow, and the summer sun caught in his golden brown hair. "Why did you agree to marry me that night, Willow? You didn't even know me."

Willow's cheeks turned crimson and her eyes filled with hot tears. She *had* known Gideon Marshall even then, had loved him because he was the man in Evadne's portrait. But how could she answer his question honestly without making even more of a fool of herself?

"I must have been moonstruck or something," she lamented.

He sighed. "Do you hate me so much, Willow? After all, I could have made love to you in that hotel room, compromised you in the fullest sense of the word, but I didn't."

The glow in Willow's cheeks grew brighter still, and she trembled with latent shame and sharp disappointment at the memory of that wonderful, terrible night.

Before she could think of any suitable response to what he'd said, however, Willow's father had returned, and his wife, Evadne, was with him.

Her fine-boned face was a study in scandalized surprise.

"Gideon!" Evadne almost wailed, wringing her elegantly gloved hands. "What in the *name of heaven?*"

Gideon sighed again and looked annoyed before he turned to face his mother squarely.

"Am I disowned?" he asked ingenuously.

Forgiveness wasn't long in coming.

Evadne, a beautiful woman with piles of dark hair and sparkling eyes the same changeable color as her son's, smiled and flung her arms out wide, enfolding Gideon in a motherly embrace. "We weren't expecting you until next month!" she trilled.

Gideon cast one look at Willow, standing there in her wedding dress, and shrugged. "From the looks of things, it's a good thing

35

I arrived early."

Evadne's gaze sliced menacingly to Willow. Probably she had already convinced herself that the whole nasty matter was the fault of her wanton stepdaughter, not her son. Gideon was Evadne's favorite; to hear her tell it, he could do no wrong. "Yes," she said, in a sandpaper voice, frowning thoughtfully now. "Well, the guests have all gone, but there will be talk of this for years. I do declare, I don't know how I'll hold my head up in polite society after this."

"You'll manage, Mother," Gideon assured her wryly. "You always do, don't you?"

Willow wanted to scream with frustration; if she couldn't get out of this close little room, away from Gideon and his mother, she would surely succumb to some sort of fit. She gathered her skirts in her hands and made her way, with as much dignity as she could summon up, toward the door.

Evadne's quiet but still piercing voice stopped her. "You haven't heard the last of this, young lady," she warned. "Please go directly home and consider what you have done to poor Norville and his family, not to mention your father and me."

The judge gave his daughter one beleaguered, sympathetic look and nodded.

Pride squared Willow's shoulders and she

walked out, through the empty sanctuary, directly across the wide, rutted road, and up the stone walk that led to the front door of the judge's magnificent brick house.

She would change her clothes first thing, she decided, still dizzy with a combination of shock and undeniable relief, and then remain in her bedroom, giving the impression of guilty reflection. When it was dark, though, she would escape to the hills.

"Miss Willow!" shouted Maria Estrada, the housekeeper, as Willow started up the main staircase, the skirts of her modest wedding gown held high.

Willow froze, shut her eyes for a moment. "Yes?" she asked softly.

"Is the wedding over? Where is your new husband?"

Deflated now, Willow turned and looked down at Maria. The woman had been so much more than a housekeeper — she'd been a substitute mother. "It seems that I'm already married," she said, and the words felt shaky as she said them, like loose floorboards under her feet.

Maria's mouth made a perfect O; then she gasped, her dark eyes wide with amazement. *"Madre de Dios,"* she whispered, aghast, crossing herself with the hasty expertise of the very devout. "How can you already be married?"

One hysterical giggle bubbled up into Willow's throat and escaped. She was going to catch hell, not only from her stepmother but from the entire town as well, but that was nothing compared to the joy of knowing that she would not, in the near future, have to share Norville Pickering's bed or endure his presence from day to day.

"What mischief are you up to?" demanded Maria, resting her hands on her ample hips now, skepticism rising in her wise and gentle face like water in a new well. No doubt, she would light candles and say many novenas for Willow's immortal soul, but for now she was set on getting answers.

Willow couldn't resist teasing a little.

Horror rounded Maria's eyes to impossible dimensions and a bluster of Spanish invective followed.

Willow laughed and took pity upon her old friend. After all, this was a woman who had held her, dried her tears, taught her to make tortillas. "Relax, Maria. I didn't set out to have two husbands, I honestly didn't."

"But . . ."

Willow wanted very much to be alone to sort out her thoughts and make some sort of plan, so she smiled warmly and promised to tell the whole story after she'd had time to collect her wits.

Ten minutes later, she was struggling with the fastenings of her wedding dress when Maria knocked lightly and then entered the bedroom with a tray and a raft of questions.

Although she would have liked more time — once she was free of the dress she prayed she would never have to wear again — comfortable in her satin chemise, Willow suppressed a sigh, helped herself to a cup of tea from the tray, and laced it with generous portions of sugar and milk.

"Are my father and Mrs. Gallagher back from the church?" she asked, mostly to stall.

Maria looked avid and exasperated, both at once. "They are in the sitting room, with Lancelot."

Willow winced, closing her eyes. Lancelot was the silly nickname she and Maria had given Gideon long ago, when they'd known him only as the figure in the painting Evadne so cherished. How embarrassing it would be, though, if that were to slip out in front of Gideon.

Thanks to the interrupted wedding, Willow was mortified enough.

"You mustn't call Mr. Marshall that in his hearing, Maria."

Maria sighed dreamily. She'd taken a seat

on the lid of Willow's hope chest, a cup of tea in hand. "He is handsome, is he not? Just as handsome as his portrait."

Willow suddenly wanted to cry. Over the years since she'd come to live with her father and Evadne, soon after her mother's death, she had made up many romantic stories, all of them centering on the painted image of Gideon Marshall that hung in the sitting room downstairs.

Meeting him in San Francisco, at seventeen, had seemed the culmination of a wonderful fantasy. Because she had loved Gideon, through the portrait, for years, Willow had agreed to his proposal with joy.

Of course, she was nineteen now and, looking back, she realized all too well how silly it had been of her to ever believe that such a man would want her as a wife, and after knowing her only a few hours, too.

He was a rounder and a rake — what other kind of man would do what he did? — but the fault had not been entirely his. Willow herself had been gullible and stupid.

Glumly, because she knew Maria would insist, Willow explained about the fraudulent marriage ceremony back in San Francisco, which had turned out to be real. She went on to tell how Gideon had stopped today's ceremony barely an hour before, leaving out an unnecessary account of her jubilation at escaping Norville Pickering. Considering what he could cause to happen to Steven, her brother, the reprieve was probably only temporary anyway.

Gideon was relieved when his mother left the judge's study. She would go off to her room, no doubt separate from her husband's, and shed melodramatic and copious tears. He didn't envy Devlin Gallagher the days and weeks ahead.

Devlin laughed gruffly as he filled a snifter with brandy the color of his daughter's eyes. "Damn," he marveled.

Gideon stared at his mother's doting husband, amazed. If the situation had been reversed, and he'd been in Judge Gallagher's position, he would have been furious. Looking to take a strip out of somebody's hide.

"Have a drink," said the judge, almost cordially.

The idea held infinite appeal. Gideon went to the side table and helped himself to a generous portion of straight whiskey. Two gulps washed a good bit of his nervousness away, along with a measure of the weariness of traveling so far.

"Sit down," prompted the judge, indicating a leather chair facing the fireplace.

41

Confused, Gideon sat. Good Lord, a man would almost think that Gallagher was *pleased* that his daughter's wedding had been spoiled, and in such a scandalous fashion, too.

"I ought to have horsewhipped you in the street," observed the older man, in companionable tones, as he settled his powerful frame in the chair opposite Gideon's.

Gideon took a sip from his whiskey. "Why didn't you?" he asked.

"I was too goddamned relieved," Gallagher replied, lifting one booted foot to rest on his knee.

"You didn't want your daughter to marry?"

Devlin Gallagher flashed Gideon a quelling look. "Damnit, would you want that pimply squirrel Pickering to marry *your* daughter?" he demanded.

The groom had been rather unprepossessing, but Gideon hadn't thought much about it until now. He'd been too intent on averting the complications of bigamy for that. "She must care for him, if she agreed to the marriage —"

The judge interrupted with a snort. "Care for him? Willow despises Pickering!"

"Then why in God's name would she consent to becoming his wife?"

Gallagher shrugged. "That's what I'd like to find out. My guess would be that it has something to do with my son."

Gideon was reminded of his other business in Virginia City — railroad business that had nothing whatsoever to do with stopping Willow's marriage to the squirrel. "Steven," he said cautiously. Admire Devlin Gallagher though he did, he couldn't afford to tip his hand now.

"No doubt, my dear wife has regaled you with an account of Steven's many sins," the judge said wearily, his blue eyes faraway and full of pain.

Gideon paid little attention to his mother's opinions of other people, as a general rule. She was inclined to look for the worst and keep searching until she found it, regardless of the effort involved. "She mentioned him," he said, in classic understatement.

The judge sighed again and took a drink of his brandy. "I suppose it's my fault. Steven is an outlaw, after all, and Willow — well, Willow is a constant reminder of my first wife. I know Evadne finds the resemblance trying."

Gideon sat back, remembering. Evadne had been delighted at the prospect of raising a daughter, when Willow first joined the Gallagher household. After Willow's ill-fated visit to San Francisco, however, her attitude had changed. Ever since the two women had returned to Virginia City, his mother's long letters had been filled with bitter references to Willow and the shameful circumstances of her birth. It seemed that Devlin and his former wife, Chastity, mother of the notorious Steven, had engaged in some sort of tryst later on, and the girl with amber eyes had been the result.

But Evadne must have known the truth about Willow's conception, Gideon reasoned. Apparently, she'd been able to overlook her husband's obvious infidelity — she'd tried to launch her stepdaughter socially, after all. When that effort failed, Evadne had turned on Willow. Permanently.

Recalling that made Gideon feel even worse, if that was possible, about the prank he and Zachary and their friends had pulled on the girl.

"Willow and Steven are close then?" Gideon dared, pretending an interest in his drink. He was uncomfortable with his thoughts; besides, he had important business in the Montana Territory beyond ruining a wedding.

"Very close. They were together until Willow was nine. Steven brought her to me then."

Gideon treaded carefully onto sensitive ground. "As Mother tells it," he began, "it came as something of a surprise, Willow's existence, I mean."

The judge's still handsome face tightened. "I knew I'd sired a second child," he said, "a daughter. But I couldn't find them. God knows I tried."

"My mother's reaction to Willow's arrival must have been interesting," observed Gideon quietly.

"It was," the judge allowed, with a sound that was part sigh and part chuckle. "But Evadne is a good woman, and she forgave me, as far as possible anyway. She tried to be a mother to Willow, and I will be forever grateful for that, but, well, things just didn't work out. It isn't as if Willow hasn't contributed to the problem — she's high-spirited and impulsive. I suppose it's natural that the two of them would butt heads." He paused and made a rueful sound. "Once Willow came to live with us, there was a lot of talk, and that made things even more difficult for your mother."

"I can imagine."

Devlin's blue eyes came to Gideon's face, their expression shadowed. "You didn't come all the way to Virginia City to stop Willow from marrying Pickering, did you?"

he asked evenly. His was the tone of a man who already knew the answer to his question.

"No, sir," Gideon admitted. Virginia City was a small community, and Devlin Gallagher was a prominent citizen. He wouldn't be able to keep his intentions secret for long.

"Railroad business, you said?"

"Yes."

"Concerning Steven?"

Gideon got out of his chair, moving to stand at one of the heavily curtained windows near Devlin's cluttered desk. There was obviously no point in lying to the judge; the man was nobody's fool.

"Yes."

The judge gave an unsettling burst of laughter. "You'll never get him," he said, with relish. "Do you know what the Indians call Steven, Gideon?"

The liquor was easing some of the tension in Gideon's shoulders, though they still ached. He remained silent, too stubborn, he guessed, to admit that he knew the enormity of the task that had been set for him.

Devlin Gallagher was only too happy to elaborate. "They call him the Mountain Fox," he said. "And not without reason, my friend. Not without reason."

"He's wanted," Gideon said spiritlessly,

not bothering to turn from the window and face this man who was, oddly, both his stepfather and father-in-law.

"By the railroad?"

"By the law. The railroad has a vested interest in his capture, of course. Steven has been robbing trains, Judge Gallagher. We can't afford to overlook that."

"I suppose not," said the judge, in a sad voice. "I don't believe Steven's your man, for what it's worth. His robberies are invariably designed to hurt me, you know. Steven inherited a great deal of money when my mother passed away. The funds have been held in trust for him, and he has full access to them, no questions asked."

Gideon turned from the window at last. After the events of this day, he'd thought that nothing could shock him, but Devlin Gallagher's words had. "And you truly believe his only aim is to cause you trouble?"

"My son hates me — and rightfully so, I'm afraid. I've never known him to waylay a train or a stagecoach that wasn't carrying something of mine — like one of my payrolls, for instance."

Beyond the window glass, the skies rumbled. The clouds that had been gathering in the distance all day were closing in.

"Two months ago Steven Gallagher and

his men held up the Central Pacific. They took twenty-five thousand dollars."

Devlin nodded. "Twenty-five thousand dollars of my money and not one damned thing else. I didn't hold the railroad responsible and I wonder why they're so all-fired anxious to see Steven prosecuted."

"The passengers were terrified, for one thing," Gideon said, albeit with less force.

"None of them was hurt," argued the judge.

"That still doesn't excuse your son — the man cannot be permitted to stop the Central Pacific at will!"

"They'll figure out a way to hang Steven if you bring him in. You know that, don't you?"

The whiskey was suddenly roiling in Gideon's stomach, and he set his glass aside with a thump. "He'll be tried fairly, Judge Gallagher."

Devlin gave a hoot of laughter. "God, you have a lot of confidence in yourself and your railroad, boy. Vancel Tudd's been after Steven for six years, and he's never even come close. Do you know who Tudd is, young fella? Well, I'll tell you. He's the best goddamned bounty hunter in the territories. How the hell do you expect to find my son if he can't?"

Gideon thought of the golden-haired, wide-eyed young woman upstairs. Thanks to all he'd done to her, here and in San Francisco, she would be seen as a scarlet woman from now on. And yet she was, he sensed, the key to finding Steven Gallagher. "I don't know," he lied, in answer to the judge's question.

Suddenly, he was bone tired, even though it was only midafternoon. He still had to write a letter to Daphne; certainly, some sort of explanation was in order, since he was supposed to marry the woman the first week in September.

Gideon went to the coat tree just inside the study doors and took down his dusty, travel-rumpled jacket. Under the circumstances, he couldn't very well stay under this roof. "I'll be at the Union Hotel," he told the still and thoughtful figure of Judge Devlin Gallagher.

"Your mother will be furious," replied the judge. He spoke wearily.

Gideon shrugged and opened one of the double doors. "Your Honor?"

Gallagher rose from his chair and turned to face Gideon. "Yes?"

"I'm sorry."

The look in the judge's eyes was incredibly patient. "I know," he answered.

Gideon went out into the rain, raising his collar against the wind.

2

The storm pounding at the single window in his hotel room, Gideon opened the packet of writing paper he had purchased at the mercantile next door and took up a pen. "Dear Daphne," he wrote. "I'm in the Montana Territory . . ."

He crumpled that page and began again: "Dear Daphne, you will never guess where I am." *Oh, and by the way, I'm already married . . . it was a joke, you see.*

Gideon took yet another fresh sheet of paper and scrawled, "Dear Daphne, I may not be back in time for the wedding —"

He stopped. It went against his grain, lying to Daphne, but how could he tell her the truth? Before their wedding could take place, he'd have to have his marriage to Willow Gallagher annulled. That shouldn't be too difficult, he reasoned, given that they'd never consummated the union.

But still.

Resolute, Gideon dipped his pen in the ink bottle and forged on, explaining that railroad business might keep him away from home longer than expected.

Even after appropriate pleasantries had been added, the letter to Daphne was very short. It seemed to Gideon that there should be more to say.

With a sigh, he signed the missive and set it aside so that the ink could dry. He didn't love Daphne Roberts and he was certain that she did not love him; his reasons for becoming engaged to her were far more practical than that. By aligning himself with Daphne's father, also a major stockholder in the Central Pacific, he would create a financial empire.

Until he had walked into the rustic church that afternoon and seen Willow Gallagher, Gideon's plans to marry for power and position, not to mention a vast increase in his personal fortune, had not bothered him in the least. Now, however, they weighed heavily on his mind and spirit. He couldn't help considering the fact that this topaz-eyed hellcat was his wife, legally if not morally. He could bed her and be well within his rights.

The thought roused an unfortunate anatomical response, and Gideon rose out of his chair, stretched his arms high above his head, and muttered a swearword. It was bad enough that he planned to use Willow Gallagher to locate her outlaw brother, Steven, bad enough that he had probably ruined her reputation forever. To seduce her in the bargain would be reprehensible.

And yet Gideon wanted her as he had never wanted Daphne or any of the dozens of more adventurous women he had enjoyed over the years of his manhood. Willow was beautiful, with her lush figure and that head of golden hair that seemed to invite his fingers to stray within it.

Gideon brought himself up short. The world was full of beautiful women; there was no need to let this crazy attraction to the lovely Miss Gallagher disrupt his well-laid plans.

Methodically, he folded the letter he'd written to Daphne, tucked it into an envelope, and penned a San Francisco address. Then, telling himself that Daphne Roberts was indeed the right woman for him, he put on his coat and left the room.

Willow rose very early the next morning, glad to see that the rainstorm had passed. She dressed quickly in trousers and a shirt. After brushing and braiding her hair into a single waist-length plait, she hurried into the hallway and down the back stairs that led to the kitchen.

Maria was there, as usual, preparing breakfast, and she inspected Willow's clothing with disapproving eyes. "Mrs. Gallagher and the judge will expect you to remain at home today, Miss Willow," she said. "It is the only proper thing to do, after yesterday."

Willow helped herself to a warm cinnamon bun and smiled reassuringly. "Just tell them you didn't see me," she suggested, wriggling into the lightweight jacket she would shed later, when the chill had gone off the morning.

"*Madre de Dios,* that would be a lie!"

"*Sí,*" teased Willow, already on her way to the back door.

"What about Señor Pickering and his people? What will we say to them?" Maria cried anxiously.

Willow shrugged, opened the door, and hurried out, consuming the cinnamon bun as she walked toward the stables on the far side of her father's property. She was going to have to face Norville again, sooner or later, but today was not the day. Today she would find Steven and tell him how Lancelot had saved her from a tragic marriage.

Maria's two young cousins, Juan and

Pablito, were already working inside the stables; Juan was milking the family cow and Pablito, the older of the two, was feeding the horses.

Willow greeted them both, ignoring their curious looks as best she could. Was there no one who had not heard of her disastrous near-wedding the day before?

Probably not.

"You will ride Banjo, señorita?" asked Pablito, resting on the handle of his pitchfork.

"Yes," said Willow, taking her bridle from its peg on the stable wall.

Pablito's grin was wide and startlingly white. "You do not marry Señor Nose Pickering?" he asked, dropping the pitchfork to lead Banjo, Willow's pinto gelding, from his stall.

Willow laughed at the name that Steven had given Norville. "I do not," she answered.

Pablito stood back as Willow found Banjo's blanket and saddle and put them deftly into place on the animal's back. "You will tell Señor Steven what has happened?"

Willow tightened the cinch around Banjo's belly, tugged at one stirrup, then swung deftly into the saddle. She didn't remember a time when she hadn't known how to ride.

"Yes," she answered.

"He will be angry."

A lump rose in Willow's throat and she nodded. Steven would be furious, but not because she hadn't been able to go through with the marriage. No, he would be outraged that she had ever intended to marry Norville in the first place.

Willow prodded Banjo into motion with a gentle touch of her booted heels. The manner in which she had come to be married to Gideon Marshall would not sit well with her brother, either.

"Be careful, señorita," enjoined Pablito, as she rode out. "Mind that you are not followed."

Willow nodded again and rode away, but she was not thinking about Pablito's well-founded warning. Her mind was full of Gideon Marshall — her husband.

As she traveled toward the foothills that rose beyond the growing town of Virginia City, Willow turned Gideon's image in her mind. She knew much about him, partly garnered from things that Evadne had said about her son over the years, partly discerned from the portrait and the brief time she had spent with him in San Francisco.

Gideon's hair, now a dark gold, would turn a crisp, toasty color in winter. He was clean-shaven in summer, but when the weather grew cold, he would wear a beard and mustache . . .

Blushing at her own daring, Willow wondered — and not for the first time — how it would feel to lie with him, as a woman lies with a man. Would Gideon's touch be gentle or rough? Would there be pain when he entered her?

Maria had warned that there would be some discomfort the first time but pleasure afterward if the man was gentle and caring. At the time of this discussion, however, Willow had been on the verge of marrying Norville, and the idea of marital intimacies had held no appeal at all.

Indeed, she'd been terrified. For all that folks seemed to see her wanton mother when they looked at her, Willow was untouched.

Sighing, Willow rode on, enjoying the bright, freshly washed glimmer of the June day. How long would it be until Gideon divorced her, or simply had the marriage declared null and void? When that day came, she would again be vulnerable to Norville's persuasion.

A full hour had passed before Willow became aware of the rider behind her. Norville?

Doing her best not to reveal that she knew she was being followed, Willow did not look back. Certainly Norville had trailed her before — that was how he'd learned of the signals she and Steven used to communicate with each other — but some instinct told her that the rider tracking her now was someone else.

Veering off the course she would otherwise have taken, Willow nudged Banjo into a gallop and then a run. She had been raised in these hills, taught from an early age to lose herself in them at will. It would be easy enough to double back and see who was behind her.

A cold shiver trickled down her spine when the rider followed without apparent difficulty. Good heavens, what if that was Vancel Tudd? Steven was within a few miles of this place. What if Tudd found him?

Still hoping to elude the one who stalked her, Willow took evasive tactics. She rode hard for the shack hidden away in a dense stand of birch and cottonwood trees, a few hundred yards away.

And the rider followed.

She led Banjo inside the shack and they cowered there in the darkness. *Please God,* Willow prayed, *don't let Steven get wind of this. Don't let him come here.*

Outside, a horse nickered, and Banjo answered companionably. Willow swore aloud, and then a burst of masculine laughter erupted beyond the shack's hanging door. A moment later, Gideon Marshall appeared in the opening.

"Who do you think you are?" demanded Willow sharply, acting on pure bravado as she stormed toward him, pulling Banjo behind her, hoping that the man would step back out of her way when she reached him.

He did, but his lips were curved into an obnoxious grin. "By all accounts, I'm your husband," he replied.

Willow let Banjo's reins drop into the deep grass and sank to the ground, angrily plucking a wild tiger lily and turning it in her fingers. Ever since she'd seen that portrait for the first time, she'd dreamed of marrying Gideon Marshall. Now, however, she felt a deep and contradictory need to plague him. "A simple annulment will fix that," she snapped. "After all, Mr. Marshall, our marriage has not been — well, it isn't *real.*"

Gideon lifted his hands to his hips, letting his own bay gelding wander free, as Banjo did. The horses nibbled companionably at the sweet, breeze-bent grass. "That little oversight could be remedied easily enough

59

— *Mrs.* Marshall."

Willow flushed and looked away. Damnit, she'd walked right into that one. "My brothers would kill you if you touched me," she said, somewhat lamely and after a long time.

Gideon arched one eyebrow and came to crouch before her, on his haunches, only a few feet away. He, too, picked a tiger lily and twirled it in his fingers. "Your brothers, plural? I understood that you had only one sibling."

"I have three — Coy and Reilly are my half brothers. Their father was Jay Forbes, but we all had the same mother."

"And they ride with Steven?"

Willow felt uneasy. She'd said too much already. There was something about this man that made her tend toward all sorts of excesses. "Are you a bounty hunter, Mr. Marshall?"

Gideon, along with his brother, Zachary, had inherited sizable interests in a number of railroad companies, founded by their paternal grandfather. While Zachary seemed to prefer to travel, among other indulgences, Gideon had always been more interested in business.

While it was unlikely that Gideon had joined Vancel Tudd's profession, he might well have a stake in putting Steven, the

60

inveterate train robber, out of commission.

Steven loved plaguing the railroads and the stagecoach lines but, as far as Willow knew, he concentrated on stealing from the judge, who had a great many fingers in a great many financial pies.

Her father was rich.

Gideon was probably richer.

"No," he answered, at some length, but so easily and smoothly that Willow found herself believing him. Almost.

"Why did you follow me?" she asked.

One of Gideon's powerful shoulders lifted in an idle shrug. The weather was warm, though it wasn't any later than seven o'clock in the morning, and Gideon had already shed his coat, if he'd worn one in the first place, and rolled up his shirtsleeves. Light brown hair shimmered on his muscled forearms. "I wanted to talk to you, without my mother and the judge and your spurned lover listening in."

Willow reddened again and dropped the bright orange tiger lily into the grass. "My *'lover'?*" she snapped.

Gideon laughed and held up both hands in a plea for peace, the wildflower still caught between his fingers. "I didn't mean to insult you, Willow. And I wasn't implying that you and Norbert had been intimate."

"Norville. His name is Norville."

Gideon sat down gracefully, flush on the ground, Indian style. "Norville," he repeated wryly. And then his wicked eyes sliced to Willow's face. "What on earth did you ever see in him?" he asked. He seemed honestly confounded, as well as amused.

The temptation to tell this man everything was great, but Willow resisted. She searched her mind for one true virtue to ascribe to Norville Pickering and came up dry. "I'm nearly twenty years old," she said, for that was the closest she could come to an explanation.

Gideon sighed. "That old?" he mocked.

She bit her lower lip.

"You were marrying Pickering because you're nearly twenty years old?" Gideon prompted when she remained silent.

"Around here, if a woman isn't married by the time she's twenty, she's considered a spinster," Willow said. She heard her own voice, as if from a distance, and marveled at the things that came out of her mouth. Before Gideon's questionable rescue, Willow had confided in Maria, in a weak moment, that she would have preferred being a nun to marrying Norville Pickering. "I *don't* want to be an old maid!"

Since when? Gideon's gaze was direct,

piercing. "Well, you're in no danger of spinsterhood, now are you? After all, you're married to me."

Willow still had that odd feeling that she'd been swept away, that she might say anything — anything at all — or, worse, *do* anything at all. "You can hardly call this a marriage," she huffed.

Gideon smiled. "No, I suppose not. Until I bed you, it's more of an arrangement, regrettably legal." He paused. "Were you planning to meet your brother today, Willow?"

"No!"

He obviously knew the lie for what it was, as he showed no sign of going away, damn him. That meant that Willow's plans for the day were in ruins, for she certainly could not risk leading this man or anyone else to Steven.

"Just out for a quiet Sunday morning ride?"

She folded her arms, stiffened her spine, and hiked up her chin. "Yes."

Gideon grinned again and it seemed that he was a bit nearer, though Willow hadn't been conscious of any movement on his part. "It isn't safe to ride in these hills alone, Mrs. Marshall," he said smoothly. "After

all, there are Indians, miners, grizzly bears
—"

"Kindly *do not* refer to me as 'Mrs.
Marshall.' "

He laughed and shifted his body in an
easy motion that brought him so close to
Willow that she could feel the warmth of
his breath on her face. "Is that any way to
talk to your husband of two years, dearest?"
he teased.

Willow had been caught in a spell of some
kind, but in that moment it was broken. She
doubled up her fists and aimed them both
at Gideon's smug and handsome face.

He forestalled the attack easily, catching
both of her wrists in his hands and then easing her backward until she found herself lying prone in the verdant summer grass,
looking up at him in amazement. The most
surprising thing of all was that she felt no
fear.

She knew Gideon Marshall would never
hurt her, not physically, anyway.

Slowly, gently, Gideon brought her hands
down to the soft and fragrant ground, but
he did not release his hold on her wrists.
He whispered her name and she felt his
hard length stretch out upon her, though
the crushing sensation she had expected did
not come. His lips came to hers, tasting.

Willow's entire body quivered with the torrent of needs that had been unchained by this one action, and she moaned as Gideon's kiss deepened, became demanding. His tongue prodded her lips to part and when they did, he explored her freely and fiercely and she found her own tongue fencing with his.

When the kiss finally ended, she stared up at him, squinting against the sunshine that framed his head like a flaming crown. "Can that make me pregnant?" she demanded.

Gideon gave a shout of laughter and rolled away to lie beside her, on his back, looking up at the china blue sky. "No, hellcat. It doesn't happen that way."

Willow was wildly embarrassed. Raised around livestock, she understood the fundamentals of intercourse, but much of it was still a mystery.

"I know how babies are conceived, Mr. Marshall!" she informed him. "I just thought there might possibly be an alternative method, that's all."

Gideon was still amused. He lay there on his back, with his hands cupped behind his head, as relaxed as could be. "There is only one way to make babies," he assured her.

Willow sat up, but it was some moments before she could bring herself to look down into that handsome, amused face. "I suppose you're thinking that I am very unsophisticated for a woman of nearly twenty."

He smiled. "Actually, my thoughts were considerably less honorable," he admitted, and when he reached for Willow and enfolded her in his arms, it seemed natural to allow him to hold her close, right there on the ground.

She let her head rest on his shoulder and hoped devoutly that he would kiss her again.

Presently, Gideon shifted, as if he had heard her thoughts, and his mouth was within an inch of her own. "Willow," he said, in a bemused and reluctant voice, and then his lips were claiming hers again.

His hand, resting on her waist, slid slowly to the outer rounding of her breast, the thumb stroking the hidden nipple to an aching alertness. She felt his groan echo into her mouth, as well as heard it, and was conscious of his desire where his groin touched her hip.

As he kissed her, Gideon undid the first button of her shirt and then the second, and Willow felt the cool caress of the morning air as he displaced the camisole beneath, baring one breast to be cupped in his hand.

Instinctively, Willow whimpered and arched her back, longing for some fulfillment that seemed to elude her. Gideon's warm, moist mouth left hers to course down over the soft underside of her chin, the tingling length of her neck, the uppermost swell of her breast. When he reached the peak that already strained for his attentions, he nipped at it, plying it painlessly with his teeth.

Willow gasped softly, in joy and in torment, and cupped the breast with one hand, offering it. Gideon withheld full satisfaction, nibbling at the sweet morsel, circling it with his tongue, raking it gently with his teeth. Finally, finally, he suckled, and instead of being assuaged, the frantic yearning within Willow's untutored body grew to torrential proportions.

Heedless of her soft pleas, Gideon bared the other breast and subjected it to the same sweet worship, tormenting Willow even as he soothed her. When he had taken full satisfaction there, he knelt astraddle her and his fingers warmed her flesh, even through the cloth, as he undid the buttons on her trousers and slid them down. She had not worn drawers, for they were too bulky under such close-fitting garb, and she was completely bared to him, waiting.

"I can't take you, Willow," he said, in a voice that seemed to be directed as much to himself as to her. "It wouldn't be right . . ."

But even as he spoke, his hand was at the vee of tangled curls, stroking, searching for the secret sheltered beneath.

What was happening?

How had they come to this?

All Willow could have said for sure was that her need for this man resembled anguish, it was so keen. "You are my husband," she reminded him.

His thumb passed through the silken down to touch the core of her need, to ply it to moist wanting. "In the legal sense of the word," he argued distractedly.

Willow's legs were parting of their own accord. "Make love to me," she whispered, shameless. "Please, Gideon, make love to me. I want to know what it's like."

"I can't," he groaned, but the motions of the pad of his thumb were sending sharp blades of desire throughout her body even as he spoke.

Her pride was gone, seared away by the heat of her wanting. "Please," she pleaded brokenly.

Gideon moved away from her, and for one terrible moment, she thought that he would leave her quivering, on the point of no return. She was about to cry out at the injustice when he caught her knees in his hands, drew them up, and pressed them wide of each other.

He bent his head and she felt his breath whisper against the secret place, his tongue wriggle through the veil to the bud beneath. Willow gasped lustily as he flicked at the hidden morsel, causing it to harden and grow very moist.

"Gideon," she choked, almost blinded by this new and never-suspected pleasure. "Oh, God — what are you — oooh!"

Gideon took his time with her, savoring her, driving her into spheres of explosive need beyond the reach of her very limited experience. He lapped and nibbled and finally suckled in earnest, his hands under Willow's bottom now, holding her up to him as though she were a chalice filled with sweet nectar.

She cried out in savage release and stiffened, and still he drank of her. The quivering began again and Willow's hips began to rise and fall, slowly, matching the meter he set for them. Her knees were draped shamelessly over his shoulders now and her hands were tangled in his hair, holding him close. When she was writhing wildly and pleading once more, Gideon stopped his suckling to part her with gentle fingers and softly kiss her over the brink and into the fire that lay beyond.

Her breath was ragged and quick as he gently lowered her back to the ground. She was still wearing her shirt and camisole, though they had both been displaced for Gideon's full access to her breasts, and her trousers lay several feet away. She had neither the strength nor the will to reach for them, and she was too dazed to be ashamed of her nakedness.

He smiled at the question brewing in her amber eyes. "No, hellcat, that didn't make you pregnant, either."

Willow's head was beginning to clear by then, and she could see Gideon's own need pressing, fierce, against the confining cloth of his trousers. "What about . . . what about you?"

His hand trailed over the curve of her thigh, threatening to begin the madness all over again. "I'll be all right," he assured her, but there was a hollow sound in his voice, and Willow found herself fearing that he would find relief elsewhere, with another woman. Though she had no right to consider such things, she was broken by the very possibility.

"You're going to be married," she remembered aloud, trying to hide the emotions that were already displacing the sleepy ecstasy she had known only seconds before. "Your mother talked of little else, until Norville proposed to me."

Gideon sighed, reached for her discarded trousers, and extended them in a mannerly fashion. "Yes," he replied quietly. "I am getting married. Once I'm free to, anyway."

Willow silently ordered herself not to cry and sat up to scramble somewhat awkwardly into her trousers. "Is she pretty?"

"I suppose so, yes."

"What is her name?" She already knew the answer, of course. Evadne was constantly singing the praises of her daughter-in-law to be.

"Daphne," Gideon answered.

Willow wriggled to button her trousers. "That is a silly name," she observed petulantly, her lower lip jutting out.

Gideon only shrugged.

"What would she say, your *Daphne,* if she knew what we just did together?"

He shifted uncomfortably in the grass. "What would Norville Pickering say?" he countered.

"He would probably challenge you to a duel or something equally stupid. Now answer my question."

Gideon's green-gray eyes were impatient now, and narrowed to slits. "How in the devil can I answer a question like that? How should I know what Daphne would say?"

"You must have some idea," Willow insisted.

"All right," Gideon said, growing impatient. "Naturally, she'd be upset. Are you happy now?"

"No!" Willow cried, swaying somewhat precariously on her knees as she did up the buttons of her shirt. "No, I am *not* happy! I have just been compromised in the grass by a man who is my husband and someone else's intended and I am *anything* but happy!"

Gideon's face reddened. "God damnit, you have not been compromised and I have the wherewithal to prove it!"

In spite of the fact that she was near tears and totally confused about everything, Willow had to stifle a laugh. "So you do, Mr. Marshall," she said, glancing briefly at the front of his trousers. When her face caught fire, she had to look away. "That will teach you to follow me through the woods like some skulking —"

Suddenly, Gideon was on his knees, too, his face within inches of Willow's. "Skulking, is it?" he broke in, taking obvious offense to the term.

Willow went on, though it would probably

have been more prudent to hold her tongue.

Alas, she had never been the prudent sort.

"And as if that wasn't enough, *Mr.* Marshall, you then proceeded to take liberties with my virtue!"

"I took liberties with *you?"* growled Gideon, even more affronted, it would seem, than before. "You practically attacked me. In fact, you *asked* me to make love to you!"

With a smug smile, Willow reached out and caressed him, taking wicked delight in his groan and the almost imperceptible motion of his hips. "I suppose some people would even say that we have consummated our marriage," she said.

Gideon caught her wrist in a grasp just short of pain and stopped her from tormenting him. The color drained from his face as he stared at her. "What did you say?"

"We were very intimate, weren't we? Just now, I mean?"

"Yes, but —"

"I've certainly never done anything like that with anyone else," Willow said primly.

"Willow!"

"I guess you'll have to divorce me now, instead of just getting an annulment. Dear, dear — Norville and Miss Daphne are going to be in a fine state when they hear about this."

Gideon's jawline was rock hard and his nose was almost touching Willow's. "Are you planning to claim that I actually *made love* to you?"

"Of course not — I wouldn't lie. But I suppose my father will see little difference between that and what we actually did."

Gideon grew paler still as he drew back and considered. Above, the shiny leaves of cottonwood trees whispered in the breeze and cast their dancing shadows down onto the soft ground. "You would tell him?" he asked at last and in wonder.

"I would do practically anything to keep from marrying Norville Pickering," Willow answered, in all honesty.

"Well, just tell him no, for God's sake!"

"I can't do that."

"Why not?"

Willow turned her head, only to have her chin caught in Gideon's hand and drawn back. Tears welled in her eyes and trickled down her face. "Because Norville knows how to find Steven," she said.

Gideon's hands rested on her cheeks now, his thumbs wiping her tears away. "Pickering blackmailed you by threatening your brother? *That* was why you were getting married?"

Miserably, Willow nodded.

74

Gideon sighed and shoved a hand through his rumpled hair. "What's to keep Pickering from telling what he knows, Willow? His price was marriage and you haven't met it."

"I think I can stall him."

Suspicion played in Gideon's features. "How?" he demanded.

Willow shrugged. "By making Norville think that I still want him, even though I'm married to you."

"That's insane."

"I'll tell him that you've never actually touched me in an untoward fashion and —"

"And he'll want to know why you don't have your father the judge arrange an annulment!"

"If-if I have to, I'll let Norville kiss me . . ."

She paused and shivered slightly.

Gideon's hands suddenly grasped her shoulders. "Oh, no, you *won't,*" he said.

And then he looked surprised by the assertion.

Willow felt a wisp of triumph. "No?"

"That's right, no. Damnit, you are my wife and you will not —"

"Will not what?" Willow wanted to know.

Gideon made an exasperated sound and got to his feet, turning away, folding his arms. "You will not go around throwing yourself at other men, just to save your

75

brother's hide."

"And you, of course, will not go to other women," Willow said reasonably, standing up. "Because that would be equally wrong, wouldn't it?"

"You forget that I am engaged to Daphne Roberts!" Gideon threw out.

"You're the one who *forgot,* Gideon. And you aren't faithful to her anyway, are you?"

His back stiffened and his head was tilted back, as though he might be challenging the sky itself. His silence was answer enough.

3

Dove Triskadden settled herself on the sofa and took a sip from her brandy snifter. There were times when it was wise to speak first and times when it was best to hold her tongue, and this was one of the latter.

Devlin stood facing the mirror over the fireplace, adjusting his string tie. Though everyone in Virginia City knew that he kept a mistress, and that that mistress was Dove Triskadden, he couldn't very well go home looking as though he'd just crawled out of her bed — which was exactly what he'd done.

Finally, he turned and assessed Dove's voluptuous body with appreciative eyes. Worry was etched in his handsome face, and Dove felt regret that her lovemaking had not smoothed it away. She sighed.

"Smile," he urged gruffly, as he always did when he was about to go back to Evadne.

Obediently, Dove summoned up the requested smile, for she loved Judge Devlin Gallagher as no other woman, including Chastity, ever had. Loved him for who and what he was, the good with the bad, and never wished to change him.

Devlin was perceptive, and he read much from Dove's wide green eyes. "You know I would live here with you always, if only I could," he said gently. "I love you, Triskadden."

Dove's smile was real this time, requiring no effort on her part. "Wouldn't that be a scandal, though, if you moved out of Evadne's house and into mine, bold as brass?"

Devlin sighed. "It would be, indeed. Between Steven and Willow, there's been enough of that sort of thing already."

"Do you think Steven's heard about the wedding yet?"

He grinned and shook his head. There was gray in his wheat-colored hair, and Dove felt a tug in her heart at the notice of it. "No — definitely not. There would have been some kind of incident if he had."

Dove looked away as Devlin reached for his suit coat and shrugged into it. "What will happen now, Dev? Will Willow still marry Norville Pickering?"

"Good God," sighed the judge, "I hope not."

"That's why you haven't tried to dissolve her marriage to Gideon Marshall, isn't it?"

Devlin was deeply troubled; Dove didn't need to look at him to know that. She'd felt it, even before she'd held him in her arms, given him the only solace she had to offer. "I'm not sure that's possible," he muttered. "Both Gideon and Willow claim they haven't consummated the union, but there's a — well, there's some kind of charge between those two. If they haven't been together already, they soon will be."

"Would you want Gideon Marshall for a son-in-law, Dev?"

His chuckle was raspy, humorless. "I don't think my personal opinion matters much, one way or the other. I can't say I dislike the man, but . . ."

"But?" prompted Dove.

Devlin gave a ragged sigh. "Gideon came here to track Steven down — at the behest of the railroad. He told me that, straight out."

The pit of Dove's stomach quivered. "Do you suppose he can find Steven? Succeed where Vancel Tudd has failed?"

"I sure as hell hope not," breathed Devlin, and then he approached Dove, bent to

79

kiss the top of her head, and was on his way out of the house.

The morning hadn't gone at all the way Gideon had planned it. He'd meant to find Steven Gallagher; instead, he'd ended up on the ground with Willow.

Swinging back into the saddle of the horse he'd borrowed from the judge's stables, he rode away from the scene of his downfall without looking back.

Willow's challenge rang through his mind and heart — *And you aren't faithful to her anyway, are you?* — all the way back to town. He hadn't been strictly true to Daphne, that was a fact, and up until now that had never seemed important. Every man had at least one mistress, didn't he?

Gideon swallowed hard. His pride smarted and his groin ached and his thoughts were all tangled up with each other. Fidelity was something Daphne, sophisticated as she was, had never demanded of him, probably never even expected.

It was the way of the world.

Men of means provided well for their wives and children; in his world, that was understood. A mistress, discreetly maintained of course, was considered his due.

But things were different with Willow, and

Gideon knew he had a bitter choice to make. He could appease his physical needs with other women and let his "wife" do as she pleased, or he could be faithful — to a woman he couldn't, in good conscience, bed.

"Shit!" he yelled to the blue summer sky.

Willow sat quietly on the ground, long after Gideon rode away, her arms wrapped around her knees, her eyes burning with unshed tears. Lord have mercy, what a mess her life was.

One tear trickled down her face and she dashed it away angrily.

A long shadow passed over her. "Willow?"

Willow's head shot up and she gaped at her brother, both alarmed and relieved. He had the most disconcerting way of appearing and disappearing, like some kind of stage magician. "Steven! What are you doing here?"

Steven crouched to face her, the wind lifting his sandy hair, his blue eyes bright with affection and mischief. He looked as Devlin must have, in his youth, powerful and handsome and arrogant, and for all of that, ingenuous.

"I came to see my sister," he answered mildly.

Willow flushed, remembering what she and Gideon had done, conscious of the possibility that Steven might have seen at least some of the exchange.

God forbid. "You took a terrible chance, Steven," she scolded, testing the waters. "What if I hadn't been alone?"

"You weren't alone," he said, taking in her rumpled clothes and misbuttoned shirt with discerning eyes, "unless I miss my guess."

Willow colored again and averted her eyes, but she was still self-possessed enough to make an attempt at throwing her brother off *that* conversational trail. "You should be more careful," she muttered. "Contrary to what you probably tell yourself, Steven Gallagher, you don't lead a charmed life."

Steven laughed and plucked a blade of grass to turn in his hands, as Gideon had turned a tiger lily only minutes before. "Lancelot is well away, m'lady," he teased. "I made sure of that before showing myself. When did he arrive in our fair town?"

Willow flinched at the mention of the silly name she'd given Gideon in her innocence; she'd forgotten how much she had confided to her older brother over the years. "He came yesterday — just in time to stop me from marrying Norville."

There was an awful silence, followed by a

breathless "To stop you from *what?*"

Willow straightened her spine, then raised her chin a notch. "You heard me, Steven. I was going to marry Norville. I was even standing at the altar. Then Lan-Gideon walked in and proceeded to inform the whole community that I couldn't be married because I was already his wife." Willow stopped the account there, closing her eyes, bracing herself for the inevitable explosion.

Instead, Steven gave a ragged burst of laughter. "I owe our Lancelot a debt of gratitude, it appears. That was brilliant!"

For a moment, Willow was puzzled. But then she realized that Steven thought Gideon had merely been bluffing. "I don't think you understand," she said quietly. "Steven, I really am married to Gideon. Truly."

Steven's mouth fell open; for once in his dashing and completely misguided life, he was speechless.

"It happened two years ago, Steven, when I visited San Francisco with Evadne," Willow rushed to explain. "You remember, don't you, when she decided to dress me up and present me to society?"

Most likely, Evadne had hoped to marry Willow off. Leave her behind in San Francisco when she returned to Virginia City.

"I remember," Steven rasped, his aristocratic face completely devoid of color.

Painfully, knowing that it had to be done, Willow explained the prank Gideon had played on her, the prank that had turned out to be a documented reality.

At the end of the account, Steven shot to his feet, towering against the morning sun like an angry Adonis. "I'll kill him!" he bellowed.

With what she hoped was a calming demeanor, Willow stood up and approached Steven, then caught his muscular arms in her hands. "Gideon could have made love to me that night, Steven," she said rationally. "I thought it was our wedding night and I would have allowed him to. But he didn't. H-he said it was all a terrible mistake and brought me back to the mansion . . ."

Steven wrenched free of her grasp, then paced back and forth in the deep, wind-blown grass, his face murderous. "Why didn't you ever tell me about this?" he demanded, after some time.

Willow ached with embarrassment and residual pain. What a bumpkin she'd been, back then. How Gideon and Zachary and the others must have laughed at her gullibility.

"I didn't want you to know, Steven. Surely you can understand how stupid I felt!"

Before Steven could reply to this, one way or the other, the hoot of a night owl rang through the bright June morning. It was a signal, of course; Coy or Reilly warning Steven that someone was coming.

Steven gave Willow one beleaguered look and disappeared into the cottonwood trees farther up the hill.

Two minutes later, Norville rode out of the brush on horseback, looking very pleased with himself. Dressed in black trousers and a smudged white shirt that was stained under the armpits, he was even less appealing than usual.

"Well," he drawled, his tone scathing. "Fancy meeting you here!"

Willow was in no mood for an encounter with Norville, and she stalked over to Banjo, who was grazing nearby, and took his dangling reins in hand. "You followed me," she accused, swinging up into the saddle, ready to flee if Norville came any closer.

"We need to have a talk, you and I," Norville reiterated, still in the saddle, placing his hands on his hips.

"About what?"

Norville flushed furiously. "About our bargain, Miss Gallagher. We had an agreement. Surely you didn't think I was simply going to pretend that didn't happen?"

Willow swallowed hard but made no move to ride away, though she longed to. This, like the confrontation with Steven just past, was unavoidable. "I can't very well marry you now," she said lamely.

"Of course not," conceded Norville. "Think what it would do to the Pickering name. Your reputation wasn't exactly pristine before; now, of course, it's probably unsalvageable. I couldn't marry you even if — *especially* if — you were divorced."

Fresh relief swept over Willow in such an intense wave that she nearly swayed out of the saddle. A previous marriage was a definite disadvantage when it came to matrimony; there were many men who would be unwilling to wed a divorcee, and thank God, Norville Pickering apparently numbered among them. "I see," she managed to say.

Norville gave her a speculative look that made her uncomfortable all over again. "I don't think you *do* see, Willow. If you don't want me to go to Vancel Tudd or the marshal with what I know about your brother, you'll have to, er, *accommodate* me."

A cold sickness welled in Willow's stomach. "A-accommodate you?"

Norville rolled his colorless eyes heavenward. "Spare me the innocent amazement,

Willow. You understand exactly what I mean and we both know it. I want you to be my mistress."

At some unconscious urging from Willow, Banjo began to dance backward, nickering and tossing his head. "I am a married woman," she reminded him.

Not that he appeared to care in the least.

"You are also the sister of a wanted man. Do you want to see your beloved Steven imprisoned, maybe even hanged, Willow?"

Just the image of Steven struggling at the end of a hangman's rope before that final, inevitable stillness made Willow squeeze her eyes shut. Grief seared the back of her throat, and she couldn't have spoken for anything.

Norville was editor of Virginia City's newspaper, having inherited both the business and the family home when his father, Mance, passed away, and there was no denying that he had a way with words. "It's a terrible death, you know, strangulation. Most hangmen are quite inept. Sometimes the poor fellow just flails a few feet above the ground, slowly spinning round and round, turning blue. Often, the tongue protrudes, and the bowels open." He paused, grinding the image into Willow's mind. "Would you like to see that happen to your *precious* Steven, Willow?"

She shook her head, sicker than ever, and forced herself to open her eyes.

"Of course you wouldn't!" exclaimed Norville, spreading his hands in an expansive, generous gesture. But then his eyes moved over Willow's full breasts and trim hips like the slithering passage of a snake. He shifted in the saddle, about to dismount. "Get down from the horse, my dear."

Would pleading save her? Looking at Norville, Willow knew that it wouldn't. She lifted one suddenly weighted leg over the horn of her saddle and slid despondently from Banjo's back.

She took one step toward Norville, then another. And the only thing that kept her from screaming in revulsion and fear was the thought of Steven with a noose tightening around his neck.

Norville, looking like the proverbial cat that ate the canary, simply leaned back against the trunk of a cottonwood tree, folded his arms, and waited.

Willow was within his reach when all hell broke loose. Suddenly, it seemed, there were horses everywhere.

Coy and Reilly were there, both of them excited.

His face taut and brutal, Steven sprang

from the bare back of his sorrel gelding, a rifle dangling from one hand. Within seconds, he'd swung the rifle sideways and pinned Norville to the trunk of the tree with its cold steel barrel.

Norville's eyes were the size of Maria's tortillas.

Steven favored his captive with a blood-chilling grin. "Hello, Norville," he said.

"Cut off his ears," suggested Coy, Willow's half brother, in an affable tone.

"Yeah," Reilly agreed.

"Shut up, both of you," Steven ordered, his eyes never leaving Norville's alternately crimson and snow white face.

Coy flung one beleaguered look at Reilly and shrugged. Willow noticed then that there was another man with them, a man she had never seen before. He was tall, with coloring much like Steven's, but there was an emptiness in his eyes that was vaguely disturbing.

Norville finally managed a strangled "For God's sake, Willow, call them off!"

Steven gave the rifle barrel an eloquent thrust into Norville's twitching neck. "One more word, my friend," he breathed, "and my brothers will have your ears — among other things."

Norville's gaze swung to Willow, pleaded

89

with her piteously.

"Steven," she ventured. Lord knew she had no great love for Norville Pickering, but if Steven killed or injured him, bad matters would certainly become worse, and in no time at all.

Her brother gave no indication that he had heard Willow at all, but he did loosen the pressure of the rifle barrel, allowing Norville to breathe a little more freely. Steven's broad shoulders moved in a deceptively casual shrug.

"You wanted me, Pickering," Steven said. "Here I am."

Poor Norville didn't know whether to reply or not. Wisely, he kept his peace.

Steven dropped the rifle; it clattered to the rocky ground at his feet. Instantly, however, his hands were at the front of Norville's shirt, gripping the fabric, lifting the object of his ire completely off the ground. "I will warn you one time," the outlaw rasped, between perfect white teeth. "If you ever touch my sister or even speak to her in a manner I consider ungentlemanly, I will find you, Pickering, and I will kick your scrawny ass up between your shoulder blades, for a start. Following that, I will let my younger brothers — bless their hearts, they're not all there, never have been — *l will let my younger brothers cut away any part of your anatomy they so desire.* Do you understand me?"

Looking sick, his skin a greenish gray, his brow beaded with sweat, Norville nodded.

Steven released him and his head swung in Willow's direction. "Go home," he ordered his sister. "Right now."

Willow lifted her chin. Norville had reason to be scared of Steven. She didn't.

"No," she said flatly.

Norville was scrambling toward his own horse, left to graze nearby. The poor man was red to the ears he probably believed he had come so close to losing, struggling into the saddle, fleeing ignobly. The delighted laughter of both Coy and Reilly rang in the air.

The other man remained silent and watchful, the brim of his hat pulled down over his face, hiding his features.

Steven, meanwhile, strode toward Willow, his blue eyes blazing. He stood toe to toe with her. "You were actually going to give in to him!" he yelled.

Coy and Reilly reined their horses around and rode discreetly away, followed somewhat reluctantly by the silent stranger.

"It didn't seem that I had much choice!" Willow shouted back, standing her ground.

They were nose to nose now, brother and sister, one's will every bit as strong as the other's.

"I can take care of myself!" bellowed Steven.

"Like hell you can!" screamed Willow.

With monumental effort, Steven calmed himself. He turned and walked away. "No more, Willow," he said hoarsely. "Damnit, *no more*. I won't have you bargaining with your virtue to protect the likes of me. I'm not worth it."

Suddenly, there were tears in Willow's eyes. She couldn't help thinking of all the times he'd defended her against Jay Forbes and others, the small gifts he'd somehow managed to present, on her birthdays and at Christmas, the way he'd reassured her when she was small and frightened. "But I love you, Steven —"

"No more," he repeated, in a voice that was hardly more than a whisper.

There was something so final in the words that Willow shivered. "Steven," she began, but he was striding toward his horse, mounting it, bending to catch the dangling reins up in his hands.

"Sometimes I think it would be better for everyone if I turned myself in," he said.

Before Willow could find words to refute

this rash statement, Steven was riding away, soon to vanish into the trees.

Tears burning behind her eyes and aching in her throat, Willow caught and remounted her horse, which had wandered some distance away during the confusion surrounding Steven's unexpected return. Dispiritedly, she rode toward home.

Not surprisingly, Evadne was waiting in the doorway when Willow reached the rear entrance to the house. "How dare you disappear like that, after the scandal you've unleashed on us all?" she demanded. "Willow Gallagher, how dare you?"

There was no point in reminding her that *Gideon* had been the one to ruin her wedding to Norville.

Too spent emotionally to defend herself, Willow simply stood there, in her trousers and her shirt and her boots, her hair slipping from its hasty braid, and awaited her stepmother's lecture.

It was not forthcoming, for, just as Evadne opened her mouth to give vent to her obvious umbrage, Devlin rounded the western corner of the house. His blue eyes touched Willow with much sympathy, then swept, in rare warning, to his wife.

"I'll have a word with my daughter," he said flatly, mounting the porch steps.

Evadne flushed and then turned in a swirl of crisp sateen skirts to disappear into the house. The only outward rebellion she allowed herself was the distant slamming of the kitchen door.

"You've seen Steven," Devlin guessed aloud, the moment he and Willow were alone.

Despite the fact that she'd been almost ten years old before even meeting Devlin Gallagher, or knowing that he was her real father, Willow found it impossible to lie to the man. Like Steven, he'd always been good to her, unfailingly generous. A firm but loving father.

She nodded miserably.

And Devlin looked uncommonly stern. "I don't want you to go near your brother again, Willow — do you hear me? Steven is a marked man, and when justice catches up with him, I won't have you caught in the crossfire!"

"Justice!" cried Willow. "You know as well as I do that Steven isn't really a criminal!"

Devlin suddenly seemed very old, and his eyes were fixed on the distant hills. "It may be that we delude ourselves, you and I, because we love Steven and want him to survive."

Willow had considered this possibility —

and discarded it. Having lived nine years of her life in the company of Steven Gallagher, she knew him better than his father ever would. "Steven is not an outlaw," she insisted stubbornly.

The weary blue eyes came searchingly to Willow's face. A beat passed, and during that fraction of a moment, the conversation changed course. "You will be careful of Gideon Marshall, won't you, Willow?"

Willow was taken aback; for a moment it seemed that her father surely knew of the illicit pleasures Gideon had revealed to her that morning in the quiet hills. "What do you mean?" she asked, as a diversionary tactic.

"I mean that Gideon is on the board of directors of the Central Pacific Railroad, Willow. He's a major stockholder. And he's here to find Steven and see that he's charged with train robbery, and most likely a whole slew of other things, too."

Willow felt as though she'd been slapped. Inwardly, she reeled, but soon enough she accepted the truth in her father's words. Gideon *had* shown a marked interest in Steven, now that she thought about it. And she'd thought he was curious about *her.*

A mingling of shame and rage turned her dirt-smudged cheeks crimson. To think she'd let that man take such unconscionable liberties with her person, to bare her breasts, to know her in ways only a husband should. Probably her surrender, such as it was, was just another joke to him.

Like their "wedding" two years before, in California.

Quickly, her father was there, drawing her into his strong arms, holding her. "I'll have this farce of a marriage annulled, Willow," he promised earnestly, "if you can just tell me that-that you and Gideon haven't . . ."

Willow wept harder, overcome by this second betrayal of Gideon's, and her father took this for an admission that the marriage had been consummated.

Still, he was patient. "There's no annulment, then," Devlin said bleakly. "I'll make up the papers and we'll go to the territorial legislature —"

Willow broke away from her father, ran sobbing into the house, and locked herself in her bedroom. She wanted more than anything in the world to be free of Gideon Marshall, but she also wanted to be his wife. God help her, she wanted more — much more — of the heated ecstasy that she had known with him that morning. Instinctively, she knew that she would never, in all her life, love another man as she loved Gideon, never feel such brutal, sweeping satisfaction unless it was he who gave it.

The knowledge filled Willow Gallagher with despair.

Gideon had lain on his lumpy hotel room bed all day long, staring up at the ceiling and wishing that he'd never been born. Though he considered it time and time again, he could not bring himself to find a whore and end the torture.

Finally, though, as the sun began to set, he rose from the bed, washed, and brushed his hair. There was still time to send the wire the board of directors was waiting for, and then he'd go to one of Virginia City's dozen saloons and get blind drunk.

Five minutes later, he entered the Western Union office and, feeling like Judas reincarnated, dictated the message that had to be sent:

HAVE FOUND THE MEANS TO LOCATE GALLAGHER. G.M.

It was that means, that whiskey-eyed, passionate means, that haunted Gideon as he left Western Union and entered the noisy, well-lighted saloon directly across the street. Gideon Marshall hadn't cried since he was four years old; now, at thirty-one, it was all he could do to keep from it.

■ ■ ■ ■

Wielding her sponge, Maria scrubbed Willow's back with a ferocity born of love.

Willow, her single braid wound into a coronet on top of her aching head, sat stolidly in the ornate tub in the special bathing chamber just off the kitchen, enduring. "I want to die," she said distractedly.

Maria spared her the lecture such a remark invited. "Pooh," she said, scrubbing harder. "You will live to be a hundred."

And every minute of it loving a man who would sell out my brother, mourned Willow in silence.

Finished scouring Willow's back, Maria deftly undid the thick golden braid and began the process of shampooing by reaching for an enamel pitcher and dunking it into the tub. "You must look especially pretty tonight," she said brightly.

Willow groaned. "Why? I'm staying in my room from now until three years after the Second Coming."

Maria shook her head, overlooking the irreverent remark, for reasons of her own. *"Sí,"* she agreed. "The señorita *would* expect a Third Coming, just for her."

Willow was silent until after she had left

the bathtub, long minutes and much scrub-bing and rinsing later. She dried herself with a thick towel and took modest refuge in a flannel wrapper. "Why did you say I would have to look pretty tonight, Maria?"

"You are not the only one who suffers. Your father, he is wearing his heart in his eyes. He, too, is afraid and worried. If you do not go down to dinner and behave like a lady, he will have only the señora to talk to. Would you wish this on a man who has been so good to you?"

Willow sighed. "I wouldn't wish that on anybody," she said, with a broken sort of wryness. Once, she and Evadne had liked each other. Everything had been so much easier then. "Why do you suppose he's here at all, when he could be with Dove?"

Maria bit her full lower lip and would make no comment.

Gideon realized, with alarm, that he was losing his taste for hard liquor; he'd been nursing the same lousy, watered-down drink for better than an hour. To add insult to injury, he felt distinctly drunk.

It was late when the traveling peddler came into the saloon. He was a very tall man, with fair hair that stuck out from under his dusty bowler hat, and his suit, ill-fitting and assembled of a bright plaid, was an assault to the eyes.

Gideon swore under his breath and looked away, blinking.

As luck would have it, the drummer set his case down within an inch of Gideon's left boot and jovially pounded on the bar with one fist. "A special!" he shouted to the bartender, in a thick Scots burr that seemed to roll on and on, like a wagon wheel racing downhill. "And one for me new friend here, as well!"

Was the bartender smirking a little? In his unlikely drunken state, Gideon couldn't rightly tell. He peered into his glass, wondering if it had been laced with poison.

"Aye and have a wet for your whistle, then!" enjoined the friendly peddler, as two enormous mugs of foaming beer were set on the bar.

Gideon looked at the Scot and thought that his mustache was just a bit off center. "Don't mind if I do," he said, befuddled, his words a bit slurred.

He took a sip from the mug allotted to him and the taste of it was so bad that he spat the stuff unceremoniously onto the sawdust floor.

"We call it panther piss," explained the barkeeper.

The peddler laughed richly. "It's an acquired taste, Mr. . . . ?"

"Marshall," frowned Gideon. "Gideon Marshall."

" 'Tis a troubled man you are, Gideon Marshall," guessed the Scot. Did he straighten his mustache? No, it wasn't possible to do that; Gideon had merely imagined the gesture.

At the back of the saloon, someone pounded a tinny piano and a woman began to sing a bawdy barroom song, the lyrics of which Gideon would normally have appreciated. Everyone except the bartender, the drummer, and Gideon himself drifted toward the music, singing along.

The peddler drained his mug and ordered another. He seemed as steady on his feet as before, a remarkable thing, considering. "You're a wee bit into your cups, Mr. Marshall," he observed, and it seemed to Gideon that his burr was slipping, just as his mustache had seemed to, moments before. "Might be good if you went back to your house, then. There are those who'll set upon a man and take his valuables, in an evil and wayward town such as this one."

"Evil?" muttered Gideon, drunker than he'd ever been in his life. Virginia City was a wild place, especially when compared to the comforts of San Francisco, but he wouldn't have gone so far as to say it was evil.

" 'Tis a sin to sell spirits of a Sunday," announced the peddler, in a jovial tone of confession, raising his glass and looking at it appreciatively before taking a deep draft.

Gideon sighed inwardly. The world was full of hypocrites and he himself was among the greatest of those. "What'd you say your name was?" he asked the peddler.

"I didn't say," came the reply, with no accent at all, and then the stranger was calmly ushering Gideon out of the bar and onto the almost deserted street.

There, he suddenly thrust Gideon up against the weathered outside wall of the saloon and landed a very respectable punch in his middle.

Though he was a fair hand in a fight, thanks to years of defending himself against his older brother, Zachary, Gideon was in no condition to do battle now. He gave a windless grunt and slid ignobly down the wall to rest on his haunches.

The drummer crouched before Gideon and, to his amazement, handed him the mustache. "I'll leave you this to remember me by," he said. "And don't be playing any more of your tricks on my sister!"

A moment later, the peddler turned and strode away into the night.

4

Befuddled and breathless from the hard blow to his stomach, Gideon stared down at the handlebar mustache in his hand. After a few minutes, the fog shrouding his brain began to dissipate, and he laughed as he lifted himself back to his feet and tucked the glue-crusted hank of fair hair into the pocket of his coat. He'd wanted to meet Steven Gallagher face-to-face, and now he had.

As he made his way back toward his hotel, Gideon tried to equate the Steven he'd just encountered with the desperado the Central Pacific wanted to see tried and, if possible, hanged. The two images simply wouldn't go together. After all, considering what had been done to his innocent young sister, two years before, Steven Gallagher had every right to be furious. Few people would have blamed the man if he'd shot Gideon for a scoundrel, but he'd only executed a gut punch, for God's sake. Was this the revenge of a vicious criminal, the merciless outlaw he'd heard so much about?

Once in his room, Gideon considered forgetting the whole idea of arresting Steven Gallagher. He'd obtained a temporary appointment as a deputy U.S. marshal before leaving his home city. Now he thought that his time might be better spent by finding some legal means of extricating himself from the sham marriage to Willow, going home, and building a life with Daphne.

Still short of breath and hurting from the punch to his middle, Gideon sat down on the edge of the bed and braced his head in his hands. Why the devil had he agreed to come to Montana, where he didn't belong, in the first place? Why had he promised to bring in Steven Gallagher?

Gideon sighed. He had promised, though; he had given his word. And that had to be respected, despite the fact that he liked Steven Gallagher, liked his father, and felt something disturbingly beyond liking for Willow.

In near despair, Gideon kicked off his boots, unbuttoned his shirt, then removed his trousers. He couldn't help drawing a parallel between himself and Benedict Arnold, and the comparison smarted.

The next morning, groggy from the excess of whiskey and the restless night, Gideon put on his best clothes and set out for Judge Gallagher's stately house.

Oh, yes, he thought. And it was his mother's fine residence, as well.

Willow stared at the disembodied mustache that Gideon had presented to her, in her father's entry hall, and then tried to suppress the smile of understanding that tugged at one side of her mouth. Once, in a poker game, Steven had acquired the moth-eaten belongings of an out-of-work stage actor. Obviously her brother was making use of the costumes.

Gideon arched an eyebrow, watching her closely.

Willow, having momentarily forgotten what her father had told her about Gideon the day before, remembered, and stiffened. This man was not the dashing and chivalrous Lancelot of her fantasies, and she must keep that in mind. Gideon was a liar and a trickster, as well as lecherous, and he'd come to Virginia City to find and arrest Steven. Period.

Even worse, he was base enough to use Willow herself to achieve this end.

"Where did you get such a thing?" she

asked coolly, handing the mustache back to Gideon.

He smiled wanly and she felt a tug in the deepest regions of her heart. "It was given to me by a Scot I met in a saloon last night," he answered, "along with a rather forceful message."

Willow longed to shove Gideon back out onto the porch and slam the door in his face, but she didn't dare. After all, this scoundrel was Evadne's beloved son, the golden one, and as such, he was welcome in the household no matter what. "Does this — this *hank of hair* have some significance, or are you merely trying to bore me to death, Mr. Marshall?"

Gideon laughed. "Does your brother often disguise himself as a peddler and walk among the law-abiding, Mrs. Marshall?" he asked mildly, his eyes dancing.

Willow grimaced at the reminder of her legal bond with this man. "I asked you not to address me that way," she said. She was turning away, intending to abandon this unwanted guest to his doting mother, who would soon descend the stairs, when he caught her elbow in his hand and forced her to stay.

"I've been thinking about our situation, *Mrs. Marshall*," he announced, in an undertone, a muscle growing taut in his freshly shaven jaw. "Perhaps it would be a good idea if we lived together as man and wife."

Willow stared at him in amazement. Her heart grew wings, soared into her throat, and flapped there like a bird trapped in a chimney pipe. "What?"

He lifted one shoulder in a shrug. "You've set some very stiff conditions — such as my remaining faithful to you. I am not a celibate man, my dear, and if I cannot share your bed, I promise you, I shall share someone else's."

Willow felt a warm glow in her cheeks and she tried to pull free of his grasp, to no avail. "You may sleep with whomever you please, Mr. Marshall," she said, and even though she knew what a wretch this man was, the image of him lying in another woman's arms seared her from the inside, as though she'd swallowed live coals. With a sniff, she added, "I really don't care what you do, as long as I can be free of you at the earliest possible moment."

His wondrous eyes assessed her, seeing beneath the surface, skimming, it seemed, over her very soul. "How you've changed since yesterday, when you were demanding my husbandly fidelity."

"I didn't know what you were really after then!"

Gideon arched one eyebrow. "What am I after?"

"I think we both know," Willow whispered angrily, as Evadne came sweeping down the stairway, dressed in a green silk morning gown and glowing at the sight of her son as she trilled a merry greeting.

Reluctantly, Gideon released Willow and favored his mother with a patient smile. "We'll discuss this again later, Mrs. Marshall," he informed his bride, out of the side of his mouth.

Willow knew real gratitude as her stepmother caught Gideon's arm and all but dragged him into the parlor, prattling cheerfully on about the "social desolation" of a place like Virginia City, where there simply was no culture to be found.

Disgruntled and very much at loose ends, Willow wandered into the sitting room and looked up at the massive painting of Gideon displayed over the fireplace. Remembering all the foolish dreams she'd nurtured, both before the debacle in California and after, she made an angry sound and put out her tongue.

This brief and impotent defiance was immediately followed by a sweep of sadness that took all the starch out of Willow Gallagher and caused her to sink despondently into a nearby chair. She almost wished that Gideon had not reached Virginia City in time to stop her wedding to Norville; if he hadn't, she would have suffered much in Mr. Pickering's bed, but she would also have known for a certainty that Steven was still safe.

She sighed, letting her eyes drift to the suit of armor that stood in one corner of the room, a relic from one of her father and Evadne's trips to Europe, and new pain filled her. How often had she actually spoken to that ridiculous tangle of iron, pretending that it was a knight?

Tears filled her eyes. The time for childish games was long past.

Evadne Gallagher nearly dropped her delicate china teacup. "Gideon!" she gasped, her eyes wide with horror. "That is the most scurrilous suggestion I've ever heard!"

Gideon sighed, ignoring the cup of tea that awaited him on the little table beside his chair. "Willow and I are married, Mother," he said dryly. "Why does it surprise you that I want to live with my own wife?"

"Married!" Evadne's hand rose to flutter,

110

fanlike, in front of her reddened face. "Merciful heavens, Gideon, you are not *married* to that-that hoyden! You were the victim of a trick."

Gideon thought of Zachary and longed to strangle him. "Willow was the victim, Mother, not I. She is my wife and I want to live with her."

"Live with her! Gideon, how can you even consider such a thing, when . . ."

Impatience filled all the spaces inside Gideon that were not already occupied by weariness, confusion, and the residual effects of his hangover. "Mother," he broke in, "I understand that Willow was conceived outside your marriage. What I can't quite grasp is why you hate her the way you do. Surely you must realize that the circumstances of her birth were no fault of her own."

"The child is impossible!"

"The *child* isn't a child at all, Mother," Gideon corrected her. "She's a woman, and I want her."

His mother looked patently shocked. She fluttered one hand in front of her face and breathed in short gasps. "Gideon!" she finally sputtered. "What a dreadful thing to say . . ."

He stood up, uncomfortable in that fussy,

cluttered parlor with its fringes and tassels and figurines, and went to the window. Recollections of the day before, with Willow, burned through him like some invisible wildfire, and he realized with a jolt that he'd been looking for an excuse to bed her ever since. "Is the judge at home?" he asked, in what he hoped was a reasonable and moderate tone.

Behind him, Evadne was frantic; the air crackled with her annoyance and her indignation. "Gideon, what about Miss Roberts?" she pleaded. "What about the woman you promised to wed?"

What indeed, thought Gideon. All his grand plans aside, the fact was that Daphne Roberts wasn't very likely to want him for a husband, once she learned the enormity of the situation. In Daphne's social circles, "complications" like Willow were frowned upon. Though he might be able to persuade the comely Miss Roberts to overlook his sins later, Gideon was not dealing with later. He was dealing with now.

"Gideon!" prodded his mother.

"Is the judge at home or not, Mother?"

"Devlin is away for the day," Evadne finally admitted. "What do you want with him, anyway?"

"I thought it would be decent to tell the

judge that I plan to move his daughter from this house into one of my own," Gideon said, and it was as though he stood back from himself, watching, marveling. What the hell was he doing?

Evadne gave a distracted little cry and swooned into her chair, her eyes rolling back in her head, her hands quivering. She'd had these spells for as long as Gideon could remember, usually at her personal convenience, but they never failed to frighten him.

He strode to the open doorway and shouted for help.

Both Willow and Maria came on the run, the latter bearing a vial of smelling salts that probably came into continual use in this house. Evadne was revived, after a fashion, and guided upstairs to her room, leaning hard against Maria.

"What on earth did you say to her?" Willow gasped, one hand to her throat. She was pale, and the worry in her eyes looked genuine.

A muscle twitched in Gideon's jaw and he swore under his breath. "I told my mother that I want you to come and live with me, Willow."

The full mouth that he had not had enough of, that he longed to kiss even now, rounded into a circle and then parted slightly.

"Pack your things, Mrs. Marshall," Gideon said decisively into the pulsing silence. "As soon as I'm sure Mother will be all right, you and I are going home."

Willow's emotions ran a gamut ranging from stunned dismay to sheer joy. "I believe I've already told you, sir," she managed to say, raising her voice a little because her heart was beating so loudly, "that I want absolutely nothing to do with you."

"Yesterday," Gideon reminded her calmly, "your body told me something entirely different."

"How can you even bring this up, now of all times, when your mother has just taken sick?"

"My mother falls ill," Gideon pointed out, his voice taut, "when it best suits her purposes."

"Gideon!"

"Once Mother adjusts to the idea of our living together, you and me, I mean, she will probably make a most miraculous recovery."

Many times over the years, Willow had seen Evadne develop a "sick headache" or the vapors when she wanted to draw attention to herself.

"Willow," Gideon persisted, *"we are married."*

"But-but, Gideon, it isn't a *real* marriage — you don't love me —"

"That is quite true," he answered, probably having no conception of the depth of the wound he'd just inflicted. "All the same, you will pack your things and be ready when I come back for you."

"I refuse to live with you just because you decree it!"

"You have two hours," Gideon said, and then he was striding out of the parlor, through the entry hall, onto the front porch. Forty minutes later, he bought a white frame house and seven hundred acres of land he'd read about in that morning's newspaper and rationalized the brash expenditure by telling himself that he was tired of living in a hotel.

Maria watched her charge with gentle amusement. "Hadn't you better start packing, señorita?" she asked. "Oh, but now you are a señora, of course. I keep forgetting."

Willow, having retreated into her bedroom, glared at the woman who had practically raised her. Her real mother, Chastity, had cared for no one but Jay Forbes; it had been Maria who had shown her unflagging love. "Packing! Are you mad, Maria? I'm not going anywhere with that man!"

"That man is your husband," Maria reminded her quietly, "and he is the kind, I think, to come up here after you if you are not ready when he arrives."

"Let him — I'll lock my door! I'll have him arrested!"

"One door would not stop this hombre, I think. And the marshal, he would only laugh at you if you asked that your own husband be hauled off to jail."

"Papa could do it! Papa could have Gideon thrown into the hoosegow just like that!" Willow snapped her fingers.

"Sí, but the papa is not here now, is he? No, he is far away, at one of his copper mines, and even when he leaves there he will not come first to this house."

Willow lowered her head. What Maria said was all too true; her father would go to Dove Triskadden when his business was through, and remain with her until morning. And by morning, of course, it would be too late.

She would be ruined.

Forever.

And what of poor Evadne? Didn't she deserve her husband's attention, feeling the

116

way she did?

"Evadne?"

"Mrs. Gallagher is resting," Maria assured her. "I gave her a dose of her medicine and she spoke to me. I've already sent Pablito for the doctor, but I feel certain that there is no more to be done."

Willow nodded, fidgety. Neither Maria nor Gideon seemed very concerned, but to her, Evadne had looked dreadful.

"You love the señor, no?" asked Maria, her tone gentle with knowing as she dragged Willow's trunk out of the wardrobe and began to fill it with drawers and camisoles, dresses and nightgowns.

"No!" lied Willow. "I do not love Gideon Marshall. Wherever would you get such an idea?"

"Ah, but I know you too well, *chiquita*," argued Maria with a smile and a pat of Willow's hand. "You have loved him always."

Willow shook her head. "No! I loved Lancelot — an imaginary man, no more real than Cinderella's prince."

"You love this one," Maria insisted, seemingly oblivious to what was about to happen.

Willow was appalled. "Maria, how can you do it? How can you stand there, calmly packing my clothes, when you know I am about to be — kidnapped?" She swallowed and hugged herself tightly with both arms. "And *worse?*"

Maria chuckled. "Kidnapped," she repeated, as though Willow had made a joke.

"Maria, Gideon doesn't love me — he told me so himself. Suppose he turns out to be a drunkard, or he beats me, or —"

"Gideon will not beat you, though you will surely try his patience many times." Maria seemed damnably certain of that, and Willow wondered why.

Despondent, she sank down onto the edge of her bed. What was happening to her? She knew that Gideon intended to track down her brother, for heaven's sake, and yet she would have gone with him willingly, glad to be his wife, if only he'd said he loved her.

Maria paused to place a gentle hand beneath Willow's chin. "Little one, do not fear. He does love you, your Gideon."

"He came right out and said he didn't!"

"Then he lies or, perhaps, he has not yet recognized his feelings for what they are. *Chiquita,* the señor burns for you. This is in his eyes. In his breath. In the way his hands want to reach for you, and he must still them."

118

"That's only lust!" Willow protested vehemently.

But Maria would make no further comment. She went placidly back to the packing, and when it was finished, she left Willow to her musings to go and make sure Pablito had gone on his errand, then to sit with Evadne until the doctor arrived.

Willow was bending out of her window, trying to decide whether she could jump and escape to freedom without breaking one or both legs, when the door of her bedroom opened behind her. She whirled, expecting to see Gideon standing there.

Instead, she was confronted with a wild-eyed, distraught-looking Evadne. Her dark hair, always elegantly coiffed, tumbled down over her shoulders, reaching past her waist.

"What did you do to entice my son?" the woman demanded, in strange, slurred tones.

For a moment, Willow was too taken aback to speak. Had Evadne — proper and temperate Evadne — been partaking of spirits? "Entice your son? Evadne, I didn't —"

"You're exactly like your mother!" Evadne broke in, and her voice was shrill now. She trembled with indignation. "Leaving one man, taking up with another, doing whatever you want, no matter who gets hurt!

Well, I won't let you poison Gideon's life the way Chastity did Devlin's. *Do you hear me, Willow? I will not permit you to spoil his chance to be happy with a suitable woman!*"

A suitable woman.

Evadne was referring, of course, to Daphne Roberts.

What made Daphne "suitable," Willow wondered, unexpectedly injured, and why wasn't *she* suitable, too?

A thousand protests leaped into Willow's mind, but she did not give voice to any of them. It was Evadne who had been poisoned, with hatred and with bitterness, but trying to reason with her now would be useless.

"I'm sorry you feel that way," Willow said finally, as compassion swept through her. "The truth is that I love Gideon very much."

"Love him?" scoffed Evadne. "No one in this misguided family has any conception of the meaning of that word!"

Willow blinked back tears. "My father loves you, Evadne."

Evadne fell against the doorjamb, and the dearth of color in her face was frightening. "Does he? Does he, Willow? They why, pray tell, does he spend every free moment with that Triskadden woman?"

Sympathy for her stepmother swept over

Willow in a crushing wave; she went to Evadne, took her arm, guided her to a chair. "Please. You mustn't upset yourself so — you don't look well —"

"Don't touch me!" Evadne shrieked.

"What is wrong?" Maria queried anxiously, from the open doorway.

Willow looked at the housekeeper in relief and pleaded, "Maria, has the doctor arrived? Mrs. Gallagher is not well."

"I am not ill!" screamed Evadne, flinging away the hand that Maria extended to her.

Over Evadne's head, Maria's worried brown eyes met Willow's gaze. "The señora needs to rest. Help me take her back to her room, *chiquita.* The doctor is on his way."

Surprisingly, Evadne allowed herself to be squired to her own chamber, but she muttered senselessly the whole way. When she had been settled on the bed, Maria and Willow left the room to confer in the hallway.

"You will go to meet the doctor, *chiquita,* and beg him to hurry," Maria commanded. "Quickly, *por favor.*"

Willow had never loved Evadne — the woman had not permitted that — but she was genuinely worried about her father's wife. "What about Papa? Shouldn't he be here, too?"

121

Maria considered. "He will be with the woman now. I do not want you going there. You go and tell the doctor that Mrs. Gallagher is worse than we thought, and I will send Juan for the judge."

Under other circumstances, Willow would have been disappointed not to be sent on such an errand, for she had always wanted a close look at the notorious Dove Triskadden, who had once been, it was rumored, the queen of a great Chicago bordello. Now, with Evadne so ill, Willow knew her curiosity about her father's mistress had to be put aside.

She bounded down the stairs, out through the front doors, and over the walk. At the gate, she encountered Gideon.

Having forgotten his ultimatum in the emergency, Willow stopped and waited for him to step aside.

"Are you ready to leave?" he asked.

"Your lust will have to wait, Mr. Marshall," she informed her "husband" in a scathing undertone. "I'm off to see what's keeping Dr. McDonald."

"What?"

"Something is terribly wrong with your mother," Willow said, though not without kindness, pushing past him, wrenching at the gate until the catch gave way.

At this, Gideon bolted toward the house and Willow was free to seek out the doctor.

Devlin Gallagher was hopping awkwardly about on one foot, struggling into his left boot. "How serious is it?" he snapped, as Juan waited just inside Dove's back door.

The boy shrugged. "I do not know, señor. My cousin Maria, she say to come here, bring you back. She sent me for the doctor earlier."

Calmly, Dove Triskadden handed her harried lover his coat. At Devlin's beleaguered look, she simply smiled, very sadly and very gently, and said, "Go. I'll be all right."

Heedless of the young man who awaited him, within earshot, Devlin kissed Dove briefly but with conviction and replied, "I love you."

"Go home," insisted Dove as her fingers brushed his cheek in farewell.

Willow grasped Dr. McDonald's frayed coat sleeve the moment he stepped out of Evadne's room. There were deep lines in the man's face and his eyes were averted.

"Well?" pleaded Willow. "What's wrong? Will my stepmother get better?"

Perhaps reading something in the doctor's manner that Willow had missed, Gideon thrust himself away from the wall he'd been leaning against and closed his hands gently over her shoulders.

"Mrs. Gallagher has suffered some sort of apoplectic fit," the physician said wearily. "She may linger a few days, a few weeks — or only a few hours. I'm sorry."

Willow looked wildly to Gideon, saw him close his eyes and saw the color seep out of his face. "Oh my God," he whispered raggedly.

Guilt encompassed Willow. Had she caused this thing to happen by being so troublesome to Evadne, always talking back, stirring things up? Oh, God in heaven, why had she baited the woman the way she had? Why?

Overcome, Willow cried out and groped down the stairs, nearly falling before Gideon caught up to her, midway down, and pulled her into his arms.

"Willow," he said, his breath warm in her tangled hair, holding on as she tried in vain to wrench free of him. She wanted to run from him and from her feelings and from the terrible thing that had befallen her stepmother. She wanted to escape the awareness that she'd never loved her father's wife, and the sense that she'd brought this calamity on somehow. "Willow!"

She cried out in anguish and then began

to sob. "I made her so angry . . . I'm to blame for this —"

"No," Gideon rasped. "No."

And then he lifted Willow into his arms and carried her back upstairs and into her room, Maria appearing in the corridor to lead the way.

Willow felt herself being lowered carefully to the bed. Her entire body was wracked by sobs, deep, dry, angry sobs that came from the depths of her and were not stopped until after the laudanum Dr. McDonald administered had taken effect.

Gideon and the doctor had both left the room by the time Maria began undressing Willow and helping her into a nightgown.

"Rest now, *chiquita,*" the older woman urged, her eyes bright with tears. "Rest."

Willow was too befuddled to speak, and the room kept going in and out of focus, while the bed seemed to have all the substance of a wispy summer cloud. After Maria had gone — did she dream it? — Gideon came into the room, sat down nearby, then touched her cheek.

Willow smiled at him and for a few moments none of the dreadful things that had been happening were real after all. It was all a bad dream.

"Lancelot," she sighed.

Gruffly, brokenly, Gideon laughed, and his fingers were warm where they caressed her face. "At your willing service, m'lady," he answered.

Willow smiled again and allowed the fog of sleep rising up around her to carry her away with it.

It was late and there were voices, angry voices. Willow listened but could not make out the words or the identities of the speakers.

Curious, she got out of bed, scrambled into her wrapper, and crept into the hallway and down the stairs.

"You were with your whore, you son of a bitch!" Gideon yelled. "My mother is dying and you were with your goddamned whore!"

Willow froze outside the closed doors of her father's study.

"Dove Triskadden is not a whore," replied the judge, with admirable evenness of tone, "and I will thank you to keep your voice down, Gideon. It's the middle of the night and this mother you speak of so fondly is gravely ill."

"You don't give a damn, either, do you?" Gideon retorted, his voice torn, raw with grief. "You're probably hoping she'll die. That would solve a lot of your problems,

126

wouldn't it, Judge?"

Fury at this cruel accusation surged through Willow's numb little frame like lightning blazing down a metal rainspout. She wrenched open one of the doors and stormed inside, pausing only when she found herself face-to-face with Gideon Marshall.

"Don't you ever speak to my papa like that again!"

Devlin sighed heavily and leaned back against his desk. "Willow," he scolded. "That's enough. Go back upstairs and —"

She whirled, glared at him. "Don't you dare tell me to go back to bed!" she warned. "I'm not a child, to be sent here and there, seen and not heard."

Devlin's look was stern, and his sorrow was plain to see. "Leave us," he said. "Please."

Willow's gaze swung, full of fury, back to Gideon. She was about to let loose with a tongue-lashing, but the words were stopped in her throat by the anguish she saw in his face. She knew then that Gideon had attacked her father because of this, because he was in terrible pain, and not because he'd meant any of the awful things he'd said.

One glance at Devlin revealed that he had understood all along.

"I'm sorry, Gideon," Willow said softly. "About your mother, I mean."

Gideon looked haggard; he was pale and his eyes were distracted and his shirt was so rumpled he might have slept in it. Yet he smiled. "I did like it better, I admit, when you called me Lancelot."

Willow flinched, then felt color pound over her cheekbones. Oh, Lord in heaven, had she really said that? Had she really called him by that silly, treasured name? "I guess I'll go to bed," she said, averting her eyes.

Devlin grasped the half-filled glass of whiskey on the edge of his desk and took a deep draft, then turned away to stand, shoulders slumped, at the window. Gideon and Willow might not have been within a hundred miles for all the notice he paid them.

Outside the study, in the darkened hallway, Willow looked up at Gideon's shattered face and longed to comfort him, in the way a woman comforts a man. "I'm sorry about your mother, Gideon," she said again.

Torment darkened his eyes to a deeper shade of green, and he rubbed the back of his neck with one hand. "Why wasn't I better to her, Willow?" Gideon asked hoarsely. "Why?"

Because she loved Gideon Marshall, no matter what he had done in the past or meant to do in the future, because he needed her, Willow lifted her hands to the sides of his face. "Hush," she said, and when his lips fell to hers, with desperation, she welcomed them. Welcomed him.

When the kiss ended, Willow caught her husband's hand in her own and led him slowly up the stairs. If Gideon wanted her now, she would give herself, without any regrets.

But, at the door of her bedroom, he balked. "Willow . . ."

She pulled him inside the room; slowly, in the silver light of the moon, she unbuttoned his wrinkled shirt, then removed it. "I love you," she whispered, even though she knew that she shouldn't have confided such a secret.

Showing no sign that he'd heard her, Gideon groaned as Willow's hands smoothed the mat of golden maple hair glimmering on his chest, stopping to toy with his nipples, caressing the powerful muscles of his shoulders and upper arms.

Acting strictly on instinct, Willow tasted one of the masculine nipples cosseted in toasty down and knew wonder and delight when it grew taut against her tongue. Gideon moaned; heartened, she stood on tiptoe, then caught his earlobe lightly between her teeth.

With a hoarse cry of response, Gideon took her face between strong hands and lifted it. "Willow, do you know what is going to happen if you don't stop? If you don't stop right now and order me out of this room? God help me, if you don't tell me to, I won't be able to go!"

"You did say we were going to live together as husband and wife, didn't you?" Willow whispered back. "Just this very day, in fact."

"Yes. And I behaved like an obnoxious idiot."

Willow reached up to trace his taut lips with an index finger. "Hush, Gideon," she said.

5

Devlin Gallagher finished his drink and set the glass aside resolutely. Then he made his way up the stairway to Evadne's room, the room he had been barred from since the night Steven had appeared, with Willow and Maria, the servant woman, in tow.

A long time ago, now.

A decade.

He lifted his hand to knock, shook his head distractedly, and opened the door.

Evadne was awake. Devlin sensed that as he approached the bedside, struck a match, and lit the fancy globe lamp on the nightstand.

There were no words to say, not at first. For almost a minute, Devlin simply stood there, staring down at the ravaged face framed in dark, tangled hair, and saw accusations flare in the eyes that had once adored him without reservation.

Devlin drew up a chair and sat down at

the bedside. He had loved this woman once, in a comfortable, settled way. She had been a good wife to him, restored his faith in her gender, tried hard to accept Willow as a daughter.

He despaired, truly and deeply, at her suffering. "I'm sorry," he finally managed to say, in a gruff undertone.

One side of Evadne's face was slightly out of line with the other and she couldn't speak. Still, it was as though she had shouted an ugly challenge; Devlin flinched and momentarily closed his eyes.

Cautiously, he reached out and took Evadne's hand, held it. Even now, in this desperate hour, he could not find words to reach her, to comfort her. She seemed to hold herself apart from him in some inexplicable way.

He knew he deserved it.

His eyes clouded with tears of frustration and grief. Devlin kept his vigil through the night hours.

Just before dawn, with no fuss at all, Evadne Gallagher died.

Willow sat up in bed, arms wrapped around her knees, and studied the man sleeping naked beside her. Who would have thought, to see them in this intimate state, that they had not made love during the night? No, Gideon had talked, in the hoarse tones of bereavement, and he had even wept a little once, in Willow's arms, but he had not taken her.

With a sigh, Willow ran one hand through her sleep-tousled hair. She had been so willing to come to Gideon as a woman, but now, in the light of day, she felt gratitude for his forbearance. It wouldn't have been right, she supposed, for them to make love now, in this house where there was so much confusion and pain.

Leaving Gideon sleeping soundly on his stomach, his broad back uncovered, Willow slipped out of bed, found a wrapper, and put it on. In the hallway outside her room, she encountered her father.

Knowing he was well aware that Willow had not spent the night alone, she lowered her eyes for a moment. It hadn't been proper, sharing her bed with Gideon Marshall, but surely it hadn't been wrong, either. They were, after all, legally married.

"Willow."

The whispered word made Willow lift her eyes to her father's face in questioning dread. He was still wearing yesterday's clothes.

"She's gone," Devlin said raggedly, as the

last of the night gave way to morning.

Willow swallowed hard and managed a nod. Then, with a strangled cry, she flung herself into her father's arms.

He held her close and they shared a silent sorrow, totally in accord, and then they broke apart. Devlin went slowly down the stairs, his shoulders straight and strong, and Willow turned and forced herself back into the bedroom she had just left.

"Gideon," she said, touching his bare shoulder, wishing that she didn't have to tell him. "Gideon, wake up."

It rained the day of Evadne Gallagher's funeral, but almost a hundred people came to mourn, including Gideon's brother, Zachary, who had arrived by train just that morning, after receiving a summons by telegram.

At the graveside, standing between her husband and her father, her face shrouded by the thick black veil Maria had provided, Willow studied Evadne's elder son. Zachary was dark, an inch or so shorter than Gideon, and his clothes fit his well-made frame with tailored perfection. His eyes were a deep, compelling green.

Knowing that this was the man who had arranged the prank that had changed both her own life and Gideon's, Willow wavered between anger and heartfelt gratitude. Though Zachary Marshall was clearly grieving as deeply as his brother was, he still managed to fling an occasional speculative look in Willow's direction.

It was much later, at the Gallagher house, when he finally approached her. "My brother's wife?" he asked, in a smooth, deep voice.

Willow was very conscious of Gideon, even though he was on the far side of the room, enduring the gushy condolences of one of Evadne's friends. Not since the night of his mother's death three days before had he shared her bed, touched her, or spoken more than a few words.

"Yes," she said, though the word was, in many ways, a lie.

"You've changed," Zachary remarked, in flat tones that betrayed neither approval nor disappointment. "I wasn't sure you were the same person we knew in San Francisco."

"The same gullible, smitten schoolgirl, you mean?" Willow retorted evenly, for it was easy to be angry now.

Zachary winced good-naturedly and his straight white teeth flashed in a brief, boyish smile. "It was a shameful thing to do," he confessed. "How can I make it up to you?"

Willow was aware of this man's fundamental charm and totally unresponsive to it. "Can such a thing ever be made up?" she asked, with a coldness that she couldn't help, even though she knew it was entirely out of keeping with the mood of the day.

Zachary was about to respond to this when Gideon suddenly intruded, and the look he gave his brother was decidedly unfriendly.

"Zachary," he said.

Zachary nodded in response. "Gideon," he replied.

To Willow's intense surprise, Gideon slipped an arm around her waist — an almost proprietary arm — and drew her close. "You've met my wife?" he drawled sardonically.

The dark-haired brother nodded again. "Under different circumstances, it would have been a pleasure."

Gideon's jaw went taut, and his grip on the glass of liquor he held in his free hand whitened his knuckles. In contrast, his voice was flat when he spoke, asking Zachary when he had arrived and where he was staying.

Zachary made some reply; Willow didn't

take note of it, because all her attention was fixed on Gideon's face. The play of emotions she saw there was unsettling, even considering the loss he had just suffered. His hostility toward his brother went beyond the justified resentment of a childish jest, it seemed to Willow.

Finally, Zachary went off to another part of the crowded parlor, probably in search of more amicable company, and Gideon surprised Willow again by turning to her and muttering, "I've got to get out of here — I can't breathe."

Willow felt the impending loss of him, even for a few hours, like a blow, but she managed a comforting smile. It was a peculiarity of funerals that people insisted on clustering together just when the grief-stricken wanted most to be alone. "I understand," she said.

He caught her elbow in his hand and ushered her through the mingling friends of Evadne Gallagher's, toward the front doors. "Will you come with me, Willow?" he pleaded, somewhat after the fact, as he took her cloak from the coat tree and draped it over her shoulders.

There was nothing Willow wanted more, but she was conscious of her father, somewhere in the crowd, distraught and trapped among the mourners in the parlor, many of whom would take sanctimonious delight in dropping Dove Triskadden's name wherever possible.

"But, my father —"

Gideon looked at once broken and annoyed. "Your father left half an hour ago," he pointed out brusquely. "No doubt Miss Triskadden is soothing his tortured brow even as we speak."

Willow flushed but did not speak in defense of Devlin Gallagher, for with this man at this moment, it would have been a waste of breath. Lifting her chin, she allowed her husband to escort her out of the house and down the walk to a waiting horse and buggy.

After lifting Willow into the creaky seat, Gideon rounded the rig and climbed in beside her, taking the reins into practiced hands. His smile was given with an effort that tore at Willow's heart. "I bought this the other day, Mrs. Marshall. How do you like it?"

Willow only shrugged, for a horse was a horse and a buggy was a buggy and there were weightier matters on her mind anyway. "What would you be wanting with a rig when you don't plan to stay in Virginia City?"

"When did I say I didn't plan to stay?"

Gideon retorted as he guided the vehicle away from Devlin Gallagher's house.

Hope leaped in Willow's heart, then sank again. Gideon, as deeply as she loved him, was an enemy, and she must not allow herself to forget that in the emotional upheaval of the day. "Once you've found my brother, there won't be much reason to remain here, will there?"

They were leaving town, jolting and jostling over the cattle trail that was generously referred to as a road.

"I bought a house," Gideon announced, his eyes on the far mountains, with their craggy, snow-traced peaks. "And several hundred acres of land."

Again hope surged in Willow's confused heart. "Why?" she demanded.

"To tell you the truth, I don't know," Gideon answered, and then they drove in silence for a long time.

The house, a spacious, wood-framed structure with two stories and a porch that nearly encircled it, had belonged to the widow of a prosperous rancher until her death a few months before. It was surrounded by tall cottonwoods and willows, and there was a pond within easy walking distance.

Willow felt a surge of delight as she took

it all in. "You bought Mrs. Baker's place!" she cried, forgetting, for the moment, that there had been a funeral that day.

Gideon smiled a slight, bruised smile and nodded.

"I used to come here for piano lessons," Willow said, suddenly shy and quite at a loss. "Did you buy the furnishings, too?"

"Yes," Gideon answered, as the horse splashed through the rain-filled ruts on the driveway leading toward the house. "But you can replace them, if you want to, with things of your own. Mrs. Baker's daughter has already been here to collect her mother's personal belongings — pictures and the wedding china and things of that sort."

Willow gaped at this man who was and yet wasn't her husband as he drew the rig to a stop at the base of the house's front steps. "I?"

"If you'll live here with me," Gideon said quietly. "Will you do that, Mrs. Marshall?"

Willow was totally confused. For how long did he mean? For a day, a week, a year? Until after he had found Steven and seen him tried and imprisoned?

She stiffened.

Gideon caught one hand under her chin. His flesh felt warm and pleasantly roughened, an indication that he worked with his hands, if only sometimes. "What is it?"

A single tear welled up and trailed down Willow's cheek. "You want to put my brother in prison," she whispered, reminding herself as well as Gideon. "You might even want to see him hanged."

Gideon looked away for a moment, wrapped the reins around the buggy's brake lever, and sighed. "I'm not certain that I even want to look for Steven now," he admitted. "God help me, I'm not sure of anything, except that I need you very much, Willow Gallagher Marshall."

Willow studied him. "You could have had me," she pointed out, in her confusion, all too aware of how vulnerable she'd been to this man ever since that morning in the hills. "You slept in my bed, Gideon Marshall, and you didn't so much as touch me. Exactly what is it that you need me for?"

Gideon laughed. "You're *angry*," he marveled hoarsely. "Good God in heaven, *you're actually angry* because I didn't make love to you, aren't you?"

"I must admit," Willow said loftily, "that I don't understand."

"It's simple, hellcat. I couldn't let you give yourself to me that way just because you wanted to comfort me. And knowing that your father and-and my mother — who happened to be dying at the time — were under the same roof didn't exactly help."

Again, Willow was confused. What an enigma this man was, first planning to use her to find her brother, then denying his own physical needs to protect her virtue.

Gideon smiled at the bemusement in her face, leaped to the ground, and helped Willow down after him, his hands strong and sure around her waist. Neither of them noticed the drizzling rain as they hurried up the wooden walkway and into the tall white house that awaited them.

The neat, uncluttered rooms inside Mrs. Baker's house smelled of lemon verbena and cinnamon, and Willow was delighted to see that the piano still stood near the parlor's bay windows. She paused before it, lifted the cover, and idly played two bars of a favorite song. When she looked up, Gideon was watching her with quietly mischievous eyes.

"Can you play 'My Love Lies Dead on a Sawdust Floor'?" he teased.

"I'm afraid not," Willow replied, with a sniff of disdain. As Gideon caught her hand to pull her through the other rooms, though, she vowed to learn the piece as soon as she could find the sheet music.

■ ■ ■ ■

The rain beading on his long canvas coat, Devlin Gallagher rode into the hills that were his solace whenever life became too much to bear.

This day, however, Evadne's spirit seemed to follow him, accusing and full of hate.

Finally, when his horse was on the verge of collapse, Devlin stopped before a cave in the mountainside and solemnly began to make camp. As he gathered wood for a fire and assessed the dark skies, he thought of Dove and wished that he could be with her now, as the whole town of Virginia City probably thought he was.

Love Dove Triskadden though he did, there was no room for her on this particular day. He had taken Evadne for granted, had never expected her to die before he did, and now he needed time and silence to deal with the reality of her passing.

Had he loved Evadne after all? Devlin didn't think so, but she had been his wife, there for him in every way except one, and the bond between them had run far deeper than he had ever imagined.

No, Evadne hadn't shared his bed.

But she'd stood straight and proud at his

side, whenever they were together in public. Evadne had been a gracious hostess, often entertaining both friends and business associates, and although she'd probably never been truly fond of Willow, she *had* tried to mother the girl, especially early on.

Willow, so young and so frightened, wanting Steven, her protector, and finding herself among virtual strangers, hadn't made things easy.

The rain didn't let up but it did not hinder Devlin, for the cave he'd chosen as his refuge for the rest of the day and the long night that would follow was sheltered by the tall mountain pines. He built his fire, staked out his horse to graze, and sat down on the ground to think.

Memories of Evadne roiled in his mind, prickling like splinters. Dear Lord, what a comfort she'd been to him in those early days of their marriage. He'd been in jagged pieces after Chastity's departure, and very slowly and with gentle care, Evadne had put him back together again, hope by hope, dream by dream.

Evadne had longed for another child, at first anyway, and Devlin would gladly have given her one, but no baby was ever conceived.

Devlin did not ask himself when things

had changed between them; he knew. He'd encountered Chastity and succumbed and Willow had been conceived. He didn't regret that, for the simple reason that he couldn't begin to imagine a life that didn't include his daughter, but he did regret the pain his betrayal had caused Evadne.

Why, he wondered, couldn't Willow have been *Evadne's* child? Chastity hadn't wanted her. Evadne, on the other hand, would have adored, *cherished,* a daughter.

Things might have been so different.

At first, Devlin *had* tried to reach his heartbroken wife, to earn her forgiveness. She had given that, after a fashion, and tried even harder to be a mother to the confused and rebellious little girl who had quite literally been dropped on her doorstep, but Evadne had drawn the line at letting Devlin share her bed.

For a time, he had managed to deal with that, too. But there came a day, or more properly, a night, when his loneliness and his needs could no longer be subdued by copious doses of whiskey and self-directed anger. He'd still been a young man, and a virile one, and into the void that was his life then came Dove Triskadden. Soft, willing, admiring Dove.

She'd been a rancher's widow, back then.

She'd come to Virginia City simply because she'd longed to live in a town again.

When had he grown to love her? He wasn't sure, but one day the feelings he bore toward Dove were more than liking, more than desire. Devlin Gallagher had realized that the woman could stop the universe, realign the stars, and spin his world on the tip of one carefully manicured index finger.

Now, sitting at the mouth of a mountain cave, before a crackling fire, Devlin wept for all that he had not been to Evadne, for all his wrongs, for all the tears he had caused her to shed. Because he believed himself to be alone, he gave free rein to his grief, sobbing hoarsely, shouting the occasional broken curse word.

The tall man came boldly to the fireside, sank to his haunches, and helped himself to a mug and coffee from the small pot simmering in the embers.

Devlin dragged one arm across his face, offering no verbal greeting even though he was glad, very glad, to see Steven.

Steven drank cautiously from the metal mug to avoid burning his mouth. "Willow is all right?" he ventured, after a long interval designed to let his father recover his composure.

Devlin nodded. "Your sister is fine."

Steven sat down on the ground, crossing his legs like an Indian. The silence that ensued was more soothing to Devlin than any words of consolation his son might have offered.

When the time came to end that silence, the older man said, "Evadne died four days ago."

"I'm sorry," Steven replied. He must have heard about the death; he didn't seem surprised. But then, Steven was a hard man to surprise. He'd grown up tough, learned to play his cards close to his chest.

Devlin sighed, his head down. "I'm afraid I wasn't any more of a husband to her than I was a father to you."

Steven said nothing. Having heard second-hand the story of Jay Forbes's hanging and the way Chastity had died trying to protect him, he'd always blamed Devlin for his mother's death. It still amazed Devlin that, feeling the way he did, Steven had entrusted him with the person he loved better than anyone in the world — his sister.

There was another long silence, again broken by Devlin. "I want you to stay away from Willow, Steven," he said, recovered. "You're a danger to her now, and she to you."

Steven's blue eyes were intent and narrowed. "Why?"

"I think you know, but I'll explain it anyway. The law is after you, Steven, and so is Vancel Tudd. Eventually, one or both are going to catch up with you. Do you want Willow to be there when that happens?"

Steven tilted his head back, sighed wearily, and then met his father's gaze again. "Of course I don't," he answered finally. "I would do anything to keep her safe and you know it."

There, perhaps, was the explanation for Steven's bringing Willow to his father that long-ago night. He'd known that a little girl couldn't be raised to womanhood among outlaws, and he had done what he thought best for his sister.

"Willow is married now."

Steven's jaw tightened. "I heard about that," he said, after a long, charged interval. "Gideon Marshall tricked her into it, she said."

"That he did," admitted Devlin presently. "But he loves her."

"She doesn't seem to believe that," remarked Steven.

Devlin chuckled gruffly, despite the thickness in his throat and the gnawing ache in his heart. "Gideon doesn't think so, either, but he does. It isn't safe to use any flammable substance around those two."

Grudgingly, Steven smiled. "You think he's good for her, then?"

"I know he is," answered Devlin, with surety. "And she's good for him, too. Which isn't to say there won't be an earthquake or two before they get the knack of being married."

Steven laughed, then sobered at the expression on his father's face.

"Steven, be careful," Devlin said. "Gideon owns a share of the Central Pacific Railroad, and he's as much as admitted to me that he'd like to hand you over to their agents for prosecution."

It was several moments before Steven answered. "That puts Willow in one hell of a position, doesn't it?"

"If anything spoils their chance to be happy, it will be that, I think," agreed Devlin pensively. "Steven, will you lay off the goddamned trains? I'm a rich man and you'll never bankrupt me that way."

Steven grinned. "So you're on to that, are you?"

"It wasn't hard to figure out who you were trying to hurt. Everything you've ever stolen has been mine. Damnit all to hell, you don't have to steal from me — you're my son and anything I have is yours for the asking."

The handsome face, a masculine version of Chastity's, stiffened. "I don't want — or need — anything from you."

"Well, I want something from you, God damnit!"

Steven was on his feet, flinging down his coffee mug. "What?" he demanded furiously. "Do you want to make me a partner in your many businesses, Papa? Do you want to acknowledge me, the notorious outlaw, as your son?"

Devlin rose no less furiously to his feet. "What the hell do you mean, do I want to acknowledge you? I've never denied you!"

Fury crept, crimson, up Steven's muscular neck. "No?" he bellowed. "Then tell me, dear Papa, why you never even looked for me? Tell me why you didn't come for us!"

For the first time, Devlin realized the full depths of his son's animosity toward him. In the face of the man, he saw the hurts of the child. "My God, Steven, I *did* look for you! I hired detectives, I —"

"You're a liar!"

"And you're a hardheaded smart-ass!" Devlin yelled back. "I did find your mother, Steven. In '63. She was dancing in a hurdy-gurdy house. I begged her, Steven, I *begged* her to tell me where you were. She was afraid to, and rightfully so, because I would have stolen you from her without a second thought!"

"Why didn't you keep trying?"

"Because I was a fool, that's why. I spent the night with Chastity. God help me, I was married to Evadne and still I couldn't resist your mother — and when I woke up, she was gone, along with every hope I had of finding you."

Steven turned away, and an old grief moved in the powerful shoulders and tall frame he had inherited from Devlin. "I don't believe you."

"Believe what you like, Steven. Throw your goddamned life away to spite me. But keep in mind that, one of these days, it will be too damned late to put aside what you're doing and make something of yourself."

"What about Coy and Reilly?" Steven asked, in distracted and more moderate tones. "They don't know anything but running with me."

"You'll get them killed if you keep this up. Is that what you want for your half brothers, Steven? Do you want Willow to see the three of you hanged?"

Steven shuddered involuntarily and tilted his head back to search the gray skies. "It's already too late for me," he said, after a long time. "If I turn myself in, can you get them pardoned? Coy and Reilly, I mean?"

"Yes," Devlin said, without hesitation. "I could get you pardoned, too, if you'd just stop robbing trains and overturning wagon-loads of copper ore."

Steven turned to face his father and, for a moment, hope flashed in his eyes, but it was almost immediately displaced by the old skepticism and disbelief. God in heaven, did he think Devlin was trying to draw him and Jay Forbes's two half-witted sons into some kind of trap?

The idea filled Devlin with raging anguish. "You think I'd sell you out?" he hissed incredulously. "You think I'd see my own son arrested and maybe even hanged?"

Maddeningly, Steven shrugged. "Just think how peaceful your life would be if I were dead," he said.

Half-blinded by his hurt and his anger, Devlin stormed over to his son and back-handed him so hard that Steven, caught off guard, stumbled and almost lost his footing.

Pale, the younger man bellowed a curse and doubled up one lethal fist.

"Go ahead, boy," Devlin breathed. "Go ahead and beat the hell out of me. Do it. And you'll see that nothing, *nothing,* Steven, is changed!"

Slowly, his blue eyes dark with an anguish

to match Devlin's own, Steven unclenched his fist.

Devlin wanted to grasp his shoulders, but he didn't dare; the moment was too fragile. "I love you, Steven," he said quietly, and in all truth. "For God's sake, let me help you before it's too late."

Steven wavered visibly, but again the trust in his face was fleeting. "It's already too late," he said, and then he turned and disappeared into the surrounding woods. Devlin knew that he would not be back.

This time, the tears Devlin Gallagher shed had nothing whatsoever to do with Evadne's death.

The last room that Willow and Gideon toured was the master bedroom, and not by accident, Willow reflected, unnerved.

Grinning slightly, because he always seemed to understand so much more than he should have, Gideon left his wife to stand at the windows nearest the huge four-poster bed.

"You can see the mountains from here," he said presently.

Unconcerned, for the moment, with the distant Rockies, Willow was staring at the bed. Would she lie here, with Gideon, for a thousand nights, a million nights? Would she bear his children here?

Or would he leave her, once his apparent penchant had been appeased?

Tears filled Willow's golden eyes and the sob she couldn't hold back made Gideon turn to face her. In two strides, he was standing before her, pulling her close, burying one hand in her hair. The pins that held her heavy tresses in place were thus displaced, and thick tendrils began to fall around her shoulders and down her back.

Gideon was somehow moved by this, and his mouth came to hers, swiftly and with hungry desperation.

Stricken and yet unable to stop herself, Willow returned his kiss, greeted his conquering tongue with her own. His hands made fiery magic along her rib cage, rising to the rounding of her breasts, sliding down to cup her bottom and press her lower body into the searing evidence of his desire.

"Willow," he said, when the kiss ended at last. "Willow."

She closed her eyes, enclosed in a delicious blaze of heat, as his hands came to the bodice of her simple black dress and began working the buttons from their tiny loops. When the dress had been opened, he unlaced the camisole beneath, revealing the full, passion-weighted breasts that awaited him.

Gideon drew in his breath and his hand rose shakily to close over the sweet mounds, his palms chafing their rosy peaks to a hard wanting. "Do you want me to take you home?" he asked, in a voice that was barely audible. And even as he spoke, he drew Willow to the bed, sat down, then positioned her gently on his lap.

"This is home," Willow answered, and his mouth came to the peak of her breast, greedy and warm and wholly welcome.

6

A voice deep in Willow's mind pleaded caution, but she could not heed it, for her newly awakened body was making demands of its own. It was caught in a cascade of craving that could be met only by this man.

She had no memory of shedding her clothes, nor of Gideon shedding his, but now they lay together on Mrs. Baker's bare mattress, naked and strong in the breeze that floated in through the window Gideon had opened.

Willow knew a moment of fear, sensing the strength of this man, a strength that was not just physical but mental, too. What elemental forces would be unleashed with his passion?

As if he'd looked into Willow's mind and read her deepest thoughts, Gideon traced the outline of her jaw, smoothed back the dense dark-taffy hair he had freed from its thick braid. "I wouldn't hurt you, ever," he said. And his mouth went to the sensitive length of her neck, making a tender exploration there.

A shudder of unqualified need went through Willow. "Gideon," she whispered, "I've never — I mean —"

"I know," he murmured, into the hollow above her collarbone.

Willow sighed and then gasped as his lips moved softly over the swell of her breast to nibble tentatively at its dusky rose peak. Once, long ago, she had overheard Steven and one of his women making love in a hayloft. They had not known that she was there, of course, and she had not been able to run away, for she had been held in place by a bond of curiosity and by her fear of being caught.

There had been much movement and much noise, and both Steven and the woman had cried out at intervals, as though they were in the throes of unendurable agony. Willow had been terrified, but to her amazement, Steven and his woman had seemed fully recovered when she saw them later. There had been a certain shine in the woman's eyes, and Steven had smiled at her a great deal, as though the two had shared a private joke.

Now Gideon's hands were making magic

along Willow's rib cage and his mouth feasted at her breasts, first one and then the other, that sweetly scandalous way that he had before, that day in the hills. She began to thrash beneath him. She had cried out then. Was that why Steven's woman had moaned and pleaded, as if in anguish?

Willow was filled with confusion and need, dread and wanting. "Gideon, Gideon," she said senselessly.

His answer was a hoarse chortle. "Soon, hellcat. You aren't ready yet."

And his mouth coursed downward, planting warm kisses that knifed all the way through to Willow's backbone, so fierce was the pleasure they gave. "R-ready?" she whispered, her hands tangled in his hair.

He was at the very portal of her womanhood now, his breath heating her entire body, despite the breeze from the window, causing every inch of her flesh to glisten. "Ummm," he said, and then he took her full in his mouth. The gentle motion was piercing, creating a comfort that was almost pain.

Willow writhed and twisted, though the last thing she wanted was to break away. Gideon's hands caught her hips and held them high and still and the pleasure grew keener, until Willow was certain that she could not bear it another moment.

"Gideon, Gideon!" she cried, as a shattering, burning tumult broke within her, then slowly faded, leaving her trembling and shaken.

Gideon lowered her gently back to the bed. His eyes were slumberous and veiled as they swept over her nakedness, claiming her. Careful not to let his full weight rest upon her, Gideon lowered himself and she felt the muscles in his sun-browned body ripple with need and restraint. The heated length of his manhood was both alarming and welcome where it pressed against her thigh.

"Beautiful," he murmured, as though spellbound, burying his face in the bright, silken tangle of Willow's hair.

She lay still beneath him, sated and yet knowing that the fullness of her womanhood was awakening again, drawn up from her depths by the hard power of his body, the scent of his hair and skin. "Come to me," she whispered, bold even in her relative innocence.

With a groan, Gideon nudged Willow's legs apart and sought entrance gently. "Sorceress," he rasped, and then he was within her, though just barely.

Instinct caused Willow to grasp his taut,

muscular buttocks in her hands and press him closer.

He moaned, as if in terrible pain. "Easy — for God's sake — this will hurt you if we go too fast."

Maria's words of warning loomed suddenly in Willow's mind. There would be pain the first time, she had said. But Willow's yearning was greater than her fear. "Please, Gideon," she said, in a hushed and tender voice.

Gideon came to her fully, in a cautious thrust. Willow felt a quick, tearing sting, but the sensation soon passed and she clutched at him as he made to withdraw. Surely, this wasn't all there was to this magical, puzzling rite — she had expected, dreamed of so much more.

But Gideon returned, this time with more power and force, and Willow was consumed in wildfire despite the tenderness of the passage he traveled.

The movements of Gideon's body were metered by his passion now, quickening with each thrust. He began to repeat her name over and over again in a strangled voice, and Willow, half-blinded by a bevy of new sensations, new emotions, allowed that voice to guide her through to the shuddering, raucous fulfillment that awaited them both.

They lay still, in sweet exhaustion, for some time. Then, with a nervous giggle, Willow announced, "You're squashing me."

Gideon immediately shifted away to lie on his back. His breath came ragged from somewhere deep in his chest, and he stared up at the ceiling as though he could see through it to the unbounded skies beyond. "Small vengeance," he answered, "for what you just did to me."

Willow sat up; if there had been covers, she would have clutched them to her. "I beg your pardon?" she asked; perhaps because her passions had been aroused, she was quick to anger.

"Relax, hellcat," Gideon said. "I meant no offense by that remark. And, just in case you're about to ask, yes. What we just did could make you pregnant."

Willow swallowed. Their alliance was an uncertain one, for all its fire, and she suddenly felt very much alone, even though Gideon was within touching distance. "What if I did have a baby, Gideon? What would happen then — between us, I mean?"

He cupped a strong and undeniably masculine hand over one of her still-pulsing breasts. "Then I would have to share this," he answered.

Tears smarted in Willow's eyes and Gideon saw them; he drew her down so that her head rested on his shoulder. His flesh, too, was moist with the exertion of climbing to the heights.

"What do you think would happen, Willow?" he asked softly, entangling a hand in her hair. "Do you imagine that I would leave you and my child, without even looking back?"

Willow shivered. "How do I know what you would do, Gideon Marshall? You're a stranger to me, a portrait come to life."

He laughed; the sound was deep in his chest, rumbling under Willow's ear. "I'm Lancelot," he said.

Willow would have bolted upright again if he hadn't stayed her. "You know about that?"

"It wasn't hard to figure out, hellcat. I hope you realize that I'm not made up of oil and canvas and paint thinner, but flesh and blood."

Willow colored richly, for there was no denying what this complicated, exasperating man was made of. "I imagined a lot of things about you, but I never *dreamed* of anything like this," she confessed.

Gideon laughed. "What, pray tell, did you

imagine, fair damsel?"

Willow's throat ached over the girlish naivete of the answer she had to give. "I — I thought you would just — well — I knew you would be inside me, but I didn't know how it would feel. I didn't know we would move like that . . ."

This time Gideon did not laugh, and the humor in his voice was tender. "You thought I was just going to jump on you and then lie there?"

"Yes," admitted Willow.

They were silent for a time, lying close, Gideon's hand moving softly in Willow's hair. Finally, turning to lie above her again, his lips not an inch from her own, Gideon breathed, "Never fear, m'lady. I will stay with you, and I will slay dragons for you."

A feeling of lush well-being swept over Willow, but beneath this lurked a niggling doubt. Promises made when the two of them had just made love were one thing, but she knew from bitter experience that reality was another.

Gideon meant to hunt down her brother. Would he slay Steven, too, like the dragons he'd mentioned?

His mouth came down to cover hers then, searching and hungry in a sleepy sort of way, and it was nightfall before they both labored back into their clothes and returned to town.

To Gideon's immense relief, the mourners, strangers all, had gone by the time he and Willow reached Judge Gallagher's house. Only Zachary remained and, though he was not in the mood to spar with his brother, Gideon could at least deal with his presence.

Zachary remained silent until Willow had bounded up the stairs, her hair trailing loose behind her, her cheeks glowing. Then, in the quiet of the Gallagher parlor, he lifted his brandy snifter in a wry and patently unfriendly salute. "Some people deal with grief in very interesting ways," he remarked.

Gideon stiffened, then willed his taut muscles to go loose. To aid in this, he helped himself to a glass of his father-in-law's imported whiskey. "Willow is, after all, my wife," he said, with an ease he did not feel.

"Who would know that better than I?" countered Zachary. Leaning back against the mantel over the fireplace, he gave the impression of a relaxed man, but Gideon knew that inwardly his brother was coiled like a snake, prepared to strike at any moment.

Gideon pinioned Zachary with a scathing

look. "Listen, Zachary, I've been patient about this. When I found out what you did, I wanted to kill you. I didn't, obviously. So why don't you just let well enough alone and shut up while you can?"

Zachary made a contemptuous sound deep in his throat and smirked. "Do you, perchance, labor under the delusion that you're any kind of match for me, little brother?"

"It's no delusion, Zachary, and you know it."

Zachary smiled, showing his dazzling white teeth, but he paled slightly, too. "All right, Gid, all right. We're neither one of us thinking straight, what with Mama buried just today."

There was a barb hidden in those words and it caught on Gideon's sense of honor, smarting. Had it been wrong, his losing himself in Willow's sweet fire on this grim day? Carefully, he hid the fact that Zachary had hit his mark. "Don't be maudlin, Zachary," he said hoarsely, "we weren't close to our mother, either one of us, so let's not pretend to be devastated by her loss. She virtually abandoned us, after all."

Zachary took a long draft from his appropriated brandy. "Gideon, she didn't abandon us. According to the terms of our granddad's will, we had to remain in San Francisco, under the Marshall roof, until we were of legal age. She didn't want us to be cut off from our inheritances."

That was the reasoning, but it didn't quite hold up, in Gideon's mind at least. Evadne had married Devlin Gallagher within a few years of her first husband's death and installed both her young sons in boarding school. They'd spent vacations in the San Francisco house, under the care of a variety of servants.

Still, the fact that Evadne had been able to walk away from her own children without putting up any kind of a fight nettled him.

"Maybe the judge wouldn't have let her bring us along on the honeymoon anyway," Zachary suggested into the resounding silence. "Did you ever think of that, Gideon? Maybe he didn't want another man's get underfoot all the time."

Gideon had considered that possibility often, over the years, but now, having met the judge, he didn't see him in that light. For all his riotous ways, Devlin Gallagher was not the kind of man to shirk responsibility, even if it was only indirectly his. "No," he said aloud. "The lawyers managing Granddad's estate brought pressure to bear, and Mama folded under it, that's all."

"She's dead, Gideon. Let's just give poor Mama the benefit of the doubt and assume that she did the best she could — all right?"

It was the only sensible approach and Gideon was more than ready to put his little-boy thoughts and feelings aside. Right or wrong, the past was the past, and Evadne was gone forever. "You're right," he conceded, facing his brother with a pensive frown. "Frankly, I'm still a little surprised that you're here at all, brother. I didn't think anything — even our mother's death — could drag you away from the gaming tables and — what's her name — Melanie?"

Zachary grinned wearily. "Melanie married a fifty-year-old shipping magnate with a belly and an even bigger bankroll than mine. And I made the journey because — well — because I felt guilty about that little trick I played on you. I thought there might be something I could do to help, but you seem to have things under control."

Control? Gideon almost laughed at the word. He was anything but in control; he was acting at odds with his own plans, in fact. He had intended to find Steven Gallagher, to marry Daphne Roberts, and to unite his shares of Central Pacific stock with her father's, thus gaining a controlling interest.

Instead of pursuing these objectives, he had bought a house, for God's sake, and on top of that he'd bedded Willow. He hadn't told her he loved her, but he'd come damned close, and he had as much as promised her that they would grow old together. Have children.

What the hell was wrong with him? He'd always been able to think decisively, but now he was torn between two vastly different goals. He *did* want to live on that small ranch he had so rashly purchased. He *did* want to see Willow swell to lush roundness with his children.

And yet he wanted to pursue his other desires, too. Not knowing how else to approach his quandary, Gideon turned on Zachary.

"Do you have any inkling of what a hell of a mess you've made of my life?" he growled furiously.

Zachary looked amused rather than contrite. "May I remind you that you went along with the idea willingly? You were ready to bed that sweet little morsel, no matter what you had to do to accomplish the purpose. Unless I miss my guess, which I'm sure I haven't, you've been rolling around in the hay with her all afternoon. You could have just quietly annulled the marriage, you know. Obviously, you've chosen to do otherwise."

Gideon scowled. "Did you tell Daphne about this, by any chance?"

"Of course I did. I couldn't have the poor girl running around town, telling everyone that she was engaged to a married man."

Gideon closed his eyes and drew a deep breath. "How did she take the news?"

"Colorfully. I could still hear the bric-a-brac shattering when I got into the carriage to leave."

"Wonderful. And her father?"

Zachary smiled, enjoying his memories. "The old man wanted to have you publicly flogged. Then shot. Then flogged again."

So much for uniting two financial empires, despaired Gideon, in grim silence.

"That isn't all, I'm afraid," said Zachary, with thinly veiled relish. "They're coming here to Virginia City, Daphne and her papa, presumably to make you see the error of your ways and seek some kind of redress for their grievances."

Gideon swore again but was stayed from further comment by the sudden appearance of Willow in the parlor doorway. The bright smile on her beautiful face was adequate proof that she hadn't overheard any of the conversation.

169

"We'll have to stay here tonight, Gideon," she announced cheerfully. "Maria says there simply isn't time to gather up all the sheets and towels and other things we'd need to be comfortable at the ranch house. She and I can take care of all that in the morning."

Gideon felt as limp as an unstarched shirt, and he avoided the knowing look he knew would be gleaming in Zachary's eyes. "Fine," he said, with a sharpness he hadn't intended.

Willow was visibly stung, and her smile wavered slightly, threatening to come unfixed. "Is something wrong?"

Zachary leaped into the conversation, with his usual dashing aplomb. "No, no — nothing is wrong, love." He took her hand, bent his head, and brushed his lips lightly across her knuckles. "And may I say, welcome to the Marshall family."

Gideon winced, but fortunately Willow's attention was focused on Zachary and she didn't see.

"Thank you," she said softly, and her lovely eyes came to Gideon's face with a timidity that made him ache inside. With the brusqueness of a single word, he had hurt her, and he hated himself for it. Himself *and* Zachary.

"We'll stay here tonight," he told his wife,

with a gentleness calculated to make up for his earlier brusque tone, "if you're sure your father wouldn't mind."

For a moment, Gideon thought Willow would come to him and put her arms around him in an embrace. He wouldn't have been able to bear the sweetness of the gesture if she had. But stopped by the coolness of his manner, she simply summoned up another tremulous smile and said, "He won't mind — we're married, after all."

This time, Gideon could not hide his reaction to the reminder; it struck his troubled conscience like a lash.

Willow's face literally crumbled, but she left the parlor doorway with a dignity Gideon immediately admired, her shoulders straight, head held high.

"You bastard," said Zachary. "Why didn't you just come right to the point and slap her to the floor? She didn't deserve that."

"Will you shut up?" rasped Gideon, at the end of his patience. "None of this would have happened if it weren't for you."

"I may have started it rolling, brother," Zachary answered dryly, "but I didn't bed that girl, and I didn't get her hopes up, either. You did those things, Gideon. You."

Zachary was right, though Gideon would never have admitted it aloud. And suddenly, he felt as though Devlin Gallagher's house was closing in around him, choking the breath from his lungs.

"I'm going out," he said crisply. "Are you coming with me?"

Arching one eyebrow, Zachary shrugged. "Why not?" he intoned.

Fifteen minutes later, they entered the same saloon where Gideon had encountered Steven Gallagher, then wearing his peddler disguise.

"A special," Gideon said, to the grinning bartender. "For my brother, that is. I'll have whiskey."

Zachary was about to protest when the bartender slid a brimming mug of panther piss in front of him, from which he obligingly took a deep drink.

His violent reaction did much to ease Gideon's beleaguered spirit.

"Son of a goddamned bitch!" roared Zachary, alternately spitting and eyeing his glass with horror. "What is this stuff?"

Gideon only grinned.

Maria's hand was soft and warm on Willow's shuddering shoulder. "What is it, little one? Why do you cry?"

Willow's response was a wail of indignation and pain.

"Already you and the husband have quarreled?"

Willow sat up on her childhood bed and sniffled. "Not exactly. He just — well . . ."

Maria took a seat beside Willow and enfolded her in a motherly embrace. "What, little one? What has he done?"

"I don't know — I can't explain it."

A warm, understanding laugh escaped Maria. "You will not worry," she ordered.

"Not worry?" snapped Willow, stiffening in the housekeeper's arms. "Maria, Gideon is my husband and he doesn't love me!"

"Hush. Gideon does not know what he feels, and neither do you. Tomorrow there is time to settle things, always there is time. Why do you not get into bed, and I will bring you supper here, no?"

"No," Willow answered stubbornly.

But when Maria returned, only minutes later, with a tray, Willow was snuggled down in her bed, sound asleep and dreaming that Sir Lancelot, riding a white charger, was saving her from a great, scaly dragon, breathing fire.

Gideon opened one eye and groaned. He was sprawled out on the narrow settee in his mother's sitting room, and his own portrait smirked at him from above the fireplace. He'd been not quite seventeen when he'd posed for the likeness, and at school. Evadne had forced him to submit to days of excruciating stillness by promising, from a distance, to withhold his allowance unless he cooperated.

Sickness rolled in his stomach and pounded beneath his temples as he sat up. In one corner of the room stood a polished suit of medieval armor, silently mocking him. He arched one eyebrow, which ached as badly as his head, impossible as that was, and idly wondered if that iron garb would fit him.

Not likely, he thought ruefully, as a lusty snore rose over the top of a brocade chair a few feet away.

Gideon grinned. His only comfort lay in the fact that Zachary was going to feel every bit as bad as he did, if not worse, and he clung to that. "Zachary!" he said loudly.

His brother moaned and stirred in the small chair. "Next time you offer me a drink, little brother," he rasped out, "I fully intend to shoot you."

Gideon lifted whiskey-reddened eyes to the ceiling, thinking of Willow. Chances were, Zachary wasn't the only person in this house inclined to do him violence. He sighed. At least he hadn't gone to his bride's bed the night before, though he'd been sorely tempted. In the end, he'd decided that Willow deserved better than the pawing of a drunk.

Zachary lumbered out of the fussy chair and stretched, giving a painful groan as he did so. "Why the hell did you sleep down here," he demanded testily, "when your curvaceous little wife was right upstairs?"

Gideon colored up for the first time in his memory and concentrated on wrenching his boots onto his feet. He said nothing, for at the moment he was too ashamed even to speak Willow's name.

"I sure wouldn't have spent the night on a sofa if I'd been in your situation," grumbled Zachary, who never knew when to keep his mouth shut.

"That's the difference between us," Gideon answered shortly. With a baleful glance at the suit of armor, he wondered what your average, everyday, run-of-the-mill knight would do in circumstances like these. Chivalry aside, his impulse was to grovel.

"There aren't as many differences between you and me as you would like to believe," Zachary replied, with an insight that was both uncanny and fundamentally disturbing. "The sooner you admit to that and act accordingly, little brother, the better off you're going to be."

"Go to hell," muttered Gideon.

"Good morning," sang Maria, from the sitting room doorway and, even though she was smiling, her velvet-brown eyes fairly snapped with malice. Gideon knew that he had ruffled her chick, and he was going to be pecked severely for the indiscretion. "You will have breakfast, no?"

"*No!*" chorused Gideon and Zachary in unison.

Maria's smile grew broader. "But is eggs!" she crowed, knowing full well how she was tormenting them, "scrambled eggs, still warm from the nest, with nice peppers and many onions to give flavor!"

Zachary slapped one hand over his mouth, groaned, and ran for the nearest exit.

Maria's vengeful gaze was fixed on Gideon now. "Eggs are funny things, señor," she commented. "Once, I get one that is all rotten and runny inside —"

Gideon made a strangled sound and bolted after Zachary.

"Weren't Gideon and Zachary hungry?" asked Willow brightly, as she sat down at the kitchen table to enjoy a hearty breakfast. Now that it was morning and the sun was warm in the summer sky, she felt optimistic again.

Maria, standing at the stove, chuckled, the sound vibrating through her great bulk. "No, they are not hungry, little one. They are, I think, looking at the petunias we planted by the fence."

Willow frowned. Neither Gideon nor Zachary had struck her as the type of man to be particularly fond of flowers. She shrugged. Later, she would show them the white lilacs and the rose arbor. "Did Papa come home last night?"

"No," replied Maria.

"Do you think he's with Dove Triskadden, so soon after — ?"

Maria shook her head firmly. "No. The judge took a bedroll with him. Food and a coffeepot, too."

"I wish he would come back," said Willow. "I don't like the idea of going to live in Gideon's house without telling Papa first."

Maria's smile was fond as she came to the table and poured hot, fresh coffee into Willow's cup. "Your papa will not be angry. He knows that a bride must live with her husband."

"I'll miss you when I go, Maria."

Bright tears glistened in Maria's kind eyes. "You will not be far away," she said, possibly as much for her own benefit as Willow's. "And perhaps I can come and work for you there, on the ranch."

Her fork poised halfway between her plate and her mouth, Willow was immediately cheered. "I'm going to speak to Gideon on your behalf at the first opportunity," she said.

But Maria looked sad now. "I was forgetting my duties here. Who will look after your papa, if I leave?"

Willow had no doubt that Dove Triskadden would be ensconced in this house as soon as propriety allowed, but then Dove probably wasn't the kind to devote herself to baking bread and scrubbing floors, and it wasn't as if there were a lot of unemployed housekeepers in Virginia City, just waiting to be offered a job. Willow conceded Maria's point silently and concentrated on eating her breakfast.

When that was done, the two women turned to gathering linens and cooking utensils and extra curtains, all to be taken to the house outside of town, the house that would now be Willow's home. Despite the fact that she had had Maria to look after her all these years, and was thus not only somewhat spoiled but also domestically inept, she was eager to try her hand at homemaking.

Willow was humming as she folded blankets and quilts, but she stopped abruptly when she sensed Gideon's presence in the bedroom doorway. Considering his treatment of her the night before, she stiffened, unwilling or unable to speak first.

"I seem to be apologizing to you at every turn," he said, from just behind her, his voice husky and low.

His very nearness made Willow ache inside. "You were out all night," she said. There was no accusation in her words, no anger.

"I was out *most* of the night. I slept in the sitting room."

Willow felt a sudden urge to whirl around and slap her husband soundly across the face, but she suppressed it. Her knuckles, though, turned white where she grasped the wedding-ring quilt she had been folding into a linen chest. "Why didn't you come to my room?"

There was a short silence, "Would you have welcomed me, Willow?"

She spun to face him, pulling the quilt with her, her eyes shooting golden flames. "No!"

Gideon shrugged and spread his hands. "I rest my case," he said. He hesitated, then thrust a hand through his hair. "Forgive me?"

The room seemed to be filled with the scent of white lilacs, flowing in through the open window. "Are you going to be a good husband, Gideon Marshall," she countered, "or a shameless rounder?"

"My fate hinges on my answer, I presume?"

Willow reddened. "It does," she confirmed.

He smiled wanly. "Then I'm going to be a good husband," he answered.

Against her better judgment, Willow believed him.

Perhaps because she wanted to so much.

7

When Devlin Gallagher returned from his sojourn in the mountains, it was to find Juan and Pablito, the stable workers, loading various trunks and crates into the bed of a buckboard. Understanding immediately, Devlin was filled with a sweeping loneliness.

Willow was leaving home. His little girl was all grown up now, and married — for better or for worse.

Wearily, Devlin waved away Pablito's quick offer of help and stabled his horse himself, seeing that it had water and a little extra feed. He was just bolting the stall door when Gideon Marshall approached him, looking nervous and determined, both at once.

"You'd best be good to my daughter," Devlin said gruffly. There was no point in mincing words, especially when the discussion concerned Willow. The girl was strong and spirited, even wild at times, but she had a fragile, innocent side, too.

Devlin would not see her hurt, and he wanted to make sure his son-in-law understood that.

Gideon smiled somewhat weakly. It wasn't hard to guess that he didn't like knowing that he was putting Willow between her husband and her brother, and that comforted Devlin in an odd sort of way. Most likely, the man had a conscience.

"I'll see that Willow never wants for anything," Gideon promised.

Devlin was quiet for a few moments, absorbing that. "Thought you'd be gone by now," he observed, rubbing the back of his aching neck with one hand as he strode out of the shadowy barn and into the bright sunshine. He was getting old; too old to go trekking around in the mountains like some young buck with the sap still flowing through his veins, cooking for himself over a campfire, and sleeping on the ground.

Gideon's hands were wedged into the pockets of his trousers. "Willow didn't want to leave without speaking to you first." He paused, cleared his throat. "Neither did I, as a matter of fact."

Devlin eyed his son-in-law with wry appreciation. "Thank you."

Gideon only nodded; there was a muscle leaping in his jawline and his eyes kept straying away from Devlin's face and then being drawn firmly back again. Clearly, there was more the man wanted to say, but he was having a hell of a time coming out with it.

"I believe I'd enjoy a cup of Maria's coffee right about now," Devlin commented mildly. "Join me?"

Again, Gideon nodded, and color seeped up from his open collar to pulse in his ears.

Devlin, understanding, or at least figuring that he did, smiled to himself.

In the kitchen, Maria silently served coffee and left the room. Gideon and Devlin sat at the table, cupping their hands around their mugs.

Presently, Gideon cleared his throat again. "Sir . . ."

Devlin waited, biting his lower lip to keep from smiling or, worse, laughing out loud. "Yes?" he prompted when he dared, unable to resist arching one eyebrow.

Gideon squirmed miserably in his chair. "I — well — Willow and I have already been . . . together."

Devlin feared for the mouthful of hot coffee he'd just taken. It burned as he swallowed it. "You must have some reason for telling me that, boy, but I can't rightly think what it would be," he finally managed to say.

"You had a right to know that this isn't some kind of sham, this marriage, I mean," Gideon blurted out, looking defensive and once again red at the earlobes.

"Isn't it?"

Gideon shook his head forcefully. "I can't honestly say that I love your daughter — that is, I don't know if I do or not. But I'll be good to Willow, I promise you."

"That's a promise you'll want to keep," warned Devlin quietly. "There're two things I won't tolerate, Gideon, and the rest is your business. Don't lay a hand on that girl, ever, for any reason, in anger. And don't betray her with another woman."

Gideon's strong jaw tightened and he started to speak, but Devlin cut him off briskly.

"I know what you were going to say — that I'm a fine one to be advising a man to be faithful to his wife. But I've got the right, because it's my daughter who would be hurt and because I know better than anybody how much pain and trouble that kind of self-indulgence can bring on."

"Are you saying — ?"

Again, Devlin interrupted. "I'm saying

that I'm sorry for what I did to your mother, Gideon. I said it to her and I'm saying it to you. Bring shame to Willow in that way and I'll horsewhip you for it, and if you think that's an idle threat from an old man, you'd damn well better think again."

Gideon averted his eyes, absorbing in silence what Devlin had said.

"Not long before she took sick, your mother said something to me that'll be carved into my memory, no matter what I do, until the day I die," Devlin went on quietly. "She said it wasn't the straying that she couldn't forgive me for, but the fact that my actions made other people pity her. Evadne despised me for that, and I don't blame her."

The younger man's gaze sliced back to Devlin's face, unreadable and slightly narrowed. "When you married my mother, did you ask her to leave my brother and me behind in San Francisco to attend boarding school?"

Devlin was taken aback by the directness of the question, but he recovered quickly. On some level, he'd expected it to be asked a long time ago, though he hadn't spent much time in the presence of Evadne's sons. "Of course I didn't. And she didn't want to, either — she cried for weeks."

"She could have challenged my grandfather's will," Gideon said.

Devlin sighed, sitting back, remembering. "There were still a lot of Indian raids out here then, Gideon, and the only law we had was the vigilante kind. Your grandfather's lawyers convinced Evadne that the two of you were better off in San Francisco, for a great many reasons. As for the will, it was ironclad. I went over it myself, at Evadne's request, of course. You and Zachary would have lost your inheritances if she'd defied the terms of that will."

Gideon looked away for a moment and, in that brief space of time, Devlin realized how much alike Steven and this young man really were. Again, he was comforted.

Into the silence came Willow, looking flushed and happy. As she thrust herself into Devlin's arms, nearly toppling his chair in the process, he laughed and hugged her. For now, he smiled and shared her obvious joy; later, though, he knew that he would grieve at the loss of her.

Willow was like music, filling the house.

When she was gone, there would be silence.

Some instinct made Vancel Tudd turn away from both his favorite saloon and the room

186

he kept at Mrs. Porter's boardinghouse that late June morning, despite the fact that he was hot, thirsty, and very discouraged. Annoyed with himself, he went instead to the general store for cigarette papers and some tobacco.

The very fetching face of the Gallagher girl brought him up short as soon as he entered that mercantile. She was there alone and immersed in the inspection of a set of china. This afforded Vancel the option of watching her freely, without her taking immediate notice.

Remorse swept over him, displacing the fatigue of tracking Steven Gallagher for days, without avail. She'd been here all the time, this girl — Christ, why hadn't he thought about her before? If she was close to her brother, she would eventually meet with him, and all Vancel would have to do would be to follow. He'd assuage his wounded pride and collect the bounty from the railroad, all in one easy move.

She turned then, saw him, and the almost imperceptible curl of her lip convinced Vancel that he'd been right. She knew him, and despised him, and that meant that she probably saw her brother on a regular basis.

The scrawny, simpering storekeeper was trying to divert the woman's attention from

Vancel. "Will that pattern serve, Mrs. Marshall?"

"It will do just fine, Mr. McCullough," the whiskey-eyed scamp answered, with a Gallagher-proud lift of her chin. "Will you send the entire set, along with my other purchases, out to our house as soon as possible, please?"

"Yes, ma'am," replied the shopkeeper, darting one nervous look in Vancel's direction. "Will there be anything else?"

"Not today, thank you," she answered crisply, and then she was leaving the store, shifting her skirts aside as she passed Vancel.

Tudd was not a prepossessing man, and he knew it, but the woman's casual snobbery sealed his determination to use her to find the Mountain Fox. *They all thought they was better than the next one, them Gallaghers.*

"What'll it be, Vance?" the shopkeeper asked politely as Vancel approached the long, dark-wood counter. "Tobacco, maybe?"

Vancel laid a sizable bill on the countertop. "That woman that just left — she's Judge Gallagher's girl, ain't she?"

Surreptitiously, McCullough swept the bill into one hand. "Willow? Sure, but her

188

name's Marshall now — she got married a while back. Damnedest ceremony you ever saw! Why, there was ol' Norville Pickering, standing at the altar and all ready to tangle some blankets with her soon as the two of them were alone . . ."

Vancel's throat was dry and his head ached. No, sir, he just wasn't the man he'd once been; he needed to get out of this business and get himself a place in Mexico, soon as he could. The high bounty on Steven Gallagher's head would make that possible. "Shut up!" he rasped, catching McCullough's starched shirt in his hands and lifting the little man several inches off the floor. "I'll ask you what I want to know!"

McCullough sputtered and turned bright red. "Why, 'course, Vancel. I just thought —"

"Don't think, McCullough. You might hurt your head." Vancel eased the man back down to stand on his own feet. "This Marshall fella she married — who's he?"

McCullough tugged his vest and his dignity back into place, but he had an aggrieved air about him, too. "That's what I was fixin' to tell ya, Vance. He's got shares in the Central Pacific, and the talk is that he's out to get Judge Gallagher's boy, just like you are."

189

"Is he a fast gun, this Marshall yahoo?"

"I ain't seen him shoot, but he's a big 'un, like you, Vancel. Shoulders like a bear. No, sir, I wouldn't want to tangle with that one."

Vancel couldn't help smiling. So Marshall was big, was he? Most likely he was tough, too. But he had a weakness Vancel Tudd didn't share — a fondness for that saucy scrap with the brandy-colored eyes. "Where did these newlyweds set up housekeepin'?" he asked.

"They bought the Baker place, and for cash money," grumbled McCullough. No doubt the Marshalls paid cash for their goods, too, thus depriving him of the exorbitant interest rates he charged for credit.

In a fine mood, Vancel turned and left the store. He'd have himself a bath, a woman, and a good meal, though not necessarily in that order. By tomorrow morning, he'd be ready to start keeping a much closer eye on Judge Gallagher's girl.

Yes, sir, if he watched that little bit of a thing long enough, she was sure to lead him right to Steven Gallagher.

Leaving the horse and buggy at the gate, Willow ran up the walk to her own house and burst through the door. "Gideon?"

There was a distant answer, and she followed the sound through the parlor and the big kitchen and finally out onto the narrow, weathered back porch.

Gideon was standing just a few feet away, at the wash bench, wearing only trousers, his bare chest and back glistening with little beads of spring water. He gave Willow a sidelong grin and flung the soapy contents of the basin into the tall grass. "Where have you been, wife?" he demanded, with mock annoyance.

Willow's insides pulsed in unison with the beat of her heart, just to remember how they had made love the night before. And she was remembering with a lot more than just her brain.

"I went to town," she said, as color seeped, warm, into her cheeks. "To buy china."

He grinned again. "China? Did you buy Siam, too?"

Willow swatted at him and laughed. "That was a very bad joke. I hope I can expect better in the future, Gideon Marshall."

Gideon wrenched a snow white towel from a peg on the porch wall and began to dry his arms, his back, his shoulders. Willow felt such delicious discomfort that she had to look away.

"What else did you buy?" he asked, aware of her sweet distress and clearly enjoying it.

Willow managed a shrug. "Flour, sugar, coffee — all those things."

His voice was low, reaching out to Willow even though she knew that he had not drawn a step nearer, and he was toweling his hair with motions that made the muscles in his chest and stomach ripple. "Are you a good cook, Mrs. Marshall?"

Willow lifted her chin. "Fair to middling," she replied honestly. "Maria does most of the cooking herself, but she taught me a few things, like how to brew tea and make tortillas."

He grinned. "Tea and tortillas? I'm even luckier than I thought." His warm eyes swept over her breasts, her stomach, her hips, turning to a deep green as they passed. "Let's make love in the grass, Mrs. Marshall."

Willow's crimson cheeks not only burned, they ached, too. "In broad daylight?"

Gideon laughed. "I think I'd like to see you bathed in sunlight," he commented, and he set aside the towel in a measured motion that made the pit of Willow's stomach leap and gyrate like a circus performer dancing on a high wire.

She stepped backward into the kitchen. "But we haven't — we haven't had any breakfast," she stammered stupidly.

Gideon followed her inside, stalking her like some magnificent mountain beast, his eyes teasing her as he came nearer and nearer. "I am ravenous," he said, in a gruff voice.

Only too aware that he wasn't talking about food, and more than a little frightened by the reckless intensity of her own desire, Willow wrung her hands and managed a nervous smile. "Gideon, I-we —"

He caught her hand in his, pulled her against his chest, and won the victory in that moment. His mouth came down to cover Willow's, to take it, and he tasted of spring water and sweet grass and sunlight. Her heart spun inside her and her traitorous loins leaped to life with a force that was almost painful. She wrapped her arms around his neck and succumbed to his kiss, to him.

Somehow, without breaking the astounding depths of that kiss, Gideon maneuvered his wife outside again, into the sun. They fell together into the lush grass near the back porch, bruising it with their bodies, stirring its scent to mingle with those of pitch and fresh air and wild honeysuckle.

He covered both her legs with one of his own, pinioning her to the soft ground, but not in restraint, for there was no shade of resistance in Willow. In fact, she whimpered and strained to be bared to his touch even as he undid the tiny buttons that closed her calico dress.

Willow felt the cool summer breeze on her breasts as her muslin camisole was unlaced, and Gideon's mouth left hers, at last. Sitting up, he smiled, and his fingers deftly worked each succulent nipple into readiness for his taking. When the peaks were pebble hard, he bent to taste them, one at a time and at his torturous leisure.

In the meantime, his hand smoothed Willow's skirts up over her knees and her thighs, trespassed into the satiny confines of her drawers, unerringly found the very core of her need. Ruthlessly, he plied her until she thrashed and whimpered and reached blindly for him.

He laughed tenderly and removed her drawers with a slow motion of both hands. That done, he undid the strained buttons of his trousers and fell gently to her, seeking her with fire and quiet majesty.

Willow arched her back and cried out as he took swift, forceful entry. He was filling her and she clutched at his bare shoulders and his muscle-corded back.

Mischievously, he held back, watching her, savoring his dominion, and Willow's passion was suddenly shot through with a singular sort of rage. She grasped his taut buttocks and forced him to drive deep inside her.

Gideon groaned and closed his eyes and his magnificent features tightened as he struggled to withhold the full heat of his own need. "Wench," he rasped, and there was a hoarse tenderness in the word. It almost sounded like love.

Willow showed no mercy; instead, she began to rise and fall beneath Gideon, increasing his pleasure as she increased her own, demanding, commanding that he give up his seed. And he moaned in joyful anguish as he moved upon her, captured, forced to surrender as she was surrendering.

Finally, driven to be fused to this man at the deepest possible level, Willow cried out and flung her legs around his powerful hips, holding him in final conquest.

Gideon called her name and shuddered violently upon her and she replied with a shout of mingled triumph and defiance, her own body quivering in the soft grass.

Presently, Gideon left her to lie still on the ground, his breath rasping in and out of his lungs, his manhood still proud and strong in the bright sunlight.

Willow was suddenly angry, with him and with herself. She sat up, blushing and fumbling with the laces of her camisole and the buttons of her dress. Laughing gruffly, Gideon grasped her arms and hauled her on top of him, so that she sat upon the already swelling rod that had conquered her so completely.

"Where do you think you're going?" he demanded.

"Inside the house," Willow whispered, wretched with embarrassment, squirming.

Gideon held her fast. His smile flashed white in his tanned face, and for some reason she noticed that his beard was growing in. "Keep doing that. It feels good."

"Why, you reprehensible lecher," Willow retorted, but she nearly laughed.

His hands were firm and strong on her hips. "You're not going anywhere, hellcat. Not yet, at least."

Willow made to rise from him and he allowed it, to a point. Her cheeks flared again as she realized that he had only wanted to get a grip on her skirts, which he promptly lifted to her waist.

She glared at him in furious triumph, even as a heat that would not be denied surged through her. She was astraddle him, after all, and there was the small matter of her drawers. What did he intend to do about them?

The answer came in the form of a soft, ripping sound; he'd torn the appropriate seam, and now was prodding her, seeking sanction. Willow groaned helplessly as Gideon entered with a fierce upward thrust, then clutched him as he pitched beneath her like a raging stallion, muttering raspy, senseless words in the delirium of his own quest.

Finally, they convulsed together, their cries intertwining into one shout of desperation and victory.

Even when it was over, and their breathing had returned, somewhat, to normal, Gideon would not free her. He lay there, under her and yet wholly in command of her, body and soul, his hands kneading the firm plumpness of her bare bottom.

"Are you going to fix my breakfast or not?" he asked finally, grinning.

Willow reached out and slapped his smug face, though not with much force or purpose.

Willow saw the buggy coming a long time before it reached the far gate and the driveway leading up to the house, and she was very pleased. Gideon had gone to town and she was done with her cleaning and baking and eager to have a visitor.

When the horse and buggy came to a stop at the small picket fence bounding the yard itself, Willow drew in a startled breath and stepped back from the window. She had no woman friends, with the exception of Maria, as the ladies of Virginia City viewed her background with jaundiced disapproval, but she had not, in her wildest dreams, expected this particular caller.

Still, she was lonely — the house seemed big and empty without Gideon there — and she was used to living in town, where there was a lot of coming and going. Willow hastily dusted her floury hands on the apron she wore over her calico dress. Then, with decorum, she walked to the door to admit Dove Triskadden.

Dove was not a young woman, but neither was she old; Willow discerned that she was somewhere in her early forties. And yet, standing there, with her curly mane of pale blond hair, wearing a tailored dress of mint green silk and nervously twirling a parasol to match, she was as attractive as any lady in town. Her waist was narrow and her bosom was full; it was disturbingly easy to understand why Willow's own father found Miss Triskadden so attractive.

Poor Evadne, Willow thought as she summoned up a questioning smile and greeted her father's mistress politely.

Dove's dark green eyes danced as she stood there on the front porch, resplendent in her splendid dress and a dramatic hat with long feather plumes for accent. "Hello, Mrs. Marshall," Dove responded, in a voice that was sweet and somehow lush.

"W-won't you come in?" Willow asked, stepping back and wondering what on earth one served to such a guest? Tea? Brandy? Something frivolous, like sherry or a fruit cordial?

Alas, Willow had none of those things on hand; she could offer nothing but tea.

Dove smiled and stepped inside the house, tugging at her fine kid gloves as she came. "This is a right nice place," she said, in that musical voice of hers, looking around. "Of course, I've never been inside before."

Willow didn't know what to say to that, so she said nothing at all. She simply started toward the parlor and assumed that Dove Triskadden would follow.

Which she did.

There, in that spacious and only partially furnished room, Dove settled herself into a chair and sighed. Almost immediately, her round, spirited eyes fell upon the piano. "Do you play?" she said, mostly, Willow suspected, to put her hostess at ease.

Willow did not know whether to sit or stand. "A little," she confessed.

Dove laughed. "I play a little, too. That's all it takes to make Devlin beg me to stop."

Willow leaned forward, forgetting her awe and confusion for a moment. "Do you know 'My Love Lies Dead on a Sawdust Floor'?" she asked, her eyes wide.

Again, the green eyes danced. "Now why would a sweet little thing like you want to play a bawdy tune like that? It's a drinking song, sung in saloons, and it isn't often heard in a lady's parlor."

Willow blushed, but something in this woman's manner told her that she could be honest, so she blurted out, "My husband, Gideon, asked me if I could play it. I think he was teasing, but I'd love to surprise him by learning the piece."

Dove's full lips quivered with restrained amusement. "It'll be a surprise, all right. But, sure, I'll show you the notes."

"Thank you," said Willow, delighted.

With that, the two women went to the piano, and by the time Willow had mastered the boisterous and somewhat suggestive song, they were fast friends.

After numerous cups of tea and much

chatter, Dove came to the point of her visit.

"Your father and I," she announced crisply, "are going to be married as soon as it's proper. That'll be about a year yet, but I wanted you to know."

Willow reached tentatively across the kitchen table and touched Dove's soft, jewel-laden hand. "I'll welcome you as a stepmother," she said.

Dove suddenly stiffened, and her rouged lips puckered into a circle. "Oh, mercy, I almost forgot. When I said I was on my way out here, Charlie Evans overheard me and asked if I'd bring this wire." She opened her beaded handbag and began rummaging through it, finally drawing out a folded piece of paper. "It's meant for your husband, but you'll see he gets it, won't you?"

Willow felt some unaccountable alarm tickle its way down her spine, just touching the telegram, but she smiled and promised to give Gideon the message the moment he got home.

Long after Dove took her leave, Willow was drawn again and again to that sealed missive lying in the middle of the kitchen table. She was a ninny, she told herself, even to think about it, and nosy, too.

Finally, though, when the feeling of foreboding became too great to bear, she peeled away the wax seal and unfolded the crumpled white paper. The message was hand copied, and it read:

Gideon. Father detained in San Francisco. Hilda and I will arrive soon. You have some explaining to do.

Daphne

Daphne. The very name made Willow ache all over. Until this moment, she had denied herself any thought of the woman who had been engaged to Gideon, but that luxury was no longer possible. Daphne had obviously seen fit to fight for what she regarded, with some justification, as hers.

Tears welled in Willow's eyes and she slumped into a chair, her chin propped in her hands. What chance was she going to have against someone like Daphne, someone raised in a cosmopolitan city, someone educated in the finest schools, someone who knew how to behave as a lady should?

Willow tried to comfort herself with the memory of Gideon's lovemaking that morning, in — she flushed to recall her own lusty responses — the yard. The reassurance this gave her turned quickly to biting mortification. Good Lord, what man wouldn't avail himself of a pleasure so wantonly offered, with or without loving her?

Seeing that telegram through tear-blurred eyes, Willow knew for a certainty that Gideon had used her and that love had had no place in that using.

After a few minutes of recovery, Willow heated the wax seal with a match and pressed it back into place. When Gideon came home from town, she was at the parlor piano, playing the song Dove had taught her with a gusto designed to hide her broken heart.

Gideon laughed with amused recognition and came to stand behind her, his strong hands warm and wounding on her shoulders. When he bent to kiss the length of her neck, she shuddered and nearly burst into tears. Willow hammered at the keys.

He sat down beside her on the long bench, his thigh hard against hers, and she felt those inquisitive eyes raking her, reaching inside her, searching the secret regions of her heart and soul. Gideon caught her chin in his hand and made her face him, and the music died away in miserable discord.

"What is it?" he asked, frowning. "Willow, what's happened?"

Willow's vision was blurred and shifting, but her pride sustained her. "You have a wire, from San Francisco," she said, amazed that she sounded so calm.

Gideon's withdrawal was instant, and it was alarming. The color drained from beneath his tan and his hand fell slowly from her chin. Only a moment later, he was rising from the piano bench, looking down at Willow as though she were a stranger, an intruder.

"Where is it?" he asked.

Willow managed an idle shrug, though on the inside she was already breaking into a thousand splintery pieces. "On the table," she answered with dignity, "on the kitchen table."

He hurried toward that room with an earnestness that wounded Willow even further. In less than a minute, Gideon was back again, though it seemed to Willow that a month had passed.

"Daphne is on her way here," Willow said, making no attempt to hide the fact that she'd read the wire intended for her husband.

"Yes," he replied, in a faraway, expressionless voice.

Willow lifted numb, bloodless fingers to the piano keys and began to play. The song was too sad to share, and Gideon promptly left the house.

8

The Marshall house was out in the open, except for a stand of cottonwood trees rising around the pond, and it was there that Vancel Tudd took refuge in the predawn hours of a summer morning. Just after the sun came up, he saw the husband leave by the back door and stride toward the barn.

Vancel thought dispassionately that for once the storekeeper, McCullough, had been right about something. Gideon Marshall was big enough to fight grizzlies with a butter knife, and he was probably meaner than hell, too. Here, the bounty hunter reflected, was a man who, for all his obvious polish and good looks, was tough clear through. It was there in the way he moved, the way he carried himself.

He wasn't afraid of anybody.

Marshall came out of the barn presently, mounted on a dancing black gelding, and tossed one lingering look toward the house before riding out.

Vancel, still safely hidden from view, sighed. The weather was cold, since it was so early, but, as the day wore on, it would get hot, even under the shelter of those whispering cottonwood trees. Sometimes he wondered if Steven Gallagher's hide was worth all the trouble and discomfort he'd already endured, not to mention the danger. That Gideon Marshall fella hadn't looked like the kind to cotton to finding a man idling on his property and watching his house.

Especially when he had a little woman in there, all by herself.

Hatred and the twenty-five-thousand-dollar bounty on Gallagher's head sustained Vancel. All he ever had to do, when he started having doubts, was to remember that time in Bannack, when the outlaw had surprised him in a whorehouse. He'd been wearing a nightshirt, Vancel had, and Steven Gallagher had literally nailed that garment to the wall — with Vancel still inside it.

Vancel seethed with the remembered humiliation of hanging there, six inches off the floor of that whorehouse bedroom, bound by his own clothes. One way or another, no matter what he had to do, he would see Steven Gallagher dead. In the final analysis, it didn't matter whether the bastard was shot or hanged, just as long as he died.

Painfully, of course.

Over the coming half hour or so, Vancel took pains to calm himself. If he was going to keep a clear head, he couldn't be thinking about how much he hated Gallagher. No, sir, the thing to do was keep an eye on the man's sister.

She was the key to everything.

When the rider first appeared, Vancel laid a hand to the butt of his pistol. He flexed his fingers, though, when he saw that this caller, whoever he was, was a stranger, a dark-haired man with fine clothes, tailor made to fit him.

"Who the hell . . . ?" muttered Vancel, squinting into the bright sunshine. But he still didn't recognize the man.

The rider dismounted at the front gate of the Marshall house, tethered his mount to the picket fence, then took off his fancy round-brimmed hat to run one hand through his hair.

Vancel grinned, relaxing a little. Whoever he was, that feller sure looked nervous. Maybe that saucy little bundle inside the house was more like her old daddy than people thought. Sure would be interesting if

207

the man with the big shoulders was to come back right about now, the bounty hunter thought. Sure would, indeed.

If Zachary Marshall had had any doubts about the advisability of calling on Gideon's bride, they were dispelled by the puffiness around her pale amber eyes and the pallor in her cheeks.

"What are you doing here?" she asked at the door, with a directness that neither surprised nor unsettled Zachary.

"I'm looking for Gideon," he lied, easily. He knew that his brother was already in town, involved in some kind of consultation with Mitch Kroeber, the marshal. "Is he at home?"

The small, defiant chin lifted and there was a suspicious light in the gilt eyes. Willow's dark honey hair had been pinned up loosely, and it appeared ready to fall down around her shoulders. Zachary's fingers ached to pick forbidden fruit even as he reflected mundanely that Gideon and his heart-stopping little wife would surely have fair-haired children. "My husband has gone to town," she said stiffly.

Zachary flinched and worked up an engaging grin. "I see you haven't forgiven me for my part in that unfortunate episode two years ago," he said, properly sheepish.

The lovely face relaxed a little, humor leaping in the dark-lashed golden eyes. "You were a scoundrel to take part in such a thing," she announced, "and so was Gideon. Frankly, I'm surprised that my father hasn't shot both of you dead."

Zachary felt it was safe to laugh. "He would have been justified in doing that, I'm afraid. The judge must be a generous-minded man."

Willow's full breasts were tantalizing as they pressed against the fabric of her modest cambric dress; Zachary was careful not to look at them, even though they were bared in his imagination. Damn, that Gideon was a lucky bastard, and Zachary wondered if his brother had the good sense to realize that.

She was about to close the door in his face, Willow was, and Zachary moved quickly to block it with his right boot. At the same time, he was careful to look ingenuous.

"Couldn't I come in, Mrs. Marshall?" he enjoined. "It's a long ride back to town —"

"At least ten minutes," she retorted, with acidic humor, but then she stepped back out of the doorway and admitted Zachary to his brother's house.

"You must be pretty bored out here, all alone," Zachary observed cautiously, as he removed his hat and followed Willow into a spotless parlor full of morning sunshine.

Again, she gave him a suspicious appraisal with those remarkable eyes. Way back when, he'd envied Gideon this young woman's obvious adoration. He'd gladly have played the groom's role at the wedding two years ago, even knowing, as his brother hadn't, that the ceremony was authentic. "What is the real purpose of your visit, please, Mr. Marshall?"

Of course she didn't trust him, and why would she?

On the other hand, she didn't seem to have any trouble trusting *Gideon,* now did she?

Quiet, keen resentment surged through Zachary.

He was the firstborn son, the rightful heir to the Marshall legacy, but Gideon had always been the golden boy, the bold one who acted first, who never hesitated to speak up and offer an opinion. Right from the first, it was simply assumed that Gideon would be the one to do great things.

Zachary, for his part, was the charmer, the bon vivant, the good-natured but spoiled womanizer, of whom little or nothing should be expected. His mother, always and forever doting on Gideon, had merely tolerated him, often remarking that he was more like his father's side of the family than her own.

He shook off the troubling thoughts and took a seat in the chair he suspected would be Gideon's favorite. He eyed the piano in a surreptitious glance and again felt envy, imagining Willow playing soft ballads at the instrument for the pleasure of her husband. "My name is Zachary," he insisted, "*not* Mr. Marshall, and I want, to be honest, to get to know my new sister-in-law, that's all. You're not afraid of me, are you, Willow?"

She seemed to be weighing him again. "No, I'm not afraid of you," she answered, after several moments. "You do get your way with the ladies as a general rule, I rather think. No doubt you depend on flattery and the like, though, instead of force."

A muscle in the pit of Zachary's stomach knotted tight and then leaped. Sweet triumph washed over him, only to be instantly displaced by the sound of boots on the front porch.

As Gideon entered the house, Zachary sank down deep in the chair and devoutly wished that he'd spent the morning hunting rabbits — or doing just about anything else.

■ ■ ■ ■

Willow's throat constricted as she looked into her husband's face. She had known a moment of hope that they might be able to talk. God knew the night before had been a miserable and lonely one, with them sleeping in separate bedrooms, but the cool flash in Gideon's eyes boded ill. There would be no tender reconciliation this day.

"I wasn't expecting you until dinnertime," she said, because someone had to make an effort. Besides, they had company, even if it was only Zachary, who was not, in her opinion, a person of substance.

"I can see that," said Gideon, his gaze fixed on the slouching Zachary and then slicing back to Willow herself.

It was a moment before she realized what he was implying. When she did, she was furious, but before she could give voice to her outrage, Zachary rose diplomatically out of his chair and faced his brother.

"Gideon, calm down. I came out here to see you, not to court your wife."

Gideon's broad shoulders relaxed just a little, though there was no change in his face. "Who is that fool hiding by the pond?" he asked, giving Willow a cool inspection.

Willow lifted her chin high. Gallagher high. For Lord's sake, did the man think she had a lover lurking on the property? "Unless you've been there yourself, I wouldn't know," she replied.

Zachary gave a snort of laughter and then wisely recovered himself.

Gideon was seething. Without a word, he strode to the closet in the hallway and pulled a pair of holstered .45s down from a high shelf. He strapped on the gun belt and then calmly loaded each pistol.

"Christ," breathed Zachary, "you hunting bear, or what?"

Gideon's answer was double-edged and sharp as a new razor. "Nobody creeps around on my land without giving me an explanation," he said. "A damned convincing explanation."

Zachary paled a little. "Damnit, Gideon, it's probably just some poor yokel watering his horse. You mean to gun down a man for that?"

A muscle in Gideon's hard jawline twitched ominously. "You'd be surprised at what I'd gun a man down for, Zach. Or maybe you wouldn't."

The warning wasn't lost on anyone in the room — it sent an ominous chill skittering down Willow's spine — but when Gideon walked out of the house to investigate the trespasser, Zachary followed him.

When the time came, Willow would be furious with her husband; for now, she was quietly afraid for his safety. The man by the pond would feel called upon to defend himself, and surely he was armed. What if he shot Gideon?

The very possibility made Willow's blood run icy cold through her veins. Gideon was a rake and a rounder, but she loved him too much to see him die.

Let him live, God, she prayed, as she ran for the back door. *Please. Even if he means to leave me and go back to San Francisco with Daphne, please, please don't let him be hurt . . .*

Zachary and Gideon were walking toward the pond with long strides, both of them unaware, it seemed, that Willow was scrambling through the high grass behind them.

She froze when Vancel Tudd came boldly out of the trees, his gun hand at the ready, his spindly Indian pony walking obediently along behind him. Tudd was a huge man, with a bulbous, misshapen nose and wild brown hair that hung almost to his shoulders. His clothes were of filthy buckskin and his reputation as a marksman was unmatched. He'd sworn to collect the bounty on Steven by whatever means necessary; everybody knew that.

Once a friend of her late stepfather, the outlaw Jay Forbes, Tudd was a feature in Willow Gallagher Marshall's private nightmares.

"Mornin', little lady," he said, with a tip of his battered hat.

Though Gideon stiffened at the revelation of his wife's presence, he did not look back. "State your name and your business," he said, his tone frigid.

Tudd smiled. "No need for trouble now," he said, and then he spat a stream of brown tobacco juice into the shifting green grass. "The name's Vancel Tudd and I was hopin', to tell ya the truth, for a glimpse of the lady's brother."

Willow shuddered to think that this vile man had been so near her house, watching. Waiting.

What if Steven had gotten wind of her move to the ranch and had taken it into his head to pay her a visit?

"I'll thank you to stay off my land in the future," Gideon said, in a hard voice. But there was no sympathy in him for Steven, Willow knew. He wanted to make that enviable catch himself, that was all.

Tudd shrugged, and despite his easy manner, Willow was afraid. In six years this man hadn't given up seeking Steven and he wasn't about to throw in his hand and call it quits now. "Didn't mean to offend," he said.

Some instinct made Willow draw nearer. Gideon had turned his back on Tudd, apparently satisfied that the matter was closed. And the bounty hunter's gnarled hand was moving, almost imperceptibly, nearer and nearer the knife in his belt.

"Gideon!" Willow screamed, and he whirled to face Tudd. One of the .45s seemed to leap into her husband's right hand of some volition all its own.

Tudd slowly lowered his hands, still grinning, his manner so falsely obsequious that Willow's revulsion grew. "You're mighty fast, Mr. Marshall," he observed, spitting again. "Mighty fast." The small eyes darted to Willow's flushed face. "Maybe even faster'n Steven Gallagher himself."

Cold dread washed over Willow's spirit in a crushing cascade. In that moment, she knew what was most likely to happen when and if her brother and her husband met. Steven would not willingly be captured. There would be a gunfight and one of them would be grievously wounded, perhaps even die.

216

She stood there in the middle of that grassy expanse of ranch land, one hand clutched to her mouth, watching as Vancel Tudd swung onto his paint pony and rode away without looking back.

"Willow?" The strong, gentle hands that came to her shoulders were not Gideon's, as they should have been, but Zachary's. "Willow, are you all right?"

Willow pulled herself free of her brother-in-law's concerned grasp, staring in frustration and consternation at the cold and unforgiving face of her husband. She made a strangled sound deep in her throat, lifted her skirts, and whirled to run toward the house. Gideon caught up to her in a few strides, grasping her elbow and staying her flight.

Frantic, half-hysterical in the full realization of what this man could do to her family, Willow bared her teeth like a cornered animal and kicked at him as she twisted in his unbreakable hold, trying to break free.

"Gideon," protested Zachary, from somewhere just outside the range of Willow's vision. "For God's sake, what's come over you? Let her go!"

Gideon loosened his grip, but his eyes never left Willow's face. "Get out of here, Zachary," he said. "My wife is in no danger from me and you damn well know it."

Willow sensed Zachary's reluctance, but she also knew he was about to leave.

She stared at Gideon, imagining him facing Steven in a shoot-out. The picture was so real that it might have been happening right then; the reports of the bullets thudded against her eardrums and she could actually smell the acrid scent of gunpowder.

"I won't let you kill my brother!" she cried.

Something moved in Gideon's hard face, but his grasp on her arm, though still not painful, tightened a little. "Stop it, Willow," he ordered. "Get ahold of yourself."

But Willow was seeing new visions now — crazy, kaleidoscopic visions. Steven, dangling at the end of a dirty rope. Both of them, her brother *and* her husband, lying dead and bleeding in the street. She screamed again, and Gideon gripped her shoulders and shook her, firmly albeit gently.

She pulled free, stumbled backward, toppled to the grass, and when she lost her footing, accidentally bit her lip. She tasted blood on the inside of her mouth.

Terrible pain played in Gideon's face as he crouched on the ground and reached for her hand, then gasped her name.

She began scooting back from him — *get away, get away* — rocks and twigs clawing at the palms of her hands. "Don't touch me, Gideon Marshall. *Don't you touch me!*"

Gideon gave a ragged sigh and lowered his hands to his sides. "Willow," he pleaded, in a tormented whisper. "You're hurt. Let me help you."

Shaking her head, Willow scrambled to her feet, desperate to flee this man and the awful, dangerous mistake she'd made by falling in love with him. But as she turned to run, he grabbed her skirts in one hand and hauled her back down so that she toppled into his lap.

"You're not going anywhere until you calm down," he said, in a gruff and quiet voice.

She raised both fists to assault him; he caught them in his hands and held them fast.

"Willow," he said again.

Tears were trickling down Willow's face by then; she wondered distractedly how long she had been crying. "You can't shoot Steven!" she sobbed. "I'll never, never let you shoot Steven!"

"Who says I want to do that?" Gideon asked, still holding her.

Fresh hysteria filled her. She'd seen more

than her share of gunplay before she'd gone to live with her father, and the terror was almost overwhelming. "I saw the way you drew that pistol just now — it was as if the thing was already a part of your hand!"

Gideon sighed again and drew Willow close, holding her in his arms as though she were a child. "I promise that I won't shoot Steven," he said, very slowly and very clearly. "I won't even go after him."

Willow pulled back to look up into his face. Was this man telling her the truth, or was he simply a liar? God help her, since he wasn't really Lancelot, she had no way to know. She tried to speak, but words were beyond her.

Gideon stilled the impotent motion of her lips with the touch of an index finger. "You have my word, Willow. Unless it means my own life, or yours, I won't shoot Steven."

"A-and you won't look for him?"

Clearly, this last was not so easy for Gideon. Still, his hand came, tender, to cup Willow's cheek, the thumb smoothing the corner of her mouth. "He has to give me something in return if that's going to be the agreement, Willow. When you see him again, you tell him that I won't come after him if he doesn't stop any more trains."

With another man, Willow would have

denied having any access to Steven, but there would have been no use in it with Gideon. He knew the truth. "I'll tell him."

"When you do, make damned sure Vancel Tudd isn't trotting along behind you."

Willow nodded, but there was deliberate warning in her eyes, too. "You'd better be telling me the truth, Gideon Marshall. I'm trusting you, though God knows why, and if you betray me . . ."

He arched one eyebrow, and there was a mischievous light in his eyes. "Do you really think I would do that?"

"Why wouldn't you?" countered Willow. "That's why you came to Virginia City in the first place, isn't it?"

"I came to Virginia City for a closer look at my bride," he said, caressing her cheek.

"Just because you say a thing," she protested, "that doesn't make it the truth!"

Gideon sighed philosophically, his arms still tight and strong around her. He propped his chin on top of her head and gave a second sigh. "I guess I have a lot to prove," he said, after a long time. "And a lot to make up for."

Willow bit her lower lip and swallowed. It would be so easy to trust him.

But he was still the man who had played a thoughtless trick on her, back in San Francisco. And he was still a railroad magnate, with a vested interest in putting a stop to her brother's career as an outlaw.

"Gideon —"

His lips touched the tip of her nose just briefly, and there was tenderness in his gruff "What?"

She swallowed. "What's going to happen when Daphne arrives?"

For a moment, Gideon stiffened, and Willow thought that he was going to thrust her away from him. Instead, however, he held her closer. "She'll scream at me, slap my face, probably, and then she'll get back on the train and go home, her honor avenged."

"You won't go with her?"

Gideon's hand came to Willow's chin, lifted it. "Is that what all this was really about? You thought I was going to let Daphne take me by the hand and lead me back to the straight and narrow?"

Miserably, Willow nodded. "It did cross my mind," she said.

Gideon gave a raucous, startling shout of laughter and fell backward into the grass, pulling Willow with him, rolling onto his side to look down at her. And when his amusement had abated a little, he lowered his mouth to hers and kissed her thoroughly.

"Was that the kiss of a man who wants to leave his wife?" he teased.

"It surely wasn't." Willow smiled through her tears, and then she wrapped her arms around Gideon's neck and pulled him downward, so that their lips met again.

Willow lay wide awake in the darkness, her head resting on Gideon's shoulder. Far off in the distance, she heard the wail of a train whistle. Or had it been the cry of a night owl?

Careful not to awaken her sleeping husband, Willow slid out of his arms and then out of the bed. It had been a full week since the confrontation with Vancel Tudd, and though she had been wildly happy the whole time, Steven had been in her thoughts often. She needed to talk to her brother, to relay Gideon's message, but aware now that Mr. Tudd would be watching her, she hesitated to approach any of their usual meeting places.

Standing very still, in a pool of moonlight pouring in through the open window, Willow listened hard. The owl cry sounded again and she knew then that she would not have to seek Steven out at all — he had come to her.

But she could have throttled him for taking such a chance, and her motions were quick as she reached for the thin silk wrapper that lay at the foot of the bed. The rustling sound of the fabric caused Gideon to stir in his sleep and mutter something.

The last thing Willow wanted was for her husband to awaken now. "Gideon?" she whispered, as a precaution.

He turned away from her, mumbling and burrowing deeper into his pillow, and the meter of his breathing assured her that he was still sound asleep.

Carefully, Willow left the bedroom, her hair rumpled, her feet bare. Passing through the parlor to the kitchen, she stubbed her toe and had to bite down hard on her lower lip to keep from crying out in pain.

The back door creaked on its hinges, and Willow opened it very carefully. Although Gideon had given his word that he would not shoot Steven or even seek him out, there was no telling what he would do if he were to awaken and encounter him now.

The yard, the outhouse, and the clothesline took on spectral shapes in the moonlight, and Willow gasped, in spite of herself, when a tall shadow slid across the grass at her feet.

Steven spoke quietly. "Did I scare you, little sister?"

"Shut up!" Willow whispered. "We're too close to the house — Gideon might hear you."

With a shrug, Steven caught his sister's hand and they began walking toward the pond. There, at some distance from the house and shielded from view by trees, should Gideon awaken and look out, they sat down together on a fallen log and watched the moonlight shift and sparkle on the rippling water for a time.

"Steven," Willow began finally, "why did you come here? You must know it's dangerous."

"I wanted to see you," he answered blithely.

She turned to face him. "Did you know that Vancel Tudd has been watching me? Gideon caught him right here, not a week ago."

Even in the darkness, the sparks in Steven's blue eyes were unmistakable. "Tudd? Here? Willow, did he lay a hand on you?"

"No," Willow said quickly. She couldn't help squinting into the darkness, shivering a little. Suppose Tudd was out there, even now? Suppose he was about to pounce? "But, like I said, he's been watching me. That means he knows that I see you,

225

Steven."

"I know what it means," Steven said, tugging lightly at a lock of her hair.

"One would never guess it," retorted Willow sharply, jabbing an elbow into his ribs. "And will you please shut your mouth and listen to me? I have a message for you, from Gideon."

Steven's look was an amused one, almost patronizing. "Oh? And what, pray tell, is that?"

"He won't try to track you if you agree not to stop any more trains, Steven."

Steven laid one hand to his chest in feigned gratitude. "I'm overwhelmed. Gosh, Willow, now I'll be able to sleep at night, my conscience clear."

Willow's patience had reached an end; she stretched out one hand, shoved hard at Steven's chest and sent him toppling backward off the log. "Idiot!" she scolded, still keeping her voice down, just on general principles. "Gideon isn't old and slow like Vancel Tudd, and he can shoot, Steven. As well as you can!"

Steven, with typical grace, was rising out of the grass, dusting himself off, and looking almost comically regretful. "No more trains?"

"No more trains, Steven. If you won't

leave them alone for your own good, will you do it for mine?"

Steven swore softly and turned away, his hands on his hips.

"You only steal to get under Papa's hide anyway," Willow went on, when he didn't speak. "Oh, Steven, won't you please grow up?"

He whirled to face her, the back of one hand affixed dramatically to his forehead. " 'Tis much you ask of me, me bonny lass," he bewailed, in his faultless Scots burr. "But, alas, I'll be after desistin' for love of your fair charms!"

Willow didn't laugh as she might have at another time; she faced her brother and caught his hands in her own. "Steven, I'm serious. *Promise me* you won't stop another train, ever."

He cupped gentle hands around her face. "I promise, Button," he said. And then he kissed her forehead and stepped back from her. "I love you," he said, and then he was gone.

Willow sat down on the log again and clasped her hands in her lap. She had done all she could to avert disaster; now there was nothing more to do but wait and pray.

After a long time, the chill of the night began to reach through Willow's thin wrapper, and she walked slowly back toward the house, her head down. Though there was no light burning in the kitchen, Gideon was up, standing near the stove. His hair was sleep-rumpled and he was naked except for a pair of misbuttoned trousers.

"Coffee?" he asked companionably.

Willow, taken aback, could manage nothing more than a nod. When Gideon calmly poured coffee for both of them and sat down at the table, she followed suit.

"You saw Steven," he said, after a long silence.

"Yes," Willow replied, for Gideon had not been asking a question but making a statement.

"And?" Gideon's spoon clattered as he stirred coarse brown sugar into his coffee.

"And I told him what you said about the trains. He promised not to stop the Central Pacific again."

"Is he a man of his word, your brother?"

Willow's cheeks flamed at this quiet challenge, although it seemed like a reasonable thing to ask, given Steven's criminal history. "Yes!"

"Good. Then our only problem, for the moment, is Tudd. I trust you warned him about that weasel?"

"I did."

"Excellent. Drink your coffee."

Willow had no interest in refreshment. "You were awake when I got out of bed, weren't you? You knew that Steven was here."

There was a short silence, and then Gideon owned up with a hesitant nod. She felt his eyes touch her in the near darkness surrounding the circle of lantern light in which they sat, but she could not read their expression.

"Why didn't you follow me, then?" Willow persisted, truly curious.

"I, too, am a man of my word, Willow. Besides, I knew Steven wouldn't hurt you."

Willow reached out for her coffee and took a cautious sip. "Thank you, Gideon," she said.

"For the coffee?"

"For trusting Steven and for trusting me."

"Don't mention it, Mrs. Marshall."

"There is something I do want to mention, as it happens," said Willow.

"Oh? And what is that?"

"The way you treated Zachary the other day. You were very rude, Gideon. I mean, he is your brother, after all, and you acted as though he and I were carrying on or something."

"I was the classic jealous husband, wasn't I?"

"Yes, and without reason, too."

Gideon sighed. "If I wronged anyone that day, it was you. I remain convinced, however, that Zachary, on the contrary, was almost certainly up to no good."

"How do you know that?"

"I know Zachary."

"You don't mean that he would . . . that he would force himself on me?"

Gideon chortled without humor and shook his head. "No, he wouldn't do that. But he is very persuasive, Willow, and you of all people should know how devious he can be."

Willow cupped her hands around her coffee mug and allowed herself a brief smile of triumph. Gideon was jealous — he'd admitted it himself — and to be jealous one had to care, at least a little. "I'll try not to notice how handsome and charming he is," she said ingenuously, "though, Lord knows, it won't be easy."

"What do you mean, it won't be easy?" Gideon demanded. His voice was quiet, but there was a smile hiding in his eyes.

Willow only yawned and stretched her arms high above her head, not about to dignify such a question with an answer.

When she started back upstairs, Gideon was
quick to follow.

9

Daphne Roberts sat stiffly in the train seat, looking out at the seemingly endless prairie. Her backside was sore and her corset was cutting into her right hipbone, and inside her spotless kid gloves, the hollows between her fingers were sweating. Dear Lord, if this was first-class travel, she hated to think what tortures of the damned those poor souls in the cars farther back must be suffering.

In the aisle seat next to Daphne's, her cousin Hilda snored loudly and then sat bolt upright, looking around in wild confusion. "Where am I?"

Daphne was weary of Hilda, after almost a week of rattling along the endless rails leading west, but she was determined to be charitable. After all, if it hadn't been for Hilda, her father would have escorted her instead. For mercy's sake, it was a fool's mission anyway, traveling to this wild and remote place. Gideon was married to another woman and there didn't seem to be much point in making a great fuss about it.

Besides, she was missing the Andersons' lawn party and the bicycle races, and how could Miss Millicent Parnult be expected to finish her new gowns in time for the opera season if Daphne wasn't there to be fitted on a regular basis?

She gave an irritated sigh and settled back in the hard seat, intending to feign sleep so that she would not have to endure a spate of Hilda's chatter. Just as she closed her eyes, however, the train came to a lurching halt and there were gunshots fired outside.

Hilda, who had been flung into the seat ahead by the impact, was huffing inelegantly and trying to right her bonnet, the brim of which was resting on the tip of her nose.

At that moment, the door leading into the car ahead burst open and a masked man appeared in the chasm, brandishing a pistol. "This is a robbery, ladies and gentlemen," he said, in cultured tones, "and if you'll all put your money and other valuables into this bag, I'll be obliged."

"Highwaymen!" cried Hilda, her extra chins quivering.

"Hush," muttered Daphne, who was already pulling the bracelet from her wrist.

"Do you want to be shot over a few trinkets?"

The bandit moved calmly along the aisle, helping himself to the contents of purses and pockets and valises. Daphne was glad she'd had the foresight to stitch most of her traveling money into the hem of one of her nightgowns, safely packed away inside a trunk in the baggage car. Indeed, this was a rather colorful experience, all in all; she would recount it at tea parties, she supposed, for the rest of her life.

And she'd never cared much for the bracelet in the first place.

But it gave her pause when the highwayman came back to stand in the aisle beside Hilda, and his dark blue eyes assessed Daphne with a brazen languor that made her forget about the glamour and drama of the situation. He reached out, with a gloved hand, past a trembling Hilda, to lift one of Daphne's raven-black ringlets in his fingers and let it fall back to her shoulder.

Daphne sat perfectly still, trying not to show the sudden and deep fear she felt.

There was no telling what would have happened if it hadn't been for the man bursting through the rear door of the train at just that moment. The clatter drew every head around, including Daphne's.

"Drop that gun, Gallagher!" the earnest, middle-aged man ordered hoarsely.

Instead of obeying, the outlaw trained his weapon on the man's chest. Daphne caught the silvery glint of a star-shaped badge before the pistol went off and the older man fell face-first into the aisle, blood spraying in every direction.

Several women screamed and Hilda swooned sideways onto Daphne, nearly crushing her. The outlaw turned and fled, his bag of loot in hand.

After drawing three or four deep breaths and working her way out from under Hilda, Daphne left her seat to hurry to the back of the car and see what could be done for the marshal.

Gideon slammed the blood-specked badge down on Devlin's desk with a crash. "Swear me in," he bit out, in a voice that had to be forced past his clenched jaw.

Devlin spared the badge one look and then sat back in his squeaky chair. "Mitch Kroeber?" he asked.

"The marshal is dead," Gideon replied, "and I'm going to take his place."

"What happened?" Devlin insisted calmly.

Gideon made a conscious effort to relax, but he was too furious to really accomplish the feat. God damnit, he had made a fair deal with Steven Gallagher, and this was what he got for it. The Central Pacific had been robbed and a good man, Marshal Kroeber, was dead. With great effort, he managed to convey what had happened just outside of town, less than an hour before, in civil tones.

Devlin swore and pain etched deep lines into his face. "You think Steven did this thing, Gideon?" he rasped, after a long time. "My son is no killer!"

"I *know* it was Steven. Everybody in the second car heard Kroeber call the outlaw Gallagher."

The judge bolted out of his chair and turned away toward the open window, where lacy white curtains danced in a soft summer breeze. "God *damn*it, Gideon, that isn't proof!"

"It's proof enough for me — Kroeber would have recognized Steven if he saw him. Now, are you going to swear me in or not?"

"You're a deputy U.S. marshal," Devlin pointed out. "You don't need poor Mitch's badge — or my permission — to go after a train robber."

Gideon widened his stance. "It's for Kroeber," he said quietly.

"This isn't your fight!" argued the judge

brokenly.

"It is my fight, Devlin," Gideon insisted, and pity for the man before him gentled his voice. "It was my train."

Misery writhed in his blue eyes as Devlin Gallagher turned to face Gideon. "You'll bring him in alive?"

Gideon thought of Willow and ached. "If I possibly can," he promised hoarsely.

Gallagher looked down at the badge, then up at his son-in-law's face. "Raise your right hand," he muttered.

After depositing a very shaken Hilda at the hotel and sending a wire to San Francisco to apprise her father of their safe arrival — she would save the account of the robbery and that poor man's murder for when she got back home — Daphne set about getting her most unpleasant duty out of the way. Once she'd faced Gideon and spoken with him, she could get on the train and be back at home in just under a week.

The rough town of Virginia City filled her senses as she walked toward the livery stable; there were cowboys everywhere, businessmen in dusty suits and bowler hats, pale ladies of the evening trudging through the sunlight. The excitement and newness of the place intrigued Daphne; she had expected more primitive surroundings — log cabins, perhaps, and renegade Indians riding painted ponies.

She shivered even as perspiration tickled the tender flesh between her shoulder blades. Although she hadn't mentioned the train robbery in her wire to her father, the horrible memory of the senseless shooting would be with her to her dying day. Until she'd heard the fatal shot and looked into the marshal's waxen, lifeless face, it had been an adventure.

At the livery, Daphne rented a horse and buggy — she had been something of a tomboy when she was younger and she could drive or ride with the best of them — and asked for word of Gideon Marshall's whereabouts. She was informed that he had bought property south of town and was directed to it.

Shaking off the unnerving feeling the stable man's frank assessment had given her, Daphne climbed into the hired rig, took the reins firmly into her hands, and set out for a confrontation she wanted no part of.

Willow dusted the piano with furious effort, knowing that, when that was done, there would be nothing to occupy her for the rest of the day. Despite her love for Gideon, she was tired of straightening bric-a-brac and scrubbing spotless floors just for something to do.

She visited in town whenever she could, but the prospects there were limited. She dared not call on Dove Triskadden, and her father was seldom at home during the day; he kept an office over the jailhouse and often had cases to try in the town's small courthouse. Having no real friends besides Maria, who was busy with her own household duties, Willow was at a loss. One could only go into the mercantile and inspect ribbon and fabric so many times and still remain sane.

The sound of an approaching rig brought Willow's heart surging into her throat. She prayed that Dove was coming to call; in fact, she was so lonely and bored that she would even have been glad to see Zachary.

After smoothing her hair and the skirts of her yellow and white gingham dress, Willow walked to the front door with as much decorum as she could manage. The smile on her face was genuine, until she saw the elegant young woman making her way up the walk.

The visitor had dark, glistening hair, styled in ringlets that rested on her shoulders, and her clothes were richly tailored, if somewhat travel mussed. Once she drew near enough, Willow realized that this woman's eyes were the deepest shade of lavender she had ever seen.

"Daphne," she said, with resignation, as her caller came up the steps.

The beautiful visitor smiled, revealing straight white teeth. "Yes," she answered, in friendly but weary tones. "Are you Gideon's wife?"

At the moment, Willow felt more like Gideon's concubine than his wife. She felt, in fact, like a trespasser, and this in her very own home. "I am," she answered, wondering how she could talk when her stomach was spinning wildly inside her and her heart was pressing up into the back of her throat. "Won't you come in?"

Daphne sighed. "I would be ever so grateful for a cup of strong tea," she said, following Willow through the immaculate hallway to the kitchen. "I've just had the most horrendous experience, you see."

Wondering how this woman could speak so calmly and mundanely when she herself was dissolving into a state of sheer panic, Willow gestured for Daphne to take a seat at the table and began to make the requested tea.

"Do you love Gideon, Willow?" Daphne

asked directly, some minutes later, when they had been seated, their cups steaming before them.

Willow managed a nod, unable to speak because of the lump of dread and shame lodged in her throat.

Daphne smiled, incredible as it seemed. She was, it appeared, determined to be not only civil about the matter but warm, too. "I see," she said, sipping her tea and rolling her beautiful eyes in a humorous sort of ecstasy at the taste. "Mercy me, I needed that."

Willow couldn't help returning the smile, though there were tears gathering in her eyes. "I . . . I'm sorry, Daphne," she struggled to say.

"Sorry?" echoed Daphne, arching her perfect, featherlike eyebrows.

"For . . . for . . ." Willow's words fell away in misery. She'd been about to say that she was sorry for taking Gideon, but she couldn't quite do it. She loved him, for all their problems and their tempestuous disagreements, and she couldn't truthfully say that she was sorry for anything.

"I shall be eternally grateful to you, Willow Marshall," Daphne said easily, her eyes sparkling.

Willow nearly choked on the tea she'd just

taken in an effort to steady herself. "Grateful?" she croaked, wide-eyed.

Daphne laughed. "Oh, yes. Gideon is a fine fellow, and he's handsome, not to mention rich. But marrying him wasn't my idea or even his. It was Papa's, with input from Gideon's mother and his grandfather, of course. I was never actually consulted in the matter, and I doubt that Gideon was, either."

Having anticipated an ugly scene of recriminations and possibly even hair pulling, Willow could only gape at Gideon's former fiancée in amazement.

Apparently amused by her expression, Daphne laughed again. It was a vibrant, musical sound. "Dear, dear," she exclaimed. "This is quite a mess, isn't it?"

Willow nodded woodenly. "Why on earth did you come all the way to Montana if you didn't want to be with Gideon?"

Beneath the rich, rose-colored silk of her dress, the bodice of which was fitted and hand-smocked, Daphne's shoulders affected an idle and very appealing shrug. "Papa insisted that I come. I do think he thought Gideon and I would fall into each other's arms and all would be well, like in a fairy tale. I'm here, too, because my father would have given me no peace if I hadn't and because — well — I wanted to see the wild frontier."

Willow was trembling, and she took another gulp of her tea. "You aren't at all what I expected," she said. Her relief was fleeting, though, for while Daphne had avowed no romantic interest in Gideon, there was no telling what *his* reaction would be. He had planned to marry Daphne, and he had said so, straight out. Suppose he put his accidental wife aside to take one on purpose?

Of course, pride wouldn't allow Willow to present this possibility aloud, so she thrust her misgivings aside, to deal with later. She was about to ask Daphne about her journey when Gideon suddenly bolted into the house like a raucous wind, roaring his wife's name.

For the second time in the space of half an hour, Willow was alarmed. She forgot all about Daphne and turned in her chair, bracing for the new crisis she knew was about to break over her life.

Gideon didn't see Daphne at first; his eyes, fierce and angry, were fixed on Willow's face. On the lapel of his coat was a star-shaped badge. "Did you or did you not tell your brother to lay off the Central Pacific?" he snapped.

Willow paled, lifted one hand to her

throat. "I told him, Gideon — you know I did."

"Then it's a pity he didn't listen to you," Gideon retorted furiously. And his gaze caught on Daphne, stopping at her face.

"Daphne," he said, looking more resigned than startled.

She nodded. "Gideon," she replied sweetly. "I'd say it's good to see you again, but . . ."

The high color in Gideon's face drained away, though the muscles remained hard and ungiving.

Willow broke into the conversation rudely. "What has Steven done?" she cried in her desperation.

"He robbed the morning train, Willow," Gideon answered coldly, as though he blamed her for the crime as well as Steven. "This time, he added a new touch. He took everything — not just a payroll or a shipment that belonged to Judge Gallagher. And if that wasn't enough, he shot Mitch Kroeber to death."

The room swayed and shifted around Willow, stopping at crazy angles and then moving again. "No," she choked out. "Steven wouldn't do that. I *know* he wouldn't."

"Yes," Gideon said harshly, and began going through a drawer, most likely rummaging for the bullets he kept there. "He would, Willow, because he *did*."

Willow could see nothing, it seemed, but that polished silver badge. "That's a lie!" she cried. "Gideon, you know it's a lie!"

He had removed his gun belt and begun sliding lethal shells into the casings that lined the outside of it. "I'm afraid it's all too true, hellcat. And as God is my witness, he's going to pay for this one, in spades."

Willow bolted out of her chair, forgetting Daphne and everything else except that Gideon was preparing to go after her brother with guns. "W-why are you wearing that star, Gideon?" she asked, even though she knew the horrible answer.

He paused and looked down at the badge with grim, callous humor. "I guess this makes me Marshal Marshall," he replied.

Willow grabbed at her husband's arms. "Gideon, please —"

He shook free of her, no more conscious of Daphne's presence than she was. "I'm sorry, Willow," he said gruffly. "I really am. I'll be back in a few days. It might be a good idea for you to go on into town and stay with Maria and the judge until this is over."

"No!" Willow burst out, nearly frantic with

fear and foreboding. "I want to go with you!"

Gideon arched one eyebrow. "Why? So you can lead me away from your brother? Not this time, sweetheart. I'm going to bring him in, either sitting upright in his saddle or draped across it: the choice is his."

With that, Gideon left the kitchen by the back door.

"Fool!" Willow screamed after him. And then she fell into her chair and covered her face with both hands.

Her sobs brought Daphne out of her chair and around the table to say softly, uncertainly, "Everything will be all right, Willow. Why don't you do what Gideon said? I'll take you to town in my buggy and —"

Willow shook Daphne's comforting hands from her shoulders. "I don't want to go to town!" she wailed.

"Is there someone I can fetch for you, then?" Daphne persisted reasonably. "Your mother or father or —"

"No!" sobbed Willow, undone.

Daphne sighed and refilled her own teacup and Willow's from the china pot on the narrow table next to the stove before returning to her chair. "Then would you mind explaining what's going on around here?"

After a few minutes of recovery, Willow

told Daphne about the many robberies that had been attributed to Steven Gallagher in the past six years.

"Mercy," said Daphne, when the tale was ended. "That must have been your brother I saw —"

Willow gaped at her guest. "What?"

"I was on that train, Willow, with my cousin Hilda. We were stopped and a robber came into our car, demanding everyone's money and watches and things." She paused and stared sadly at her right wrist. "He took my amethyst bracelet, as a matter of fact. The marshal came in and ordered him to disarm himself and the outlaw shot the poor man dead."

"Steven would *never* do a thing like that!"

"All the same," Daphne sighed, "the marshal did address the man as Gallagher. I remember that distinctly."

The sun was going down; Willow saw shadows creeping across the kitchen floor. "Steven wouldn't," she whispered rawly. "I know he wouldn't."

Daphne managed a smile. "You know him and I don't," she conceded, "so perhaps that robber wasn't your brother after all. In any case, he was wearing a mask."

"What did he look like otherwise, Daphne?"

"He was very tall and he had fair hair and blue eyes. That's about all I can tell you; he was, as I said, wearing a bandanna or something over his face and I was too scared to notice much more than that."

Bleak despair thundered over Willow's spirit in a cruel stampede. Daphne had described Steven.

"Are you sure you don't want me to drive you into town?" Daphne asked gently, breaking the painful silence. "I think Gideon is right — you shouldn't be here alone, feeling the way you do."

Willow had no desire to go anywhere if she couldn't go with Gideon to find Steven. She preferred to remain in the privacy of her den, like a wounded beast, to lick her wounds. "I'd rather stay here," she said.

Daphne's reaction was brisk. She stood up and gathered her handbag and her parasol. "In that case, I'll go back to my hotel, get a few of my things, and explain the situation to Hilda — she's probably sound asleep, anyway — then I'll come back here."

Having never had a real friend, not one close to her own age anyway, Willow couldn't quite credit that she'd just made a very good one. "You would do that, a-after everything that's happened?"

Daphne smiled. "It isn't your fault that Zachary and Gideon played that reprehensible trick, now is it? And, besides, I happen to like you very much. So why shouldn't I spend time with you?"

"Thank you," Willow breathed.

Daphne had only been gone a few minutes when Maria and the judge arrived in the family buggy, both their dear and familiar faces worried and full of pain.

"You will come home with us," Maria said firmly, following as the judge climbed down from the buggy and crossed the yard to climb the porch steps and wordlessly pulled his daughter into a gentle embrace.

"No," Willow said firmly. "I can't."

Maria and the judge exchanged a look and then Maria nodded. *"Sí,"* she said, with gentle resignation. "I will make supper, then, and we will decide later what is best."

The last thing Willow wanted at that moment was food, but she nodded at Maria in mute gratitude. Her presence, like the judge's, was a great comfort.

By the time Daphne returned, with a valise, there was a fine meal on the table.

Numbly, Willow made introductions, without explaining Daphne's relationship with Gideon, and then they all sat down to eat their supper, as though this were a party and not a death vigil of sorts. Willow could do no more than trail her fork despondently through her food.

"Eat," the judge urged hoarsely, his eyes dark with a pain to match Willow's own as he watched her.

"I couldn't —" Willow began, only to have her words broken off by a shuffling sound just beyond the kitchen door. Automatically, she got up to investigate.

Steven himself was standing there, in the darkness, pale as a specter. There was a bloody wound in his shoulder and yet he managed a weak smile. "Am I late for supper?" he asked, and then his knees buckled and he slumped, unconscious, to the floor.

Willow stepped back, staring, but her father overturned his chair in his haste to reach his son. "Jesus God, boy," he mourned, in a soblike voice, "what happened? What happened?"

Maria knelt on Steven's other side and gently opened his shirt. There was a deep, jagged slash in his right shoulder, seeping blood. *"Madre de Dios,"* she whispered. "We must have a doctor."

"No!" Willow gasped, suddenly mobile again. "No, we can't bring a doctor here!"

"She's right," said Devlin calmly, his eyes at once stern and imploring upon Maria's face. "The doctor would have to report this. Is it safe to move him, Maria?"

Maria sighed. "*Sí,* we must. I will tend the wound myself. But if there is infection . . ."

Devlin was already hauling the inert Steven to his feet. Together, he and Maria half-dragged him up the back stairs and into the spare room Willow indicated.

There they laid him out on the narrow bed.

"Bring hot water and some cloth," Devlin said to a stricken Willow. And, as Steven moaned and stirred on the guest room bed, he added, "Whiskey, too, if you've got it."

Daphne was already at the stove, putting water on to heat, when Willow reached the kitchen and began gathering her pretty new dish towels, bought from Mr. McCullough at the general store just a few days before. Clutching them to her breast, Gideon's one bottle of liquor in hand, Willow forced herself to meet her new friend's gaze.

"It wasn't him," Daphne confided.

"What?" Willow breathed, hardly daring to hope.

"This is not the man I saw onboard the train today, Willow. It was someone else, someone thinner and not as tall."

Willow's heart pounded with hope. "You're sure?"

251

Daphne nodded. "Do you want me to bring this water upstairs when it's hot?"

Willow couldn't move. Biting her lower lip, she looked toward the door, then back at her friend. "Daphne, you wouldn't — ?"

"No," broke in her friend, with good-natured impatience, "I'm not going to go racing off to town and tell everyone that your brother is here. Stop worrying."

"If Gideon comes back —"

Daphne grinned wanly. "If Gideon comes back, I'll keep him busy by listing all the wrongs he's done this innocent maiden. Go to your brother, Willow."

Thinking what a fine thing a friend was, Willow bolted back up the stairs with the dish towels and the bottle of liquor.

In the little bedroom at the opposite end of that hall from the one Willow and Gideon shared, Steven was writhing on the blankets and murmuring in delirium. Devlin was holding his hand and looking down at his son in a way that said he'd give his soul to change places with him, and bear the pain in his place, while Maria held a needle over the flame in the bedside lamp.

"Was he shot?" Willow dared, drawing nearer to Steven.

"No," answered her father, without looking up. "Looks to me like somebody used a

252

knife on him."

Willow shuddered with revulsion and hatred, but then promptly took herself in hand. He had managed to escape the person who attacked him. Perhaps he'd had to kill to do it. "Will he die?" she whispered brokenly.

"No," said Maria, when the judge didn't respond. "Steven will not die."

A few minutes later, Daphne arrived with the hot water and Maria began cleaning Steven's wound. That done, she threaded the needle she had been holding over the lamp flame and began to stitch the sundered flesh neatly back into place. Though he was still unconscious, Steven groaned and tossed so violently on the bed that Devlin had to use all his strength to hold the patient still.

When the last stitch had been tied off, Maria drenched a cloth with whiskey from the bottle Willow had brought and began saturating the wound with it.

Steven gasped as though he had been touched with fire, tossing his head back and forth on the pillow, making a low, garbled sound in his throat. The judge held him firmly, and shameless tears trickled down his face as he spoke to Steven in hoarse, tender words.

Willow paced back and forth across the small room long after both Daphne and Maria had retired to some other part of the house, leaving the judge and his daughter to keep the vigil.

Finally, Steven awakened. He looked at his father and sister in surprise and swore under his breath.

"What happened?" the judge demanded instantly, his voice roughened by the long hours of anxiety. "Steven, did you rob that train?"

"What train?" countered Steven, looking bewildered and sick. He was ghostly pale, almost gaunt, Willow thought.

Devlin made an exasperated sound and turned away from the bed, but Willow drew nearer and took Steven's hand in her own. "A Central Pacific was robbed yesterday, Steven," she said. "A man was killed."

"Dear God," breathed Steven.

"Did you do it, damn you?!" demanded the judge, tormented.

"No, he didn't!" shouted Willow before Steven could answer. "Daphne saw the bandit and she said it wasn't Steven!"

"But they're blaming me, aren't they?" Steven guessed, in a weary tone.

"Yes," answered Devlin harshly. "And if you aren't guilty, how did you happen to be wounded?"

Steven laughed raggedly without amusement and fixed his eyes on the shadowed ceiling. "I was in the mountains, in the Shoshone camp. We were gambling and I won."

"It certainly looks like it," rasped the judge, with bitter sarcasm.

"I did. Got all of Red Eagle's horses and his woman, too. He didn't take very kindly to the loss."

Willow drew in her breath, horrified.

"I was leaving camp with everything but the woman and Red Eagle came after me. We fought." Steven paused, sighed philosophically. "I lost and Red Eagle took everything back, except for his hatchet . . ." There was another pause and Steven's lips twisted into a wry grin. "He left that with me."

Willow reached out and touched his damp, tangled hair. "You fool. Don't you know better than to gamble with Red Eagle? He's a bad loser."

Steven grimaced. "That he is, little sister. Could I have a shot of that firewater?"

Willow followed his eyes to the bottle and nodded. "I'll get you a glass."

"Never mind the glass. Just give me the bottle."

She complied.

"Where were Coy and Reilly during all this?" the judge asked, drawing close to the foot of the bed. Now that the crisis was past, he looked as though he might be wishing that Steven were a few years younger, so that he could haul him off to the woodshed.

Steven shrugged, then winced at the pain the motion stirred in his bandaged shoulder. "I don't know," he answered. "But I sure hope I find them before little sister's husband does."

"Don't we all," sighed the judge, and, since it was a statement and not a question, no one answered.

10

He was sleeping, or so it appeared to Daphne. Wanting a closer look at a man who could run afoul of the law and still be so thoroughly and completely loved by his family, she crept nearer the bed, holding her breath, and bent to look into the face of Steven Gallagher.

His frame, only half-covered by the tangled bedsheets, was long and lean, yet incredibly muscular. His hair appeared, in the shadows, to be roughly the color of raw honey.

Daphne found herself wishing that he would open his eyes so that she could see into them. That was, she had found in her eighteen years, the easiest way to get the true measure of another person.

Steven stirred on the narrow bed and something inside Daphne moved in response. The feeling so alarmed her that she took a step back from the bedside and let her breath out in a long, soft sigh.

This man was a desperado, she reminded herself, even though she was certain that he was not the same person who had robbed the train the day before. Steven Gallagher had a price on his head; Willow and the Mexican woman, Maria, had said so. And yet he did not have the look of an outlaw; indeed, to Daphne, he resembled the storybook princes of her childhood fancies.

Slowly, Daphne turned, her skirts whispering as she moved, to make her way out of the little room. Mercy, she thought, if one could bring a specimen like that into existence by kissing toads, she'd get nothing else done for raiding lily pads.

Willow was standing at the well when Gideon rode in, and the quiet despondency in the angle of her head and the set of her shoulders caused him a tender sort of despair.

As Willow looked up and saw him, he felt her brace herself against him, somewhere deep in her spirit, and was doubly wounded. Had he, between Daphne and the pursuit of Steven Gallagher, driven some eternal wedge between himself and this woman? Opened a breach that could never be closed?

Dismounting, Gideon held the reins of his

horse in one hand and walked slowly toward his wife. In the three days spent apart from her, he'd learned the painful truth: a world without Willow was a world without air, sunshine, or music.

"Willow," he said, because everything else was beyond him. His search for Steven had been fruitless, as she no doubt knew, and his face was scratchy with the stubble of a beard. Every muscle in his body ached from sleeping on the hard ground. He wanted to eat, to bathe in a tub filled to the brim with hot water, to die, and then come to life again in the arms of this woman.

The golden eyes were remote as they touched on him. "Did you find him?" she asked.

Gideon's voice was like gravel in his throat. "You know I didn't."

"Yes," she said, with a small nod.

He took the water bucket from her hands and carried it inside, into the quiet, spotless kitchen. "You've seen Steven, haven't you?" he asked, injured by the space she kept between them.

"He was here," she said, with a slight tilt of her obstinate little chin. "How do you like that, Marshal Marshall? While you and your posse were scouring the hills, Steven was here under your very own roof."

The words were intended to nettle him, he knew, but he felt nothing beyond the faintest sting; he was numb. It would have been better, he thought, if Willow had flung herself at him in a screaming rage. "And now he's gone again, like any good outlaw," he guessed calmly.

"Long gone," said Willow. "And Steven didn't rob your damnable train, either, Gideon Marshall."

Gideon's shoulders ached as he reached for the bright new coffeepot that sat on the back of the stove. "What makes you so sure of that?" he asked evenly.

"He was wounded in a fight with an Indian. If you talk to the Shoshone, you'll find that Steven was in their camp when the train was stopped."

Gideon froze. "Wounded? Steven is wounded?"

Willow's eyes were shooting topaz fire now. "Do you imagine that that will make him easier to find? Don't delude yourself on that score."

"How was he hurt?" Gideon insisted, hoping that the pain her words and bearing caused him didn't show.

"Steven was gambling with Red Eagle. He won the warrior's horse and woman."

"Naturally," rasped Gideon, annoyed.

"The Indian came after him, they fought, and Steven was the loser."

"That's novel," said Gideon wryly. "What transpired then, pray tell?"

"Red Eagle struck Steven with his hatchet and left him to die."

Gideon turned a chair around and sat astraddle it, his weary arms braced across its back. Thoughtfully, he sipped his coffee. "A fact that no doubt dooms a certain ill-guided redskin to the wrath of the close-knit Gallagher family."

"We look after our own," she said, again with that provocative lift of her chin.

The statement excluded Gideon; he knew that and was hurt, though he hid his inward reaction. "I suppose it would be foolhardy of me to ask you to heat water for a bath?"

"Heat your own water, Gideon Marshall. Fix your own breakfast, too."

Philosophically, Gideon finished his coffee and strode outside to the well. When he returned with the first bucketful of water, he found that the washtub had been set in the middle of the kitchen floor. Willow was in some other part of the house, probably feeding the fires of a never-to-be-forgotten sulk.

Almost forty-five minutes later, the tub was full of hot water; Gideon stripped off his clothes and sank into it. Damnit, it was almost funny — he'd been riding all over the foothills for three days and all the time the object of his search had been right here in his own house. The irony of it brought a grim smile to his lips.

Presently, Willow swept in, her full lips drawn into a tight line. Her expression said all too clearly that she hadn't forgiven him, but what she did next shocked Gideon anyway.

She strode to the side of the tub, which was much too small for anyone over the age of three to bathe in, pulled off the simple wedding band Gideon had given her the day he'd brought her to this house, and dropped it into the water.

"Good-bye, Gideon Marshall," she said, and then she turned on her heel to march out of the kitchen.

With one straining grab, Gideon caught her skirts in his hand. "Wait a minute!" he barked, holding on as if for dear life. "What the hell do you mean, 'good-bye'?"

"It's a simple word, Gideon," she answered, too damned stubborn to turn around. "It means I'm leaving you. Now, if you'll just let go of my dress . . ."

A thousand courses of action whirled through Gideon's mind, but none of them was workable. If Willow wanted to go he couldn't keep her; that was the dismal fact of the matter. He opened his hand and her skirts fell into place, stained by soapy water. "Where will you go?" he asked, summoning up every shred of dignity he possessed.

"To my father's house," she snapped back. "Where else?"

"Hell, how would I know? Devoted sister that you are, you might have been planning to join your brother in a life of crime and become the next Belle Starr."

She stepped out of reach and turned to face him, her arms folded, her face flushed. "I was a fool to come here with you, when I knew that you wanted to be Daphne's husband and not mine. I was even more the fool to think there could ever be any sort of peace between you and Steven."

"Willow —"

"Don't say anything more, Gideon. You're free now. You can court your Daphne, though I must say that I don't think you'll have much luck. And you can hunt Steven till your hair turns gray. But know this, Gideon Marshall: it won't be an easy task, because they don't call him the Mountain Fox for nothing. Furthermore, I will do anything in my power to stop you."

Gideon was outraged, but there was no

point in arguing that he didn't care a whit about Daphne Roberts or any other woman besides Willow herself. Even if they'd managed to settle that, which would be a miracle in itself, it appeared there was still the matter of Steven.

"I'll find your brother," he said icily, regretting his tone even as he spoke, "and when I do, I'll see him hang."

"Good luck," she replied, with brisk contempt. And then she was gone.

When Gideon heard the front door slam behind her, he fished the wedding band out of the bathwater and flung it across the room with a bellowed curse. Then he sat back in the cramped tub and squeezed his eyes shut tight.

The sorrow got through anyway.

Maria met Willow at the front door of Judge Gallagher's house, casting a quietly disapproving look at the valises she carried, one in each hand. "I will make your room ready," she said, with a sigh.

"Thank you," replied Willow, in a steady voice. "Is Papa at home?"

Maria took one of the valises and started wearily up the stairs. "No, señora. He is hearing a case today."

Willow maintained her composure as she

followed the housekeeper up to the second floor and into the room that had been hers before Gideon Marshall, damn his hide, changed everything. "I could sleep for a thousand years," she confided, sitting down on the edge of her bed.

"Sleeping will solve nothing. When you awaken, *chiquita,* all your problems will be waiting."

Willow unpinned her modest, wifely hat and flung it across the room. From now on, she would wear low-cut dresses and fancy millinery, the way Dove Triskadden did. Maybe, just to annoy Gideon, she would become someone's mistress.

"I will bring tea," said Maria, pursing her lips just as if she'd heard Willow's scandalous thoughts.

"I would rather have sherry," parried Willow. If she was going to change her image, she might as well start by putting aside temperance.

"That is too bad," retorted Maria. "You will have tea."

"I said I wanted sherry!"

"I don't care what you said," came the brisk reply. "And I would advise the señora to remember that a lady respects her elders."

Willow blushed and bit her lower lip, but when Maria brought the tea, she drank it without protest. Following that, she stripped to her chemise and waited for the solace of sleep to enclose her.

When it did, it was fitful, and when Willow awakened again, all her troubles were there waiting for her, just as Maria had warned. She cried as she put her dress back on.

She spent the day alone, reading in her room, but her books did not provide their usual solace. Her mind kept straying back to Gideon.

She rested.

She paced.

She finally went downstairs to help Maria do housework.

That evening, there were guests for dinner: Dove Triskadden, Daphne and her cousin Hilda — and Gideon.

Willow would have turned and fled the dining room if her father hadn't caught her elbow in his hand and muttered, out of the side of his mouth, "Oh, no you don't, sugarplum. Running away is no solution."

Gideon looked up from his wineglass, which had seemed to intrigue him deeply until that moment, and his eyes were unreadable as they swept the length of Willow and came back to her face. Almost as an afterthought, he rose halfheartedly from his chair and then sat down again, turning his attention to Daphne, who had been seated beside him.

Daphne sparkled in her pale lilac dress, and there were little amethyst ribbons tied among her dark curls. She smiled at Willow and then turned graciously back to Gideon, relating some story about a mutual friend in animated tones.

Willow forced herself to sit down.

Daphne and Gideon continued to chat, seemingly absorbed in each other.

Willow, thinking her own dismal thoughts, soon lost track of their conversation.

"You may keep your cursed railroads, darling," Daphne was saying. "I think they're absolutely dreadful."

"Darling!" muttered Willow, under her breath, and it wasn't until her knuckles began to throb that she realized she was gripping the sides of her chair with all her strength. She darted one outraged look at Daphne.

"We all have our personal opinions," Gideon replied, smiling into Daphne's beguiling face like a besotted idiot. "But surely the train has some redeeming features."

"I can't think what they would be," Daphne answered blithely. "I declare, the thought of journeying all the way back to San Francisco in one of those cramped seats inclines me toward staying right here in Virginia City for the rest of my life!"

Willow choked on her asparagus, but it was Hilda who spoke in protest.

"You promised that we'd leave tomorrow!" she wailed, fixing a piteous gaze on Daphne.

Daphne shrugged and turned a winning smile on Gideon. "Promises are made to be broken — aren't they, Gideon dear?"

Gideon merely smiled, flattered by Daphne's attention; Willow had to grip her chair seat again, even harder this time, to keep from flinging a wineglass at his head.

"I have wronged you sorely," he said to Daphne. "Perhaps I can redeem myself."

There was a silence, during which all eyes except Gideon's and Daphne's swung to Willow. She forced herself to sit still, though inside she was in a screaming rage.

"However would you do that?" trilled Daphne, bending so that Gideon might avail himself of a glimpse of her full and shapely bosom, displayed to considerable advantage by the fashionably low neckline of her lovely dress. The garment was the palest purple, nearly the same color as her eyes.

Gideon's answer would have led any sensible person to believe that he and Daphne were alone. "There is a supper dance tomorrow night. Will you let me escort you?"

Daphne flushed prettily, looking for all the world as though she had never even pretended to be Willow's friend. "Would that be proper?" she countered, lowering her eyes and fluttering her thick lashes. "I mean, you are a married man."

Gideon's gaze sliced, menacing, to Willow's bloodless face. "You couldn't prove that by me," he said evenly.

At this point, the judge cleared his throat and diplomatically swung the conversation in another direction. Despite his efforts, the remainder of the evening was the purest misery for Willow. At the first opportunity, which came when Gideon and her father retired to the parlor for an after-dinner brandy, she sprang out of her chair and fled up the stairs, her skirts wadded in her hands, to hide behind the heavy door of her bedroom.

The knock that came a few minutes later was too subdued and refined to be Gideon's, so Willow opened the door.

"Good Lord," said Dove briskly. "Splash some cold water on your face before that rounder downstairs gets a look at you."

Willow went to the pitcher and basin immediately, for she would have died before letting Gideon know that she had been crying over him. When she had flung a few handfuls of water over her aching face and dried it with a towel, she turned to look at her father's mistress.

"Did Gideon leave yet?"

"No. He's closeted away with your father, in Devlin's study, and I must say that I hope Devlin puts that young scoundrel in his place, once and for all."

There seemed to be no strength at all in Willow's knees, so she sat down in her rocking chair. She had spent many hours in that chair, reading or just dreaming, but it seemed foreign to her now, just as the rest of the house did.

As familiar as it was, the place wasn't home anymore.

"If he didn't say anything during dinner, I doubt that Papa will come to my defense now," she mourned.

Dove sighed and folded her slender, snow-white arms across the bodice of her striking black dress. The neckline was trimmed with real pearls, and they shimmered like milky prisms as she paced back and forth in front of the small fireplace. "Men," she exclaimed, in happy agreement. "They do tend to side with each other more often than not, and that's a fact, I'm sorry to say."

Willow drew her knees up and wrapped her arms around them, heedless of the way she was crumpling her very best gown. "I thought Daphne was my friend," she whispered, in mourning. In some ways, the end of that illusion was as crushing as the demise of her marriage.

"You're like me in that way, I think," Dove commented pensively. "I've never had any female friends — not before you, that is. I know why women don't like me, Willow, but that doesn't explain why they don't take to you."

Willow shrugged. Even in San Francisco, where she had diligently followed Evadne's instructions on manners and spoken to the few people who bothered to speak to her, she'd never had an actual friend.

It was one of the great sorrows of her life.

"Having an outlaw for a brother doesn't help," she mused, "and everyone has always known about Mother, too. She left Papa and created an awful scandal. She took up with Jay Forbes . . ." Willow paused and shivered at the shadowy recollection of a man she couldn't completely remember.

"But you were born," prodded Dove gently. Her smile was soft, and it made Willow feel a little better.

"Yes, I guess Papa and Mama met somewhere and I was the result. Evadne hated me for that and everybody else just sort of fell into line and hated me, too."

"Do you love Gideon, Willow?"

She raised swollen, miserable eyes to Dove's face. "Yes, God help me. But you can see how he feels about me. It's Daphne he wants."

Dove was quiet and introspective for several seconds. "I think perhaps he was just trying to make you jealous. Worked, too, didn't it?"

Willow flushed. She was so inexperienced in matters of the heart; the possibility hadn't even occurred to her. "That doesn't explain Daphne's behavior," she protested. "Why, that woman told me that she never wanted to marry Gideon in the first place, and the next thing you know, she's throwing herself at him —"

"She may be in league with Gideon," mused Dove, one finger pressed to her chin in speculation. "In any case, if you want Gideon Marshall, you'd better stop running off to your bedroom to cry like a little girl whenever you're challenged. Believe me, with a man like that, you'll have more than one Daphne to fend off during your lifetime."

Willow stared at Dove, mouth agape. Was

this woman turning on her now, too? "You make it sound as though I was the one who did something wrong!"

"You did," Dove affirmed. "You should have walked straight up to Gideon and slapped that man silly, for a start."

"I couldn't very well do that when I was the one who started all this by leaving him!"

Dove smiled. "Exactly," she confirmed, and then she came and knelt beside Willow's chair. "Sweetie, if you want to own that man more than the devil ever could, I can tell you how. And if you love him, then you'd better fight, because it's plain that you love him in the forever way, and that means your life could be mighty long and mighty empty if you don't do something."

"Tell me," Willow pleaded.

Dove explained, and Willow's eyes widened as she listened.

"I don't like this, Gideon," Daphne said, wringing her hands as she looked up at the bright moon and drew the scent of Willow Marshall's lilacs into her nostrils. "I don't like it at all. That woman is my friend."

Gideon was standing a few feet away, his hands in the pockets of his trousers. "I don't deserve any favors from you, Daphne," he conceded gruffly, "but if you don't help me,

I don't know what I'm going to do."

Daphne was filled with frustration. She had hurt Willow, and badly, and she hated herself for it. "You know I'm not the type to hold grudges, Gideon, and it probably wouldn't have been good if we'd married anyway. But I still think you should go back inside that house and tell your wife that you love her."

His broad shoulders stiffened beneath his pristine white shirt, and the fabric of his silk vest strained across his back. "She wouldn't care," he said. "No one is more important to Willow than her thieving, murdering brother."

"Oh, Gideon, don't be such a *fool.* You *must* know how deeply Willow cares for you — it's in her face, in everything she says and does." She paused, drew a deep breath. "Besides, she came right out and told me."

"She'll have to choose between Steven and me, Daphne," Gideon broke in. "And I don't mind telling you that my prospects aren't very good."

"You're not going to increase them by flirting with other women under her nose, Gideon." The mention of Steven Gallagher made Daphne uncomfortable; she'd visited him several times while he was recovering at Gideon's house, attracted to him like fil-

ings to a magnet, and they'd laughed together in the quiet. Once, he'd drawn her
down to lie beside him on the bed — he
was that bold — and he'd kissed her.
Daphne knew for a shattering certainty that
if she hadn't heard footsteps on the stairs at
the very last moment, she might have given
Steven Gallagher what she had never given
to any other man — herself.

Gideon turned to face her, and she shuddered to think that he might know what she
was thinking and feeling. "Tell me, Daphne,
what's keeping you here in Virginia City?
You obviously know as well as I do that our,
er, association is over."

Daphne lowered her eyes. It wouldn't be
wise to admit that she hoped to see Steven
Gallagher again, but she couldn't lie, either.
For that reason, she said nothing at all.

"It's Steven, isn't it?" asked Gideon, who
could be damnably perceptive. "Christ in
heaven, it's Steven Gallagher!"

"Yes," admitted Daphne lamely.

Gideon swore again and sat down on the
marble bench beside her, taking her hand in
his own. "He's an *outlaw,* Daphne. Life with
him would be foreign to everything you've
ever been taught, everything you've believed
in —"

Daphne laughed, despite the tears sliding

down her face. "Yes, Papa will — well, you can imagine how Papa would react, I'm sure."

Gideon squeezed her hand. "Can *you,* Daphne?" he countered gently. "Can you even *begin* to imagine the way society would respond?"

Glumly, Daphne nodded her head.

In a brotherly fashion, Gideon took out his handkerchief, unfolded it, and dabbed away the tears that wet her cheeks. "Daphne, does Steven feel the way you do?"

Again, Daphne laughed, but the sound was one of anguish. "No, I'm sure he doesn't. No doubt, I'm just another potential conquest to him."

"Potential?"

Daphne swatted at Gideon in reprimand. "Yes, *potential.* I didn't give in to him, if that's what you want to know."

Gideon gave a ragged sigh and released Daphne's suddenly moist and quivering hand. "God damn. Now I suppose I'm going to have to do constant battle not only with Willow but with you, too."

"If you mean to hang Steven Gallagher," Daphne said bravely, "you'll get no help from me. And that includes this silly charade you want to put on for Willow!"

"Daphne —"

"*No.* I won't go to the supper dance with you, Gideon Marshall, and I won't lie to Willow anymore, either. I've already told you — she's my friend!"

Gideon stood up, looking hard and imperious in the bright moonlight. "I'm your friend, too, Daphne, and I'm warning you. For your own sake, stay away from Steven Gallagher. Go back to San Francisco and marry someone — suitable."

"And if I don't heed your advice?"

Gideon sighed. "Despite what I've done, your father will listen to me, Daphne, and if I wire him that you've taken up with a man who makes a habit of robbing Central Pacific trains, he'll be on his way here within the day."

"You would do that to me, after humiliating me in front of the whole city of San Francisco?"

"In a heartbeat," replied Gideon, and then he disappeared into the shadows of the garden, leaving Daphne alone with her very disturbing thoughts.

Gideon stood at the base of the stairs, his hand gripping the newel, and stared up into the shadows of the second floor. Watching him from the doorway of his study, Devlin knew that he should be bone-angry with this young rascal, but the truth was that he was amused instead. Any fool would have seen through that act he'd put on at dinner.

"Problems?" Devlin intoned, with a grin. He had long since removed his dinner jacket and now, to make his comfort complete, he was rolling up his sleeves.

Gideon flung him a look and tore himself away from the newel. "Just one," he answered caustically.

"About so high?" jibed the judge, holding one hand, palm down, to Willow's approximate height.

"I need a drink," said Gideon, with a distracted shake of his head.

"Nope," countered the judge good-naturedly. "What you need is to march up those stairs and make some kind of peace with that wife of yours before it's too late."

"Are you crazy? She'd probably shoot me on sight."

"Can't say I'd blame her much, the way you behaved at dinner tonight."

"The way *I* behaved?" growled Gideon. "What about *her behavior*? She left me!"

"That she did. But you're not going to get Willow back by carrying on like a road-show Romeo, my boy. She's too proud to take that, and if I know my daughter, she'll give as good as she gets if you try."

"What the hell do you mean by that?"

"I mean that you aren't the only young fellow around these parts with eyes in his head. Willow is a beautiful young woman."

Gideon laughed, though he didn't sound too amused. "Are you telling me that she might take up with Norville Pickering again?"

The judge indulged in a slow smile. "Never. But your brother, Zachary — now there's a possibility, though it would probably take some time. He's good-looking, and he's a hand with the women, from what I've seen. Seems to me that if you didn't want Willow, he'd be more than happy to take her off your hands."

Gideon's jaw clamped down like a vise, and his eyes once again were fixed on the top of the stairs. A visible tremor went through his frame before he bolted up them, taking three steps at a time.

11

The knob on Willow's bedroom door turned sharply. With her heart in her throat, she snuggled down deeper in the blankets, waiting, her eyes on the brass key jutting from the lock.

"Open the door, Willow," Gideon commanded evenly, from the hallway.

"No," replied his wife, in a clear voice.

"Do you want me to kick it in?"

"You wouldn't dare!"

"Wouldn't I, Willow?"

"My father would —"

"The hell with your father! Besides, he's the one who sent me up here."

"I don't believe you."

"Fine," he answered, from beyond the sturdy barrier that separated them. "Do you believe this?" There was a short, ominous silence, followed by a thundering crash that sent the door rattling against the inside wall, hinges whining.

Willow sat up in bed, her eyes wide. "Gideon!" she gasped.

He executed a mocking bow. "Good evening, my dear," he said.

Despite the violence of his action, Willow was not afraid of her husband. No, if she was afraid of anything, it was of her own vulnerability to him. "How dare you?" she breathed.

Gideon shrugged, a shadow-draped giant, and began undoing the string tie he had worn to dinner. Then he unfastened the top buttons of his shirt and shrugged out of his suit coat. "How dare I what?" he asked, with a gruff insolence that chafed Willow's pride.

Willow ignored the question, since the answer was so obvious. "Get out of my room," she said, through her teeth.

As though she had not spoken, Gideon closed the door, walked over and sat down on the edge of the bed with a long sigh, and began pulling off his boots.

"Gideon!"

He smiled at her, his teeth gleaming winter white in the thick shadows. "Yes, dear?" he asked pleasantly.

"I told you to get out!"

"I know what you told me, hellcat," he replied, without a whit of concern. "Move over, will you? I'm especially tired tonight."

"I will *not* move over. If you think you're going to touch me, Gideon Marshall, after what you did tonight —"

"I've no intention of touching you," Gideon interrupted. "But I'm not going to ride out to the ranch tonight, either. Nor do I plan to sleep on that damn settee in the sitting room again."

"Sleep in one of the guest rooms, then!"

"I'll sleep here, thank you very much. Now, move over."

Outraged, Willow untangled herself from the covers and made to scramble off the bed, muttering about audacity and people who thought they ought to have their own way no matter what.

Grinning, Gideon caught her arm in a light hold and eased her back onto the pillows.

Willow glared up into his handsome face, her shoulders imprisoned beneath his hands. "If you don't let me out of this bed," she warned, on a hissing breath, "I will scream for my papa!"

"That would be embarrassing for everybody," crooned Gideon, his eyes twinkling with quiet merriment, "wouldn't it?"

"Most of all for you, I think!"

Gideon arched an eyebrow. "Nothing embarrasses me, Willow," he said. "And kindly stop acting as though you were still in pigtails."

Recalling Dove's gentle reprimand concerning her tendency to behave like a little girl, Willow subsided. She rolled away from Gideon, pulled the covers up over her head, and bit back the screaming tantrum that was brewing on the tip of her tongue.

Calmly, Gideon finished undressing and crawled into bed, stretching out beside Willow with a contented, husbandly sigh. "Good night," he said.

Good night? Willow fumed beneath her share of the covers. Good night indeed, when she could feel the length of him in every one of her senses, feel the hard, masculine prowess that summoned traitorous things deep inside her even though they weren't touching at all.

"Humph," she said.

Silence.

Unsettled, Willow waited, then finally began to wonder if Gideon had gone to sleep. If he had, damn him, she would be even angrier than she would have been if he had made unseemly advances. After all, he owed her some kind of explanation for his behavior that night, if not a full and preferably abject apology, perhaps sweetened by a bouquet of flowers. "Gideon?"

His breathing was deep, even. And he said nothing at all in response.

"Gideon!" Willow repeated, with rising consternation.

Nothing.

Willow twisted into a sitting position, her fists clenched. He had a nerve, forcing his way into this room and then just lying there *sleeping,* for heaven's sake, leaving her to stew in her anger like a cabbage in a pot of soup. Now that he had proved his alleged dominance, Willow concluded, Gideon meant to rest as though nothing had happened.

Biting her lower lip, Willow studied her husband. The things Dove had told her about "owning" a man sifted into her mind. Did she love Gideon enough to do that? Was she angry enough?

Willow had affirmative answers for both questions, contrary though they were. "Gideon," she whispered sweetly, pulling the blankets down to his waist, trailing feather-light fingers through the swirls of tarnished gold down on his chest.

He groaned and stirred slightly. His eyes were still closed, but Willow knew that he wasn't sleeping at all — he'd been pretending. Somehow, this made the prospect of conquering him all the more appealing.

"Poor darling," she crooned, "so tired . . ."

A muscle in his jaw tightened, then relaxed again. Willow allowed her hand to stray lower, over his hard stomach . . . farther. She clasped him tight and knew sweeping satisfaction at the way he tensed involuntarily and grew to magnificence in her hold.

"So tired," she said again, slipping beneath the covers, trailing victorious kisses over his taut flesh as she went.

Gideon made a strangled sound and arched his back when she reached her destination; in that wildly triumphant moment, Willow knew that Dove had been right. The dominion, always Gideon's before, had shifted. His powerful legs moved in unqualified surrender and his hands were tangled in Willow's hair, making a plea all their own.

At the same time, hoarse, senseless words came from deep within him; Willow could feel them shuddering through his hard frame long before they reached his throat.

On and on, she gloried in the knowledge that she was pleasing him, that she and she alone existed for him now, in this treacherous, excruciatingly beautiful moment.

Gideon began to writhe and twist like a man in delirium, his fingers frantic in her hair, his cries oddly muffled. Finally, a great shudder racked him and he gave a guttural growl of mingled satisfaction and defeat. Again and again he tensed, gasping Willow's name as though it were a chant for salvation.

Flushed with the ferocity of her victory, Willow sat up and smiled down into his face. He was breathing very rapidly and his eyes were fixed on something far beyond the dark ceiling of that bedroom.

Deliberately patronizing him, Willow reached up and patted his cheek. "Good night, dear," she said. Now she would be the one to sleep, while Gideon lay wondering in the darkness.

Except that he caught her wrist in an inescapable hand and his eyes glittered like a tiger's in the silvery moonlight. "Where did you learn that?" he demanded.

Willow executed a theatrical yawn. "Dove told me. Good night, darling."

"Good night nothing!"

"I'm very tired, Gideon."

"You're going to be a lot more tired before I get through with you," he answered.

Willow would have scooted away if he hadn't held her so firmly. "What — don't you want to sleep?"

Gideon laughed low in his throat. "Sleep? After that? You must be joking."

"But —"

He arched an eyebrow and held her wrist while his free hand came to the buttons of her prim flannel nightgown and deftly began to undo them. "But?" he mocked, in a drawl.

"Dove said you would sleep —"

Again Gideon laughed. "Did she?" he teased, baring both of Willow's breasts and tracing the nipples with the tip of one finger, rousing them to a hard, crimson response. "Well, my dear, Dove passes her evenings, you must remember, with a man almost twice my age."

Willow blushed hotly and swatted at his plundering fingers with her free hand. "Gideon Marshall —"

In a lightning-fast grappling motion, Gideon caught both of Willow's wrists in one hand and held them behind her. Then, slowly, gently, he drew the shoulders of her nightgown downward until they were tight around her upper arms. A calculated thrust at the small of her back made her captured breasts jut forward in proud surrender. He bent to take suckle at one peak, echoing the groan this brought from deep within Willow.

When he had feasted at one brazenly beautiful fount, he turned to the other, plying it to obedience with his lips, his teeth, his tongue. The pleasure was so piercing that Willow had to bite down on a thick strand of her own hair to keep from letting him know the full scope of her need.

But if she could control the cries that rose repeatedly into her throat, demanding utterance, she could not stop the primitive responses of her body itself. Each time Willow shuddered, Gideon grew greedier at her breast, renewing his efforts to drive her beyond the portals of paradise.

Finally, however, his greed was sated. They knelt in the middle of the bed, facing each other, Gideon naked, Willow still imprisoned in her disheveled nightgown. The peaks of Willow's breasts, moist, thoroughly tongued, and suckled, pulsed in the night air. She sat motionless as Gideon deftly pulled the flannel garment up over her head.

Slowly, almost reverently, he drew her to kneel astraddle his lap, his lips warm in the hollow beneath her right ear. "Sweet vengeance awaits you, little pagan," he promised hoarsely. "Sweet vengeance indeed."

At his entry, which was a gentle one, Willow gasped and let her head fall back, knowing that her passion was visible to him and beyond caring. "Oh, Gideon," she choked out, already transported. "Gideon, Gideon!"

"Soon," he said, bending to attend one straining nipple even as his hands lifted Willow and slowly lowered her again.

She cried out softly and tried to accelerate the motion of her hips, only to be held to the slower pace Gideon had set for them both. When satisfied that she would obey this meter, Gideon released her hips to catch both of her breasts in his hand and press their lush fullness together. Now he subjected both peaks to the searing forays of his tongue.

"Gideon," moaned Willow, "Gideon — please — I can't bear any more."

He merely continued the sweet menacing, bringing his teeth and lips into play, too.

Finally, driven by a force greater than her will and her pride combined, Willow began to move upon him. This time he permitted it, and their bodies left their minds far behind as they soared toward a ferocious release that encompassed them both and sent them spinning through a universe void of all but their own stifled, throaty cries.

When she could coerce her lax muscles to move again, Willow fell back, ready to sleep. This, Gideon would not allow. He was insatiable and his tender vengeance carried them both to peak after breathless peak. Their fevered gasps and whispered pleas echoed far into the night.

Steven Gallagher sat back in the rickety wooden chair, his wounded shoulder and his mind aching in time with each other. Even though it would have been too dangerous to stay at Willow's place, he'd returned to the hideout, a cabin way back in the hills, almost as soon as he could ride. He was getting too old for the outlaw life.

The thought made him sigh.

It wasn't as if he had a lot of other choices.

Behind him, at a small table, Coy and Reilly were engaged in a game of cards and yet another of their almost constant arguments.

Steven sighed and covered his eyes with one hand. God, he was tired of them, tired of this life, tired of hiding and being hunted like a rabid wolf.

And now there was Daphne. Since he'd met her, the bone-deep loneliness — as much a part of him as the color of his eyes or the pitch of his voice, it had been with him so long — had become almost unbearable.

Stretching out his long legs toward the empty hearth, he remembered that dark-haired, violet-eyed wonder and, for the first time, wished that he had lived his life differently. If he'd been the upright and law-abiding sort, after all, he would be free to go to Daphne now, with flowers in his hand.

Flowers? Steven lifted the back of one hand to his forehead to see if he was fevered. Next he'd be wearing suits and bowler hats, passing out calling cards.

Devlin would like that, Steven told himself, but the old, bitter magic didn't work. Spiting his father, always a major source of satisfaction, just wasn't enough anymore. The hell of it was that Coy and Reilly had been dragged into a life that would, more than likely, get them killed one day, just because they were his half brothers.

His head throbbing, Steven listened to the boys as they argued over a stupid turn of the cards. They weren't children, as he'd so often reminded himself, they were men — Coy twenty-five years old, Reilly twenty-two. They should have jobs, homes, wives, children by now. Instead, by virtue of their association with Steven himself, they had prices on their heads.

"Steven," whined Coy, "two aces don't beat three of a kind, does it?"

"No," Steven answered, too tired to grapple with his brother's convoluted grammar. Chastity had taught Steven to read when he was little, from a stack of dime novels someone had left behind in one of the hideouts, and he'd devoured virtually every book he could get his hands on ever since.

Thanks to Willow, who had no compunction about pilfering the judge's fine library, there had been plenty.

His younger brothers, by contrast, were practically illiterate.

"I can't stand this place no more!" blurted Reilly, out of the blue. "No women, no whiskey — I'm going to Mexico with Blanchard."

Steven let the front legs of his chair strike the floor. "What?"

Both Coy and Reilly were glaring at him now, flushed, braced for some sort of challenge. "You done wrong, tellin' him to ride out, Steven," complained the latter. "Blanchard was a good man."

"Good?" Steven rasped. "He robbed the Central Pacific and they're blaming us for it. He killed a man, for no reason —"

"So what?" countered Coy petulantly. "Ain't that what an outlaw's supposed to do?"

"My God," muttered Steven distractedly. *Look what you've done to them,* said a voice deep in his mind. *Look what you've done.*

"I'm leavin' this place," said Reilly, with

unusual spirit. "You wanna spend your life plaguin' your rich daddy, that's your affair. I don't wanna hide out anymore, and I don't care to be all the time lookin' over my shoulder for Vancel Tudd, neither."

"I feel the same," said Coy.

"Fine," Steven said raggedly. "You're men and I'm not about to tell you what to do. But mark my words, both of you — if you take up with Blanchard, you'll get yourselves killed before you ever get as far as Mexico."

"You're the one that said he could ride with us in the first place, Steven!" Reilly reminded him as he began gathering up his rifle, his bedroll, his few personal belongings. Coy soon followed suit.

There was no denying Reilly's remark, and Steven, still recovering from Red Eagle's hatchet attack, didn't have the spirit to argue with his brothers. Besides, where had his advice gotten them so far? "Go," he said, "get out of here."

"We'll find a way to send word when we're out of the country, maybe through Willow or the judge," promised Coy. "Okay, Steven?"

The last two words echoed through Steven's spirit like the toll of some grim funeral bell. *We're trusting you — okay,*

Steven? We'll live the way you do — okay, Steven?

"Good-bye," he said, closing his eyes.

"You'll be all right, won't you?" Reilly asked, hesitating. "What're you gonna do now, Steven?"

He sighed, wishing they'd go, wishing they'd stay, wishing he'd done things differently after Chastity and Jay Forbes had died. "I can take care of myself," he said.

"Sure," said Coy, like he really believed it.

"So long, Steven," added Reilly.

And then they were gone, the shack door closing quietly behind them.

After he'd heard them ride away, into the thick darkness, Steven got out of his chair, went to the small stove in one corner of the old cabin, and poured coffee into a chipped enamel mug. As he drank it, he pictured himself knocking on Devlin Gallagher's door. *Hullo, Pap,* he imagined himself saying.

The ridiculousness of that made him laugh ruefully. It was too late to go home. Maybe, despite Devlin's constant pleas and protestations, it had always been too late.

Willow felt the sun touch her face and squeezed her eyes shut, at the same time flailing one arm in Gideon's direction. If he was there, beside her, she would pretend to be asleep until he left.

But the bed was empty and so, Willow soon realized, was the room. She felt mingled disappointment and relief as she yawned and sat up.

She supposed Gideon was prancing about like a rooster, after last might. He'd be insufferable and pompous, probably, and just imagining the glitter of triumph in his eyes made her simmer.

There was a knock at the door and Willow stiffened, thinking that she might have to face her husband after all. Then it came to her that, with his gall, Gideon wouldn't have bothered to knock. "Come in," she said, expecting Maria.

Instead, Daphne swept into the room, looking insistently friendly. "About what happened at dinner last night —"

Willow stopped her with an upraised hand. "If you want Gideon Marshall, you can have him," she said. "With my blessings."

"But I *don't*. Willow, you must know that Gideon put me up to that — he only wanted to make you jealous."

So Dove had been right. Willow tossed back her covers and wriggled her feet into the slippers that waited beside the bed.

"How nice of you to oblige him," she muttered coldly.

"Willow —"

"It was an underhanded thing to do, Daphne Roberts, especially after you pretended to be my friend!"

"I *am* your friend."

"Then I shall not need to cultivate any enemies — you, no doubt, will serve in either capacity," Willow said loftily.

Daphne lowered her head. "I thought it would help at the time, Willow, I honestly did."

Willow was pulling on her wrapper. "Sure," she scoffed.

Daphne came nearer and folded her arms. "Have you so many friends that you can spare me, Willow Marshall?"

"Are you going to let Gideon escort you to the supper dance tonight?" Willow countered.

Flushing, Daphne eyed the rumpled bed. "You don't mean that — that things haven't changed between you and Gideon?"

Willow lifted her chin. "Things haven't changed. And if you are my friend, as you claim, Daphne Roberts, you will insist that Gideon keep his word and take you to the supper dance."

Daphne's mouth fell open. "Willow —

what on earth . . . didn't you and Gideon
— ?"

Willow could not suppress a grin. "Yes,
we did. No doubt, Gideon is certain that he
has put me in my wifely place. Well, he has
some surprises coming!"

"Such as what?" asked Daphne warily.

"For one thing," replied Willow, "I am not
going to trot obediently back to our house
and cook and clean and warm his bed. For
another, I am not going to that supper
dance on his arm, smiling and wearing
calico!"

Daphne looked really worried now. "Willow, I've known Gideon for a long time.
He-he thinks for himself, but there are
certain conventions he'll expect you to ob-
serve."

"He can expect whatever he likes," replied
Willow with a toss of her head.

Daphne shrugged and left her friend to
her morning ablutions.

Gideon stood outside the dust-streaked
window of the largest general store in
Virginia City, totally at a loss. Faced with
the prospect of buying Willow a gift, he realized how little he knew about her.

Recalling her fondness for wearing trousers and letting her hair hang down in a

single braid, he smiled. Not for her the jewels and frilly geegaws so well received by other women of his experience.

Gideon sighed, shifted from one foot to the other, and wedged his hands into his pants pockets. Indeed, that was the only thing he could be certain of: Willow was unlike any woman he had ever known.

"The law business must be slow," drawled a voice beside him, "if you've got time to window-shop."

Gideon focused on his brother's face, then frowned. "I'm trying to find a gift for my wife," he said defensively, putting a slight emphasis on the last two words.

"Trouble?" beamed Zachary.

"No!" snapped Gideon, too quickly.

Zachary held up both hands, palms out. "Easy, Gideon, easy. I was just trying to make polite conversation."

"Sure. When are you leaving, by the way?"

Zachary shrugged. "Tomorrow, next week, whenever the mood strikes me." He was assessing the array of goods displayed beyond the store window. "Just how much Dutch are you in with Willow, anyway?"

"What do you care?"

"I want to help, that's all. Are we talking the kind of sin that calls for diamonds and rubies, or is this transgression in the hair-ribbon range?"

Exasperated, Gideon grinned anyway and shook his head. "You never quit, do you, Zach?"

Just the slightest flicker of triumph flashed in Zachary's eyes. "Never, little brother. Willow probably doesn't care much about jewelry or hair ribbons, but I know she likes music. Why don't you get her one of those?"

Gideon took note of the music boxes Zachary was pointing at, and he knew that Willow would like one, but he was stung that he hadn't thought of the idea first. "Maybe," he said.

Zachary laughed. "Buy the one that looks like a little piano," he suggested affably, and then he was on his way again, his hands in his pockets, whistling a song Gideon had heard Willow play on the spinet at home.

Gideon swore under his breath, went inside the store, and bought the piano music box. While the storekeeper's wife was wrapping that, a display of toy monkeys caught his eye. When wound, each mechanical creature chattered and clapped two tiny brass cymbals together.

Smiling to himself, Gideon bought a monkey, too. There was enough of the child in Willow that such a thing would make her laugh.

He was leaving the store, his purchases bound up in a brown paper parcel, when he saw Willow entering the small dress and millinery shop across the street, with Daphne. It was odd, those two being friends, but he was glad they were. The burden of her mother's reputation and Steven's notoriety had been a heavy one for Willow to bear, he knew. It was too bad that Daphne would be going back to San Francisco soon.

"Marshal?"

Gideon turned and was jarred to find Vancel Tudd standing beside him, grinning his gapped mocking grin. "Tudd," he responded, glad that the music box and the mechanical monkey he carried had been wrapped, because they suddenly seemed so powerfully intimate.

"I'm ridin' out to look for Gallagher again. Just thought I'd tell you, so's you could wire the railroad and make sure the bounty money's on hand when I bring him in."

"You don't lack for confidence, do you?" asked Gideon dryly.

Tudd shrugged, chewing on a soggy wooden splinter. "I figure I'll find 'em today — Gallagher and those Forbes boys that ride with him."

"Do you know something I don't, Mr. Tudd?"

The bounty hunter shifted the splinter to one side of his mouth and spat out of the other. "I reckon I know lots of things you don't, Marshal. You just round up that money, 'cause I'll be bringin' in all three of them wasters 'fore mornin'."

"I want them alive," Gideon replied.

Again Tudd shrugged. "Maybe. Posters say they can be dead or kickin', no matter which."

A feeling of cold dread crept up Gideon's spine. Tudd could be bluffing, but on the other hand . . .

"Good day to you, Marshal," drawled Vancel Tudd, tipping his hat before starting to walk away.

Gideon caught his arm and held on. "I'll ride with you," he said.

Tudd shook his head. "No, sir. I ain't sharin' that bounty with nobody."

"I don't give a damn about the bounty. If you know where Gallagher is . . ."

The grizzled old man looked almost innocent. "Why, Marshal. I don't know where Steven Gallagher is, not rightly. I just got me a hunch I'm about to find him, that's all."

"Tudd . . ."

"He's your brother-in-law, ain't he? 'Pears you might be forgettin' your duty. A man would, with a bit o' fluff like that Willow lyin' in his bed."

Gideon felt cold rage, but he kept his manner calm. "I haven't forgotten my duty, Mr. Tudd, you can be sure of that. I'm having the conditions of Steven Gallagher's capture changed. If you gun him down, I'll call it murder."

"You can call it whatever you might like, I reckon. The people of this here town, though, they'll feel different. They'll know ol' Vancel was just tryin' to make Virginia City a little safer for their kids and their womenfolk."

Gideon caught Tudd's filthy shirt front in his free hand but let go again. Disgust unfurled inside him, like a cobra rising out of a basket. "Bring in Steven Gallagher — alive, Mr. Tudd — and I'll double the bounty."

Tudd grinned. "Will you sign a paper sayin' that?"

Gideon sighed and nodded his head. As he and the bounty hunter walked toward the marshal's office down the street, he wondered whether Willow would see his deal with Tudd as a favor or a betrayal.

12

The dressmaker's shop was small and jammed with bolts of fabric, every surface dusty.

"You can't wear that to a supper dance!" cried Daphne, taking in the rich, wine-colored velvet Willow was holding up. "The neckline is too low and —"

Willow smiled at her friend's alarm. The bodice *was* rather revealing and was trimmed with a sprinkling of glistening, diamondlike crystals, as was the hem. "I think it's a beautiful gown," she said stubbornly.

"It is," conceded Daphne, sounding slightly choked. "And if you were Dove Triskadden, that dress would be perfect but . . ."

Willow lifted her chin and turned back to the dress-shop mirror, assessing the lush dress again. The deep burgundy shade of the velvet gave color to her fair complexion, accented the gold of her eyes, turned her

hair to spun silk. "I like it," she said decisively.

"Willow, everyone else will be wearing
calico and cambric!"

"I don't care what everyone else wears.
And I'm tired of dressing like a mouse just
so the townswomen will approve of me. So
far, that strategy hasn't worked, anyway; I'm
still Steven Gallagher's sister and my mother's illegitimate daughter!"

Daphne gnawed at her lower lip, still
uncertain. Finally, she made a last, lame effort. "You'll be too warm," she protested.
"Velvet is for winter."

Willow didn't care. She'd never felt the
way that dress made her feel — beautiful,
exquisitely feminine, and at the same time
powerful.

The dressmaker, a small, thin woman with
wispy hair, was fluttering her hands. "But it
is so lovely," she put in, anxious no doubt,
to make the sizable sale. "And I could manage the alterations in less than two hours."

The little bell over the shop door jingled,
and a fresh breeze stirred the dangling ends
of a rainbow of ribbons gracing one wall.

"Take the dress," interceded a smooth,
masculine voice.

Willow and Daphne both turned quickly,
but their reactions to Zachary Marshall

were quite different. Daphne looked openly hostile, but Willow smiled.

By then, she'd decided he was harmless. He simply enjoyed flirting, that was all.

Zachary removed his immaculate black hat, fixing all his considerable charm on his brother's wife. "Willow," he said cordially, looking as lithe as a sapling tree, standing there.

"Good morning, Zachary," she replied with warmth. "Do you really like the dress?"

Zachary's eyes widened slightly as he took in the gown. "Like it?" he echoed. "My dear, it takes my breath away. *You* take my breath away."

"No doubt she does," put in Daphne, in a rather tart tone.

Zachary favored her with a blinding white smile, somehow brittle and more than a little condescending. "Don't be jealous, little one. It doesn't become you."

"Jealous!" sputtered Daphne, incensed, drawing nearer to Willow, as though to protect her from some dreadful fate. "That will be the day, Zachary Marshall. And since when do you frequent dress shops?"

"Since I walked by the window and caught a glimpse of my gloriously beautiful sister-in-law."

Daphne was as bristly as a porcupine.

"You'd do well to remember that that's *exactly* what Willow is — your brother's wife."

Willow, who had been watching this subtle, verbal fencing match in silence, now felt compelled to join the conversation. "Zachary knows I'm married to Gideon," she said, in hasty and lighthearted defense. "Don't you, Zachary?"

Zachary looked poetically wounded. "Oh, yes," he replied. "The fact of your matrimonial status allows me no rest; indeed, even in sleep it torments me."

"Oh, for heaven's sake!" snapped Daphne, jamming her hands hard onto her slender but womanly hips. "Aren't you overdoing this just a little, Zachary?"

Zachary's attention had again turned to Willow. "Will you be at the supper dance tonight?" he asked, for all the world as though they were alone. Daphne and Miss Collins, the dressmaker, might have been part of the woodwork, for all the notice he paid them.

Willow knew a moment of trepidation; to follow through with her plan was to play with fire. But follow through she must, if she was going to awaken Gideon to the fact that he could not treat her in any fashion he chose and then expect to be welcomed into her bed. "I'll be there."

"With Gideon, of course?"

"Quite alone, I'm afraid," countered Willow, in a distracted tone. Daphne's sidelong glance said clearly that Zachary wasn't the only one overdoing things around here. "You see, Gideon has asked Daphne to accompany him."

Zachary looked stunned, then hopeful. "I see," he said softly.

"Willow Marshall!" warned Daphne, flushing to the roots of her raven hair.

Every inch the cavalier, Zachary bowed low, his handsome face a study in knightly humility. "As Gideon's brother," he said, "I can but offer to rectify this shameful situation in the only possible way. Will you do me the honor, Willow, of attending the dance as my guest?"

This was what Willow had planned on, hoped for. Indeed, she had even considered approaching Zachary with the idea herself. Now, however, faced with the actual prospect of attending a public function on the arm of a man who was not her husband, she was nervous and more than a little reluctant. "Yes," she said firmly, determined to see the daring enterprise through to the end, however rash it might seem now. "I'm staying at my father's house."

"I know," said Zachary easily, touching the brim of his stylish hat. "I will call for you there at seven."

"Seven," confirmed Willow, her voice shaky.

Zachary kissed her hand, flung one triumphant look at the simmering Daphne, and turned to leave the dress shop.

The little bell jingled hard to mark his departure.

"Willow Marshall, you *are* a fool!" Daphne accused heatedly, turning on her friend with folded arms and angry lilac eyes. "Gideon will be livid when he finds out about this!"

"That is exactly what I want him to be," said Willow, with a lofty bravado that was almost wholly feigned. "Livid." Then she turned her attention to the dressmaker, who was very busy pretending not to have noticed the small drama that had just been played out in her cluttered little shop. "I'll take this dress, please."

"You don't understand — about Gideon and Zachary, I mean," Daphne persisted, practically atwitter with anxiety now. "Willow, they aren't like most brothers . . ."

Miss Collins hummed to herself, clearly delighted to make the sale, oblivious to the charge of anger arching between the two younger women, scurrying to fetch pins and a measuring tape.

Willow went into a curtained cubicle to change. Daphne, her face pale except for two splotches of bright crimson flowering on her cheekbones, accompanied her to help with buttons and other fastenings.

"Do you have any idea what you're starting, Willow?" she demanded, in a rather feverish-sounding whisper. "I'm not exaggerating when I tell you that there is bad blood between those two. They're more like enemies than brothers — their names might have been Cain and Abel, rather than Zachary and Gideon!"

Willow felt only the faintest flinch of alarm at Daphne's words before discounting them completely. She was fond of Coy and Reilly, her half brothers, and she adored Steven.

How could brothers be enemies? After all, blood was thicker than water, wasn't it?

"That's silly," Willow said, turning her back to step out of the dress.

They despise each other, Daphne repeated. "If you go through with this, someone is surely going to be hurt — perhaps even killed!"

A memory sniggled into Willow's mind; Gideon taking his gun belt down from its high shelf, the day he'd caught Vancel Tudd prowling near the pond. *You'd be surprised at what I'd gun a man down for, Zach,* he'd said.

Willow squared her shoulders, pulled her everyday dress back on over her head, and put aside her misgivings, turning her back so Daphne would fasten the buttons. Gideon and Zachary were *brothers,* despite any minor differences they might have.

Willow couldn't imagine that not mattering deeply to both of them.

"Do you think I should wear my hair up?" she asked, lifting the heavy tresses to survey the effect in the murky dressing room mirror. "Or should I have Maria curl it into ringlets?"

Daphne, whose flush of conviction had given way to pallor, only sighed and shook her head.

"What do you mean she's already left for the dance?" barked Gideon Marshall, taking no note of the fear he was inspiring in poor, timid Hilda, who had made the hapless mistake of answering the door.

Daphne, standing on the stairway of Judge Gallagher's house, worked up a brave smile. "Gideon, don't plague my cousin so. She's merely a guest in this house, as I am, and knows nothing of the intrigues that concern the rest of you."

Gideon, basically a chivalrous sort, subsided with an audible sigh. Hilda saw her chance and scampered off toward the kitchen and the safety of Maria's presence.

Daphne drew a deep breath and held on to the banister, in case the winds of Gideon's anger should blow her away. "I tried to reason with Willow, Gideon," she said quietly. "I really did. But she was angry about what happened last night and she wouldn't listen to me."

Color surged beneath Gideon's deep tan. "What are you trying to tell me, Daphne?" he demanded, turning his freshly brushed, round-brimmed hat in his hands.

"Willow went to the supper dance with Zachary," confessed Daphne, in a rush of carefully enunciated words.

Now Gideon paled. His eyes narrowed. "What?" he whispered.

"Please don't make me repeat it," Daphne said, not knowing whether to approach him or keep her distance. It wasn't that she was afraid of Gideon, but she sensed the strength of his emotions, knew that he wasn't merely angry, he was afraid.

"Son of a bitch!" rasped Gideon, half under his breath.

Daphne decided to be firm, and she came down the stairs rapidly, careful of her long, silken skirts. "What did you expect, Gideon, after the way you behaved last night?"

"I behaved rather well last night," he muttered, his tone bleak, his thoughts elsewhere.

Daphne remembered the rumpled bed she'd seen that morning and the flush in Willow's cheeks, but refrained from comment. "You asked me to go to the supper dance with you, Gideon, just to spite Willow. Now, I'm afraid, she's determined to spite you in return. You brought this on yourself."

Gideon's hand was already on the doorknob. "You didn't warn her?"

"I told Willow that you and Zachary are different from most brothers, and that this would be a mistake. What *else* was I supposed to say, Gideon? That you suspect your brother of all manner of secret sins, things I only know as hearsay?"

Gideon's aristocratically handsome face tightened for a moment, but then, with extraordinary self-control, he relaxed a little, even smiled.

"It appears that we have no choice, then, but to play by Willow's rules," he said. "Are you ready to leave?"

Daphne swallowed and nodded. With a gesture of one hand, she indicated her shawl, draped over one of the hooks on the coat tree there in the entryway.

Gideon brought it to her and set it gently over her shoulders.

Daphne looked up at him in trepidation and concern. "I hope you know," she said, "that you will only make this situation worse if you pretend that you still care for me."

"Pretend?" Gideon retorted smoothly, wearing his lawn-party smile. Daphne could almost smell freshly cut grass and hear the click of croquet balls. "I assure you that my attraction to you is not feigned, my dear. You are a very beautiful woman — not to mention a *good* one — and the man who eventually becomes your husband and fathers your children will be fortunate indeed."

Daphne rolled her eyes and took his offered arm. "Gideon, Gideon," she reprimanded, under her breath. "What will become of you?"

He smiled, but only faintly.

Together, they set out for the supper dance on foot, for the distance was short and the night was warm.

The reaction of the townspeople to Willow's wine-colored dress and unexpected escort was notable. It was also, considering all the times they'd slighted or ignored her, very satisfying.

Zachary drew his sister-in-law inordinately close for the first waltz of the evening. The dance hall was filled with noise and color and the enticing smells of the pies, cakes, and other delectable dishes brought by the local women. "They're all talking about you," he told Willow, in an intimate whisper.

"That's nothing new," she replied, drawing back from him a little way and looking around. "Do you see Daphne? She should be here by now."

Zachary grinned. "No. And I don't see Gideon, either. Perhaps they've worked out their differences and gone off to start anew."

Willow flinched slightly, then recovered herself. Daphne had, after all, categorically denied having any romantic feelings for Gideon, and her fascination with Steven, during his brief stay at the ranch house after his grievous injury at the hands of Red Eagle, had been obvious. "Zachary," she said directly, after yet another struggle with her conscience, "I must apologize. You see, the fact of the matter is that I'm using you."

"I know that," he answered smoothly, as they continued to dance.

She was stunned. Was she as transparent as that? "You know? And you aren't angry?"

"Of course I'm not angry. I'll stoop to any depths to spend time with you."

If she'd had any doubts before, now Willow knew for sure that she had gone too far. Although he'd spoken in a light tone, there had been a worrisome note to Zachary's words.

"I love Gideon," she reminded him. "I love him very, very much."

Zachary didn't miss a step. There was something in his eyes that made Willow feel out of her depth, even cornered. "Ah, but does Gideon love *you,* my dear? Will he do battle for you, or will he simply shrug and turn back to the fair Daphne? Or any one of the women he knows back home in San Francisco?"

Willow didn't miss his subtle emphasis on the words *back home* — the message was clear. Gideon didn't belong in the wild Montana Territory; he was a man of wealth and sophistication, used to the culture and the comforts of a major city.

She paused to collect her wits, then raised her chin a notch and countered, "What do you hope to gain by this, Zachary?"

"You've aroused my protective instincts, that's all," Zachary said easily. They were still dancing, and although Willow wanted to break away, she wasn't about to make a scene.

The gossip was bad enough as it was.

"Gideon is a grown man," Willow heard herself say, "quite capable of deciding where he wants to live, and he *did* buy a ranch right outside of town, after all. Furthermore, Daphne doesn't have any romantic feelings toward him."

Zachary arched one raven black brow. Still, the music went on. Still they danced.

"Gideon is extremely wealthy," Zachary said. "He owns property all over the map. As for Daphne and her sentiments, are you *sure* she doesn't care for my brother? The two of them have been a pair, in one way or another, since childhood."

"Of course I'm sure," whispered Willow, who, all of a sudden, was not sure at all. While she didn't believe for one moment that Daphne had been lying about the state of her affection for Gideon, she supposed it was possible that her friend had spoken in anger, or from bitter disappointment over the dashing of her own hopes.

In Daphne's place, loving a man the way Willow loved Gideon and then finding out that he'd been married to someone else all along would have left her devastated.

Zachary still wore a benign, satisfied

smile. One that made Willow want to slap him.

"I don't believe you *are* sure," he said. "And Gideon is very persuasive with the ladies, as I'm sure you would agree. Isn't it possible that my brother has been dallying with both of you?"

Willow remembered — nearly *relived* — making love with Gideon in the sun-spangled grass behind their house and blushed. There was no arguing with the fact that he was adept at getting his way. Even when she was wildly angry, as she had been only the night before, Gideon could get past her defenses with very little effort; he'd already demonstrated that more than once. It wasn't so hard to imagine that he might be just as successful with Daphne.

"Don't look now," Zachary said smugly, "but they're here, Gideon and Daphne, I mean. Little wonder that they're late."

The implication in Zachary's last words made Willow defy his warning and crane her neck to look. Daphne was a vision in pale blue silk, though her smile appeared a bit fixed, and Gideon stood tall and proud beside her, the last word in solicitous escorts. Seeing Willow, he nodded as though they had only a passing acquaintance and turned all his attention on Daphne.

"Thunderation," muttered Willow, into Zachary's fragrant neck.

At that point, Judge Gallagher brusquely cut in, waltzing his daughter well away from a surprised Zachary Marshall. "What the devil are you up to?" he demanded sharply. "And that dress. Did you borrow it from one of the dance-hall girls over at the Golden Feather Saloon?"

Willow worked up a faltering smile, relieved that her father had broken Zachary's strange spell over her, and stung because Daphne and Gideon looked so right together. "What am I *up to?*" she echoed innocently, hoping Devlin would mistake the tremor in her voice for mischief, rather than heartbreak. "Why, Papa, I can't imagine what you could possibly mean, saying such a thing —"

"Don't you 'Why, Papa' me, you little imp," Devlin broke in sternly. The set of his face was grim. "You're trying to make Gideon jealous, aren't you?"

Willow blushed. A lie would have been more prudent, but it was her private curse to blurt out the truth, whether the moment was opportune or not. "Yes."

Devlin thrust out a sigh of exasperation and shook his head. "That's foolish," he declared, though he did keep his voice low

318

under the lively flow of the music. "Now he'll feel obliged to return the favor."

Willow couldn't summon the spirit to argue the point. Between Zachary's warning and the sight of Gideon and Daphne together, her bravado had deserted her. "What shall I do?"

Devlin softened a little, and there was warmth in his eyes. "For a start, you could go to Gideon and tell him, straight out, what you were trying to do. And then you could go home and get into a dress that doesn't make you look like a hurdy-gurdy dancer!"

Willow didn't care for her father's suggestions, though she supposed they might have made sense to some people. She'd let the remark about borrowing her gown from a dance-hall girl pass, but saying she resembled a hurdy-gurdy dancer was going *too far.*

She stiffened, pressed her lips together, and stood stock still, glaring up into her father's face.

Devlin sighed again and shook his head. "I should have known you wouldn't listen," he said.

Willow's color was high. Insult heaped upon injury, that was the substance of her evening. And she'd looked forward to it so much, felt so womanly in her splendid velvet dress.

"You don't seem to object to dresses like this one when Dove Triskadden wears them!" she accused.

The music stopped, then started again. Someone sawed industriously on a fiddle, and people stepped lively all around Willow and her father, but neither one of them moved at all.

Devlin arched one eyebrow. "You're not Dove Triskadden, in case you've forgotten. And watch what tone you take with me, young lady. I can still send you off to find a switch."

Despite everything, Willow couldn't help smiling. In all her life, she'd never been spanked, but there had been one near miss, long ago. "Remember the last time?"

Devlin smiled. "How could I forget? I sent you to find a stick I could spank you with and you came back dragging a fence post!"

Willow was smug. "You didn't spank me, either — you were laughing too hard."

Devlin shook his head, his eyes dancing at the memory. "I figured an eleven-year-old with that much gumption ought to be let off with a warning."

Out of the corner of her eye, Willow saw Gideon whirl by with Daphne in his arms and felt subdued again. If she approached Gideon now, as her father had suggested, he would probably only laugh at her.

And that would be worse than anything.

"Oh, Papa," she sighed, "I've done it this time."

"I'm afraid so," agreed the judge, but his tone was tender and his eyes smiled at her. "Do you want me to talk to Gideon?"

The day when Devlin Gallagher could fight her battles for her was past, and Willow knew it. She shook her head and they finished the waltz in silence.

Overheated and tired of dancing to Gideon Marshall's tune, Daphne hurried outside. Hell's bells, had the whole town come to this affair? It certainly seemed so, but the grassy yard surrounding the dance hall was empty and quiet, and the breeze was deliciously cool.

Drawing in a deep breath of fresh air, Daphne wished that she'd been able to reason with Willow and Gideon and end this stupid game they were playing, once and for all. Alas, they were both as stubborn as a miner's mule.

Inside the hall, a new set was beginning. Daphne slipped into the shadows edging the porch, lest Gideon see her and insist they dance again. It was then that she saw the rider, sitting statue still on his horse, perhaps a dozen yards distant, the two of them bathed in moonlight.

Daphne's heart leaped into her throat. Steven? It *couldn't* be. Not now, not here.

Heedless of the dangers of approaching a stranger, on horseback or not, Daphne swept off the porch, skirts in hand, and marched forward.

"Steven?" she marveled, hardly able to believe her eyes when she was within a few steps of him.

He tilted his head slightly in suave acknowledgment. His fair hair shone silvery gold in the light of the summer moon. "Daphne," he replied in greeting, as calmly as if he hadn't endangered his freedom — possibly even his very life — by coming there.

She stared at him, amazed and stricken by emotions she'd never felt before, as he swung one leg over his saddle horn, gained his footing on the soft ground, and strode toward her.

"May I have this dance?" the outlaw asked, after executing one dashing bow.

"Are you insane?" fretted Daphne, breathless because her heart was bounding around inside her, now surging into her throat, now plummeting to her stomach.

The distant strains of a waltz came to them, over the whispering prairie grass, swirling around them, enclosing them like an embrace. They came together slowly, surely, as though they'd danced like this before at some point just beyond the reach of their memories.

In a dream, perhaps, or another lifetime.

When the music stopped, however, the strange magic shattered instantly. Daphne, ever practical, faced the dismal facts. Enthralled as she was by this magnificent man, he was a thief with a price on his head — a price that had been put there by her own father.

"Leave, Steven," she whispered. "Please — get out of here before someone sees you and . . ."

He was still holding her hand; his fingers, remarkably gentle fingers, moved idly over her knuckles, sending little molten shivers into every part of her. "Daphne —"

"No!" cried Daphne, as much to herself as to him. "Don't say it. Don't say anything at all, because I won't be able to bear it if you do!"

With that, she turned to flee for her life and for her sanity, only to be restrained and then wrenched full into Steven Gallagher's

323

broad chest. The impact took her breath away.

Moonlight glimmered in his eyes as well as his hair as he caught her chin in one hand and tilted it upward. In the next moment, he was kissing Daphne with a commanding sort of gentleness, molding her soft frame to his hard one with magical hands.

It wasn't easy, but after some concerted effort, Daphne finally broke away from his kiss. "Steven, I'm not one of your loose women. I . . ."

His hands, his brazen, strong hands, were still cupping her bottom, still holding her to the devastating evidence of his desire. He cocked his splendid head to one side and his smile was slow, sensuous, and very, very sad. "Come with me, Daphne," he said. "Right now. Tonight."

Daphne actually considered the suggestion. The idea of riding away with this man, on his horse, and surrendering to him in some isolated, moonlit place had definite appeal. "No," she answered. She might have been smitten — and worse — but she wasn't stupid.

"You're a virgin," Steven guessed, his hands kneading her plump, firm derriere.

Daphne flushed. "Of course I'm a virgin!" she sputtered. The frankness of country folk, she thought distractedly, was going to take some getting used to.

"I will love you gently," he said. "In fact, Daphne Roberts, I will make you plead for more."

Somewhere, Daphne found the strength to draw back one hand and slap Steven Gallagher's face, and soundly. "Of all the *arrogant,* ill-mannered, presumptuous —"

He arched an eyebrow, silently urging her to continue her quiet damnation. Laughter burned blue in his eyes.

Far away, in the dance hall, the music began again. Daphne realized, with horror, that Gideon would soon notice her absence and come in search of her, if he hadn't done so already.

"You've got to get away from here!" she said desperately, forgetting her ire, her indignation, and, partly anyway, her foolish yearning for this man. "Please, Steven, go now! I couldn't bear it if —"

"If they caught me?" he said, his lips perilously near her own again, drawing her. "But I'm arrogant and ill-mannered. Not to mention presumptuous. Surely you don't care if I hang —"

"Steven!" Daphne pleaded, and the word was a sob of terror.

He kissed her forehead. "You're staying at

my father's house, aren't you?" he asked.

Feverishly, Daphne nodded. What had she been thinking, tarrying here with a wanted man, allowing him to take such a risk? Dear Lord, if he didn't go, and go soon, someone was sure to see him.

Blithely, he patted her pulsing bottom with both hands. "Are you sharing a room with your homely cousin?" he inquired, as though they had all the time in the world.

"Yes!" she said. "Please —"

"I'll be waiting in the judge's stables, Daphne. When the dance is over, come to me."

Daphne would have agreed to almost anything by that time, so desperate was she to see this handsome, infuriating outlaw safe. "All right, all right!" she choked out, and then she turned and fled, and this time Steven made no move to stop her.

She had almost reached the dance hall before she dared to look back.

Steven had vanished.

Daphne sighed and looked up at the star-speckled sky, as if in search of a sign. She didn't have to meet Steven Gallagher in his father's stables; indeed, she would be a fool if she did, an utter fool. He was on the run, an enemy of her father's, and they certainly had no future together.

No doubt, deflowering her would be sport to him, nothing more.

Again, Daphne sighed. She could stand there and philosophize all she wanted, she knew. But when the dance was over and the Gallagher house was quiet, she would go to meet Steven.

"If you ever wear a dress like this in public again," Gideon intoned, his smile rock hard as he danced with his wife, "I will turn you over my knee!"

Willow was hurt, but she tossed her head defiantly and glared up into Gideon's face. "You'll have heart failure when you get the bill," she said. "Or, at least, I *hope* so."

The familiar muscle pulsed in his jawline. "You charged that getup to me?" he said through his splendid and tightly clenched teeth. "Good. That gives me the right to tear it to shreds."

"You wouldn't dare, Gideon Marshall!"

"Watch me, hellcat."

Willow felt tears burning in her eyes. "I thought you would like this gown," she said, unable to hide her feelings. "I thought I looked — well — rather nice in it."

Gideon's face gentled, and he held her just a little closer. "Oh, you look a lot better than rather nice," he assured her.

"Then, why — ?"

He reached up and touched the tip of her nose with an index finger. "Hush," he interrupted quietly. "I'm trying to explain my churlish and reprehensible behavior, here."

Willow only looked at him, waiting, praying that this cruel and foolish game they played could be ended.

Gideon smiled, maneuvering her toward the open door and the privacy outside the dance hall. Gripping her hand, he led her across the shadowy porch and toward a familiar buggy. Reaching that, he lifted Willow into the seat and climbed up beside her.

"Willow, I know that one person can't own another," he said raggedly. "I know it and yet I try to own you, and I'm sorry."

"What does that have to do with my dress?" she asked, truly confused and still a little hurt.

She loved that dress.

Loved the way she looked and felt wearing it.

Gideon caught one of her hands between both of his own, there beneath the dark canopy of the buggy. "Everything," he confessed. "Willow, I try to be objective about you, I really do. But when you wear something like that and other men are looking at you, seeing everything but your tonsils . . ."

Willow blushed and swallowed hard. "You *were* jealous," she said, and though that had been her end, there seemed to be no satisfaction in the knowledge that she had achieved it.

"Jealous?" he drawled. "God, that is a pitiably inadequate word for what I felt! The only time I had any peace this whole night was when you were dancing with your father."

Having said that, he took up the reins, released the brake with a motion of one booted foot, and urged the single horse into motion.

He drove in silence until they were out of town, hidden in a copse of trees. The creek flowing past — Willow had always known that creek — seemed strange and somehow magical.

Willow was conscious of Gideon, more conscious than she'd been even on the dance floor, when he had held her so close. "I'm sorry," she said, and the tears on her face were audible in her voice.

"Why?" chided Gideon in a tender whisper.

"I was hoping to make you jealous."

Gideon smiled. "I guess we're even, then,"

he said. He hooked a finger in the neckline of her velvet dress — which was suddenly a bit too warm for comfort, just as Daphne had warned it would be. "It's a wonder you didn't fall right out of that thing," he teased. "Half the town was probably praying you would."

Willow gave an involuntary, sniffling laugh. "Were you hoping that, Gideon?"

He chuckled. "Yes. But I was going to shoot the first man who looked."

"A-are you really going to tear up my dress?"

"Ummm," he replied hoarsely, considering. "Definitely not. I want you to wear it for me. And not wear it for me." Gideon set the brake lever again, then let go of the reins. The patient old horse bent its head to graze on sweet grass sprinkled with stray shards of moonlight.

"W-what about Daphne?" Willow asked.

"What about her?" retorted Gideon, his right hand coming to rest on the full softness of Willow's left thigh.

"You can't just go off and leave her at the dance —"

"Seems to me I've already done that," Gideon said. He seemed to be looking at her mouth with great interest, as though it had qualities he'd never noticed before.

Then, mumbling, he added, "Don't worry. Devlin will see Daphne home when the dance is over."

Unaccountably nervous, Willow intertwined her fingers in her lap.

Their house was in the opposite direction.

Gideon smiled and took in the dancing leaves of the cottonwood trees all around them. They were completely alone, but because they faced the broad spring moon, the interior of the buggy was filled with silver light.

"Fall out of your dress, Mrs. Marshall," he said quietly.

Willow sat very still, transfixed, staring at this man who had such incredible power over her.

"Now," he added, in companionable tones.

Fingers trembling with desire and with a rebellion that would not quite come to life, Willow reached up and took hold of the daring neckline of her gown. A slight downward pull made her lush breasts spill out, milky white in the moonlight.

Gideon drew in his breath and tentatively touched one of the crimson buttons that awaited him with the tip of one finger. "Mine," he said, and he sounded wonder stricken rather than proprietary.

Willow quivered as keen pleasure shot through every part of her. "Yes," she answered. "Yours."

Gideon bent, scraped the pulsing morsel with gentle teeth. "Only mine," he prompted.

Willow felt her body preparing itself to accommodate, to welcome him. "Yes," she conceded, breathing the word instead of speaking it. Dear God, how was it possible to want a man so desperately, against all reason and good sense?

Swiftly, Gideon positioned her so that she was facing him, kneeling, astraddle his lap, on the narrow buggy seat. With another motion of his teeth, he claimed the untested bud, stirred it to a fiery hardness. "Let your hair down," he ordered.

Willow shivered, and when she reached up with both hands to unpin her heavy hair, he caught the nipple he'd been toying with between his lips and attended it with his tongue. With his left hand, Gideon caught her wrists together at the back of her head.

"Gideon," she whimpered, deliciously vulnerable.

He worked her hair free of its pins, somehow, but retained his firm hold on her wrists. "Lean back, little pagan, and let me feast."

Willow groaned, resisting.

But Gideon's hand had found its way under her voluminous skirts, inside her satiny drawers. With a gentle thrust, he claimed her. "Lean back," he repeated.

And this time Willow obeyed.

Gideon bent his head to take suckle at one breast, delved deep with his fingers, and plied her to a brutal, scalding release with the pad of his thumb. Her throaty cries obviously pleased him.

Soon enough, though, it came Willow's turn to rule. Kneeling on the floor of the buggy, brazenly undoing the nearly bursting buttons of his trousers, she had her way with Gideon Marshall, and had it well.

And afterward, they went home to their little house.

The night was long and sweet and neither Gideon nor Willow slept a wink.

13

Maria greeted Willow in the Gallagher kitchen the next morning, her smile as bright as the sunlight streaming in through the windows. "What are you doing here so early?" she asked, in kindly surprise. "Last night, the judge told me you'd gone home with your husband when the dance was about to be over."

It didn't surprise Willow that her father had taken note of her departure the night before.

"I'm here because Gideon had business in town, and I wanted to see Daphne — and Hilda, of course."

Maria, seeming a little distracted, took a cup and saucer down from the cupboard and poured coffee for Willow.

Willow blushed a little and sat down at the kitchen table. It struck her, not for the first time, what an odd thing it was to feel like a visitor in this house, this dear house that had been, until Gideon, the only real home she'd ever had. Even with Evadne there, the place had been a refuge.

"Papa did bring Daphne home from the dance last night, didn't he?" Willow asked. It was her understanding that shy and reticent Hilda had preferred to stay behind, reading in the guest room she and Daphne shared.

"*Sí,*" replied Maria, but there definitely *was* a perplexed shadow in the depths of her dark eyes.

"What is it, Maria?"

Maria sighed and shrugged her thick shoulders. "It is Señor Steven. He was here, *chiquita.*"

Willow set her cup back in its saucer with a nervous rattle. "Here? In this house?"

"No." Maria shook her head ruefully, and her blue-black hair glinted in a shaft of sunlight from the windows. "He came to the stables. And the señorita — Miss Roberts — I believe she went to him there."

Worried for Daphne, angry that Steven would take such a brazen chance, Willow bit her lower lip and paled. "Oh, Maria, you don't suppose —"

"*Sí,*" said Maria sadly. "Something must have happened between them. The señorita cries much when she is back in the house."

335

"Did you go to her, Maria?"

"No. What was there for me to say, little one? I could not tell the señorita that things would be all right, because I know that they won't. Not if she throws in her lot with an outlaw."

Now it was Willow who shook her head. Her coffee forgotten, she rose out of her chair and started up the back stairs. Moments later, she was knocking softly at Daphne's door.

"Come in," said Daphne, in a thick, miserable voice.

She sounded nothing like her normal, confident self.

Willow opened the door and paused uncertainly just inside. Where was Hilda? Probably out for one of her early-morning constitutionals.

Biting her lower lip, Willow wondered how to broach the subject of her brother in a diplomatic way.

Daphne, her eyes swollen and red, sat up in her bed and blurted out, "You know what happened — don't tell me you don't, because I can see it in your face."

"Yes," answered Willow, frozen in the doorway. "I think I know."

At this, Daphne burst into tears.

Willow was able to move again; she hur-

336

ried to the bedside, sat down, and pulled her friend into her arms.

Daphne sobbed, childlike, into the shoulder of Willow's calico dress.

"Go back to San Francisco, Daphne," she whispered, when she was sure the worst of the outburst had passed, feeling this other woman's pain and confusion as keenly as if they were her own. "Buy a train ticket and go home, while you still can."

"I couldn't," Daphne sniffled. "Oh, Willow, how could I bear to go, after-after . . ." A great shudder went through her, and she began to cry again, harder than before.

"After Steven?" Willow asked gently.

Daphne nodded into Willow's shoulder, sniffling. "Oh, Willow, I love him and I . . . last night —"

"I know," said Willow, in complete sympathy. Lord knew, Daphne's obvious assignation with Steven had been ill-advised, but after her own experiences with Gideon, Willow Marshall was in no position to stand in judgment. "But you must leave, Daphne. If you don't, this will happen again. And what if there was a child?"

Daphne looked up, her wet eyes flashing now, darkened to purple by the intensity of her feelings. "I don't care. I won't go — I can't!"

Willow felt rage, not toward Daphne, but toward her handsome, charming, and totally irresponsible brother. What had he been thinking of to do something like this? Weren't his notorious women enough? "Did Steven ask you to meet him again?"

"Yes," Daphne admitted, after a few moments of moist hesitation. "Tonight."

"Where, Daphne? Tell me where."

"Do you mean to tell Gideon?"

"Of *course* not. But I've got a few things to say to that brother of mine, and say them I will!"

Daphne drew out of Willow's embrace and covered her face with both hands. "It was so wonderful, Willow, and leaving him was so awful . . ."

Some of Willow's angry impatience spilled over in Daphne's direction. "Awful? If you think it was awful after one night, Daphne Roberts, just think how awful it will be if it becomes a way of life. Do you really want to wait in some shack, while Steven robs your father's trains, knowing all the while that he might never come back? Do you want to be alone all the time, and hunted, possibly even named a criminal in your own right? Do you want to share all that sorrow and misery and danger with an innocent little baby, Daphne?"

Willow knew, of course, what that sort of life was really like, because she'd lived it, in the years before Steven brought her to their father's house.

"It wouldn't be like that," moaned Daphne, but her wide, hollow eyes belied her words.

"It would," Willow insisted, "and *worse*, too. Steven carries on with half a dozen different women, Daphne, although I'm sure he's sworn his undying devotion. You would have to share him, sooner or later." At the look of protest rising in her friend's face, she went on. "And even if that didn't bother you, what about the danger you yourself would represent to him?"

"Danger?" Daphne frowned, dashing away her tears with the back of one hand. "What-what do you mean?"

"I mean, Daphne, that a lot of people are looking for Steven. There's a bounty on his head. And that means that every time you came to town, for any reason, someone would try to follow you back to him."

Daphne paled. "My God."

"Go home, Daphne," Willow pleaded earnestly, taking her friend's hands in her own. "For your sake and Steven's, I beg you to get on today's train and go home to the life and the people you know."

"I won't," Daphne reiterated, tight-jawed, after a brief period of solemn reflection. "Hilda wants to leave — she says this is the back of beyond, not a fit place for civilized people — but I'm staying right here."

"Daphne!"

"I'm staying!"

Willow sighed and stood up to leave the room. "Then there isn't anything more to say, is there?"

"Will you still be my friend, Willow?"

Willow paused in the doorway. "It's because I'm your friend that I begged you to leave, Daphne. I want you to tell me where you're supposed to meet Steven tonight."

Daphne blanched and bit her lower lip. "The p-pond. The one near your house."

Willow trembled. "God in heaven, that fool! Gideon will be —"

Daphne stiffened, and her eyes were wide with alarm. "You must keep Gideon from knowing. Willow, *he mustn't* get word of this, no matter what!"

"How do you expect me to do that, Daphne?" snapped Willow, in a whisper. "Steven may be an idiot, but believe me, Gideon isn't. If Steven sets foot on our land, he'll know it. And if I try to distract him, he'll guess instantly what reason I have for doing that!"

"Then what are we to do?" choked Daphne, in near panic. "Steven *will* come to that pond, Willow!"

"Yes, he'll be there," Willow conceded, in exasperation. "But he won't find you waiting. No, *I'll* meet Steven, and it will be up to you to keep Gideon away."

Daphne sucked in a breath. "However will I do *that?*" she demanded. "It isn't as if Gideon Marshall does my *bidding,* you know."

"The 'how' part is your problem, I'm afraid," Willow answered succinctly. And then she left the bedroom, closing the door behind her.

Back in the kitchen, she related the essentials of the problem to Maria.

"You must go to your papa without delay and tell him everything!" advised the housekeeper, every bit as frantic as Daphne had been minutes before, and as Willow felt in that moment, although she hid it well. "The judge would never betray Steven, and he is wise — he'll know what to do."

"I hesitate to do that, Maria. Papa and Steven don't get along at all —"

"If you do not tell your father," Maria warned, "*I will.* This is the choice I am giving you — either you ask for the judge's help, or I do."

Willow knew by Maria's tone and manner

341

that she'd made up her mind, and no power, either on earth or in heaven, could change it. She took a few moments to absorb the realization; then, with her shoulders slumping, she started toward the door. Another time, she might have been angry with Maria, might have felt that the woman was betraying her trust. Now, however, she knew her dear friend was right. Cursing Steven, Willow went outside, reclaimed her horse and buggy from Juan, and turned the rig toward the main part of town.

She found her father in his office, immersed in a stack of documents.

Seeing her standing in the doorway, he pulled off his reading glasses and assessed her solemnly.

"What are you doing here?" he asked, straight out. Willow did not often visit her father's office and, besides, he probably saw something in her face.

She was so very worried.

Judge Gallagher stood, rounded his desk, and took his daughter lightly but firmly by one elbow, squiring her to a chair and sitting her down. She wondered if he'd felt the trembling she couldn't seem to suppress.

"Tell me," he ordered gruffly, once he was seated in his own chair again.

Willow blushed a little as she alluded to Steven and Daphne's assignation in the stables the night before, and went on to say that the two had planned a second meeting for that very evening, beside the pond on Gideon's ranch.

In truth, Willow hated revealing all this, because it was so embarrassingly personal, but she knew Maria hadn't been bluffing. If Willow hadn't told her father the truth herself, the housekeeper would have done it.

"Great Zeus," Devlin exclaimed hoarsely, when Willow had related the situation in its entirety. "Your brother must be suffering from brain fever or something."

Willow bit her lip and nodded in teary-eyed agreement. She had always been uncomfortable in her father's downtown office, mainly because it was situated above the jailhouse. Now that Gideon was the marshal, having taken over poor Mitch Kroeber's job for the present, her unease was worse. "Papa, what are we going to do?"

"I'll tell you this much," blustered the judge, pacing the length of his small, cluttered office, "it won't be either you *or* Daphne who meets Steven by the pond tonight. By God, he'll find me there, and he'll give an accounting for all of this!"

"Papa, you know how stubborn he is," Willow protested. "You could lecture him all night long and he'd just go right on doing as he pleases!"

The judge stopped and gave a despairing and ragged sigh. "You're right," he conceded, after a time, "but I've got to try."

Suddenly, they heard the sound of boots pounding up the outside stairs from the street below. "Judge! Judge Gallagher!" shouted a masculine voice. "Judge Gallagher!"

Devlin frowned as Charlie Hennings, the blacksmith, threw open the door and erupted into the office. "What the devil?"

Charlie was pale, but excitement glimmered in his eyes, too. "He got 'em," he said, sparing a brief glance for Willow and then stepping back onto the threshold at the expression on her father's face. "By God, Tudd got 'em!"

Willow felt as if the floor had disappeared from beneath her; she was in free fall.

"Who, damnit?" demanded the judge hoarsely, though he must surely have known the horrible answer as well as Willow did.

"Your boy and them two what rode with him, that's who," Charlie said, and then he must have thought better of staying, because he turned and fled back down the stairs.

Devlin bolted after him, only to pause in the open doorway. "Willow?" he rasped, remembering, looking back at her. "Are you all right?"

Willow sat upright in her chair, breathing deeply. She had known this day, this moment, would come, but knowing had not prepared her for the shock of it. The room shifted and swayed around her and the tears clustering in her throat and spilling down her face were scalding hot. She dismissed her father with a motion of one hand.

He understood and clattered away from her.

Willow remained still, certain that if she moved a single muscle, she would fall to pieces — pieces that would not ever fit together again.

She heard nothing, she saw nothing beyond the images spinning at the forefront of her mind. Hand over hand, she made her way from one heartbeat to the next.

She sensed Gideon's presence long before he spoke to her. He took her hand. "Willow?" he whispered. "Sweetheart?"

A tremor went through Willow. She didn't look directly at Gideon, though she knew he was crouching in front of her chair, their fingers interlaced.

"Steven?" she asked dully, barely breathing the name.

"I'm sorry," Gideon said. "He's dead, Willow. So are the others."

Willow swallowed hard, still unable to meet Gideon's gaze, knowing that if she did, she would probably tumble head over heels into helpless grief.

"Coy and Reilly," she said. "Their names were Coy and Reilly Forbes. My half brothers."

"Let me take you home," Gideon said, straightening, but never letting go of her hand. Instead, he pulled her up with him, gathered her close against his chest. She could feel his heart beating, strong and true.

But Steven's heart, Coy's and Reilly's — they were forever stilled.

Suddenly, Willow's control splintered. She tore herself from Gideon's arms, ran for the door, started down the steps, and nearly fell because she couldn't see for her tears.

Gideon was close behind, but he didn't try to stop her.

A hot breeze blew, and dust devils whirled along the street. A crowd had gathered, and yet the silence was profound, and it was dense, and it thudded against Willow from all sides, like it would smother her.

Three horses stood wearily at the hitching post in front of the jailhouse. And over their saddles lay the lifeless bodies of Coy, Reilly — and Steven.

Devlin stood with his forehead resting against the side of Steven's horse, one hand on his son's back. Sickness burned in Willow's throat as she forced her way past the spectators to reach her father's side.

"The hood," Judge Gallagher choked out, when he'd straightened again, possibly for Willow's sake, tears slipping down his face as he took in the cloth bag that covered Steven's head.

Vancel Tudd looked quietly apologetic. "I'm right sorry about that, Judge. Right sorry. Bullet hit him right between the eyes, though, and it seemed the only decent thing to do; you wouldn't want to see . . ."

Willow cried out and started toward Steven's body, only to be restrained from behind. Gideon's arms were like steel bands around her waist and she didn't have the strength or the spirit to break free.

"No," he whispered into her hair, and the sound was raw and hoarse, like a sob. "No, Willow, don't. It's over. Please — let me take you home. There's nothing you can do here."

"Where'd ya hit this one?" a drifter asked Vancel Tudd, pointing to Coy as though he were a game animal instead of a human being.

"Through the heart," said Tudd, chewing on his tobacco. "Same with the other 'un."

"Fine shootin'," remarked another man, and something broke within Willow, something that gave her the impetus she needed to tear herself loose from Gideon's grasp.

"You vultures!" she screamed, to the town in general. "You filthy vultures! They never hurt any of you — the railroad wanted them alive."

Gently, Gideon caught her elbow, turned her. His face was ravaged. "Willow, please, don't. Don't do this to yourself."

Willow remembered then that this man — God, he seemed a total stranger now, for all their intimacies — had taken up the badge, had sworn to find Steven, and all for his blasted railroad. She began to kick and claw, screaming hysterically.

And Gideon made no move to defend himself. He just looked at her, his broken soul reflected in his eyes, enduring the assault in silence. It was the judge who finally restrained her.

From somewhere in the pulsing fog of horror and utter desolation surrounding Willow in those moments, Vancel Tudd said, "I reckon I don't qualify for that double bounty you offered, Marshal."

Double bounty? Willow struggled in her father's firm embrace, wanting to attack Gideon again, wanting to kill him. When the judge wouldn't let her go, she spat at her husband's feet and gasped, "I'll see you in hell for this, Gideon Marshall!"

Gideon's face contorted; he extended one hand and muttered her name.

"Not now," interceded the judge coldly, and even though Willow could not see her father's face, she knew that his gaze, like her own, was fixed on Gideon. "We'll look after our own."

Men were lifting the three bodies from the backs of the horses and carrying them away. And as Devlin tried to guide Willow toward home, she glared back at Gideon, and spat again, cursing the man with her eyes and her heart and her whole being. "Judas!" she cried in parting.

Gideon knew that Willow, his wife, was there, in that house. A primitive part of him wanted to rip the place apart, wall by wall, with his bare hands, to uncover her and gather her to him and comfort her.

Another, wiser part counseled him to keep his distance, leave well enough alone, at least for now. Willow was in her room upstairs and, as distraught as she was, she was safe there.

So he concentrated on Daphne, who sat trembling and white as the first snow of winter, on a settee in the Gallaghers' seldom-used parlor. Maria hovered nearby, weeping silent tears and wringing her hands.

She started for the stairs, stopped, stood in the parlor doorway again.

"No!" cried Daphne, looking small and broken, like a bird with an injured wing. "No, it can't be true, Gideon! You're lying to me. You're only saying that Steven is dead because you want me to go home. You're —"

"Steven is dead, Daphne," Gideon insisted, casting one glance at a very distraught Hilda, who sat straight-backed beside Daphne, one arm around her cousin's waist, trying to be strong. "There's nothing you can do to change that. Get your belongings together, and I'll take you and your cousin to the depot. You can still catch the afternoon stage to Helena if you hurry, and catch a train in the morning. You belong in San Francisco, not here."

Hilda, who could have made a mud fence look good, especially with her eyes swollen from sympathetic weeping and all the color gone from her face, nodded in helpless agreement.

But Daphne wasn't so inclined to be reasonable.

"No," she objected, shaking her head. "I'm supposed to meet Steven tonight."

Gideon took her shoulders in his hands. "Steven is dead," he said, yet again. He'd seen the body and yet he would have had to admit, if pressed, that he, too, found it hard to believe.

He had encountered Steven only briefly, in the peddler's disguise, but he remembered how vibrant Willow's brother had been — like he was just a shade more alive than everybody else.

At Daphne's statement — she still expected to meet Steven — Hilda began to wail, a heartrending sound, reminding Gideon of an animal in pain.

"Daphne," Gideon said.

"Leave me!" Daphne cried, slapping away his hands when he reached for her. "I won't listen to your lies! *Steven Gallagher loves me, and he is* not *dead.*"

"Hilda," Gideon said, encircling Daphne with both arms, holding her by force as she struggled, "get the trunks ready, please."

Hilda hurried away and Daphne gave one cry of pain and protest and then seemed to collapse against Gideon's chest, sobbing wretchedly. It was horrible to hear. He held her, though, until the first storm of grief had passed.

Willow's head ached and there seemed to be a hollow place where her soul had been. The bright summer sun, always such a joy to her, seemed garish now. It was mid-afternoon, and Steven and Coy and Reilly had been dead for one full day.

She entered the undertaker's establishment with her chin held high.

"I would like to view the bodies," she said, dry-eyed and empty.

The undertaker was a heavy, balding man, and the front of his shirt was sweat stained. "Right down the street, Mrs. Marshall," he said, shuffling papers on his desk and keeping his eyes averted.

"Down the street? What?"

"They was outlaws, ma'am," the mortician reminded her, in tones that were at once whiny and dismissive. "You wanna see them, that's just fine. They're in front of your husband's office."

Sick, Willow turned on her heel and hurried back outside into the cruel sunshine and the breeze that failed to comfort. She had forgotten, in her shock, the gruesome custom of putting the bodies of transgressors on public display.

The wages of sin, she thought.

Sure enough, Steven, Coy, and Reilly were strapped to boards and propped up on the wooden sidewalk outside the marshal's office — Gideon's office — facing the street. Coy and Reilly, whose heads had not been covered, stared blankly into eternity, their faces bloated and grayish blue.

Heedless of the bustling photographer who was setting up his huge box camera a few feet away, Willow calmly approached her dead brothers. Tenderly, she reached up and closed Coy's eyes, and then Reilly's.

She had not been close to them, these children her mother had borne Jay Forbes, between Steven's birth and Willow's own. But they had no one else in the world to mourn them; she and Steven had been their only kin.

They would have followed him anywhere — and here was the proof.

Both of them were dead.

"Willow?"

Like a sleepwalker, Willow turned to see who had spoken to her. Norville Pickering stood at her elbow, looking like the newspaper editor he was, his pencil and notepad in hand, his face shaded by the green visor he wore.

"Are you writing everything down for your father's newspaper, Norville?" she asked, in a voice that didn't sound like her own. "Have you made space in this week's edition for an accounting of their sins — Steven's and Coy's and Reilly's?"

Norville sighed and reached tentatively for her arm but drew back at the look of warning the motion brought. "I thought your father took you home," he offered miserably, his Adam's apple jumping up and down in his throat.

Was it possible that he *felt sorry* for her? It would have been easier somehow, Willow thought bleakly, if he'd gloated instead of showing sympathy.

"He did," answered Willow, in that same lifeless voice and with a lift of her chin. "But that was yesterday. Obviously I didn't stay put."

"Let me take you back there now, please? You don't belong here, you shouldn't see —"

"What shouldn't I see, Mr. Pickering? That the wages of sin is death?" She paused, the wind ruffling her skirts, and then went on. "Are you going to write about me, my deepest personal thoughts — especially in my sorrow? After all, they'll every single one, the people of this dreadful town, come to stare at the bodies and shake their heads and say that God is not mocked."

"Willow!" rasped Norville. "Please — let me take you home. Right now."

Gideon had said virtually the same thing the day before.

Why did everyone seem to think that going home was the answer?

Would that undo her loss, her father's loss? And Daphne's?

"Step aside!" grumbled the traveling photographer, a fat man sweating in a too-tight suit, from the dusty street. "I have pictures to take, and the light will be gone pretty soon."

Willow whirled on the man, suddenly alive again, and crackling like a bolt of lightning. She lunged toward the rotund stranger and overturned his camera, a great black box supported by a wooden tripod, stomping on the lens with one foot and then the other, knowing enormous, broken satisfaction as the apparatus caved in.

"Stop that," bellowed the photographer. "Damnit, that's an expensive piece of equipment!"

Willow ground her heel into the last gleaming shards of the lens. The glass made a crunching sound and then spread into a veined web.

And changed nothing.

Nothing at all.

Steven was still gone.

Coy and Reilly, too. Any chance they'd had of turning their lives around, of marrying and having children and living like decent men, was lost for good. And they'd had that in them, her stepbrothers, the capacity to change.

At a word from Steven, they would have forsworn their outlaw ways.

Now, they would never get that chance.

Livid over the destruction of his equipment, the portly photographer made a grab for Willow, only to be forestalled by a most unlikely champion — Norville Pickering. Trying to hold back the furious daguerreotypist and keep Willow away from the camera at the same time, he bellowed, "For God's sake, somebody go fetch Judge Gallagher or the marshal!"

"Get that little she-cat off my camera!" screamed the photographer.

Willow bunched her skirts in both hands and jumped up and down on the already shattered black box in much the same way she'd jumped on beds as a child.

"That cost a hundred dollars!" came the outraged protest.

Suddenly, one strong arm encircled Willow's waist, held her tight against a rock-hard hip. She kicked and struggled and shrieked, but to no avail. This time, Gideon wasn't going to let down his guard for so much as a moment.

His narrowed eyes were fixed on Norville and the nearly apoplectic man he was trying to restrain. "I'll pay for the camera," he said evenly.

"Well and good!" roared the photographer. "But what about my pictures of the Gallagher gang? How the hell am I supposed to get my goddamned pictures?"

A crowd had gathered by this time; probably, the townspeople had been watching the drama unfold for several minutes already, but Willow hadn't noticed them until now.

Without even glancing at the wife he was holding prisoner with one arm, Gideon answered coldly, "I guess you're just out of luck this time." His gaze sliced to the two men who stood nearest. "Get these bodies in off the street. Now."

"But, Marshal, we always —"

"Get them in," Gideon ordered.

Looking petulant, the men moved to do as they were bid, and the mob of onlookers began to disperse. Norville bent to pick up his spectacles, which had fallen off during the scuffle, and the photographer blustered, "I'll be by for that hundred dollars, Marshal!"

"Fine," answered Gideon, and the thwarted picture taker went off, grumbling, toward the nearest saloon.

"Let me go!" Willow finally managed to sputter. Her feet were still well off the ground, and Gideon's arm felt like a giant steel manacle circling her waist.

Gideon held her easily, seemingly paying her no attention at all. "Norville?"

Norville straightened, his spectacles crooked on his nose. He blinked several times. "Yes?"

"Thank you," Gideon said. "Thank you for looking after my wife."

Norville glanced at Willow's flushed, furious face and smiled sadly. "You're welcome, Marshal," he said, and then, embarrassed, he turned and sprinted back toward the newspaper office.

"Take your hands off me, Gideon Marshall," Willow seethed.

Coldly obliging, Gideon released his hold, and Willow nearly collapsed, her legs were so bloodless, so weak.

"Go home, Willow," Gideon said as she turned on him.

"Don't you tell me what to do, you, you

wretched, bloodthirsty . . ."

Gideon's eyes never left Willow's face, but his hand rose to the star-shaped badge on his coat and deftly unpinned it. "You will go home," he bit out, "and you will stay there, Mrs. Marshall, until I come for you."

"The hell I will!"

"The hell you won't. Move your bustle, my dear, before I forget everything you've been through today, haul you into my office, and turn you across my knee!"

Something in Gideon's eyes gave Willow pause, and she bit down on the rebellious words that sprang to her lips. "My brothers are dead," she said woodenly, without intending to.

"Yes," Gideon replied, his gaze still locked with hers.

Neither one moved, or spoke, for a long moment.

Then Willow said, "T-thank you for making those men take them inside, Gideon. It isn't right, everybody looking at them."

Gideon didn't respond. He just nodded. But everything he felt — the despair, the regret, the pity Willow didn't want — was in his eyes.

"I want to see my brothers." Willow threw the words into the silence and they seemed to crackle in the weighted air, with its strong scent of blood and death and, already, decay. "Please. Just once, before — before they're buried."

He extended one hand. "All right," he said, and then he ushered Willow inside his office, where Steven, Coy, and Reilly lay now on the floor of the marshal's office. They were still strapped to their wooden slabs.

Hilda stood blubbering in Virginia City's tiny depot, overcome by her second devastating experience in the West. "Please, Daphne," she wailed, over the steam whistle of the approaching train. "Don't make me go back to San Francisco all alone. What if there's another robbery along the way? What if —"

"Hush," Daphne broke in, quite gently, squeezing her cousin's plump hands in an attempt to reassure her. She was calmer, Daphne was, now that she knew it was impossible.

Steven Gallagher could not possibly be dead.

She loved him too much for that to be true.

"You'll be perfectly safe, Hilda," she told her cousin.

"Not when your father finds out that I left

you here, I won't!"

Daphne sighed, too spent to argue. "God-speed, Hilda. And please tell Papa that I'll be all right in Virginia City."

"All right!" prattled Hilda, her color darkening to a mottled red. "Daphne Roberts —"

"All aboard!" shouted the train conductor.

Steam from the great, coal-fed engine billowed around him.

"Good-bye," insisted Daphne firmly, kissing her cousin's moist cheek. "God go with you, Hilda."

Knowing that she would be left behind if she continued to plead, and that such pleading was entirely in vain, Hilda reluctantly boarded the outbound train, a handkerchief pressed to her face.

Daphne watched as the train pulled out, waving long after she couldn't see Hilda anymore. Then, slowly, she turned back toward the main part of town.

His sobs, deep and dry and raw, tore at Dove Triskadden like the claws of some merciless beast. What words could she offer Devlin, now that the inevitable had finally happened, now that his only son was dead?

There were none, of course. Dove could

do nothing more than hold her man in her arms and share his pain. And as great as that suffering was, she would have borne it gladly, if Devlin could have been spared.

He pulled away from her, just far enough to brace his head in his hands, and Dove stroked his broad, heaving shoulders with tender hands and looked deeply into his tormented eyes.

"He was wearing a hood — shot in the face," he mourned.

"I know, Devlin," Dove murmured, stroking his hair. "I know."

"They're glad. All those leering, gutless squirrels are glad it happened, glad Tudd shot my boy."

Dove knew he was referring to the townspeople. "No, Devlin," she said. "Not the ones who matter."

"Evadne would have been glad. She hated Steven —"

"Shhhh," Dove said. She continued to soothe this man she loved more than she could have loved herself or, God forgive her, a child they conceived together. She felt the muscles in Devlin's powerful shoulders begin to go slack as, almost against his will, he began to give up the fight. "You don't mean that, Dev. You know you don't. Evadne was doing the best she could to get by, just like the rest of us."

"I looked for my son for years. Did you know I looked for him, Dove? And he didn't believe I cared. Steven — my own son — didn't believe I cared."

"He knew, sweetheart."

"No! He died thinking that his own father didn't give a damn what became of him."

Dove drew back on Devlin's shoulders and he came to rest against her generous bosom like a child, broken by his loss. "Shhh," she said softly. "Shhh."

The room was shadowy and, because of the heat, beginning to smell. Willow passed Coy and Reilly, having said her fare-thee-wells to them, to stand beside the hooded figure that had once been Steven — her beautiful, errant Steven. God in heaven, what would the world be like without her dashing, chivalrous brother, without his friendship and his laughter and his love?

It didn't bear thinking about.

It didn't bear facing.

Tears misted Willow's eyes as she took Steven's limp hand in her own, smoothed the cold, rock-hard flesh repeatedly with her thumb. Something quickened within her, inexplicably, and she looked down at the bloodied hood that hid the dear, handsome face, then at the hand she had been holding.

"Thunderation," Willow whispered, and, after tossing one glance toward the outer office, where Gideon and the undertaker were waiting, she slowly unbuttoned Steven's soiled shirt.

The loud crash jolted Gideon right down to his raw, aching soul. He bounded out of his desk chair and pushed past the undertaker to enter the room where the bodies had been laid out.

Willow was lying on the floor in a faint.

Gideon gave an involuntary cry and knelt to draw her into his arms. "Water," he rasped, to the gaping undertaker. "Get some water."

She stirred against him, whimpering softly. "Steven," she said.

And Gideon let his face fall to her hair, weeping into its softness. It was over now, it was over. And he had lost her forever.

"Marshal? Here's the water."

Gideon sniffled, lifted his head, then took the dipper with a shaking hand. "Willow?" he nudged her lips softly with the brimming cup. Then, pleading, "Willow!"

She opened her marvelous golden-brown eyes slowly and smiled, just as though her world hadn't ended. As though she didn't hold her husband personally responsible for the death of all three of her brothers.

"Gideon," she said, as though surprised to see him. Or was she simply surprised that he was showing her even a modicum of kindness?

Shame gnawed at him.

"Drink this," he urged, in a gruff voice, still holding the ladle to her lips.

Her head cradled in the crook of his arm, Willow sipped the cold water obediently, as if to indulge him. "C-could we go home now, please?" she asked in a voice more like that of a child than a woman.

Knowing that his face was wet with tears and not caring, Gideon nodded.

She blinked. "Will you hold me, Gideon, until I sleep?"

A sob ached in Gideon's throat. "Yes," he said, and then he set the dipper aside and stood up, lifting Willow in his arms.

The buggy ride back to their house, the house Gideon had bought with such high and unfounded hopes, was a quiet one, and it seemed endless to him. Willow, perched beside him, her back straight and her shoulders rigid, stared into the distance, her eyes dry.

Once they'd arrived at home, she allowed

Gideon to carry her inside, up the stairs, into their bedroom. Such a short time before, they had made love there, with all the restraint of savages, but now they simply lay together, holding on, despairing.

They slept finally, and Gideon was swept up in a howling nightmare that became real when he awakened to the thick darkness of the night.

Willow was gone.

14

At first, Gideon thought that Willow had left him, once and for all. After a few sleep-drugged seconds of helpless grief, however, he heard the distant, tinkling chimes of a music box.

The room was black-velvet dark, but Gideon did not pause to light a lamp; instead, he groped for his trousers, wriggled into them, and made his way out into the hallway. The sprightly tune of the music box drew him toward the steep rear stairway leading down into the kitchen.

Willow sat alone in a pool of platinum moonlight, her toasted-gold hair trailing down over her back and shoulders, a strange half smile curving her lips. Gideon knew a moment of paralyzing, unaccountable fear, and he stood very still, waiting for the feeling to pass, letting his eyes adjust to the darkness.

After a few seconds, he could see quite

clearly. Willow wore a white nightgown, and the hem was darkened by dampness. She had been outside, walking in the deep, chill grass, wandering.

Unsafe. Vulnerable to a world where mercy was often in short supply.

Gideon ached to speak to his wife, to touch her and comfort her, but he was afraid. There was an ethereal look about Willow, as though she might dissipate into a shimmering fog if he startled her.

His attention caught on the music box. It was not the one he had bought for her but another that he had never seen before. Atop its round silver base, a tiny lady turned, her satin dress imprisoning stray beams of moonlight. Distractedly, Gideon wished that he had given her his gifts — the mechanical monkey and the piano music box — but they were still wrapped in their brown parcel and tucked beneath the seat of his buggy.

Cautiously, Gideon crept back up the stairs. At the top, in the shadowy hallway, he braced both arms against the wall and buried his face in them, breathing deeply, raggedly. Then, resolute, he found a lamp, lit it, and made as much noise as he possibly could on his way back down the steps.

"Couldn't you sleep?" he asked, with

forced cheer, when he reached the kitchen again.

Willow smiled, not even looking up from the music box. "Steven gave me this," she said dreamily. "Don't you think it's lovely?"

Gideon knew a brief, quiet terror, then quickly recovered himself. "Yes," he agreed, frightened, setting down the lamp and making a great clatter with the lids of the cook stove. "When was that, Willow?"

"Just after I came to live with my father," she said, and it was as though tragedy had not touched her this day or any other. She seemed spellbound, almost bewitched, sitting there in the moonlight, smiling.

Gideon lit a fire in the stove and then crossed the room to ladle water from a bucket into the coffeepot. "I'll bet you were scared," he prompted carefully. "Leaving everyone you knew and going to live with the judge and my mother, I mean."

Still, Willow did not look at him; he would have felt it if she had. "I was frightened at first, but Steven promised me everything would be all right, and Maria was with me. Your mother tried to make Maria go away, you know, but she wouldn't."

His throat ached. "My mother was a trial to you, wasn't she, Willow?"

Willow nodded as Gideon passed her to

set the pot back on the stove and spoon coffee grounds into the basket. "I was a trial to her, too, though. Every time Evadne looked at me, she must have seen Chastity."

Gideon sighed and the lid of the coffeepot clattered as he replaced it. "Yes," he said. And he stood that small distance from the woman he loved and wished that she would look up from that blasted music box, that she would spring at him or call him names as she had earlier. That would have been so much better than this odd enchantment that seemed to be upon her now.

"Sit down," she said, finally, as though he were a neighbor come to tea and not a man she had loved into insanity in the seat of a buggy, in the lush depths of the grass, in the empty bed upstairs.

Gideon sat wishing that she would look at him instead of through him. "You've been outside," he ventured, after a long, long time.

The coffee boiled over, making a hissing, snapping sound on the iron stove top. "Yes," she answered as he bounded out of his chair and grasped the handle of the coffeepot. "I was."

The metal seared Gideon's hand, and he gasped in pain and muttered a curse.

Willow's spell was immediately broken;

she bounded out of her chair, insisting that he let her look at his burn. "Thunderation," she said, sounding almost like her old self, and then she ushered him across the room to the water bucket and plunged his hand into it.

The other muscles in Gideon's body, tensed at the moment of the burn, went slack with relief. Even greater, though, was the relief that he had been able to draw a response from Willow.

"I love you," he told her.

She stared up at him, as though surprised. "What did you say?"

Gideon made to lift his hand out of the water and it stung as though set afire. Quickly, he submerged it again. "I said I love you," he admitted.

"Oh," Willow replied, and that frightening, vacuous look was back in her eyes.

Stung, Gideon took the offensive. "What were you doing outside, in the middle of the night?"

"I went to the outhouse, Gideon Marshall," Willow answered, with just a spark of the old spirit. "Is that all right with you?"

Gideon knew that she was lying through those flawless white teeth, but he didn't challenge her; he was too glad to see that there was still some fight in her. He only prayed that it would be enough to see her through the grim and difficult days to come.

The day of Steven's funeral was picnic bright. All during the graveside service, his own grief a heavy ache within him, Devlin watched his daughter and worried.

Willow was a brave young woman, he knew that. But there was something disquieting about the way she stood so stolidly beside Gideon — the man she had spat at and called "Judas" only a few days before — her face placidly void of all expression.

Feeling as though he might have collapsed if Dove Triskadden hadn't been there to hold him up, Devlin tried to shake off his own fathomless sorrow long enough to consider what it was about Willow's firm composure that bothered him. Why wasn't she weeping, like Daphne was? Had she accepted the fact that Steven was gone forever, or was she pretending that her brother still rode somewhere in the hills, still stopped trains and gambled with Shoshone braves?

When the graveside service ended at last, it took all the strength Devlin Gallagher had just to leave the churchyard and cross the road to his own house. There, Maria, tearful and repeatedly crossing herself, had set out a mourners' repast.

She had not attended the funeral.

The food Maria had spent the morning preparing was ignored by everyone except Willow, who went straight to the table, almost as soon as she entered the house, and began filling her plate. Devlin caught Gideon's eye and beckoned him with a toss of his head.

They entered the study together, Devlin closing the double doors behind them, Gideon helping himself to a shot glass full of whiskey from the decanter at the side table.

"Willow hasn't cried once," Gideon said hoarsely, before Devlin could summon the strength to ask. "I don't think she believes he's really gone."

"My God," breathed the judge, filling a glass of his own, gazing bleakly into its depths before tossing back the contents. "What has she said?"

"Nothing," Gideon ground out, his gaze distant. "Before we came to town this morning, Willow was setting bread to rise and humming as though none of this had happened."

"It isn't healthy," fretted the judge. His own anguish had torn him, pummeled him, humbled him, but it was already easing up — a little.

"I know. I've tried to talk to her, but if I

mention Steven's death, she changes the subject. Last time I brought it up, she asked me if we could plant cherry trees in the front yard next spring."

Devlin sighed and set his drink down with a thump.

"She-she wanders, too," Gideon went on.

"What do you mean, she wanders?" snapped Devlin, gruff in his concern.

Gideon's broad shoulders moved in a weary shrug. "Almost every night, I wake up to find that she's gone off somewhere. Sometimes, she sits in the parlor and plays the piano, but once I found her halfway between our house and the pond."

"You must have asked where she'd been. What did Willow say when you questioned her?"

"She told me she'd been to the outhouse."

Devlin poured another drink. He would have welcomed intoxication, but it didn't come. No matter how much whiskey he drank, the hurt didn't leave him. "People handle grief in a lot of different ways, but there's something about this that unnerves me. It isn't like Willow; the way she behaved when Steven and the boys were brought in was more typical."

"I know," agreed Gideon, remembering. Longing for that other Willow, the one he'd found so unpredictable, so impossible to handle. "Did you hear what she did to the photographer's camera?"

Devlin managed a parody of a grin. It was, Gideon thought, the saddest expression he had ever seen on a human face.

"Yes. And I'd have done that myself if I'd been there. Destroyed that camera, I mean. Damned buzzard, wanting *pictures*, for God's sake."

"It's a custom I've never understood," Gideon confessed. He hesitated, then finally went on. "Photographing corpses, displaying them like some kind of warning." He paused, cleared his throat. "I've been thinking that it might be a good idea to take Willow away somewhere, just for a while. We could go back to San Francisco — maybe even take a ship for Europe or the Far East."

The prospect of losing Willow swept through Devlin's grief-hollowed soul like a bitter wind. "San Francisco," he mourned. "The Far East?"

"Just for a change of scene," Gideon put in quickly. "We'd be gone a year and a half, at the most."

The judge shook his head. It seemed an incomprehensible length of time, a year and a half.

And yet, if Willow would benefit . . .

"Do you think it would help her? Traveling to foreign places, I mean? She's always wanted to see the world, but . . ."

Gideon lowered his head. "To be honest, I don't know. I don't even know if Willow would agree to leave Virginia City. But I've got to do something to reach her — she's drifting away, Devlin. Like a ship that's come unmoored."

Before the judge could respond to that, a soft knock sounded at the study doors. At Devlin's gruff invitation, Maria entered.

"There is a telegraph message for Señor Marshall," she said, approaching Gideon, extending a folded sheet of cheap paper.

His hand trembled as he accepted it.

Devlin watched with distracted interest as Gideon scanned the message, wondering what it contained. In the final analysis, he didn't give a damn.

Steven was dead and Willow was probably going to go away, maybe never to return. Desolate, Devlin turned his back and folded his arms across his chest.

"I can't believe you want to go riding, now of all times!" cried Daphne, her mourner's handkerchief poised within inches of her puffy, reddened eyes. She was all in black, and it made a startling contrast to her white face. She watched in stricken amazement as her friend turned from the window of her bedroom, looking determined. "Willow Marshall, your brother is dead. Can you grasp that? We saw Steven buried today, with our own eyes, and there's a *wake* going on in this house."

Willow knelt and began digging through the trunk at the foot of her childhood bed, hauling out trousers and a shirt to replace the black sateen dress she had been wearing since morning. "Daphne, just shut up and change your clothes, will you?" she snapped. "It will be dark soon."

"Do you really believe for one infernal minute that Gideon and your father are going to allow you to go *riding? Now,* of all times?"

Willow shimmied out of the hateful, restrictive dress and began pulling on the trousers. She paused long enough to fling a second pair across the room to Daphne. "Papa and Gideon won't even notice that we're gone," she said. "They're shut up in Papa's study, both of them, drowning their sorrows in whiskey no doubt, and they will probably stay there half the night."

Daphne looked appalled. "Willow, how can you be so callous, so, so blithe! I thought you loved Steven!"

"I do."

"You mean you did," insisted Daphne.

Willow sighed, tugging on her riding boots. "I mean I do," she corrected firmly.

Daphne went completely white. Then, at last, she began divesting herself of her dress and petticoats to don the trousers and shirt Willow had tossed her.

Gideon folded the telegraph message and tucked it into the inside pocket of his coat. Jack Roberts had heard about Daphne's affection for Steven Gallagher, most likely from Hilda, and he was on his way to Virginia City. Probably, it was already too late to send a return wire and inform him that the danger to his daughter's virtue had been permanently removed.

Having wandered outside into the garden encompassing one side of the judge's property, Gideon sat down on a marble bench. What with everything else that was going on in his life right now, he really didn't need a confrontation with Daphne's father. On the other hand, he was going to have to explain everything sooner or later anyway. It might as well be sooner.

"Señor?"

Gideon looked up to see one of Maria's

cousins standing near the lilac bushes, his hat turning nervously in his hands. "Yes — Juan?"

"I am Pablito," said the boy stoically. "Señor, I come to tell you that the señora — Willow — she rides toward the hills."

Gideon was alarmed. "Willow? Is she alone?"

"No. She is with the other señorita, the one who visits here."

"I see." Gideon ground out the words.

Pablito looked worried. "You will not follow them? Bring them back home?"

Gideon sighed. If going riding would help Willow deal with what had happened to her beloved older brother, and to the younger ones, he wasn't about to get in her way. Nothing he'd said or done so far had been of any comfort and, besides, she was with Daphne.

There was some comfort in that.

"No," he heard himself say. "Let them go."

Approval flashed in the dark eyes — along with something else that was harder to recognize and define. "*Sí,*" Pablito said, and then he turned and left the garden as quietly as he had entered it.

Gideon sat for a while longer and then rose from the bench. It wouldn't be right to go chasing after Willow, yet he couldn't remain in or near this house much longer, either. The sense of loss was oppressive.

First his mother, whom he missed more than he'd expected to, and now Steven and his and Willow's young half brothers.

Would the dying stop now? Gideon wondered.

He thought briefly of his brother, wondering where Zachary had gone without so much as a word of farewell, let alone explanation. But he was used to the distance between himself and his brother, whether that distance was measured by miles or by the human heart.

Finally, at a loss and not one for sitting still, he decided to walk to the office that had been his until he'd resigned the day of Steven's death, to see how the new marshal was getting on.

Lot Houghton had seemed a good man to Gideon, a stalwart sort who could handle the rigors of such a job. Today Houghton greeted his predecessor with a shy smile and a hoarse "howdy."

"Afternoon," replied Gideon, removing his hat.

"Have a chair, Mr. Marshall," urged the young lawman. "I'll get you some coffee."

Gideon took the chair but declined the coffee, wishing that the cattle he'd bought for the ranch would arrive so that he could herd them or brand them or something. He'd always had plenty to occupy him, and he wasn't used to having to look for things to do to kill time.

"I was sorry about the judge's boy," Lot ventured. "The others, too."

"Thanks," Gideon replied. He hadn't know Steven, really, only having met him once, but he felt the loss because Willow and the judge did. "Did you know Steven?"

Lot grinned sadly. "Sure did."

"What did you think of him?"

The young man, in the midst of setting out his belongings, put a daguerreotype of a plain young woman and a plump baby on the shelf behind his desk and paused to admire it. "Liked him," he said succinctly.

"Even though he was a train robber?"

"He wasn't no train robber," the lawman parried defensively. "He only took things to devil his old man."

"Steven Gallagher killed Mitch Kroeber," Gideon reminded the new marshal quietly, hoping the days ahead would be peaceful ones, not only for Houghton's sake, but for the woman and the baby in the picture. "And the loot he took that day belonged to the passengers, not to Devlin."

"That weren't Steven, that done that robbery and that killing," came the flat and certain reply.

"Kroeber called the man Gallagher."

Lot pulled a face. "Hell, if you'd lived here any stretch of time at all, you'd know old Mitch was half-blind. This feller was just somebody that looked like Steven."

Gideon knew a deep sense of disquiet, though he couldn't quite figure what had spawned it. "Do you know of anybody who looks that much like Gallagher?" he asked, almost afraid of the answer.

"Sure," said Lot, riffling through a stack of wanted posters and then extending one to Gideon. "Here's one right here."

Gideon took the tattered poster and studied the drawing in amazement. The face sketched on it belonged to a man named Silas Blanchard, and he was wanted for a list of crimes as long as the railway between there and Butte. If the witnesses were frightened, and he was wearing a mask, Blanchard probably would resemble Steven Gallagher. "You ever seen this man?"

"No, I was just looking through these after I took over the job and I thought this feller reminded me of somebody. Showed it to my Alice, when she brought over my lunch earlier today, and she said she reckoned he bore a real strong likeness to Steven."

Again Gideon felt uneasy, though he couldn't have explained why. Twilight was coming on, and he wondered if Willow and Daphne were back from their ride yet. "Kroeber kept a record of every crime committed while he was marshal, according to Judge Gallagher," he reflected. "Mind if I take those journals of Kroeber's home and look them over? I'll bring them back tomorrow."

Lot, who looked more like a farmer than a lawman, with his open, friendly face void of suspicion, seemed amenable. "Can't see what it would hurt," he said, tilting in his chair to the three dusty books Gideon had mentioned. "You see that you bring those books back here, though, like you said. Mitch's family will want them for remembrances, most likely."

"Thank you," Gideon said, with a nod in place of a promise, rising from his chair to take the journals and his leave.

"My sympathies to the judge and Miss Willow," replied Lot Houghton. His farmer's face was ingenuous, burned red by the sun.

Gideon nodded and left the marshal's office. Climbing into the waiting buggy, he remembered the parcel containing the music box and the mechanical monkey he'd bought for Willow, then bent to reach under the seat and see if it was still there. It was.

With a sigh, Gideon released the brake lever and set Mitch Kroeber's journals aside to take up the reins. He'd feel like a fool giving Willow a toy monkey; what in hell had possessed him to buy a thing like that in the first place?

Passing the Gallagher house, Gideon considered stopping by to make sure that Willow and Daphne had returned safely from their ride, then decided against it. They had to be back. Daphne would have pitched a fit the moment it started getting dark and insisted on going home.

In his own kitchen, out on his lonely ranch, Gideon lit a lamp and started a pot of coffee perking. Then, after assuring himself that Willow needed this time with her father, he sat down at the table, opened one of Kroeber's remarkably detailed logbooks, and began to read.

Again and again he found entries mentioning Steven Gallagher. He'd stopped the train twenty-eight times in the past five years, and if Mitch Kroeber's neatly written account could be believed, he'd never taken so much as a nickel that didn't belong either to Devlin Gallagher himself or one of his companies.

It was very late when Gideon closed the last book, but he was too riled up to sleep, so he just sat there at the table, drinking the dregs of his coffee and wondering about things and feeling anxious. Upon finding out that Daphne had witnessed the last train robbery and the murder of Mitch Kroeber, Gideon had, of course, questioned her. She'd said that Kroeber had called the robber Gallagher, but she'd also insisted that the late marshal had been wrong.

At the time, because he'd already guessed that Daphne cared for Steven, Gideon hadn't believed her. Willow and the judge, too, had had valid reasons for denying Steven's guilt, and he had discounted their views as well.

Now, alone in that dark and empty house, with the lamp burning low, Gideon felt more than just a hollowed-out kind of loneliness. He felt a growing conviction that Steven Gallagher had not been a vicious criminal but an angry, hurt little boy hiding inside the body of a man. Oh, he'd been a nuisance to the railroad, all right, upsetting their schedules, scaring their passengers, that sort of thing. But he wouldn't have been hanged for that, nor would a bounty have been offered for his capture. And if a reward hadn't been put up, Steven Gallagher wouldn't be dead.

Sick inside, Gideon took up the lamp and went out onto the back porch. There, he stripped off his shirt and filled the washbasin with tepid water that had been sitting in the sun all day and gave himself a bath of sorts. He wondered again if he should go back to town and fetch Willow, bring her home.

No, he decided, after a long time. She probably felt that she needed to be close to her father now; if she wanted to be with Gideon himself, she would come to him on her own.

Gideon had been in bed for about ten minutes when Willow appeared, big as life, wearing trousers and a man's shirt and sitting down on the edge of the mattress with a sigh to haul off her boots. Her hair trailed down her back in a thick, single braid. Watching her, Gideon half-believed she wasn't there at all, that he was seeing things.

"Did I wake you up?" she asked blithely.

Gideon stared at her, amazed. He couldn't make out her expression, since there was only strained moonlight to see by. "Hell, it's only two in the morning or thereabouts," he rasped, furious and oddly shaken. "Why would I be sleeping?"

The sarcasm in his voice didn't seem to

bother Willow. She pulled the braid over one shoulder and began to unwind it. That done, she took off her shirt and those god-awful trousers and crawled into bed beside Gideon in bloomers and a camisole, just as though she didn't have a thing in the world to explain.

"Where have you been, damnit?" Gideon demanded through his teeth. He raised himself onto one elbow and squinted, trying to look into her eyes.

"Riding," she said, sweetly. With a little yawn.

"At this hour of the night?"

She sighed contentedly and snuggled down into her pillow. "The moon was huge," she said, as if that settled everything. "It was bright as day out there."

Gideon was about to explode when the sheets rustled and Willow suddenly reached out and splayed the fingers of one soft hand over his chest.

"Make love to me, Gideon," she said, chafing one of his nipples with the side of her thumb, causing him to groan involuntarily.

His voice was so rough that it hurt his throat, coming out. "Willow, today —"

"I know what happened today, Gideon. Believe me. And now I need to have you touch me and kiss me until I can't see or breathe or think."

He understood and came to her, kissing her deeply. Her tongue immediately met his in a brief, spirited foray. Having lain beside her, wanting her and yet denying himself because of her loss, for three torturous nights, Gideon's body was taut with hunger for hers. He trailed his mouth to Willow's left breast and was greedy there, suckling the warm, hard tip, drawing at it with his lips, teasing it with his tongue.

She arched her back in unqualified surrender, crooning. She caught fire so easily — a touch, a word, a look.

It was one of the many things he loved about her.

"Oh, Gideon. God, God, Gideon."

He turned to the other breast, not devouring it, not mocking it with whisper-soft kisses. It was an obedient little morsel, straining to be captured.

"Have me," Willow whimpered. "Oh, Gideon, have me soon."

Stubbornly, Gideon continued to pleasure the breast, to draw from it.

"Oh, Gideon, please!" Willow wailed, clutching at his shoulders with frantic hands.

He caused her to kneel in the middle of

the bed, placed his hands full on her breasts, and began to attend her with soft, quick strokes of his tongue. She gave a choked, desperate gasp and began to move upon him, back and forth, up and down.

She chanted his name in a fever of need, writhing, moaning when he plucked gently at the points of her ripe breasts, spurring her on.

When he sensed that the most important moment was near, Gideon began to draw upon her earnestly. She gave a keening, wild-animal cry, stiffened, and then convulsed. He waited, and then parted her again and kissed her softly until a low, growling whine came from her throat.

"No, oh, Gideon, not again."

"Again," rasped Gideon, between kisses.

"Ooooooh."

He tongued her thoroughly, then kissed, then tongued again. She was maniacal, writhing and pleading, clawing at the bedclothes with her hands. "Oh, stop —"

"No," he said gruffly, from the moist sanctuary of her sweetness. "I'm not going to settle for less than everything you have to give."

She whimpered and thrust her knees out wide and Gideon was greedy to the very last.

■ ■ ■ ■

As always, there was a certain cautiousness in Gideon's eyes when he was poised above Willow. No matter how obvious her yearning for him, no matter how feverish the moment, he never failed to await her bidding.

"I love you, Gideon," she whispered, "I want you. Now."

He moaned and she felt the heated strength of him touch her, ease inside her waiting body, so ready to receive him. "Willow," he breathed, struggling to withhold the full length of his shaft. He seemed to be caught in her name, entangled in it. "Willow, Willow."

She was stroking his taut, muscular hips, urging him gently. "More, Gideon, please, more."

The planes of his magnificent face were shadowed, but she could still see the effort he was making to prolong the searing pleasure for both of them.

Willow trailed the tips of her fingers over his buttocks and knew sweet satisfaction when he trembled and bit back a cry of undisguised need. "You think to make me plead for what you have to give, sir," she teased huskily. "Instead, you force me to take it."

"Don't, oh, Willow."

But she did. She gave a powerful, upward thrust of her hips, at the same time pressing him to her with her hands.

"Oh, God," he pleaded, but he was lost, forced to move with her by the savage demands of his own body and the sweet, soft treachery of Willow's. "I've needed you so much, oh my God, my God, slower, so much . . ."

His senseless words were a sonnet to Willow, fanning the flames of passion inside her to ferocious, searing blazes. His powerful hands moved to grasp her bottom and guide her fiercely; where he had pleaded before, he now commanded. Again and again he withdrew his magnificence, sheathed it again.

Willow thrashed and wailed beneath him, craving each thrust of his sword, welcoming it. Suddenly, she was racked, body and soul, by the fiery, pagan release he had driven her to. She shivered, flailing atop the flames of passion, and then glided slowly back to earth, weeping softly as she fell.

Gideon continued to move upon her, but his control was very tenuous now. Soon, he, too, would be flung to glory, and watching that happen was a joy Willow craved as much as she had her own climax. She began to urge him toward the borders of heaven, with her hands, with soft, wanton words.

Finally, a great shudder moved through Gideon's frame. His eyes were closed and his head was thrown back and his lips were drawn tight across his teeth. His cry of triumph was a hoarse and lengthy one, infinitely beautiful to Willow. And as his hard body buckled against hers, helpless in the throes of his fulfillment, she whispered wicked promises to make the sweet suffering greater.

At last, he was still upon her, exhausted. She ran her hands up and down the moist, muscle-taut length of his back until he was breathing normally again. When he lifted his face from the dark gold fan of her hair, there was a mischievous note in his voice.

"Would you really take advantage of me on the piano bench, Mrs. Marshall?" he teased.

Willow blushed in the deep darkness. "Gideon!"

"That's what you said."

"I was speaking in the heat of passion!" she protested, wildly embarrassed that she could have made such a brazen remark.

"Nevertheless," Gideon chortled, sliding

down to bury his face in the lush fullness of her breasts, "I'm going to take *you* on the piano bench, Mrs. Marshall."

15

The cattle reached the ranch just outside Virginia City on Monday morning, filling Gideon Marshall's too-quiet world with noise and dust. Willow perched on the rail fence beside him, watching their approach, her eyes wide with wonder.

"Thunderation, Gideon," she called, over the shouts of drovers and the bawling of beasts exhausted by the overland trip from Denver, "there must be ten thousand of them!"

Gideon laughed and braced his forearms against the top rail of the paddock fence. "Roughly six hundred, hellcat," he corrected. "Remind me not to let you keep the books."

Just then, the trail boss rode up. He was a lean man, his rough clothes coated with dust, and his hat looked as though every one of those six hundred Herefords had stepped on it at one time or another. "Mr.

Marshall?" he shouted, over the glorious din.

Gideon extended his hand, and the cowboy, thin and wiry and somehow mournful in countenance, bent from his saddle to shake it.

"Name's Tyson Riggers," the drover announced, and his coal-black handlebar mustache twitched.

At that point, Willow burst into the conversation. "Come on inside, Mr. Riggers, and have some coffee and pie. Bring your men, too."

Riggers looked amused. "There's twenty-four of them, ma'am," he pointed out. "Might be better if they stayed outside."

"Won't you come in, at least?" Willow persisted, watching Tyson Riggers.

"I'd admire to, ma'am," replied Riggers, tipping his hat. His gaze, brightly melancholy in a long, gaunt face, shifted to Gideon. "We lost twelve head to Injuns, Mr. Marshall," he explained. "Considerin' how far we came, that ain't too bad."

Gideon frowned. "Indians? Were any of your men hurt?"

"No, sir," said Tyson, finally dismounting. "The Ute was real polite, all things considered. We gave 'em the dozen head of beef they asked for and they let us keep our hair."

■ ■ ■ ■

The men — Gideon and Mr. Tyson Riggers and Zachary — sat at the kitchen table, drinking fresh coffee and consuming remarkable amounts of dried apple pie. Outside, the cattle bawled and the drovers shouted and the air roiled, thick with dust.

"You gonna fence your land, Mr. Marshall?" Tyson wanted to know.

Willow watched as Gideon shook his head resolutely. "The other ranchers like an open range, and I agree with them."

"Got plenty of water?"

Now Gideon nodded. He was proud of the wide creek that ran through the center of his seven hundred acres.

"Drovers?" pressed Tyson Riggers, obviously a man of experience, familiar with the needs of cattle.

Gideon smiled. He was proud of the brand-new bunkhouse, too. He and Harry Simmons, the foreman he'd recently hired, and Zachary had built it with their own hands, suffering with patience Willow's eager efforts to help. "I've hired a half dozen men so far," he said.

Willow and Zachary exchanged glances. How, Willow wondered, could so few men handle so many cattle?

"Sounds like plenty for now," remarked Mr. Riggers. "Guess getting them critters branded will be the first order of the day."

Gideon's triumphant grin took in both his brother and his wife. "The second," he said politely. "I'll get you your bank draft, Mr. Riggers."

"I'll fetch it!" Willow volunteered eagerly, wanting desperately to do more than serve pie and coffee.

Gideon seemed to sense her need to be part of the general excitement. "Thank you," he said softly.

Willow felt no small measure of shame as she averted her eyes and hurried into the parlor, where Gideon's brand-new desk sat facing the windows. He trusted her, was willing to share every part of his life with her. And he was never, never going to forgive her if he found out about the secret she was keeping.

The draft, signed only that morning and tucked under the paperweight — a simple creek stone that Gideon had fancied and brought back to the house — fluttered in Willow's nervous hand as she took it up. Maybe if she told him the truth straight out, things would turn out all right. On the other hand, tender husband though Gideon was, there was a ruthless side to him, too.

Willow sighed and lifted her eyes to the dusty distance, neither seeing nor hearing the several hundred cattle and their shouting drovers. And what of her father? Devlin was wasting away with grief, despite his claims that the loss of Steven was getting easier to bear with every passing day.

"Willow?"

She started guiltily at Gideon's gentle inquiry, unable, for the moment, to answer.

"Is something wrong?"

The lump in Willow's throat permitted a hasty "No. I was just watching your cattle."

Gideon stood behind her in the quiet, clean parlor, his hands resting on her shoulders. "The herd is yours, too, Willow," he said.

Willow stifled the sob that rose, completely unexpected, into her throat, making the backs of her eyes and the inside of her nose burn. She loved this man so much that she thought she'd surely die of it, and keeping a secret from him, however crucial, was hell on earth. "No," she managed to say, "you bought them. This ranch, the cattle, everything is yours, Gideon. Not mine."

He turned her to face him, caught an index finger under her drooping chin, and lifted it. "Do you think anything I own would matter to me if you weren't there to share it, Willow?"

Tears smarted in her eyes. "Oh, Gideon," she protested.

Gideon looked puzzled. "Are you all right?"

She knew that he had been watching her closely, wondering. Try though she had, she had not been able to comport herself as a bereaved person should. She was no actress.

"I'm fine," she said, extending the bank draft. "Pay Mr. Riggers, Gideon. I-I think I'm going to go to town and see if Daphne's father has arrived yet."

"Willow . . ."

Willow bit her lower lip and prayed that he would not make her stay here and lie to him.

The prayer, for whatever the Lord's reasons, was answered. Gideon gave her another questioning, ponderous look and took the bank draft from her hand. "You'll be careful, won't you? Those drovers have been on the trail for a while, and there's no telling what kinds of people they might be."

Willow found a smile somewhere inside herself and tacked it to her face, where it clung shakily, seeing her through the moment but doing not one thing more. "I won't go near the drovers, Gideon," she promised. "And I'll be home in time to fix your supper."

For a moment, it seemed that he was going to say something else. In the end, however, Gideon simply gave his wife one more pensive look, shrugged, and returned to the kitchen.

Daphne's father had definitely arrived; Willow heard him shouting even as she drew the buggy to a stop at Devlin Gallagher's front gate and secured the reins.

Maria met her in the entryway, her dark eyes wide with excitement. "The señorita's — Daphne's — papa says he will shoot our Gideon!" she cried.

Willow squared her shoulders and lifted her chin. "Nonsense," she scoffed, but she was furious all the same as she marched straight into her father's study, shoving the heavy double doors open without pausing to knock.

Daphne's father, Jack Roberts, turned out to be a tall man, like Devlin, and had probably been handsome in his youth. Now, however, he was exceedingly heavy, his hair was thin, and outrage mottled his otherwise pasty face, with its muttonchop whiskers bulging under each of his ears. Near the windows, Daphne almost cowered, looking as though she would like to bundle herself up in the draperies and never come out. Except, of course, for the purple blazes of defiance beginning to kindle in her eyes.

"Willow!" she cried, as if overjoyed to see her friend. "Willow, Papa says he's going to take me back to San Francisco — and I *refuse* to go along!"

"We'll see," said Willow, with calm dispatch, unpinning her new and very fashionable hat and setting it carefully aside.

Mr. Roberts glowered at Willow, his large jowls quivering. "So you're the one who started all this, spirited my Daphne's intended away —"

"Papa!" Daphne cried in protest.

"It's all right, Daphne," Willow said evenly. "Mr. Roberts, the simple fact of the matter is that Daphne wishes to remain here in Virginia City with us."

Tiny, purple-red veins seemed to sprout all over the man's face. "I won't have my daughter living in this place, with the family of a notorious outlaw!"

A fearful shadow moved in Daphne's wide lilac eyes, and there were smudges beneath them. Willow almost thought that it would be better if her friend did return to California, once and for all. The secret obviously caused her even more distress than it did Willow.

"My brother is dead," said Willow steadily. "Therefore, of course, he presents no danger to Daphne."

"You were involved with that criminal?" thundered Jack Roberts, his eyes bulging.

Willow stared at the man. She'd been so sure he knew about Steven.

Don't say anything, Daphne! she thought frantically.

"Yes, Papa," Daphne said, with spirit. "I *love* Steven Gallagher. I will *always* love him!"

"You love him?" echoed the rich and imposing man before her. "A wanted man? An outlaw? A *dead* outlaw?"

Daphne was trembling, keeping her eyes carefully away from a meeting with Willow's. "I will always love Steven," she repeated.

"What about Gideon?" Jack Roberts asked, surprisingly calm. "I thought you came here to Montana to win him back?"

"You would have approved of that, wouldn't you, Papa?" spouted Daphne, clearly out of sorts with her father. "I could have traveled a thousand miles and seduced another woman's husband and that would have been all right with you because it would have fattened your purse! You and Gideon could still control the Central Pacific Railroad, just like you planned."

For one awful moment, it seemed as though Jack Roberts was about to collapse. When that frightening moment passed, Willow scurried to the side table and poured a generous portion of brandy, which she held out to Daphne's furious father.

He scowled at her, then took the snifter and downed a great gulp. Somewhat recovered, he lamented quietly, "Together, Gideon and I would have controlled most of the railways west of the Mississippi."

There was a silence, a thunderous one, soon broken by Daphne. "I didn't love Gideon, Papa, and he didn't love me. Like you, he wanted to control the railroad. I was incidental to the plan. Furthermore, I think both of you were despicable, planning such a thing, using me!"

"Daphne," her father began awkwardly, looking somewhat contrite but still determined.

"No!" she broke in. "I won't go back to San Francisco with you, like the dutiful daughter — like, like some *child.* I have to stay here with —"

Willow's blood froze and she cleared her throat loudly.

"With Willow," said Daphne.

"Why?" cried Jack Roberts. "This woman spoiled everything — she ruined your life."

"If saving me from a loveless marriage can be called ruining my life, I suppose she did. Willow is my dearest friend and I will not leave her."

The travel-weary, overwrought man drew a deep breath. "We'll talk about all of this tomorrow, Daphne. And I'll try to be more rational, though I can't promise I'll succeed."

After casting one look of mingled question and warning at Daphne, Willow discerned that it would be a good time to leave father and daughter alone and promptly did so. Feeling uneasy, she went to the flower garden and picked an armful of fading zinnias to carry across the street to the churchyard.

Vancel Tudd stayed well out of sight, watching Judge Gallagher's daughter approach the graves of Coy and Reilly Forbes. They were only half brothers to her, he reflected, and since she'd been raised mostly in Devlin's house, she probably hadn't known them all that well.

The sun was hot and high that day, and Vancel took out his handkerchief, then mopped his forehead and the back of his neck. Soon as the reward money came through, he'd strike out for Mexico. Even though it would be even hotter there, there would be plenty of cold drinks and pretty señoritas to offer comfort. Maybe he'd find himself a nice little town by the ocean and buy himself a real nice hacienda and live like some sort of a *patrón.*

After the hardscrabble, hand-to-mouth way his life had gone so far, the idea appealed to Vancel.

Damn, but the judge's daughter was a fetching thing, trim through the waist and nice and round at the hips and bosom. Her soft hair, pinned up loose and soft around her head, glimmered like corn silk under a summer sun.

Willow Marshall was carrying flowers, and she knelt between the two graves, laying half the blooms at one stone, half at the other. She didn't so much as look toward the fenced-off resting place marked with Steven Gallagher's name, and that struck Vancel as odd. More than odd, considering the way she'd acted the day he'd brought those wasters in.

Vancel was pondering that when rock-hard hands suddenly closed over his shoulders, whirled him around, and flung him hard against the weathered-board wall of the church. Devlin Gallagher was glaring at him, his eyes wild, his lips drawn tight across his teeth.

"What the hell do you think you're do-ing?" rasped Gallagher.

Vancel sometimes wondered if he was ever going to get to Mexico, where he could live in peace and enjoy the luxuries he'd worked so hard to secure for himself. "Doin'?" he echoed, stalling.

"You obviously didn't come here to pray," drawled Devlin, and for all the smooth soft-ness of his voice, he scared Vancel Tudd clear to the bone. It was no wonder that one or two old-timers had altered the judge's first name from Devlin to Devil. "Is there something about my daughter that interests you?"

Tudd shivered. "No, sir, Devil — Devlin — there ain't. I saw her puttin' flowers on the Forbes boys' graves and I was wonderin' why she didn't bring none for Steven, that's all."

The oddness of that clearly struck Devlin Gallagher; his eyes shifted to his daughter, then darkened. When they came back to Vancel's face, however, they were knife-sharp and clear as a mountain creek.

"You stay away from Willow, Tudd. You've done all the harm to this family that there is to do." He paused and drew a deep, raspy breath. "And so help me God, Vancel, if you so much as tip your hat to my daughter as you pass her on the street, I'll kill you."

"You'd hang for it," Tudd said, but he was bluffing, and Devlin clearly knew that.

"Maybe I would," Gallagher agreed. "Then again, maybe I wouldn't. I'm a judge, and a solid citizen, and you're a second-rate bounty hunter. Seems to me a jury might make a distinction." He paused. "Get out of here, Tudd, before I kick your ass."

It wasn't a day for fighting, as far as Vancel Tudd was concerned. He drew a deep breath, squared his shoulders, and walked away.

"Willow?"

She looked up from Coy's grave and into the ravaged face of her father. "Papa, what are you doing here? It's the middle of the day."

Devlin crouched down on his haunches, as Willow had seen Steven do so many times. "I might ask the same question of you. I didn't know you were close to your half brothers."

Inwardly, Willow sighed. She had come to town to escape lying to Gideon, and now she would have to lie to her father. "They don't have anybody else to come and pay respects," she hedged, finding it almost impossible to meet those watchful eyes of his.

Devlin pulled a bright yellow dandelion from the ground and assessed its spiky face. "I guess not. Steven was all they had in the world — except for you."

Willow lowered her eyes. She was sorry that Coy and Reilly were dead; she even mourned for them, if only in a remote way. The truth was, she had never known them well. Had never forged a bond with her half brothers like the one she and Steven had always shared.

"Yes," Willow agreed. "With Mama and Mr. Forbes both gone — and Steven, too — there's no one to remember them properly." She paused, aching with secrets that were too heavy to bear. "Have you been by the house, Papa? Daphne's father is there —"

"I've been there," Devlin broke in. "They're talking calmly and Daphne seemed to be holding her own."

Willow looked away, then sniffled once. "Good," she murmured.

Devlin stood up straight again, his knee bones making a popping sound as he did so. "Which isn't to say that Jack Roberts is going to let her stay here. Frankly, I don't understand why she wants to. Steven is gone and . . ." His voice broke. He swallowed and spoke again, gruffly. "Gideon is married to you, after all, and the two of you seem to be getting along fine."

Willow kept her eyes averted. "Daphne and I are friends. She wants to stay because of that."

"She's a mighty loyal friend, then. Very few girls her age would give up the kind of life she has in San Francisco to live on the frontier. What does she plan to do, now that Steven's . . . no longer with us?"

The bluntness of that question caused Willow's eyes to shoot involuntarily to her father's face. "What?"

"Don't, Willow. You yourself told me about Steven and Daphne, the day he was killed."

With everything that had been happening, with all her riotous feelings sweeping her this way and that, Willow had forgotten mentioning that her brother and her friend had met in the stables behind the Gallagher house after the dance.

"Yes," she confirmed lamely. Now what was she supposed to say, to do? Damn Steven anyway. "Well . . ."

But Devlin hadn't noticed her hesitation, it seemed. He broke in with, "There is nothing for Daphne here. Why in God's name does she want to stay? Virginia City is a nice town, but it isn't San Francisco. I can understand you not wanting her to go back there, but . . ."

A slow flush crept, scalding, up Willow's neck and into her face. What would happen if she told her father the truth? Surely the secret would be safe with him, and he'd know what to do about all its attendant problems.

On the other hand, knowing might be worse for him than what he was going through now.

"I don't know why Daphne wants to stay here," Willow lied firmly, and it appeared that her father believed her.

Unless, of course, that was merely what he wanted her to think.

Gideon left the saloon late, with Jack Roberts's loud lecture ringing in his ears. Even though he'd deserved every word of it, he still smarted as though he'd been pelted with small, sharp stones.

He had just reached his horse and unwound the reins from the hitching rail when Zachary stepped out of the darkness. He had the damnedest way of just *appearing* like that. "If I had a wife like yours, Gideon," he said companionably, "I wouldn't be in town right now, dallying in some saloon."

In no mood for a round with Zachary, Gideon scowled. He hung one stirrup from the saddle horn to check and then tighten the cinch around his horse's middle. "You don't have a wife like mine, though, do you?"

Zachary sighed heavily and gripped the post of the hitching rail in both hands. "Why the hell don't you go home, where you belong? Sweep Daphne off her feet again, con Jack into thinking you'll make a fine son-in-law in spite of it all. And then head back to San Francisco and your railroad shares and all your wheeling and dealing. You've had your tumbles in Willow Gallagher's bed."

Gideon had been about to mount up. Now, feeling cold all over, he turned to face his brother squarely. "Her name is Willow Marshall."

"On paper, maybe," Zachary countered smoothly. "But she's a Gallagher, through and through, and we both know that." He paused, smiled oddly. "Your Willow," he said, "is a little outlaw. Eventually, she'll get tired of being your dutiful wife, Gideon. She'll run off with somebody more exciting,

411

just like her mother did all those years ago. You might have kids of your own when she flies the coop. And, like the judge, there won't be a damn thing you can do to stop Willow from going or to make her come back."

Gideon felt a chill move through him. It had more to do with the tempestuous history he and Zachary shared than any worries he had concerning Willow.

Though, God knew, there were a few of those, too.

"Is that all you wanted to say?" he asked, refusing to rise to the bait.

"No," Zachary said, as Gideon climbed into the saddle. He never knew when to quit. "Your life is in San Francisco, Gideon, not in this godforsaken wilderness. What the hell are you *doing,* buying land and cattle, playing like you mean to settle down?"

"You know," Gideon drawled, looking down into his brother's face, "it's a curious thing, your interest in seeing me go back. And I've wondered the same thing about you — why you stay here in Virginia City, I mean."

Light from the saloon fell on Zachary's face, casting shadows that hid his expression. "Have you?" he countered mildly. "I thought you were smarter than that, little brother."

The realization was no great surprise. So why did it feel like a kick in the teeth? "It's Willow, then," Gideon said. "You want my wife."

Zachary nodded and smiled as he stepped back up onto the board sidewalk. "When you come to your senses, little brother, and go back to your board meetings and your rich mistresses, I mean to be right here, waiting to console her." His shoulders moved in a shrug. "It might take some time, I grant you, but Willow will come around. Won't that be convenient? She won't even have to change her name!"

"You're insane," Gideon said, taking up the reins but making no move to ride away. "You just told me that you expect Willow to take up with an outlaw."

Zachary's grin was somehow chilling. "I'd make a fine outlaw," he said. "Don't you think?"

Gideon swung his right leg over the saddle horn and landed deftly on the ground, face-to-face with his brother. "What I *think*," he said, "is that we ought to settle this, once and for all."

Zachary held up both his hands in affable abstention and took another step back,

413

probably to get out of fist range. "Oh, no," he averred. "I won't fight you, Gideon. I mean to wait and watch, that's all. Bide my time. You'll trip up soon enough. You'll leave the territory, or you'll get yourself killed — wouldn't *that* be a shame? — who knows which? The point is that once one or all of those things happen, Willow will be in need of consolation."

Gideon's fists ached and the blood throbbed beneath his temples. "You'll fight," he breathed, advancing on his brother. "That's the only choice you've got."

Zachary paled, but a smirk played on his mouth. "Gideon, Gideon," he scolded ruefully, "what would that do to your reputation in this town? You're supposed to be an upright landowner, a cattleman. A deputy U.S. marshal. What will people say if they see you brawling in the street like some common roughneck?"

Shrugging out of his coat, Gideon smiled. "Why, Zachary," he said, "you ought to know by now that I don't give a damn what people say about me." He undid his cuff links, dropped them into the pocket of his suit coat, then hung the garment from the horn of his saddle. Zachary backed up again as his brother calmly rolled up his sleeves. "You know, Zach," he went on, in measured

414

tones, "I've been taking all kinds of guff from you ever since you came here. Before that, too, from the time we were little kids. And I'm dead sick of it."

"Gideon," Zachary said, sounding nervous now.

Gideon advanced on his brother, filled with bloodlust, not just over the things Zachary had said about Willow, but over a lifetime of tricks and lies and out-and-out bullying. Of the two of them, Gideon had always been the one with a head for business, with the acumen to manage and increase the family fortune. Zachary, though several years older, had a less impressive set of skills.

He gambled, threw away thousands of dollars "courting" women he never intended to marry, and often had to borrow from their grandfather's vast estate to make it through to the next dividend payment.

Although Gideon doubted he'd ever be able to prove it, he knew in his bones that several of the near misses he'd had as a kid — hurtling down a flight of stairs when he was three, being locked in a shed that conveniently caught fire when he was eight, almost getting trampled by a horse on more than one occasion — had been Zachary's doing.

Zachary would have loved to see Gideon dead. He stood to inherit so much, in the event of his younger brother's tragic death. Or, at least, he *had,* until Willow came along, anyway.

Catching the lapels of Zachary's impeccable suit coat in his fists, Gideon rasped, "Thanks to you, dear brother, Willow is my wife. And I love her. So it looks like your little joke blew up in your face, doesn't it?"

Zachary's eyes went round, and his breath was quick, ragged. He tried to pull away, but he'd never been the stronger one. "Gideon, for God's sake . . ."

Gideon was half-blind with anger now, with an accumulation of memories, things Zachary had done to him, said to him, set in motion behind his back. "No. God isn't going to have any part in this," he spat out. "I mean to do it all myself."

"Wait!" Zachary cried. "Gideon, you can't; I was only —"

"Let him go, Gideon."

The voice was masculine, and somehow it reached through the fog of Gideon's fury and touched his reason like a cooling hand. He sighed and dropped his hands, releasing his grip on Zachary, stepping back.

Zachary immediately bolted, his coattails flying as he whirled around, the heels of his boots making a clomping sound on the wooden sidewalk, fading away into the night. Gideon faced his father-in-law, head-on.

"I wanted him to bleed," he said.

"I know," answered Devlin.

It struck Gideon then that Devlin looked old. He was far thinner than he had been before Steven's death, and his eyes had an unnerving, hollowed-out look, as though he'd been scraped raw on the inside.

"Is Willow all right?" Gideon asked.

"She's fine, or so she says," the judge answered. "I'd like to talk to you, though. Mind letting me buy you a drink or two?"

Gideon was brutally tired, but he sensed that Devlin would relate something important, maybe vital. "Anything but panther piss," he replied.

Much later, Gideon collected Willow from the judge's house and they drove home through the starlit night, in the buggy. The nearer they got to the ranch house, the more clearly they could hear the lowing of the weary cattle.

Gideon was pensive, the set-to with Zachary far from his mind, thinking about what the judge had told him. He'd seen Willow in the churchyard, Devlin had, placing flow-

417

ers on the graves of Coy and Reilly Forbes and never casting so much as a glance in the direction of Steven's. That bothered Gideon, as it had bothered his father-in-law.

He didn't speak of it, though. Instead, he considered odd bits and pieces torn from the fabric of the last week or so.

Grief-stricken women usually cried until the pain had passed, but Willow had not shed a tear, to his knowledge, since the day her brothers were brought in. She hummed and played her piano. She pored over seed catalogs and had already marked off plots for next year's flower and vegetable gardens.

At night, or any time he came to her, actually, Willow was more than ready to make love. That very morning, in fact, she'd followed Gideon out to the barn when he went to do the chores and — well — there was no other way to explain it: she'd had her way with him. She'd knelt in the musty hay and straw and he'd had to brace himself against the outside railing of a stall, moaning as she took her pleasure.

Just the memory of it made Gideon harden and break out in a sweat. His release had been so explosive that it had wrung a shout from him.

Now, in the buggy seat, Gideon had to

widen his knees slightly, to accommodate himself. The experience had been beautiful, and yet it bothered him for several reasons. For one thing, Willow had hated him, really hated him, the day Vancel Tudd brought her dead brothers to town. She'd spat at him and called him Judas. It was hard for Gideon to believe that her feelings had changed so completely and so rapidly.

And then there was her continuing habit of wandering in the night. Gideon had lost count of the times he'd found her outside somewhere, barefoot, her eyes haunted. Always, no matter how far she might be from that structure, she claimed she'd been to the outhouse.

Sadly, Gideon came to the obvious conclusion: Willow's behavior was irrational. It was entirely possible that, losing her brother, she might also be losing her mind.

He reached the ranch, then unhitched the horse and buggy. Just as he was leaving the barn, Gideon remembered the presents he'd bought for Willow — it seemed a thousand years ago — and went back to the rig to get them. In the kitchen, dimly lit by just one lamp, he shyly extended the parcel.

"What's this?" Willow asked, and it was impossible to read her face.

Gideon sighed. He'd given a thousand

presents to a thousand women and never once felt this way. He might as well have been a little boy, for God's sake, presenting something he'd made with his own hands to an adored goddess. "Just some things I bought in town a while ago," he said.

It seemed, in the half light, that Willow's fingers trembled a little as she untied the string and opened the crackly brown paper. The gifts inside were separately wrapped in white tissue, and she found the tiny piano first, gazing at it in wonder.

"Oh, Gideon," she breathed, as though he had given her a chest full of faultless gems. She turned the little key on the bottom and the kitchen was filled with the soft, chiming music.

Gideon felt deflated. This was Zachary's gift, not his; he hadn't been the one to choose it for her. He wanted to leap at the table and snatch away the still-wrapped monkey before she could see it and know what a raving idiot she had married.

It was too late, though; she reached for it, undid the wrapping. A cry of startled glee escaped her when she saw the little monkey with his brass cymbals and stupid hat. "What does he do?" she asked in a small voice.

His hand trembling almost imperceptibly,

Gideon reached out and turned a tiny key buried in the toy's woolly fur. The monkey began to chatter and clap the cymbals together with surprising exuberance.

Willow cupped the little creature in the upturned palms of her hands, watching it with wide eyes. Then she threw back her head and laughed so joyously that Gideon was completely taken aback, not knowing whether his gift had succeeded or failed.

He blushed miserably. "I'm sorry," he said.

"Sorry?" The lovely golden eyes were fixed on him now, unreadable. "Gideon, why on earth would you be sorry?"

The monkey was winding down, clapping the cymbals more and more slowly, chattering only after lengthening intervals of silence. Gideon just stood there, his hands in his pockets.

"Gideon?" Willow prompted gently.

"I should have given you diamonds or something," he burst out, unable to stop the rush of words. "Damnit, there isn't a decent jewelry store in the whole town and . . ."

Slowly, Willow began to wind the monkey up again. "Diamonds!" she scoffed.

Gideon had never heard a woman speak of diamonds in exactly that tone before. Again, he was at a loss.

Willow set the monkey in the center of the table and laughed again at its gyrations, clapping her hands in delight, like a child. "Oh, Gideon, it's so wonderful."

"Wonderful?" he echoed hoarsely.

And she flung herself into his arms, burying her face deep in his neck. "I love you!" she cried, her voice muffled by his flesh. "Oh, Gideon, I love you so much!"

Despite his relief in knowing that the gift had pleased her, Gideon was aware of the desperation in her tone. It was almost as though she feared they would be parted somehow.

Unnerved by this prospect, Gideon carried his wife up the stairs and into their bedroom, where their joining was fierce and bittersweet. Sometime later, when she thought Gideon was asleep, Willow left the house.

For a few minutes, Gideon lay still in the rumpled bed, thinking. And then it occurred to him that Willow might not be behaving strangely because she was losing her mind but because Steven Gallagher wasn't dead.

16

Willow's heart leaped into her throat as the long shadow near the house solidified into a man, and she started violently. "Gideon?" she croaked.

A cloud passed over the waning moon, moved on again. In the thin light, Willow saw the nod, made out the familiar frame. "Yes," he said.

She cast a furtive look toward the outhouse, which was so far away as to be invisible in the night. She could not say she'd been there, not again. The lie had grown and grown and now it lodged in her throat, the size of a Christmas orange.

"Steven is alive," Gideon ventured evenly, letting no emotion show in his voice.

Willow was torn between relief and terror. "How did you know?" she managed, shivering a little in the chill, drawing her shawl more closely about her shoulders.

Gideon reached out, took her arm in a

grasp that betrayed no anger, and squired her toward the back of the house, then inside. There, he lit a lamp before answering. "It was just a guess, until now. You've been behaving very strangely, for a bereaved woman — stuffing yourself after the funeral, when no one else had an appetite, riding into the hills that day with Daphne, making love with me as though you hadn't just suffered a shattering loss."

Willow sighed and sat down at the table, bracing her head in her hands. She was too tired to lie anymore; the secret was too heavy to carry, just as Steven had warned it would be. "You must have thought I was losing my sanity."

"At first, yes. Tonight, after you left our bed again, I started to think about the day Tudd brought the bodies in. You went into the back room to view them, remember? And you cried out and fainted."

Willow nodded.

"You had opened Steven's shirt; I was too worried about you then to think about it much, but that was how you knew that Tudd had shot someone else by mistake, wasn't it?"

Again, Willow nodded her head. "The hatchet wound — Steven had been injured

in a fight with Red Eagle a few days before
—"

"And there was no wound," Gideon
guessed, quite correctly. "You must have
suspected something before that, though, or
you wouldn't have bothered to look."

Willow's mouth went dry. She nodded.
There had been so many things, really, but
she'd been in shock. It had taken a few
minutes to absorb the truth — that the
hooded man sprawled belly-down across
Steven's saddle *wasn't* Steven.

"I knew almost right away," she admitted.

Gideon was standing near the sink by
then, watching her, his face expressionless,
his arms folded. His voice was like gravel
when he spoke. "Put your clothes on, Mrs.
Marshall," he said. "You and I are going
into town."

Alarm leaped through Willow like a fire,
out of control. "Why? Gideon, it's the
middle of the night —"

"And your father believes his only son to
be dead. We, or more specifically you, are
going to tell him that the man lying in that
grave in the churchyard, next to Coy and
Reilly Forbes, isn't Steven."

Gideon was right, of course.

Her father needed to know Steven was
alive — whatever the consequences of that

425

knowledge might be. Holding it in, especially in the face of Devlin's terrible grief, had been killing Willow.

So with a nod, Willow got up from her chair, made her way toward the back stairs, then climbed them and moved along the dark hallway and into the room she and Gideon shared now as married people.

It took, or seemed to take, a very long time to get dressed, but when Willow joined her husband in the kitchen again, she was clad in a lightweight woolen dress and wearing a bonnet.

Gideon hitched up the horse and buggy, saying nothing as he worked.

Nor did he speak during the drive into town.

When they reached Devlin's front door, Gideon knocked hard. His manner was cold and deliberate and he remained as silent as a stone, except for the knocking. Why didn't he rage at her? Why didn't he indicate, in some way, whether he understood what she'd done?

She'd had no choice but to pretend that Steven was dead.

Devlin himself opened the door, looking sleep-fogged and gaunt. He'd pulled on a pair of trousers, but his shirt was misbuttoned and left much of his chest bare.

Looking at him, in that brief moment while he tried to absorb the fact that he had guests in the middle of the night, Willow suddenly realized the full depths of what her father had suffered, was suffering still. A compassionate word from her would have saved him so much pain.

Impatient, Gideon gave her a slight push forward. The command was silent, but it was not to be disobeyed.

"Papa," Willow blurted out, "I-I have something to t-tell you."

Devlin peered at her, yawned, and ran one hand through this thick, graying hair. And suddenly he was completely alert. "Come in, then," he barked, leading the way into his study.

There he lit the lamps and fastened the study doors while Gideon sank into a chair, looking quietly fierce, and Willow paced back and forth along the hearth.

"Well?" demanded Devlin Gallagher, perched on the edge of his desk. Obviously, he sensed that the visit was important, but he could have no way of guessing just *how* important.

Willow flung one desperate look at her husband and knew that she would find no help from him. No sympathy. "The-the man in that grave across the s-street isn't Steven,"

427

she said.

Devlin tensed, glaring at his daughter. After a moment of thunderous silence, he stood, crossed to her, and stayed her pacing by grasping her shoulders and looking right into her eyes. "What are you saying?" he rasped, and she could see that he wanted desperately to hope, but was afraid to. "You can't mean?"

Tears began to trickle down Willow's cheeks. "Steven is alive, Papa," she said, ashamed. Why hadn't she told him? Why hadn't she listened to Daphne and Steven, who had argued that Devlin had a right to know?

A hoarse sob came from the depths of Devlin's powerful chest and rumbled in his throat. "God in heaven, how?"

Willow could not speak for her misery, and Gideon did not seem inclined to intervene.

"Why didn't you tell me?" Devlin asked, croaking out the words.

"I was afraid," Willow managed to reply, shaken in the face of her father's obvious anger and shock. "I thought word would get out, that Vancel Tudd would go after Steven again, with a vengeance, and succeed this time —"

Shaking his head, Devlin cut her off.

"Where is Steven now? He's well? Safe?"

"I don't know where he is, Papa. But he is well and as safe as can be expected."

"When did you see your brother last?"

Willow felt bereft, as though the two men in this room had set some sort of barrier between themselves and her. Perhaps neither of them would ever love or trust her again. "Steven comes to the pond s-sometimes," she finally admitted, casting one frightened look in Gideon's direction. "I've been meeting him there."

For the first time since their arrival at her father's house, Gideon spoke. "That's why you've been wandering outside," he said. He wasn't asking, though. He was confirming something he'd already guessed on his own.

Willow nodded.

"God in heaven," moaned Devlin distractedly. "I should have guessed!"

Willow searched his face for any sign of forgiveness. "Papa, I . . ."

He withdrew a step, looking at her as though she were a stranger. "Willow, I have grieved," he marveled brokenly. "I have wept and paced and anguished over the loss of my son, over all the ways I failed him —"

"I thought I was doing the right thing, Papa!"

Gideon made a gruff, disgusted sound and stood up. "Anything for Steven," he said, on his way toward the closed doors of the study.

Willow knew a swift, slicing fear, then stretched out a feeble hand toward him. "Gideon, wait, please."

He turned, surveying her in one scathing glance, and then smiled grimly at her father. "I leave you your daughter, sir," he said to Devlin. "God help you, my friend."

With that, Gideon was gone and the room seemed to pulse in reaction. Devastated, Willow looked up at her father's face, certain that he, too, would turn away from her. "Papa."

Devlin sighed and embraced his daughter. "I know, sweetheart," he conceded, after a moment. "I know you believed you were doing the right thing."

The next morning, Gideon made his way back to the Gallagher house, though he hadn't come there to see Willow.

Standing in the sunlit kitchen, he flung the careful records that Marshal Mitch Kroeber had kept directly in front of Jack Roberts, nearly upsetting the man's coffee cup. Maria, who had been about to serve the guest his breakfast, fled the room instead, her eyes downcast.

"Look for yourself," Gideon rasped. "You'll see that I'm telling the truth."

Roberts perused the neat entries on the first page of the first book. "I believe you," he said wearily, and at some length. "If the truth be known, Gideon, I'm too undone by all this battling with my daughter to think clearly."

Gideon sighed and helped himself to a cup of coffee at the stove. "Is she still pretending to be sick?"

Roberts nodded. "What's a man to do with a daughter like that?" he complained. "She's been meeting this damned outlaw —"

"Steven Gallagher," confirmed Gideon, with a meaningful glance at Kroeber's journals. "He's innocent of any crime beyond being a nuisance, Jack."

"Would you understand if I said I'd like to see the rounder hanged anyhow?" sighed Jack Roberts, looking distracted and two years older than dirt.

Gideon smiled grimly. Maybe he'd have a daughter someday. If he did, he hoped he wouldn't have to go through the things Jack and Devlin had suffered. "Yeah," he said. "I'd understand. You'll come to Helena with me, to speak to the governor? Get all this cleared up, once and for all?"

"I'm not doing any good here," admitted Roberts, looking ruefully down at the plate of bacon, fried potatoes, and eggs he'd been about to tuck into before Gideon's interruption. Clearly, the man's appetite was gone. "Might as well."

Half an hour later, the two men rode out together.

Daphne, clad in a long white nightgown, flung back the covers and sat up in bed, staring at Willow, her lavender eyes wide. "Oh, Willow, I told you so!" she cried, after she'd heard her friend out. "I told you Gideon would be furious!"

Willow hadn't slept at all after Gideon had stormed out of the house the night before, leaving her behind in her father's care. Now, she hung her head and sat slump-shouldered on the end of Daphne's bed. "I know he's never going to take me back," she said. "Never, ever."

Daphne, feeling no need to feign sickness while alone with her coconspirator, sat down beside her and draped one arm over Willow's stooped shoulders. "This is my fault, too. I'll take part of the blame."

"That won't help where Gideon's concerned, will it?" agonized Willow dispiritedly. "I've lost him forever."

"No," Daphne interjected. "Gideon loves you. He'll understand, once he's had time to think things through."

Willow remembered the cold, callous way in which he'd dismissed her, and she began to cry. "I'll have to leave Virginia City," she sniffled. "Oh, Daphne, I couldn't bear to live here, in this house, while Gideon lives apart from me, out there on the ranch."

Daphne gave her friend a sympathetic squeeze. "Gideon loves you, Willow," she reiterated. "He won't be able to stay angry very long."

Willow recalled the tender, uncertain look on Gideon's face when he had presented her with the mechanical monkey only the night before, and felt bereft. She could not credit that the very same man had walked away from her without looking back. "He was so quiet, Daphne, so cold. I would give anything if he'd shouted and raved instead of leaving me — well, *quietly* — the way he did, like he'd given up, like it didn't matter anymore."

Daphne sighed. "We're a pair, you and I. And we've made a grand mess of this whole situation, haven't we?"

Willow nodded, and the two women cried together, one loving the wrong man, the other estranged, perhaps permanently, from the right one.

Attending the play with Zachary for their escort was Daphne's idea; Willow only went along on the outing because she needed the distraction from her churning thoughts. As it happened, the traveling theater troupe's production of *Richard III* was anguish, in and of itself, so badly did the actors bungle it.

Willow whispered excuses to Daphne and Zachary and left after the first act, pausing outside Virginia City's impressive playhouse — Virginia City had its aspirations, as well as its pretentions — to draw in deep breaths and wonder where Gideon was at that moment. Had he returned to their ranch? Was he with a woman?

Her shoulders sagged slightly. It wouldn't be long, given Gideon's fondness for lovemaking, before he found someone else. And what of Willow herself? Could she ever love another man the way she loved Gideon, or would she burn with unfulfilled desire every night for the rest of her life?

"Willow?"

She felt the light touch at her elbow and turned to see Zachary standing behind her, dapper in his dark suit, his hat in his hands.

"Are you all right?" he asked.

Glumly, Willow nodded. "Please. Go back

and watch the rest of the play with Daphne. I can get home on my own."

"Unthinkable," argued her brother-in-law smoothly. "When I take a lady somewhere, I do my best to see her home again when she's ready to go."

Willow caught the veiled reference to the night of the supper dance, when she had left Zachary without explanation, and winced inwardly. "In that case," she responded, with asperity, "you certainly wouldn't consider abandoning Daphne here, with no one to escort her back to our house."

Zachary hid his annoyance well, though not quite well enough. "I'll come back for her," he suggested.

Willow was tired of arguing, and she did want to return to her father's house, where Maria was. Her childhood nurse would be a great comfort now, alternately scolding and pampering. "Do you promise?" she asked.

"Of course. Contrary to what my brother has probably told you, Willow, I am a gentleman."

"I doubt that very much, Zachary Marshall. But I do want to go home and, since you won't allow me to walk there alone, as I have done, I might add, a thousand and one times if not more, I'll trust you to drive me

435

directly to my father's house."

He laid a guiding but undemanding hand on the small of Willow's back, and ushered her toward his rented buggy. The seat squeaked as Zachary climbed in beside her and took up the reins, and she was filled with memories of another buggy, on another night. Her face flamed in the darkness.

In front of the judge's deserted-looking house, Zachary abandoned his smooth manner so swiftly that Willow had no time to prepare. His left hand cupped her chin and his mouth came plundering to hers.

Revulsion and rage filled Willow; she flailed and struggled, desperate to break Zachary's hold. He was much stronger than she was, of course, and he pressed her hard against the buggy seat, never breaking the kiss.

Willow made a whimpering sound in the depths of her throat and squirmed. His tongue entered her mouth, territory belonging only to Gideon, and wild to escape, she bit down hard, until she tasted blood.

Swearing and sputtering, Zachary drew back at last, but his hands still held Willow firmly against the dusty leather seat. She was trying to summon the breath to scream when he brazenly cupped her breasts in his palms. "You little wretch," he rasped, "you lovely, fiery little wretch, I knew you could be like this."

At last Willow had the breath to scream, though it was a high, squeaky sound, unlikely to penetrate the thick walls of her father's house.

Zachary trembled in a frightening way, lifted one of his marauding hands, and slapped Willow so hard that she tasted blood again. This time, it was her own. She spat at him and he straddled her lap, grappling with her as she twisted feverishly to get free of him, strong in her fear. Instinctively, she brought her knee up, hard, into Zachary's groin.

He moaned and grasped himself, off balance, and Willow took advantage of the moment, shoving him with all her strength. He fell, cursing and flailing his arms, onto the ground beside the rig,

Even if there was help inside her father's house, which she doubted, since Devlin was probably with Dove, and Daphne's father had gone off somewhere with Gideon, Willow dared not tarry long enough to find out. She grasped the reins in both hands, yelled to the already-fidgety horse, and was off, turning the small rig in a wide arch in the middle of that normally quiet street and racing back toward the main part of town.

Daphne was standing in front of the playhouse when Willow arrived, looking bewildered and a little worried, and Willow hailed her breathlessly, hardly stopping the buggy long enough for her friend to scramble inside.

"Willow!" Daphne gasped, holding on to the seat with a death grip as the rig bolted onward again. "What on earth is happening? Where have you — ?"

"Zachary," Willow managed to sputter, shaking now, but driving that buggy as earnestly as Ben Hur would have driven a chariot. She could still feel Zachary's hands on her breasts, taste his tongue as it plunged deep into her mouth, invading her. Filling her with terror and with fury. Her lower lip, bruised by his slap, throbbed. "Like a fool, I let him drive me home. He promised to come back, for you —"

"Oh, Willow!" Daphne whispered, her eyes wide in the light of the saloons, brothels, and hurdy-gurdy houses they were passing. "He-he tried to force himself on you?"

"Yes," Willow managed to reply, somewhat more calmly. But she did not slacken the pace she was setting for the poor horse pulling the rig.

"Where are we going?"

"To Dove Triskadden's house," answered

Willow, who had not, until that moment, known what she planned to do. Simple logic precluded their returning to her father's place, where Zachary might still be lurking, and the ranch was too isolated, too far away. "I'm praying that my papa will be there!"

If Daphne was shocked at the idea of venturing to such a notorious quarter at that hour of the night, she didn't show it. She was probably thinking, as Willow was, that neither she nor her friend had much right, or reason, to be worrying about propriety.

There were lights in the downstairs windows of Dove's two-story house, and Willow and Daphne felt hope as they sprang out of the buggy and bolted up the walk and onto the porch, side by side.

Daphne rang the bell, since Willow was overcome by a residual bout of the trembles, and when Dove opened the door, something very much like alarm leaped in the depths of her eyes.

"Is my father here?" Willow asked, with as much decorum as she could muster.

Dove stiffened. She was wearing a dressing gown, and her lush blond hair, usually so elaborately curled and coiffed, looked unkempt. "No, no, Devlin isn't around tonight."

Something quivered in the pit of Willow's

stomach; she felt the same basic, instinctive fear she had known during her struggle with Zachary. "Dove, is-is something wrong?"

"No!" Dove cried quickly, her eyes darting to the road and back again, as though to warn her callers away. "Now please leave; this is such an intrusion, and I'm tired."

Both Daphne and Willow stood stock still, staring at her. Both regretted the indulgence, only moments later, when Dove was suddenly flung backward out of the doorway, and Vancel Tudd loomed in the opening. With a quickness Willow wouldn't have believed possible, given his size, he caught each of Dove's visitors by one wrist and hauled them inside, kicking the door shut behind him.

"How dare you!" cried Daphne.

"Where is my father?" demanded Willow simultaneously. "Have you hurt him?"

Tudd let go of his captives, chewing on something. He smirked at Willow and then gestured toward Dove's satin-upholstered sofa. "Sit down," he commanded.

Daphne and Willow exchanged a look and then sat. It would be fruitless, they had silently agreed, to try to reach the door and escape. Tudd would have shot one or both of them before they crossed the small porch.

Standing behind the sofa, Dove said

gently, "Your papa is all right, Willow. Thank God, he hasn't been here tonight."

"Shut up!" yelled Vancel Tudd, glaring over Daphne's and Willow's heads to Dove.

Prudently, Dove obeyed, and there was a silence filled with fear and the cloying stench of Tudd's unwashed body.

"What do you want with us?" Daphne finally asked, her chin at a defiant angle.

Tudd was pacing back and forth, making the smell worse.

"Don't be a ninny, Daphne," Willow replied, "he wants *Steven*."

Tudd paused, favoring Willow with a lingering once-over and another smirk. "Now that's right smart thinkin', little lady."

"How did you find out you killed the wrong man?" demanded Willow.

"I had my suspicions almost from the first," Tudd answered airily, rocking slightly on the worn heels of his boots. Filthy and self-satisfied, he dragged greedy eyes over Willow once more before going on. "Then I happened to be in Lot Houghton's office the afternoon when he came back from the telegraph office with a judge's order to have the body in Gallagher's grave dug up. He said he'd bet we'd find Silas Blanchard in that coffin, not your brother, and I figure he's right." Tudd was pacing again, rubbing his stubbly chin with one hand. "The bounty on Blanchard is respectable," he reflected, "but it sure as hell don't come near what's offered for your big brother."

Willow shivered. She'd gone to such lengths to protect Steven, alienating her husband, letting her father suffer, and what had come of it? This, her worst fear. "I'll die before I'll lead you to Steven," she said, meaning every word.

Vancel Tudd laughed. "I figure you would, little lady. I figure you would. Lucky for both of us that you won't have to. No, ma'am, you won't have to, because Gallagher will come to me like a baby to a sweet-sucker, once he finds out that I've got my hands on his kid sister and his woman."

Beside Willow, Daphne flinched. But then her chin went up and her shoulders squared.

Tudd's pig eyes went to Dove. " 'Course, this one's no use," he speculated. "Might as well just cut her throat."

"If you hurt Dove in any way, my papa will hunt you till the day you die!" Willow reminded him forcefully, depending entirely on bravado. "You'll be a wanted man yourself — you'll know how it feels to have a price on your head!"

"I don't want trouble with no bounty hunters, that's true," Tudd conceded, surprisingly. "Still, I can't leave Miss Triskadden here behind to tell Lot and Devlin and the rest about tonight, now can I? No, sir, she goes with us."

"Goes where?" Daphne dared to ask.

"To the hills, of course. I know a good place for us to wait. Word'll get to Gallagher fast enough, I reckon."

Willow knew that Tudd's reasoning was sound. Steven would come, and he would trade himself, if necessary, for the bounty hunter's captives. "What makes you think my brother won't call your bluff?" she snapped. "Maybe he'll just shoot you on sight and that will be the end of it. Did you ever think of that?"

Tudd touched Willow's chin with a rough, stinking hand. "Why, little lady, I ain't bluffin'. He'll know it, even if you don't." He shook his head and grinned, as if unable to believe his good fortune. "Damn if this ain't a fine night; got the Fox's sister and his favorite woman without even tryin'!"

The word *favorite* struck Daphne with a visible impact, and she bristled a little, but she wisely refrained from comment.

"Tudd, you'll hang for this, you fool!" Dove cried suddenly, rounding the sofa, her small fists clenched at her sides. "You can't."

Tudd drew back his hand and struck Dove

so hard that she fell back against the fire-place and hit her head. Willow went to her immediately, followed by a stricken Daphne.

Dove was faint, and she was bleeding a little from a cut on the back of her head, but she was a frontier woman and she rallied soon enough. Tudd wrenched her to her feet by her hair, and the cruel warning was meant as much for Willow and Daphne as for Dove herself.

The three women allowed themselves, however much it rankled, to be gagged with pillowcases from Dove's linen cupboard and then bound at the wrists. Pleased with his handiwork, Vancel Tudd herded his three captives, single file, through Dove's darkened dining room and kitchen and into the yard beyond. There were no near neighbors, and it was an easy matter for Tudd to force the women into the bed of a waiting buckboard and drive away through the night.

Jolted and bounced about on the hard wagon bed, Willow struggled to get free of her bonds. Daphne and Dove, perhaps wiser than she, lay perfectly still.

Nausea scaled Willow's windpipe and burned in her throat. God in heaven, if she vomited with this gag pressed so far back in her mouth, she'd drown for sure. She swallowed convulsively and closed her eyes, concentrating on staying calm by mentally reciting the books of the Bible: *Genesis, Exodus, Leviticus, Numbers, Deuteronomy . . .*

It was the closest she could come to praying, she was so scared.

And the wagon moved on and on, up and up, endlessly. The sky turned from black to gray to an apricot shade shot through with pink and mauve, and still they traveled.

Finally, Tudd barked a hoarse "whoa" to the plodding team and the wagon stopped. All three women sighed with relief.

Their captor jumped down from the wagon seat and rounded the rig to haul them out, one by one. Willow's legs were shaky and uncertain beneath her, and she stumbled as Vancel Tudd shoved her toward a sizable cabin hidden in the woods. Hardly aware of Daphne and Dove staggering along beside her, she grappled with a long-buried memory of this place. The feeling that she had been here before was intense, but she couldn't think when that would have been or reason out why it seemed so all-fired important to recall that time.

Though ramshackle, the cabin had a spacious interior. There was a stove, a table, several broken-down chairs, and a sagging cot. Willow knew for certain that there was a back bedroom, too.

Sure enough, after untying the women's gags, if not their wrists, which remained firmly tied behind them, Tudd thrust them all through a doorway and into a small room with a slanting roof. Without a word, he closed the door and bolted it, safe in the knowledge that there was no window to offer an avenue of escape.

Willow did not like that room. Odd sounds played on the edges of her memory, frightening sounds countered by Steven's efforts to distract her . . .

"Willow?" queried Daphne, looking at her friend with a worried expression. "Are you all right?"

Willow shook off the eerie feeling that had come over her at first sight of the cabin and summoned up a rueful smile. "I'm as all right as either of you, I imagine."

"What do you suppose he'll do to us, Willow?" Daphne pressed anxiously. There were great, dark shadows moving in her eyes and smudges beneath them. "Do you think he's the kind to —"

"No," Dove broke in, settling herself on the edge of the old bed that took up most of the dingy room. The springs creaked and Willow gasped, prodded again by that dim and unsettling memory.

"He could rape us!" insisted Daphne,

446

unaware of her friend's terrified state, her attention fixed on Dove.

"He won't," said Dove firmly. "If he was that kind, I'd have known it last night. I was alone with Tudd for a good hour before you two blundered in."

Willow was swirling in an eddy of memory, afraid. Tears trickled down her face and she began to tremble, hearing echoes from some hidden, shadowy part of her mind. A bed — this bed that Dove Triskadden sat upon — rattling hard, slamming against the wall, springs screeching.

There had been groans and cries. It was Jay Forbes; he was killing her mama.

Willow stood helpless in the doorway, screaming.

Steven, strong, gentle Steven, had taken her hand then, and led her away. "He's not hurting Mama," he'd said, but there had been a quiet fury in his voice, all the same, and his blue eyes had burned with an ancient hatred.

"Willow!" The voice was Dove's.

Willow looked at her father's mistress with dazed eyes, feeling almost as though the woman had slapped her, which was impossible, of course, since they were all still bound at the wrists. "I was here before," she said woodenly, when she could speak.

"I know I was here once before."

Both Daphne and Dove looked at her with puzzled sympathy, and then the door opened with a crash and Vancel Tudd came in. He'd deign to untie their hands and permit them to breakfast on the dried beef and stale cornbread he presented.

Wildly hungry, despite the upsetting effects of their ordeal, they ate, hardly noticing when Tudd left them again and once more bolted the door.

17

Vancel Tudd had made a dire mistake, and he clearly knew it. Consequently, as the long day crawled by, he came and went from the room, fidgety, growing more and more irascible with every passing hour. On one occasion, ignoring glares of warning from Daphne and Dove, Willow smiled at him. "You'll go to prison for this," she said, "if the good citizens of Virginia City don't hang you first."

Tudd had been sucking at a bottle of Irish whiskey all afternoon, and he took a long gulp to finish it off. His skin was an odd shade of gray, and there was spittle gathering at the corner of his mouth. "Never met a Gallagher yet that knew when to shut up," he said. "And you're no exception."

"You'd better let us go, Mr. Tudd," Willow persisted. "My papa might look more kindly on your crimes if you release us, before any real harm has been done."

449

"Crimes!" spat Vancel Tudd, glowering at Willow, swaying on his feet. "I ain't done no crimes! And your daddy aside, the railroad wants Steven Gallagher bad enough to overlook everythin' else."

"Do you know who the railroad is, Mr. Tudd?" Willow pressed, not daring to look at her friends. "As far as you're concerned, the Central Pacific is two men, my husband and Daphne's father. Do you seriously think they're going to condone what you've done and blithely pay the reward, whether they want to see Steven prosecuted or not?"

Tudd grew a little grayer of flesh and sucked in a whiskey-rasped breath. "You hold your tongue!" he barked, gesturing with one unsteady hand.

Willow lifted her chin and started to argue, but Daphne and Dove each caught one of her arms, somehow willing her to be silent. They didn't release her until Tudd left them alone again and fixed the bolt on the door.

"Are you insane?" demanded Daphne, her eyes wide, with big shadows underneath. "That's a madman out there, Willow Marshall, in case you haven't noticed!"

Willow stiffened, then thrust out her chin. "He's also a drunk. Another few minutes

450

and we might have been able to overpower him!"

Dove sat despondently on the edge of that sagging bed, still clad in her dressing gown. "Overpower him? He's big as this mountain!"

"There are three of us!" retorted Willow.

"You know, Vancel Tudd was right!" Daphne shot back. "You don't know when to shut up!"

It was Dove who sounded the voice of reason. "Let's get some sleep if we can. We're not going anywhere tonight."

Stoically, they all lay down on the musty bed, trying not to think of the creatures that had probably nested there before them.

Gideon was exhausted from the long ride north to Helena with Jack Roberts, and he'd wondered every mile of the way there and back whether he was doing the right thing. It came as a profound surprise to him to find Steven Gallagher pacing the length of Devlin's study.

"It's about time!" the erstwhile outlaw bellowed at the sight of Gideon.

"Steven," Devlin said, in gruff reprimand.

"Tudd's got the women, for Christ's sake!" blurted Steven, glowering at Gideon and the heavy man who stood beside him.

Gideon's weariness was literally jolted out of him; he forgot why he'd gone to Helena, what he'd accomplished there, everything. "What?"

Steven was pacing again. "Are we going to talk all night?" he roared, casting furious, ink-blue glances at his father.

Devlin was amazingly calm, a virtue Gideon didn't share. "We can't afford to do anything rash," the judge reasoned. "Tudd's brain has finally melted down and seeped out his ears. He'll kill one or all of the women if we push him that far."

Jack Roberts had broken out in a sweat, even though dawn hadn't arrived yet and it was still cool, and he sank into one of Devlin's chairs, mopping his brow with a handkerchief, wheezing. His lips took on a blue tinge. "Lord God," he whispered.

Devlin poured a generous helping of brandy into a snifter and extended it to Roberts. "You'd better stay here, Jack," he said, with the compassion that one father feels for another in such moments. "We'll see that Daphne's safe."

Steven interjected an angry sound. "Right. Provided we don't stand around *here* all night, flapping our jaws."

"Steven," Devlin said firmly, "shut up."

"Where are they?" Gideon demanded in a rasp.

"Up in the hills; Steven knows where," answered Devlin quietly.

"Yes, and I wish I'd done something about it, instead of depending on you old ladies for help!" raged Steven, reddening to the roots of his hair. "Could we ride now, or do you have to tat doilies?"

To the surprise of everyone in the room, Devlin drew back his hand and slapped his son soundly across the face. "Enough, Steven," he said, in level tones. "If you can't calm down, I swear to God I'll leave you here."

Steven subsided, but grudgingly, and the men began to make the necessary plans.

It was dawn again, and Vancel Tudd allowed the women to go outside, though only one at a time. When Willow's turn came, she stumbled obediently into the woods, her throat dry, with no idea of rebellion in her mind. She'd slept fitfully during the night, plagued by curious, frightening dreams, dreams that strengthened her conviction that she had been in this place before.

"Hurry it up," complained Vancel Tudd, who was standing only a few feet away. At least, Willow reflected, he'd had the good

453

grace to turn his back.

She washed her face and hands in the narrow little creek and this, too, touched her memory. She had a fleeting recollection of coming here, long, long ago — with her mother.

Willow stood up, then wiped her hands on the skirts of her rumpled dress. Her hair was straggly and tangled and her face, despite its recent washing, felt sticky. She bit her lower lip and followed Vancel Tudd back toward the cabin.

The nearer they came, the more she remembered. A rising excitement quickened Willow's step.

Reaching the cabin, Tudd moved to open the door and was stopped cold by a shout from the tree-lined ridge nearby.

"You're a dead man, Tudd!"

Vancel Tudd turned slowly, ignoring Willow, scanning the ridge for some sign of Steven. "Show yourself, Gallagher!"

"Tudd!" This voice, to Willow's intense relief, was Gideon's. "Let the women go!"

The bounty hunter caught a hank of Willow's disheveled hair in one hand and jerked. She flinched, closed her eyes, and bit back a cry of pain. Tudd shouted an obscene and patently defiant response, then

hurled his captive through the cabin doorway.

A moment later, Willow was again imprisoned in the back bedroom, with Daphne
and Dove.

"They're here," she whispered, once Tudd
had left them to go outside and carry on his
hopeless argument with Steven and Gideon.

Hope leaped in both women's weary eyes.
"Then all we have to do now is wait," said
Daphne.

"That would be a serious mistake," responded Willow crisply. "Tudd is cornered
now, and he's more dangerous than he ever
was. He could decide to tie us up again and
set fire to the cabin, or any number of other
things."

Daphne made a little whimpering sound,
probably imagining the horrific scenario,
and Dove embraced the younger woman,
trying to lend courage from her own obviously dwindling store. "We'll be all right,"
she said, in hollow tones. "They've come
for us, the men have. We're as good as
saved."

"Yes," agreed Willow brightly, kneeling on
the floor and beginning to pry at the aged,
filthy boards with her hands. "We're as good
as saved. But we'd damn well better save

ourselves, because Tudd might be outnumbered, but he still has the upper hand."

"What are you doing?" marveled Daphne.

"We used to live here," Willow answered, in a low voice. "I was sure I remembered this place, and that's why; Mama and Jay Forbes hid out here sometimes. One night, some men came, on horseback — they must have been vigilantes — and we hid under the floor until they went away."

She shivered, reliving the fear. The men had cursed something awful, breaking the few dishes, overturning what little furniture there was.

But they'd left without finding the family.

Daphne simply stared at Willow as though she'd gone daft, but Dove was mobilized. "A tunnel," she whispered, excited. "There's a tunnel, isn't there?"

Willow was kneeling, peering under the old bed. "I wouldn't call it a tunnel," she replied softly. "It's more like a rabbit hole. There ought to be space enough to crawl to the edge of the house, though — that's how we got out, Mama and Jay Forbes and the rest of us. And once we're clear of the house, we can run for the trees."

Daphne was wringing her hands. "Run?" she fussed. "Tudd has a rifle, and we're wearing skirts —"

456

"Shut up and help us," breathed Willow. Moving the bed was a risk, considering the inevitable noise, but Tudd was still shouting back and forth with Gideon and Steven and there was a chance that he wouldn't hear what was going on in the room behind him.

Beneath the bed were two loose boards, easily displaced to reveal the cobwebs and dense darkness underneath.

"There are spiders down there!" protested Daphne as Willow helped the intrepid Dove Triskadden into the hole in the floor.

"And there's a raving maniac outside!" Willow reminded her, grabbing Daphne's elbow and thrusting her into the pit. "Thunderation, Daphne, get moving — we don't have all day!"

Traversing those dark, cramped environs was not an easy thing to do, even for someone as adventurous as Willow. There were rats scuttling through the shadows and cobwebs covered the women's faces like smothering sheets. The ground was fraught with other hazards, too; broken glass, old boards, nails — all these things tore at their clothes as they crawled toward the light.

At the edge of freedom, they paused. Willow drew a deep breath. "I'll go first," she said finally. "If Tudd doesn't shoot at me, you two follow after. Catch your skirts up as high as you can and run like hell!"

Daphne stayed Willow's departure with a tug on her elbow. "Willow —"

"It'll be all right, Daph," she said softly. "I promise it will."

Daphne's eyes were brimming with tears, but she bit her lower lip and nodded bravely in response. Willow crept out from under the cabin, bunched her skirts in both hands, and ran at top speed for the trees a dozen yards away. Just as she reached them, a bellowed curse from inside the house made her turn and beckon frantically to Daphne and Dove. Vancel Tudd had discovered their escape; within moments, he would be rounding the house, rifle in hand.

Daphne and Dove scrambled for their lives at Willow's signal and reached the trees just as Tudd bounded around the side of the house, shouting.

They scrambled up the rocky side hill, the three women, praying that the trees would hide them, slipping and falling, rising again. There was no time to look back and see if they were being pursued; escape called for everything they had.

At the top of the ridge, they lay on their stomachs, chests heaving, as they tried to regain their breath. A smile curved Willow's lips when she looked up and saw Gideon,

Steven, and her father, all on their bellies, with rifles at their shoulders.

Remarkably, they hadn't seen — or heard — the women's escape.

"They're a hell of a lot of help, aren't they?" rasped Dove. "Good God, if Tudd had come this way, he'd have them dead to rights."

Daphne was about to call out, but Willow stopped her by clamping a hand over her mouth. Dove grinned mischievously and winked, and the three women rose as quietly as they could to their feet.

"I think we should rush him," Steven was saying. "Christ, he could keep this up from now till the snow flies."

"Yeah," answered Gideon gruffly, "but if we scare him, he might do something stupid."

"He's already done something stupid," countered Steven hotly. "I'll tear his balls off for this!"

"The hell you will," put in the judge. "I meant it when I told Tudd he could ride out if he let the women go."

"Maybe you could smoke him out," said Dove clearly, her smudged face split by a wide grin.

The three would-be rescuers whirled, all at once, to stare at the ragtag trio of tired women who had been standing behind them for several moments by then.

Devlin was the first to move; he made a low, joyous sound in his throat and set down his rifle to bolt toward Tudd's escaped captives, kissing both Willow and Daphne, lifting Dove up in his arms and whirling her around.

Steven came and embraced Daphne, tangling his hand in her hair, muttering soft words. Gideon remained on the ground, sitting up now, his rifle resting across his knees.

Willow was stung by his reaction; despite their differences, she had been sure that he would be glad to see her again, to know that she was safe. She stood stubbornly in the bright sunlight, her hands caught together behind her back.

"Come here," Gideon said, in a stern tone that did not befit the occasion.

Willow responded with a bit of memorable advice. "I'd rather go back to Vancel Tudd than come to you!"

The rapid retreat of a single horse echoed up the ridge; Tudd was making an escape of his own, and not one of the men moved to stop him.

Gideon stood up, however, and favored Willow's father and brother with a grim smile. "If I might be alone with my wife . . ."

To Willow's amazement, they deserted her readily, grinning at each other, ushering their women down over the hill, in the opposite direction of the cabin. No doubt, the horses were tethered there.

"Come here," Gideon said again.

Willow took in his unkempt clothes — his shirt was open almost to his waist and half untucked from his trousers, his vest was unbuttoned and smudged with dirt — and stood her ground. "I would like a divorce," she said.

"Oh?" Gideon arched one eyebrow, then bent to pluck a blade of grass from the rocky ground and ply it between his fingers. "Why?"

"I can't live with a man who would destroy my family, that's why!"

"I see."

"You don't see!" cried Willow, suddenly too tired to hold in her emotions. "How long will it be, *Marshal* Marshall, before you arrest Steven? Now that you've finally found him, how long until you get him thrown in jail for the rest of his natural life, or make sure he hangs?"

Gideon took a folded paper from the inside pocket of his vest and held it out. "Here," he said. "Read this."

"Is that a warrant?" Willow asked suspiciously, unwilling to advance so much as a step toward Gideon.

"It's a pardon, signed by the territorial governor."

Willow stared at him. "F-for Steven?"

"It isn't for you, hellcat, you're still in major trouble. And I'm not Marshal Marshall any longer, remember? Lot Houghton is wearing my badge."

"You'll go back to San Francisco now," Willow mourned, forgetting her determination not to let this impossible man know how deeply the loss of him grieved her.

He executed a Lancelot-like bow. "With your permission, fair damsel, I will remain here, minding my ranch and cattle, siring a respectable number of children, storming the occasional castle wall . . ."

Willow stared at him, unable to speak for the dry lump of hope widening in her throat.

"I love you, Willow," Gideon said.

Willow flung herself at him and felt his arms close around her, strong and yet gentle, too. He kissed her, his lips sipping at hers, and then laughed and swatted her rounded bottom firmly. "You are a harridan, Mrs. Marshall, covered with cobwebs and all manner of dirt. What am I going to do with you?"

"Might I say that you are something less

than clean yourself, sir?" challenged Willow, smiling up at him. "As for what you're going to do with me . . ." she paused, letting one teasing fingertip stray inside his shirt and trace the circumference of a nipple, "it just so happens that I have a few things in mind."

"Beginning with a bath, I hope," said Gideon, his mouth close to hers again, drawing her lips to his, kissing her thoroughly. His hands were on her bottom again, pressing her close, forcing her to feel and acknowledge the extent of his desire.

"Beginning with a bath," confirmed Willow breathlessly. "Am I still in trouble?"

He bent to nip at her earlobe briefly. "Ummmm — dreadful trouble, Mrs. Marshall. But I think a pardon can be negotiated."

Willow trembled, but with anticipation, not fear. "Are the terms equitable?"

"Oh, yes," he breathed, "but you won't get off easy, hellcat."

Willow laughed. "I never do," she replied.

Gideon grinned, swept her up into his arms, and carried her down the hillside to his horse. The other riders, Devlin and Dove, Steven and Daphne, were far ahead. After settling Willow in the saddle, Gideon swung up behind her. Brazenly, he lowered her dress so that her full breasts were bared, and cupped them in his hands for a long, exquisite moment of very welcome mastery. He teased the straining nipples with the sides of his thumbs thoroughly before releasing her and righting her bodice again.

"To the castle," he said, into the tingling flesh of her neck. "Lancelot would bed his lady."

Daphne looked patently miserable, for all that she'd spent two full days resting and being fussed over by the proprietary Maria, who regarded her as a part of the family. "Papa insists!" she wailed. "If I don't go home with him and start behaving like a proper lady, he's going to disinherit me!"

Willow came to sit beside her friend on the stone bench in the judge's garden. "Your father knows about Steven's pardon — knows Steven is wealthy in his own right. Didn't those things make any difference at all to him?"

Daphne's lavender eyes brimmed with angry tears. "It might have made a difference to Papa, but it certainly didn't bother Steven! *He* doesn't seem to care one whit that I'm leaving for home today. I haven't seen him since . . ." she paused and blushed profusely, "since the day we were rescued."

Willow took one of Daphne's hands in her own. "We rescued ourselves," she reminded her friend archly. "And do you plan, Daphne Roberts, to leave without even talking to Steven?"

"It appears that I'll have to, doesn't it?" snapped Daphne. "That reprehensible outlaw! Now that he's free to live like a decent man, hold his head up high, and go where he pleases instead of hiding out, he's probably gone and found himself a not-so-decent woman!"

"Daphne!"

Daphne covered her face with both hands and wept softly for long moments. Then, with a sniffle, she looked up at Willow. "I think, I think I'm going to have a child," she confessed. "Whatever will I do?"

Willow ached with sympathy and with a need to strangle Steven Gallagher. "Then you must stay here with Papa and Dove, or at the ranch with Gideon and me. We'll look after you and the baby for as long as necessary. And Steven *might* come to his senses . . ."

"I couldn't bear to be so beholden to all of you," sniffled Daphne, though pride flashed in her beautiful eyes. "Besides, even if Papa does disinherit me, both grandmothers left me sizable sums, and I've done some investing of my own. I can take very good care of my child." She paused, thinking, and shook her head. "No," she said decisively, "I am *not* going to wait about for that arrogant man like some, some concubine!"

Secretly, Willow respected her friend's pride, though she was certainly going to miss her if she left. Besides Daphne, she'd miss the baby, even though it wasn't born yet. "You're not the only one, you know," she confided gently, "who is going to have a baby."

Daphne looked into Willow's eyes, gave a delighted cry, and hugged her. "Then one of us will be happy, Willow. I'm so glad for you, and for Gideon, too."

"Thank you," said Willow, with dignity, and then she and Daphne fell into each other's arms and wept shamelessly at the prospect of parting.

"Son of a bitch!" bellowed the engineer to the brakeman, grasping for the whistle cord. "Stop the train!"

Somewhat stupidly, the brakeman peered out. Seeing the blazing bonfire on the tracks, maybe three hundred yards ahead, he put his full weight into the lever, muttering an oath of his own.

■ ■ ■ ■

Daphne was nearly flung from her seat, even though her father was quick to put out an arm to protect her.

Worried murmurs broke out all over the railroad car; passengers peered out of soot-blackened windows, trying to see what was happening.

"It's another train robbery," Daphne told her father and, for all that little prickles of alarm poked at virtually every inch of her flesh, she was strangely excited, too. Everything within her quickened.

"Probably just a dead cow on the tracks or something," Jack Roberts assured her. "These things happen, Daphne. We'll be on our way again in no time."

"I wouldn't count on that, mister," allowed a rundown cowboy, turning from his window. "There's a fire on the tracks up ahead. I can see the smoke." He shifted in his seat, drew a pistol, and brandished it, causing the other passengers to gasp. Some even ducked behind the seats in front of their own.

A lone rider passed the windows on the side of the train opposite where Daphne sat. He wore a long canvas coat, gunslinger style, and his hat was pulled low over his eyes.

Daphne would have known him anywhere.

Seeing her — she had crossed the aisle and was struggling in vain to open the train window — he smiled and got down off the horse. Then he climbed the outside steps and entered the car.

No one spoke. Even the cowboy with the pistol seemed awed.

Daphne turned and watched as Steven Gallagher moved between the rows of seats until he was beside her. He took off his hat and held it against his chest, his honey gold hair rumpled and much too long, his eyes full of hope and amusement and the combined blues of every sky since the beginning of time.

Mr. Roberts, Daphne's father, finally found his voice. "Here, here, now," he said. "This is —"

"This is a marriage proposal," Steven said, never taking his eyes off Daphne's face. "I'm a man of some means, you'll find, and I'm willing to buy a ranch, or a business in town, or whatever else suits you, Daphne," he went on. "I'll be the best man I can, the best husband, and the best father, every day of my life, if you'll just leave with me now. I've got a preacher waiting over at the church."

An incomprehensible joy rose up within Daphne, something she could barely contain.

"Oh, Steven," she said, putting out her hand.

He took that hand, bent his magnificent, tawny head, and brushed his lips very lightly across her knuckles, sending sweet shivers through her entire body.

"Daphne," her father interjected, but the stern note in his voice was faltering. "Do not give in to wanton impulses."

Daphne ignored Jack Roberts, looking straight into Steven's impossibly blue eyes. "We're going to have a child," she told him, very gently.

The look on Steven's face was priceless; Daphne knew she would remember his expression forever.

"In that case," Mr. Roberts put in, "let's get back to that church so you two can stand in front of the preacher and make this right."

Steven just grinned, never looking away from Daphne's face.

She gazed at her father, though, hopeful. Even a little amused. "I thought you wanted to disinherit me," she said.

"That was before I knew I was in line for

a grandchild," Roberts said. "Go on, with your fellow," he added. "I'll figure out how to get back to Virginia City, too. This is one wedding I don't want to miss."

"Wedding?" an old woman trilled, three rows back. "You mean this isn't a train robbery?"

Steven grinned and reached for Daphne, then scooped her easily up into his arms and smiled at all the passengers. "I'm stealing this woman," he said. "And nothing else."

With that, he carried Daphne down the aisle and out of the train car. His horse waited a short distance away, and Steven hoisted his stolen bride up into the saddle before climbing up behind her and wrapping his strong arms around her as he took the reins.

He bent his head and nibbled lightly at her earlobe once before nudging the restless horse into a trot.

"Is there really a preacher waiting to marry us?" Daphne asked, when they were well away from the train, sheltered in a copse of cottonwood trees with shimmering leaves forming a moving canopy overhead.

"Yes," Steven said, but he climbed down from the saddle and stood beside the horse, holding his arms out to her.

"S-Shouldn't we go and get married, then?" But she let Steven take her by the waist and bring her down off the horse's back.

"We'll be married before the day is out," he told her, his voice husky as he drew her close. "I promise."

"And in the meantime?" Daphne asked, looking up at him, her heart going a little faster with every new beat.

"In the meantime," Steven said, "I want to make slow, sweet, *gentle* love to the woman who is carrying my baby."

Daphne slid her arms around his neck, then stood on tiptoe to kiss the cleft in his chin.

The bride and groom, as it turned out, were quite late for the wedding.

The Gallaghers' parlor was filled with well-wishers that afternoon, and even though the windows were open, it was insufferably hot, in Willow's opinion. Oh, to be in the pond at home, naked and cool.

Gideon squeezed her hand and smiled, as though he'd heard her thoughts and wanted to suggest a few touches of his own. When the pastor took his place in front of the hearth, however, he looked dutifully in that direction, as did the other guests.

At that moment, Devlin appeared beside Gideon's chair, looking distracted and impatient. "Steven isn't here!" he said.

Gideon smiled. "I'll fill in for him, Judge," he volunteered cheerfully. "Where's the ring?"

Frantically, Devlin delved through every pocket in his suit coat and finally found the requested item and brought it out. With a nervous laugh, he stretched to plant a kiss on Willow's forehead and then followed Gideon to the front of the room.

Lot Houghton's Alice sat down at the small organ under the windows and began to play, while her husband escorted a beaming Dove Triskadden into the room, resplendent in scarlet and dripping with pearls. When she had taken Devlin's arm, the ceremony began.

Willow listened in delight as the words were spoken, and felt tears of love burn in her eyes as Dove and her father drew closer together.

Finally, the pastor came to the part of the service that had proven so momentous the day Willow had almost married Norville Pickering. "If anyone here can show just cause," he boomed warily, no doubt remembering himself, "why these two should not be joined in marriage . . ."

Devlin turned and assessed the congregation of guests in comically dire warning, raising a twitter of amusement from the assemblage.

"Let him," the pastor finished, bracing himself, "speak now or forever hold his peace."

There was no answer, and the preacher actually sighed with relief, bringing soft laughter from the congregation. Reddening, he rushed on to demand the vows from the bride and groom and to pronounce them husband and wife.

Despite the fact that she was sitting at the back of the room, nearest the open windows, Willow was among the first to reach Devlin and fling her arms around his neck in congratulations. After kissing him soundly on each cheek, she turned and hugged Dove, too.

Later, in the kitchen, Willow pumped cold water into a basin and repeatedly splashed her face. Her tears, however, would not be washed away.

"Willow," Gideon said softly, from beside her. "What's the matter?"

"Nothing is the matter," lied Willow, in petulant tones, trying to turn away so that he wouldn't see her face. He turned her back, easily.

"Willow," he said, not to be put off.

She stiffened. "I'm just happy for Papa and Dove, that's all."

"I would have sworn you were thinking about our wedding," mused Gideon, and though his face was solemn, his hazel eyes were dancing.

"Our wedding!" scoffed Willow angrily, sniffling just a little. "Norville Pickering was the groom at our wedding!"

Gideon laughed. "So he was, if you don't count the other ceremony, back in San Francisco."

The memory of that was still painful to Willow. "I most certainly don't!"

"In that case, hellcat, we're living in sin." He paused, his lips twitching, and wedged his hands into the pockets of his trousers. "I'd better stop the preacher before he leaves and demand that he marry us."

Willow's face was warm. "Oh, Gideon, would you do that? Could we have a real wedding?"

"Certainly. Provided we have a real honeymoon afterward."

"We've already done more honeymooning than marrying, Gideon Marshall!" Willow scolded. "Besides, we can't go on neglecting our ranch any longer."

He lifted one eyebrow; clearly, his

thoughts were straying away from the subject at hand. "Speaking of neglect, have you seen Zachary?"

Remembering what had happened in front of her father's house, the night she and Daphne and Dove had been kidnapped, Willow blushed. Some instinct warned against telling Gideon, just yet, what had taken place. "No."

Gideon shrugged and drew her close. "Maybe he finally took my advice and went home. Go upstairs and change into that ivory dress you were wearing the day I stole you from Mr. Pickering, my dear. We're about to be officially married."

She looked so damned appealing, standing there at the stove, with a wisp of tarnished-gold hair moving against the back of her neck. Her dress was of simple calico, properly modest for a rancher's wife, and yet Gideon wanted her so badly that he wondered how in hell he was ever going to get any work done.

He paused, for if he said her name, she would turn to him and he would end up leading her off to bed or to the piano bench or somewhere, and having her. Even though it was suppertime, the chores that awaited him in the barn were far from completed, and he needed to speak with the range foreman he'd hired before leaving town that day.

"It's about time you got home," Willow chimed, surprising him. "I was beginning to think you were planning on spending your wedding night in a hurdy-gurdy house."

Gideon laughed. It *was* their wedding night, as much as it was Dove and Devlin's. Hell, a man couldn't go off and jaw with the foreman on his wedding night, now could he?

"I accomplished a lot after we parted at your father's house," he said, kissing the back of her neck and flinging aside the newspaper he'd bought from Norville Pickering in the same motion. "I hired a foreman, for one thing."

She purred at his sampling of her nape, pressing the full firmness of her delectable backside into his groin and wriggling slightly. "Good," she said, and Gideon didn't know whether she was talking about the foreman or about what he was doing.

"You should have waited there for me," he remonstrated gently, letting his hands slide up over her trim middle to her breasts.

"I had things to do here," she said, whimpering a little as he teased the pert nipples covered in calico.

"What things?" he whispered hoarsely.

"Just wifely things — cooking, dusting, that sort of — Gideon, stop that."

He began unbuttoning her dress, then slid his hands inside to fully possess the sweet mounds hidden there. "Come upstairs with me, Mrs. Marshall, and do something wifely."

She groaned. "Gideon, supper . . ."

Gideon turned her slightly and bent to nip and then suckle at her breast. "Supper be damned," he drew back to say, "that is good enough."

With that, he sat down, pulling Willow close, drawing up her skirts. After baring his manhood, he lowered her gently onto it. She sheathed it with a cry that made Gideon's spirit soar within him, moaned and nuzzled his mouth with her breasts until he supped.

It was much later that he showed her the newspaper article on the front page of the *Virginia City Sun,* evening edition.

STEVEN GALLAGHER
ROBS LAST TRAIN

Word reached this reporter, just in time for today's final edition, that the notorious bandit stopped the Central Pacific as it began the journey southward early this afternoon. The recently pardoned outlaw demanded the hand of one Daphne Roberts, late of San Francisco, and witnesses report that her father gave her over willingly, on the condition that Mr. Gallagher would marry her post-haste. He agreed, it is said, to see to this pleasant duty before nightfall.

Norville G. Pickering,
Editor in Chief

Eight and one half months later . . .

Judge and Mrs. Devlin Gallagher
proudly announce the births of their
grandchildren,
Steven Marshall, born March 28, 1884,
to Gideon and Willow Marshall,
and Charity Gallagher, born April 10,
1884, to Steven and Daphne Gallagher.

ABOUT THE AUTHOR

Linda Lael Miller is the *New York Times* bestselling author of more than eighty novels, including her bestsellers of romantic suspense, *Don't Look Now, Never Look Back,* and *One Last Look.* Ms. Miller resides in Spokane, Washington. Visit her website at www.lindalaelmiller.com.

We hope you have enjoyed this Large Print book. Other Thorndike, Wheeler, Kennebec, and Chivers Press Large Print books are available at your library or directly from the publishers.

For information about current and upcoming titles, please call or write, without obligation, to:

Publisher
Thorndike Press
10 Water St., Suite 310
Waterville, ME 04901
Tel. (800) 223-1244

or visit our Web site at:

http://gale.cengage.com/thorndike

OR

Chivers Large Print
published by AudioGO Ltd
St James House, The Square
Lower Bristol Road
Bath BA2 3BH
England
Tel. +44(0) 800 136919
info@audiogo.co.uk
www.audiogo.co.uk

All our Large Print titles are designed for easy reading, and all our books are made to last.